A Path Returns

M.S. HABER

For Jessica and Wolfgang

CONTENTS

ACKNOWLEDGMENTS

The inspiration, encouragement, and character of family and friends made this book possible. From my heart I thank all, including Alex, Chris, Beth, Joan, Margaret, and Rose. Thanks from my heart for your help.

Conscious life begins when memories exist and can be recalled. Memories are uniquely individualistic, as is the time in life at which they are recalled.

Memories containing important, life-directing events, even if not recognized at the moment of actuality, are subconsciously stored away, and from that unrealized hiding place, shape the rest of a person's life.

Memories are life, and in the end, life is memories.

Chapter One

Salzburg, Austria
World War II

The air was heavy and every intake of breath cold and damp. Thick
lumpy clouds hid the tall Alps that surround the city of Salzburg. The sky
resembled a dingy blanket. Beneath the gloomy sky, narrow cobblestone
streets wove damply between tall buildings crouched beside wet river-like
streets.

The only apparent movement in the depressing darkness of the night
was that of a German Military Patrol as it moved punctually and routinely
along specific streets. Otherwise, the city was silent, empty of people.

The approaching patrol wasn't aware of movement present in a
particular courtyard, as two men stirred the air where they hid behind a line
of almost leafless trees. The men flattened their backs against the inside of
a tall brick wall that encircled the courtyard. Both were dressed in black,
and melded perfectly into the dark dreary night.

No words were necessary. They were silent statues and waited only for
the passage of the nightly security patrol. When that patrol passed them by
their assigned mission would begin.

The two men were alerted by the approach, the noise of heavy
equipment as it rolled along, and the sound of marching feet. They hugged
the brick wall more closely as the patrol entered the courtyard. Two large
military trucks and twenty or more soldiers passed slowly in front of them.

The vehicles and the men swerved suddenly to the right in order to pass
around the central courtyard fountain. Still the two men didn't move,
didn't flinch. They knew this routine. Only when the entire patrol
disappeared out the opposite gate and the harsh sound of the vehicles and
the marching feet faded did they move. Practicing as they had, the

necessary timing now felt easy. They moved into action. Their assigned mission had started and no margin for error was allowed. Completion must be accomplished tonight.

Young, confident, and sharp, they moved deeper into the protective darkness, through the courtyard and to a path that ran out the opposite gate.

Quietly they ran forward and when they left the path behind, they stopped a moment to check for any unwanted people. They hid in the shadow of the Abbey Church of St. Peter, an ancient Benedictine monastery. It was dedicated back in the year 1147 and is one of the oldest monasteries in the German speaking part of Europe. It towered above them, its shadow as dark as the night sky.

Very cautiously, they stepped out of the shadow and into the open empty darkness of St. Peter's Cemetery, their destination.

The dark unattended cemetery provided excellent cover for the two men as they slithered silently into the main area. Seamlessly they moved ahead and passed another church, the small gothic St. Margaret's. The 15th century chapel sits right in the middle of St. Peter's Cemetery. With its eye-like windows closed and empty of light, its brick face stared blankly down at them. The two men in black passed by, gave it only a brief glance. Intent on completing their goal, filled with excitement, they raced forward. Empty backpacks clung to both men's backs.

Without speaking they moved to a specific section of the cemetery. Their target was crowded tightly against the side of the mountain on which stood the old historical Hohensalzburg Fortress, a large middle-age fortress. It perched high above Salzburg and on this night, its tall, imposing walls seemed to reach up and caress the heavy clouds. The towering white wall of the old fortress glowed faintly, and compelled both men's eyes briefly up. They were distracted.

With a glance between them and a flicker of mutual embarrassment, they got back to work, as both stared at the façade of the enclosed arcade grave. The arcade section was an important part of the old cemetery. It contained elaborately decorated trellised iron gates that enclosed the many vaults belonging to wealthy Salzburg families.

The men could care less about the beauty of the cemetery or the art of the trellised iron gates. They simply recognized that their mission was nearly accomplished. With another swift look around for any possible observers, they rushed confidently to a certain gate of the arcade. One man flashed a light on the gate for a fraction of a second. A positive glance and an affirmative nod passed between them. The name on the grave was correct. This is where it was buried.

Smoothly, swiftly, backpacks came off and small tools were removed. One man held a flashlight in place and the other began to work to open the wrought iron gate that guarded the vault. They both concentrated on quietly breaking it open. They were standing at the finish line.

Darkness shattered as a flash of light sparked and exploded. The tool dropped from the hand of the man who was trying to open the gate. His body slammed forward, smashed into the still un-opened gate. Blood splattered like rain as his brain exploded and he fell into a dead heap at the bottom of the gate.

Again light flashed. No time allowed for the second man to realize what had happened to his partner as his body then jerked forward and more blood flew into the air. He landed in a bloody wet death puddle, his body also pressed against the unopened gate.

Two shots and both men in black were stopped. Mission left unaccomplished.

The thick heavy air in the cemetery rippled, as a third dark figure emerged from the shadow of St. Margaret's Church, where he had been hiding. His gun was up and ready to fire again if needed.

Quickly he moved forward, glanced all around to ensure he wasn't being watched. His first thought, get rid of the bodies. He grabbed one, then the other and dragged them backwards, away from the un-opened grave gate. Next he raced away and immediately began to hide, to cover, any signs of the murders, any footprints, scuffmarks, blood on the ground. He grabbed handfuls of dead leaves and tall limp grass. The cover up worked well. No one must be able to discover, to find anything that had happened here tonight.

Suddenly, strong gusts of wind began to sweep through the cemetery. The leaves and grass he had already placed began to swirl wildly. He ran around, hiding the evidence of murder again. Anger flashed through him because he had planned this all so carefully, believed he had allowed sufficient time to clean up and then to drag the bodies to his hidden car. The dead men were to have ended up in the Salsach River.

Panic swept through him when he heard voices in the distance. He couldn't understand what was being said, but the excited tone, the shrill sound of pursuit, was loud and clear. Somebody must have seen the two now-dead men as they ran through the dark pathway on their way to the cemetery, or maybe someone had seen him. Time to run, the military was on the way.

Nervous, rushed, he grabbed the still-empty backpacks, and slung them onto his shoulders, grabbed the men's guns, their scattered tools, and stuffed them, along with the dropped flashlight into his pockets.

The voices were absolutely too close.

His job remained unfinished; no time left. He crouched down low and ran.

When the voices, the German soldiers, reached the cemetery he had melted away into the darkness, and was lost inside the complexities of the old city.

Chapter Two

The Future
Ana Must Decide

The telephone rang but Ana didn't stir. Motionless in her favorite chair, underneath an old soft quilt, she hid from life. The room was dim and gloomy as rain poured from the sky and drenched the world. She was still, silent, but her fair-skinned face, deep green eyes, and long blonde hair spoke beauty. Underneath the bulky quilt she looked almost non-existent even though she was in fact quite tall and slim. At this moment she wanted to be invisible.

The air around her was chilly and added to her unwillingness to move out of her hiding place, gave her another reason not to answer the ringing telephone. Ana had questions, needed answers. Her head was filled with confused thoughts and memories. It felt impossible to answer the incessant ringing of the telephone, the call of the future. She was in limbo.

The dark room she was hiding in was part of her home, had been for a few years. It was on the second floor of an old building located not very far from the university she attended. Her life had changed tragically shortly after she received a scholarship and started college.

At the end of her first semester, the local postman in her hometown found her mother dead on the front porch of their home when he attempted to deliver the mail one Monday morning. He called for help, and it was later determined that Monica Winchester, Ana's mother, had collapsed and died from a major heart attack.

Hurt and shocked intensely, Ana realized she had lost the one who loved her, the one she loved, and was now totally alone in the world. Her grandfather and her father had both died tragically when she was only a little girl. No other relatives existed.

Left alone it was immediately necessary that she depend on herself to pay all college expenses; scholarships don't cover everything needed to obtain a college degree. Desperate, she found this tiny cheap apartment and lived in it until she graduated. She made it her refuge.

Whenever she had free time, either after classes or after finishing her daily work for her Professor and Advisor, Dr. Bauer, she used that time to improve the tiny apartment. Somehow, making herself a refuge seemed to block some of the sadness and isolation she felt after her mother's death.

With no money to spare for fixing up the place, she hunted for furniture in thrift stores, collected small treasures from the area flea market and yard sales. Slowly the apartment brightened. She painted the worn out walls with bright colors and they acted as the perfect foil for the furnishings. She collected hand painted oils and slowly covered an entire wall in her apartment. When she walked into her refuge, the wall of paintings made her smile. None of the oils were valuable in terms of money. All cost maybe a dollar or two but they had style and beauty. The apartment spoke of her character and worked as her safe refuge. To that extent, she helped herself move forward. However, she was still alone.

Chapter Three

North Carolina
The Winchester Family
Ana's Childhood

The small town of Andrews, North Carolina nestles comfortably in a long valley surrounded by tall tree-covered mountains, and through the valley center flows a sparkling river; a masterpiece of nature.

In addition, defined seasons are spectacular in the area. Spring gives the wake-up call and green leaves and colorful flowers answer happily. When summer rules the meadows become lush food carpets, provide essentially for any hungry humans or animals. Later, autumn brings a bright mellow touch as trees dress up in warm colors to celebrate the year's accomplishments. Finally quiet winter creeps in with white snow, crisp air, and it strips the trees of their colorful leaves. Mountains stand naked, reveal their real shapes; nature takes a nap.

The Winchester farm sits in the middle of this natural beauty. The Winchesters were granted the property by the United States after the "Indian Removal Act of 1830" that forced the original owners of the land, the Cherokee Indians, to a new home in Oklahoma and gave the land to US citizens. The Trail of Tears robbed the Indians and rewarded the United States and its citizens.

The government removed the Cherokees because it needed their land. It had become valuable, providing space for the profitable building of railroads. In addition, the US was experiencing an exciting second gold rush. Gold had been discovered in nearby Dahlonaga, Georgia.

A few generations later the land belonged exclusively to Harold Winchester, his wife Ellen, and their son Leonard. They were the only remaining Winchesters.

Harold Winchester ruled the farm; it was his kingdom. He was always right, strict, and used criticism to control life. Early in their marriage, his wife Ellen died of cancer and her death left Harold in total control of their son Leonard, age ten.

Leonard worked hard to please his father, but whatever he achieved was never good enough. He got no praise, only criticism, and was told that he didn't live up to expectations.

Harold Winchester considered himself perfect and felt that all other people were beneath him. He was, in his own words, "One step below God in the hierarchy of the universe."

Fortunately, Leonard got an opportunity to leave his perfect father behind. World War II was raging. As soon as he became age-eligible, he signed up with the US Army. Even though the war was horrible, he wanted to be taken into the army and leave his father behind.

When he joined the army in Europe, the war was nearing its end. Germany had already been taken over by the US military, and he was placed into the US Army occupation forces in Germany at the base the US had established in the city of Heidelberg. He appreciated the distance his required tenure in the military placed between him and his father.

Life away from home gave Leonard some confidence, widened his view of the world. An exciting event occurred. By chance, soon after he arrived, he met and fell in love with Monica. They bonded at once and he asked her to marry him. She accepted and then they obtained permission for the marriage from the military. They were officially joined together there at the military base in Heidelberg, Germany.

Out of the blue, only a month later, Leonard suffered a serious leg injury in a military truck accident, and the army decided to release him from duty. They provided military flights and flew him and his new wife back to the United States.

From the moment they met at the Winchester Farm, Harold Winchester resented his son's wife Monica. The first words out of his mouth were, "What do you want from my son and me? Why'd you get him to marry you and bring you to the US? You Germans aren't worth much and you should've stayed in Germany with your family."

Monica was hurt, shocked, and barely found the willpower to answer him. "I do not want anything from you. Your son and I are married and this is his home. Now it is my home too. My whole family was killed during the war. I have no family left behind. I am connected only to Leonard."

"Well don't expect anything from me. You and Leonard get along, but leave me out of it. We're fighting against the Germans and I don't like having one living in my house."

Leonard, listening to his father, suddenly stepped forward, grabbled Monica by the arm and led her away. As they walked off into the room that was to be their bedroom he said, "Please Monica, don't let father get to you. He's king of his world and he's been treating me like this all my life. Just let it go, and we'll concentrate on each other. I love you and I promise to take care of you."

During the first year of their married life, Harold Winchester treated Monica with no respect, and it got worse when Monica and Leonard had a baby, born there at the farmhouse during their first year home. They named her Ana.

Now called "Grandpa", Harold Winchester went out of his way to cause pain to both his daughter-in-law and his granddaughter Ana. Monica was not fully aware of the extent of his cruelty to her daughter. The family situation was difficult and complicated because Leonard continued to let his father set the rules. He gave his father the opportunity to bring severe unhappiness to Ana.

On her fourth birthday Ana stood motionless, pain and sadness evident on her small round face. She gazed up at the tall man who stood beside her in the room.

He had asked her, "What do you want to do when you grow up Ana?"

With no hesitation, little Ana smiled up at her Grandfather. In a sweet excited voice she said, "Oh Grandpa, I want to be a ballerina!"

Grandpa threw back his head and laughed loudly. The laughter was not kind, not friendly, rather harsh and critical. "You won't ever be a ballerina. You're too fat and ugly."

He watched the pain his words caused and grinned.

Tears ran down Ana's face and she rubbed her eyes as she stood by herself in the room filled completely with her Grandpa. Suddenly the door from the connecting kitchen opened and her father stepped through.

Father saw her crying, and asked his father, "What happened to Ana?"

"Son, you're gonna have a lifetime of trouble with that little girl. I asked her a simple question and she gave me a ridiculous answer. She don't seem to be very smart. I know you gonna tell me she's only four, but even at four she ain't too bright."

Grandpa left the room.

Father looked down and said, "Ana, you sure don't make good impressions on people. You need to work harder and be more agreeable."

He turned and followed his father out of the room.

Ana sat on the floor and continued to cry softly, knowing better than to make noise and call more attention to herself. In a few minutes she heard another voice from behind the closed kitchen door. It was mother's voice.

Mother was coming.

Chapter Four

Back to the Present
Ana Must Decide

Intense grandfather-generated pain struck and she pulled the quilt over her head. Tears flowed. Childhood questions echoed in her mind. Fear kept her quiet. So many times when she asked her mother questions, she never got answers. Without doubt mother loved her, but mother avoided or didn't respond to questions Ana asked. She instinctively felt that mother had answers but wouldn't share them with her. Unfortunately mother's secrecy taught her never to ask direct questions and she was unable to tell mother how mean grandpa was to her. Without honesty, confusion reigned.

The phone rang again. The noise caused Doctor Bauer's face to flash in her mind because she knew he was the person calling. Dr. Bauer was not only Ana's advisor, but also one of her Professors at university, and, in addition, her employer. Mr. Elden, the man who managed Winchester Farms was a friend of Dr. Bauer and introduced him to her before she began college. This connection played an important role in securing Ana's scholarship to the university. The two men had met and become friends some time back. From what she understood both men had attended Heidelberg University in Germany. Evidently, they were not there at the same point in time, but that shared experience helped seal their friendship when they met later in life.

As Professor and student, as well as employer and employee, Ana had come to know Dr. Bauer well. With so much time spent together, she could now picture him clearly, tapping his foot impatiently, voicing his thoughts out loud, "Ana, where are you? Why don't you answer the telephone?"

The impatience of Dr. Bauer in no way reduced the high opinion she had of him. He had helped her get into the university and then had given her a job to enable her to support herself. She thought of him not only as her Professor but also as a friend.

From first grade forward, Ana loved school and maintained high grades in all subjects. However, she possessed an outstanding ability to learn and to speak languages. The high school in her hometown of Andrews officially offered only one foreign language to its students, that being French. She absorbed all the French lessons offered, and then took it upon herself to study other languages on her own. By the time she graduated from high school, she was fluent in two, French and German.

At university, Dr. Bauer, a Professor of Languages, helped her continue her love and absorption of language and cultures. His advice helped tremendously in her winning sponsorship from her university to the country of Germany. One student was scholar-shipped over per semester and Ana was chosen to go in her sophomore year. The time she spent in university abroad increased her excellence in her chosen field of study.

Recently she had received her Master's Degree. It had been her intention to skip the awards ceremony because she had no family members left to be there with her. Dr. Bauer, who was in charge of the special ceremony, demanded she attend. He talked to her and told her that she owed it to herself to celebrate her accomplishment. Reluctantly, she'd gone. It was difficult to push away the sadness as she watched fellow students surrounded by their families.

The telephone rang angrily again and she knew she had to leave limbo behind. The realization that her college life was over, and that she needed to secure a job hit her forcefully.

She had to depend on herself. That was what the angry ringing telephone was all about. Yesterday, Dr. Bauer had told her that he would call with some information about a job he thought she would be interested in. He'd given her some details about the job offer and she'd told him that she needed time to think it over. Time was up.

Ana jerked the quilt off her body and moved forward. She answered the telephone.

Chapter Five

Decision Made
Ana – 1969

By herself, Ana sat a table for two and glanced at the menu. She was at her favorite restaurant and presented a lovely sight for anyone passing by. Relaxed and smiling, she waited for her friend Maggie to show up. The weather was perfect; a bright blue sky and clear cool air. She sat outside in the open courtyard and absorbed the beauty.

Both Ana and Maggie appreciated that this restaurant offered customers a choice of where to eat, inside or outside. They always chose outside unless the weather didn't allow it. The courtyard tables sported red umbrellas and sat beneath cool green trees. Off to one side a water-fountain bubbled and gurgled. Many parents, accompanied by their children, stopped often beside the fountain. The children loved to throw coins in and make wishes.

Ana and Maggie met for the first time in the university cafeteria as they both began the morning trying to grab a quick breakfast before their classes began. Ana had already filled her tray with food and turned to walk toward an empty table she'd spotted. Maggie was trying to balance her tray of food plus a heavy book bag. She ran straight into Ana at full speed. The collision sent them both staggering backwards and food flew everywhere. Shock slapped them both and two mouths were wide open. What happened? Then they looked at each other, saw their breakfasts attached to their clothes and broke into uncontrollable laughter.

They became best friends. Maggie was vivacious and full-speed-ahead. Ana was quiet, took time to think before making decisions. The contrast of personalities was perfect and their friendship flourished. They shared good and bad times, laughed, cried, and understood each other.

During the years spent together, they also formed another bond. Ana took Maggie home with her to her farm in Andrews. They went there many times and Maggie loved it. She enjoyed the farm, the horse riding, and the beauty of nature. But Ana also noticed after only a few trips together to the farm that Maggie had also formed another attachment. She was definitely interested in Ana's life-long friend Sam. The two of them seemed to hit it off from the first moment they met. Without hesitation they talked and laughed constantly. Maggie and Sam were her two best friends. Maybe they would fall in love and then all three of them would be closely connected forever.

Ana smiled as she thought about the possibilities ahead for her friends but even as she smiled, she felt the shadowy confusion inside her creep forward. She tried to say no but she hadn't figured out how to eliminate the fear that haunted her.

Again, her mind slipped into the past. She was back to the day after her mother's funeral.

Ana became the wind, invisible, powerful, unstoppable. Her body bent forward, head lowered, she and her horse Devil raced along a track parallel to the main highway that ran through the long Andrew's valley.

She loved Devil and he returned that love. He was tall, black, and his long shining mane flew out as he raised his head ever so slightly, seeking even more speed, needing to go faster as he flew forward with Ana on his back. Devil's approval of their speed, his approval of the recklessness of the ride, was evidenced by his total participation. The reality of the moment for both the girl and the horse existed only in the intense and complete acceptance of danger. Any prior unanswered questions, any confusion was left behind.

Goal achieved.

A small stream that crossed the path they raced along suddenly loomed ahead. Ana felt a flash of panic. She shoved it away. Girl and horse raced faster, jumped the stream, rocketed forward. They were close to the highway but didn't even realize it.

Suddenly the thick barrier of trees and bushes that shielded their riding path from the highway ended. They were instantly visible to any highway traffic.

Mindless of the possibility that they could be seen, totally absorbed in the need to leave the past behind, they charged full speed ahead.

A horn blared loudly, once, twice, three times.

The race was over. Shock and reality forced them back into the present. She turned her head toward the harsh blaring horn and got a brief look at the small red car. She recognized the car and the driver.

That evening as she sat sadly alone in the home she and her mother had shared, footsteps sounded on the front porch. A loud knock struck the door. She slowly got up and moved forward to open it. No need to ask who was there, she simply pulled it wide open.

However, she pretended not to know what his visit was for. "Mr. Elden, please come in. What are you doing out this time of evening?"

He gently closed the door as he entered the room and answered, "Ana, I'm worried about you. I saw you and Devil racing so dangerously along the pathway. I worry because the loss of your mother was such a shock. I realize you're hurting. Also, I'm concerned because with the death of your mother, you don't have any family left to lean on."

Ana looked at him and realized that he was honestly the closest person left to lean on, to think of as family. She looked at him with her sad green eyes and said, "Mr. Elden, I don't really know how I'm going to get by without my mother. She loved and cared for me and I loved her so much too. Can I ask if you would please continue to take care of the farm, to manage the business like you have since my father died? I don't know what the future will bring and I need to make sure the farm is taken care of. It was important to my family and it's important to me too."

He walked forward and gave her a gentle hug, careful not to intimidate and frighten her with his closeness. "Ana, don't worry about this farm. I promise to do my best to take care of it. I want to make it possible for you to get back to your life at the university, finish your degree, and find a meaningful life for yourself. I'm here for you and promise to help you in any way I can. Please try not to feel completely alone."

Ana returned his hug and said, "I trust you completely. I'll never be able to tell you how much your help has meant to me. I feel confused and lost right now, can't seem to move forward."

He'd started to leave and was walking toward the door but he turned around and asked, "Is there anything else bothering you, besides the loss of your mother?"

She hesitated a second, attempted not to show her fear as a new thought flew through her head. Does he know something, maybe something that I should know? My mother had secrets. Did she share them with him?

She looked at him quietly and answered, "No Mr. Elden. I just miss my mother."

Chapter Six

Lunch With Maggie
Ana – 1969

When Ana made the call to invite Maggie to lunch she only told her friend that she'd received a job offer, didn't give any details. She wanted to talk face to face with Maggie. A need existed to share her happiness and excitement about the upcoming changes in her life and to see the approval and the joy on her friend's face.

Still at the table waiting for Maggie, after her flashback to mother's death, Ana forced herself back into her previous optimistic mood. The sad memory of that run with Devil, the liberation, the courage to face danger was hard but it really gave her a little strength.

At that moment, an excited Maggie came racing up to the table. "Ana please tell me everything! I can't believe you've received a job offer! You must have gone from no employment prospects to landing a job in only a day or two!"

Happy, petit Maggie plopped into the empty chair at the table. She settled her giant purse, her overstuffed bag, and then herself directly across from her friend.

Ana couldn't help it, she grinned. Maggie was so tiny and always carried far too many items. She even received offers of help from people who didn't know her. She was so small, so friendly, and always so overloaded.

Maggie laughed out loud when she saw Ana's grin. She knew exactly what Ana was thinking. It wasn't necessary to make a comment so she simply laughed some more and signaled for the server. Today was important and she intended to start this meal off with a celebratory glass of wine for both of them. Even though she didn't know all the details, she was positive this job was great news. It was definitely celebration time.

Maggie wanted details. "Tell me how this happened! Tell me everything! I was just remembering, on my way here, how you applied for that job you wanted so very much. That was like over a year ago wasn't it, and you never heard back. You know, the job at that university in Germany. Well, you've been looking and hoping for a long time and now, at last, a real opportunity. So tell me."

Ana's smile was big and she grabbed one of Maggie's hands. "Mr. Elden called me the day before yesterday. He told me about the possibility of a job offer from The German International University. That's the same university that I applied to before and didn't hear from. It's unbelievable how this worked out! "

Pure joy flashed across Maggie's face and she nodded her head, took a sip of wine, and waited for Ana to tell more.

"Maggie, you know Mr. Elden, my farm manager. Well, he told me that he was talking to a friend of his who lives in Canada. Remember, Mr. Elden used to live in Canada before he moved to Atlanta. Anyway, his friend in Canada used to be a professor at The German International University. When Mr. Elden told him about me and how I was looking for a job, his friend said he would contact the administration at the university, people he was acquainted with, and see if he could help get me a job there."

Ana paused, breathed deeply, then glowed as she continued. "Mr. Elden's friend told him that he knew the university had lost one of their teachers recently and that they needed a replacement at once. Oh Maggie, Mr. Elden and his friend worked together to help me land this job. They contacted and worked with The German International University, provided all my information, my qualifications, my fluency in languages. My advisor Dr. Bauer was brought into the attempt to get me the job, and as Dr. Bauer was speaking on the phone to the Administrator of the University, the administrator decided then and there to hire me. He gave Dr. Bauer all the information I would need to accept the offer and Dr. Bauer presented it to me." She paused for a happy sigh then finished the story. "I accepted! "

Maggie was excited but also seemed to be thinking deeply about something when she said, "Oh Ana, this is the best possible news! You got exactly what you wanted so badly! I'm so happy for you! When you told me what Mr. Elden did for you I started thinking about him. I never realized before now how connected he is, how many friends he has. He always seems so quiet and private. I wonder why he moved to Andrews and lives alone? Please don't think I'm being critical of him. He's one of the nicest men I've ever met and he genuinely cares about you and about your farm. I just wonder if maybe he lost somebody he loved or something happened and caused him to leave the life he lived before he came to Andrews. All I'm trying to say is that I'll always think of him more kindly than I've done before."

Ana sat quietly, ignored a jolt of pain, and worked hard to focus only on what Maggie had said about Mr. Elden. In a few moments she answered, "I've wondered about him too. I feel he's missing someone or something important. And you're right about his kindness. He's helped my mother and me so much over the years. I don't know what I'd have done without him. He manages the Winchester Farm business, helped me get my scholarship, plus the semester scholarship I received to go to Germany when I was only a sophomore. Now he's part of the connection that got me the very job I wanted so badly. He's truly a good man and honestly I think of him as family. He takes care of me."

They both smiled sadly and were silent. Then Maggie said, "Let's not be sad today. This is a day to celebrate your future. Tell me more about what your job will actually be when you get to Germany. And smile!"

"Oh Maggie, I've been offered the position of assistant to the Professor of language and cultural there at The German International University. I can't believe it!
They're actually going to pay me a salary to go work in the place I love best in the whole world, well except my home." She paused and shook her head, smiled. "Like I said before, I can't believe it! I get a well-paying job, and the opportunity to live abroad and expand my experience."

Maggie jumped up from her chair and rushed to Ana's chair, pulled her up, and hugged her tightly. "I'm so happy for you! You've worked hard, been through so much. It's time for you to walk a new path, find your place in this world, and do what you want to do." Maggie released her and took a step back to her chair. "Wait a minute! What about your farm? Is Mr. Elden going to keep managing it for you indefinitely?"

Maggie sat down and Ana looked into her eyes and grinned again. "I've got even more good news. The news is about…

The server interrupted as he asked what they would like for lunch.

They both ordered their usual meals and Ana told Maggie, "Let's just sit here and enjoy our food and you tell me how life is going for you. Afterwards I'll tell you my other good news."

The service was quick and they talked, ate their delicious food, and simply enjoyed each other's company. It was only as the meal was nearly finished that she simply couldn't wait any longer to share the good news.

She whispered Maggie's name, got her complete attention. "The news is about Sam."

Maggie nodded and whispered "yes". She focused intently on Ana and waited.

"I don't know how much of Sam's family history you know, but I think you realize he's half Cherokee and has had some rough moments in his life, suffered because of prejudice from some folks he grew up with."

Maggie spoke up softly, "He told me about it and how painful it's been."

"I didn't realize that Sam shared his hurt with you but I'm not surprised that he did. Again she reached for Maggie's hand. "I'm glad he told you."

She continued. "When I left the farm and went to college, I asked Mr. Elden to hire Sam as his assistant. I did it because Sam told me that he didn't want to go to college, told me he was content there in the valley where he was connected to the land and to nature. His plan was to continue working for Mr. Elden at the farm and to help his parents with their farm. Mr. Elden agreed with me and in a short period of time, Sam became Mr. Elden's assistant manager."

"From what Sam tells me, he's still totally content exactly where he is. Actually, he feels like he's at home and that's where he wants to spend his life." As she talked, she watched Maggie's gentle face, saw tears of happiness fill her eyes.

"Maggie, I had a conversation with Mr. Elden a few days ago. He told me that he was getting older, and felt he needed more free time. Then he told me something startling. He said he wanted to retire as manager of Winchester Farms."

"Oh, this isn't a good time for that. You're going to leave the country to live in Germany." Maggie tensed up. "What are you going to do?"

"Here's the good news Maggie. Mr. Elden wanted me to approve his recommendation for the next Winchester Farm manager and I did. His name is Sam." Ana's eyes now filled with tears of happiness.

They cried, talked, and celebrated the unexpected happy changes that life had sprung upon them. After years of hard work, both were graduates and ready to begin their adult lives. Ana felt she'd reached a positive point in her life and Maggie happily hugged her secret love for Sam inside her heart.

"Well Ana, you've made a good start by landing the exact job you wanted and tried to get for so long." Maggie's face was flushed and happy. Her thick brown hair framed her small beautiful face.

Ana said, "Maggie, one of the things I regret about this opportunity is that I have to leave you behind in the states."

"Oh Ana, you'll be meeting new people, traveling in your spare time. You'll be rubbing shoulders with other teachers, and who knows, maybe you'll meet Mr. Right. Plus, you'll still be putting up with me because whenever I get some free time, I'm coming to visit you. You won't be leaving me behind, I'll be following behind you."

Ana picked up her glass of wine and said, "Prost Maggie!" The she clicked her glass against Maggie's.

"What did you say?" Maggie giggled.

She giggled back. "I'm practicing my German."

Chapter Seven

Preparing to Leave
Ana – North Carolina – 1969

The logistics of actually getting prepared to move to Germany proved to be more complex, more emotional, than Ana had anticipated when she'd accepted the job at The German International University. She hadn't given herself enough time to realize that her university life was finished as were the long lonely days she'd spent in her self-created hiding place.

Now she had to clean out her apartment and get herself back to Andrews, to her farm. It struck her sharply that not only was she leaving behind her normal at- school life, but also her college best friend Maggie. Her focus had been completely on getting into the new life she wanted, but now she understood what came with that. She must leave Sam and Maggie behind. That fact hit her hard.

The amount of time she had before her job in Heidelberg, Germany began was short and unchangeable. She'd been hired to replace an already absent assistant, so she was expected there soon. When she began to realize all the loose ends she needed to tie up, and all the goodbyes to everything and everyone she cared for, she panicked a little. It felt too rushed, almost impossible.

Maggie helped her sort and pack and clean up items in her tiny apartment at college. After they worked hard and completed the job, she made Maggie promise that she'd come to visit her in Germany. Maggie agreed but also made her promise to update them on how it was going in her new life abroad.

Ana left Maggie and drove towards her farm in Andrews. As she got near the valley, she noticed that fall had already arrived. The trees were sporting glowing harvest colors.

Not much later, she pulled into the entrance of Winchester Farm. The road went directly past the farm office and then rose up gently and curved back and forth as it led to the home her father had built after his father, her Grandpa Winchester died.

She parked her car in front of the porch and pulled her suitcase out of it when her long-time friend Sam drove up in his truck.

He jumped out and ran over, grabbed and hugged her. "I saw you drive past. I've been looking out my window all day, couldn't wait for you to get home. How are you doing?"

She hugged him back, so glad to see him again. "I'm doing real good. I got everything cleared out and cleaned up at the university. Maggie helped me so much. She said to tell you hello." She watched his face carefully as she spoke of Maggie and was rewarded to see the sparks in his eyes.

He saw the boxes stuffed in her car, things she had brought from her apartment at university, grabbed an armload, and walked them toward her house. "Let me get all your things inside. Then I want us to sit down and talk and get caught up on everything. I heard the basics about your new job but I want details." He laughed loudly. His laughter made her happy. She cared about him so much.

She remembered the first time they met and how they became friends. She laughed loudly too and followed her memory back to the cow.

Ana made a good friend totally by chance one day in her young life. She woke up early one morning, got dressed, and walked outside through the fields that surrounded her home. She never gave a thought to where she was going, simply answered the childhood call of adventure.

She eventually found herself standing in front of a well-worn wooden fence. Without thought, she grabbed hold of the fence post and climbed up. She balanced herself with both feet on the bottom rail. Then her world changed as she peeked over the top. What she saw delighted her, transformed her smile into sunlight.

A large green field lay in front of her, enclosed by the fence she stood on. A herd of cattle was grazing contentedly, all around the field. However, one cow was leading a different life. It stood perfectly still, close to the fence. A young boy, maybe eleven or twelve years old, sat on top of it. Then the boy began to ride the cow, exactly as if the cow was a horse. The cow moved and responded just as a friendly horse could…it obeyed the young boy's instructions.

Ana was stunned, excited, and called out loudly, "Hello, Hello! I like cows. My name is Ana. What's your name, and can I ride the cow with you?"

The young boy jerked around and saw the little girl standing on the fence. His face showed surprise, and he seemed startled for an instant. But the happiness of the little girl was obvious, and he smiled a big smile too. "Hi there little girl, little Ana. Where in this world did you come from and are you sure you want to ride this cow?"

Giggling, Ana shouted enthusiastically as she climbed higher up onto the fence, "Yes, I want to ride the cow with you. Please."

Laughing as he rode the cow over to the part of the fence Ana was standing on, he dismounted. As he put one foot on the bottom rail he patted the cow and said, "Okay Daisymae, you stand still for a minute."

Not worried that the cow wouldn't do what he asked, he climbed up and over the fence. Beside Ana, he held out his hand.

She grabbed it and he helped her climb over the fence and down into the field. She asked, "Is that your cow's name? Is the cow Daisymae?"

"That's her name. My father named her Mae, but I wanted to call her Daisy, so we just put the two names together, and now she's Daisymae."

Daisymae waited patiently, apparently unconcerned that a stranger was getting so close. The young boy looked at her again and said, "Are you sure you want to ride my cow?"

"Yes I want to ride your cow Daisymae!" She excitedly nodded yes, yes, yes, and grabbed his hand again.

The boy helped her up onto the cow's back, and then mounted carefully and easily. He placed himself in front, Ana behind.

No more conversation was necessary as they rode toward the gate. Trust and friendship flowed back and forth between the two children.

When they reached the gate, he jumped down again, led the cow outside onto the road, then closed the gate and joined Ana back on top. The life journey of two friends began, riding the cow down the road together.

Daisymae's pace was slow and steady and as they started out the young boy spoke up. "You told me your name was Ana. Do you live around here?"

Without waiting for her answer he yelled "Giddy-up." He wanted to move faster. The well-trained cow responded with a little more speed, and smiles grew larger on both of the two young riders' faces.

She was so happy. Life was so good. She wrapped her arms more tightly around the young boy and answered, "My name is Ana Winchester and I live with my mother and father and grandpa. We're your neighbors."

Immediately the boy stiffened. The stiffness was also present in his words. "Well nice to meet you Ana. My name is Sam, and I live here with my mother and father. We're your neighbors. We've been living on our land from time's beginning. Maybe you don't know it, but I'm half Cherokee Indian. Does that make you want to get down from my cow?"

She felt confused. Her face showed it as she sat motionless behind him.

Sam couldn't see her anxious face. Even as she felt Sam's unhappiness, she didn't know what he was talking about. She didn't know anything about Cherokee Indian hardships, nothing about the Trail of Tears. She simply didn't know what he was trying to tell her.

"Don't you like me Sam? I like you." She answered softly, painfully into the back of his shirt.

Sam stopped the cow and turned around to look at Ana. On her little face he saw uncertainty and confusion. In that exact moment he became her best friend.

He didn't say anything else about his connection to the Cherokees, simply answered her, "My new friend Ana, would you like to ride even further down the road with me on Daisymae? Before today I didn't realize that there were friendly Winchesters in this world."

Laughter was her answer and Sam understood a yes when he heard it. He gave the cow another "Giddy-up" and off they went, more talking and more laughing. They were fortunate enough to be able to ride for almost a mile.

The cow belonged to Sam's father, and he regularly showed her at livestock fairs in the general vicinity of their farm. The cow had been trained to behave well around people, and was actually trained to perform as a horse might. Young Sam, responsible for much of her caretaking, had strengthened this training because he pretended to himself that the cow could actually be the horse he wanted for himself.

It felt too soon when they were halted in their tracks by the harsh voice of Ana's grandpa yelling, "What in heaven's name are you up to? Your mother's worried because you disappeared and I was forced to come and look for you."

Grandpa stood at the side of the road and his face was stern and angry. He gave her no chance to answer his question. He simply continued in his sarcastic voice, "Looks like you found another looser like yourself to hang out with. Neither one of you is worth nothing, and proves how dumb you both are, riding a cow and thinking it's a horse."

Sam and Ana sat still. Ana tensed, and her arms recorded the same tensing in Sam's body. Suddenly Sam jumped down from the cow, and with one movement reached up and lifted Ana safely to the ground.

Then he looked over at her grandpa and said, "Mr. Winchester, you aren't worth talking to, much less listening to. I'm sorry that little Ana has you for her grandpa."

With those angry words, Sam jumped back up on his cow, turned her around, and as he started back down the road, he called out to Ana, "Don't you believe anything that man says!"

Their first time together raced through her mind and ended as she looked in front of her and saw Sam dropping the boxes on her front porch. "Hey Sam, guess what I was just thinking about?"

He walked quickly back to her. "You look happy Ana. Were you thinking about your new job in Germany?"

"No Sam. I was thinking about how we met for the first time, about Daisymae. I was laughing and having fun again just thinking about it." Then she remembered how their fun together ended. Without thinking about what she said, she blurted out, "But I was also remembering the advice you gave me about my grandpa; don't listen to anything he says. It was wise for a boy your age and I wish I'd been more able to follow it."

Her laughter disappeared. She became a statue.

He saw her laughter end and a ghost fly across her face. "What's wrong? You were so happy and now you're so sad. What's the matter Ana?"

"Come on Sam. I'll help you carry my junk inside." She screamed inside her head saying, forget it! Don't think about it! She ignored his question, and then laughed at him again. "Let's get this all moved in and then I'll make us some coffee and I'll give you all the wonderful details of my new job."

Like many times before he respected her silence, didn't press her for an answer.

Chapter Eight

A Secret Uncovered
Ana – North Carolina – 1969

After all the boxes were carried in and stashed, Ana and Sam went into the small cozy kitchen of her home. He sat down at the table, she made some coffee, and they started a non-stop conversation. He wanted details about her new job, how it happened, and what needed to be done before she went to live and teach in Germany. She shared all the information along with an obvious high degree of excitement. He saw and felt that she'd gotten what she truly wanted.

They hadn't started on their second cups of coffee when they heard a knock on the front door.

"I'll get it!" Sam left the table and headed for the door.

Ana didn't sit still. She got up too because she felt she knew who was knocking. Sam's voice, his welcome, confirmed that she was right.

"Mr. Elden, it's so nice to see you. Ana just got here and we've unloaded her things and we're drinking some coffee. Come on in and have some with us." As he talked, Sam led Mr. Elden into the house.

She didn't wait for him to walk over to her, instead moved forward and quietly gave him a hug. ""Hello, Mr. Elden. It's so good to see you again. Come on in and let me get you some coffee. "

Because of his involvement in her job offer, she didn't feel it necessary to give Mr. Elden too many details. Instead she said, "Enjoy your coffee and know how much it means to me that you helped me get this job. If not for you and your friend in Canada, I don't think I'd be so happy right now."

Mr. Elden responded with a smile on his normally serious face. "It was my pleasure. You had all the qualifications required for the job. I simply happened to know someone who had the right connections and could help

25

you get what you wanted. I'm pleased for you."

More coffee, more conversation, and the three moved on to another facet of life that connected them all together, the Winchester Farm.

Mr. Elden was talking about Sam as the new farm manager. "I'm certainly glad that you agreed to take over my duties with Ana's farm. The timing was perfect. Not only do I now get more time to enjoy nature and read but I'm also finding out that this is a good time to re-start my real estate business. Well, I should say a good time and a bad time. The real estate market is much busier than before when I worked it and that helps pay for groceries. That's' the good part. The bad part is that it takes more of my time than it used too. Thanks again Sam, for taking my place. I appreciate it greatly."

Ana spoke with feeling. "Just like we agreed Mr. Elden, Sam is a natural for the job. You made so much progress over the years, and now Sam's doing the same thing. You taught him well. The farm is flourishing because of you Mr. Elden, and now, because of your hard work Sam."

Mr. Elden had taken on the farm with all its responsibilities when Ana's father died and he must have been thinking about that point in time because he started talking about her father. "Your father was an intelligent man. He made some excellent decisions when he inherited everything from your grandpa. I think the most important decision was when he added a new dimension to the farm income. I remember that a friend of his, a man he served with in the war, contacted him with an idea for selling fresh produce. His friend Tom had a grocery store that constantly needed fresh produce. Tom lived in Atlanta, relatively close to your farm, and he wanted your father to promise to grow certain vegetables that he needed. Then he wanted your father to truck it down to Atlanta on the weekends. He promised to buy a specific agreed upon amount of the produce and then he helped your father get set up at the Farmers Market. That way, lots of other stores could and did purchase the rest of the produce your father brought down every weekend."

Ana asked, "But Mr. Elden, I never really heard how the produce trucking to Atlanta got started. Did mother tell you this when she asked you to help us manage the farm after father died?"

"Yes she did share this with me when I agreed to manage the farm for her. She provided me with facts like the name of your father's friend and how your father got started. I needed all available information so we could continue the good profit your father had started and grow the profit of the farm to care for you and your mother."

Ana spoke up again. "I guess I was too young to understand all the business stuff at that time." She smiled gently, and then continued. "Actually, I think the best decision father made was to agree with mother and let us use that old vacant barn and meadow to start boarding and caring for horses." Then she laughed at her comment.

Sam laughed with her. "I agree with you! Your mother asked me if I'd like to help out and boy did I want to. Every minute I spent there helping you and your mother was a pleasure. Oh, remember how the horses used to react when you came up Ana? Remember how they'd all look at you, shake their heads, and then start to walk directly over to you. Trust me, it wasn't a matter of food. You weren't feeding them, I was. They just wanted to talk to you."

More fun and lots more laughter erupted, even from the normally quiet Mr. Elden.

Ana got up and started to gather up the now empty coffee cups and put them in the sink. She had her back to them when Sam started talking again.

"Mr. Elden, maybe this is not the right time or maybe I shouldn't ask, but do you know why the police never found the person who caused Ana's father to die in the accident?"

Silence. Ana turned around and faced them both. "Mother filled me in on what happened but she also never could understand why the police couldn't find out who killed him. If you know anything Mr. Elden, I want to hear it."

"I only know what you know Ana. When you mother asked me to help, she also told me what she knew. She said that your father was driving to Atlanta with a load of produce. It was really early in the morning. There in the mountains, before he crossed over into Georgia, his truck was struck by another vehicle. The hit was powerful and your father's truck ran off the road and then crashed down the side of the mountain. The coroner said that your father died instantly. And, like we all know, the driver and the vehicle that hit him vanished. I also never knew or could understand why they never caught the person who caused his death."

"This is too sad. I'm sorry for asking. Forgive me and let's get back to the good things that are happening here today." Sam looked at Ana. "I'm a sorry friend!"

"I won't agree that you're a sorry kind of friend. You're my friend. You're the brother I never had. Maybe you don't understand that talking about these sad things in my past helps me a little. Actually, this has been a warm and loving homecoming, spending time with you and Mr. Elden."

A few days later, alone in her home, Ana decided that is was time to clean out some of her mother's things. Since mother died, she couldn't seem to feel ready to sort out her left-behind belongings. Her mother's bedroom remained exactly as it was before her death.

She pushed herself to deal with it now. Too much time had passed. Perhaps part of the new life-path she'd chosen to pursue was forcing her to deal with the past. A new life in another country forced her to shove aside her loss, to deal with the hurt, and sort out mother's things before she left for Germany. She knew that sadness would be attached to everything her mother's hand had ever touched.

Prepared, or so she thought, she was still shocked by the depth of sadness that saturated her body when she sorted mother's clothes. Memories were clinging to each dress, every piece of clothing.

Pictures were scattered around the bedroom, of Ana, father, the farm. Then the books! Everywhere. Stacks filled any place available in the room, and then in the closet even more. Mother had filled up the closet with row after row of books. Books had provided mother with happiness and serenity.

Ana decided to look at every one. A few were books mother had read or shared with her and these Ana pulled aside into a stack she meant to keep with her.

Finally, the books were sorted and the closet was empty. She started to close the door. Wait. Suddenly she stopped.

A tiny white-painted wooden knob at the top right of the closet caught her eye. She fully re-opened the door and stared at it. It wasn't actually a safe, but it was obvious that it had been hidden carefully. Ana had never seen it or heard about it. Suddenly, she felt nervous.

Be strong. She pulled hard on the knob and opened the small door it was attached to. She reached up and put her hand into the inside of the cabinet and felt something. In her hand was a box. It was fairly large and it wasn't locked. When she opened the lid, she found a few pieces of jewelry, some pictures, some of mother's special memories.

At the bottom of the box sat a notebook. Without any thought of secrets, of deliberate hiding away, she opened the notebook and found numbers and dates. Was this how mother kept a record of income and expenses? Then she saw another notebook, this time underneath a thick piece of cardboard. She pulled it out and opened it.

Life, breath, time all stopped. The notebook was slim, and the first pages were filled with mother's writing. Ana recognized immediately that the language was German. Oh! Maybe this is mother's journal, her diary! Quickly she flipped through the book but she saw quickly that all the pages were not written on, half of the book was blank.

She sat on the bed and began to read, to translate what mother had written.

She finished. Slowly she walked out of the room and back into the kitchen. She sat down at the table and stared blankly out the window. She floated, abandoned in a massive dark sea.

Chapter Nine

Goodbyes
Ana – North Carolina – 1969

Sam knocked, knocked, waited, and then he knocked again, harder this time. Ana was supposed to meet him here at her home. They'd made plans to spend this afternoon together.

It had been Ana's idea. She wanted, needed to go to the barn and re-unite with her horse Devil. Sam's horse was boarded there too and so she asked if he wanted to go riding together, friends on their favorite horses. Time to talk, ride, and enjoy the countryside.

At the exact moment he was ready to yell out to her, she opened the door. "Hi Sam! I bet you thought I'd forgotten about our horse riding together."

He grinned. "I wondered why you didn't answer the door but I knew you didn't forget about our plan. I know better than anyone exactly how much you love your Devil."

Even as he spoke to her, he paid close attention to her body language, watched her face and looked into her eyes. He knew it; she was hiding something again.

Over the years they'd grown up together, Sam had learned that she kept lots of her thoughts and emotions to herself. She didn't share. He gave her respect for being able to deal privately with her life and believed that maybe that was how she managed to move forward when she was distressed.

He didn't ask what was bothering her. Instead he waited to see what their afternoon ride together would reveal.

"I'm running behind Sam. Could you wait while I change clothes? I lost track of time. I've been working on sorting out mother's bedroom this morning."

He moved inside the house, her words stopped him. "I didn't know you were working on that today. I'm sorry you had to deal with all that. Can I help you with it?"

Again, as he talked, he also watched her. Maybe that overload of emotion, her mother's death, was why she seemed off balance. "Do you still want to go on our ride?"

"I'm fine Sam. I really want to get out and enjoy our ride together." She peeked out the window. "It looks like the weather might seriously be cooling down out there. The air will feel good."

"No hurry Ana. This afternoon belongs to us and to our horses. Take your time and change clothes."

Sam drove them to the horse barn a short time later. He stood back and watched her run to Devil's stall. Devil had already spotted her and his head stretched forward, trying to reach her, to welcome her. They reconnected powerfully.

After the horses were saddled they climbed on and he asked, "Which way do you want to go?"

"It doesn't matter to me. I just want to breathe the air, feel the beauty of things, and spend time with you and Devil. Go any direction you want to Sam."

"Okay, then let's ride on up to my place. I want to show you some changes I'm making. Thanks to you, my life's gotten better and I want you to see the good changes you've helped me make."

"I'd love to see your land and the changes you're making but don't credit me with what is really your success in this life. You get the credit for what you accomplish, not me. In fact, you also get credit for helping me get to where I am today. You've got the thanks backwards; it comes from me to you, not you to me."

He stopped his horse and reached out to grab Devil's bridle. "You and I are both trying to argue our way to what's right."

They sat on their horses and looked at each other. He spoke first. "I don't know if you believe in God, in luck, or in spirits, but we need to agree that we're bonded together. We both get help from each other. That's been true from that first time when we sat on my cow."

"I don't know exactly what I believe so I won't argue with you. You're right. We do help each other. I promise not to argue anymore. Let's ride!"

No further words required. They turned the horses and dashed off to look at the new home Sam was building for himself on his own land. He'd inherited his farm from his father, the white man and from his mother, the white man's Cherokee wife.

The rest of the afternoon they rode and talked. As they neared the horse barn Sam made a request. "Promise me that you'll keep in close contact with me after you move away. I know how strong you are but I want you to understand that I'm here for you anytime you need me. It's a long way to Germany but I'll get there fast is you need me."

"I'll remember and remind you of those words if I need you!" She laughed out loud at him. "Seriously, I'm trying to check out the life I've always dreamed of. I need to see if the reality lives up to my dream. I know you're there for me and it means so much. I know you have my back."

Later as they unsaddled the horses she asked him, "Would you do me a favor and check up on Maggie for me? She landed a great job at a Certified Public Accounting firm in Atlanta. She starts next week. Maggie loves it here on the farm, so maybe you could invite her to stay at my house when she has time free from work. Would you do that for me?"

Sam laughed and shook his finger at her. "Let me be very clear on this. Inviting Maggie to stay here and to take care of her while she's here will most definitely be my pleasure."

They understood each other perfectly.

Chapter Ten

A Little German Girl
Ingrid – Heidelberg - Early 1930s

The little girl Ingrid lived in the Neuschwander family home in Heidelberg, Germany along with her parents and her grandparents. The house stood proudly on the north side of the famously beautiful Neckar River at the base of a large mountain that rose up steeply, directly behind it. It was a tall beautiful house and blended perfectly into its natural background.

Their home rested on a raised parcel of land above the Neckar River and provided a wide and open view that made the river an intrinsic part of daily life, gifted the family with a daily dose of beauty and joy.

In addition, the river attracted animals. Beneath the flowing water fish swam and periodically broke the surface with a flash and a splash. Birds flew above the water, on the lookout for food, then swooped low to grab it and soared swiftly off into the clear blue sky with their captured meal. So many aspects of nature were framed and highlighted by the mountains that rose up on both sides of the river.

The City of Heidelberg is an old and important part of European history. It was inhabited as far back as the fifth century BC. Remains of a large Celtic Fortress are still identifiable where they exist at the top of the Heiligenberg, (the Holy Mountain). Later in time, after the occupation by the Celts, a Monastery, named "St. Paul's" was built on top of the original old Celtic Fortress. The Holy Mountain was important to generations of people who lived in the Heidelberg area.

Ingrid's ancestors were not directly descended from any of the original inhabitants of the area, had only arrived in Heidelberg in the mid-fifteen hundreds as immigrants. They were French Huguenots who fled France, their homeland, to escape waves of religious persecution. Everything they knew and loved was left behind in order to save their lives.

Even though they left so much behind, they managed to bring many assets with them, including moderate wealth, intelligence, and a passion for hard work. At once, with no time wasted, they put down roots, opened their imagination to new possibilities, and purchased land in the Old Town of Heidelberg where they started a business. Over time they flourished and built a large family home.

At this point in history, the early 1930s, the Neuschwander family was recognized as part of the history of Heidelberg. They'd contributed greatly to its growth and heritage.

Ingrid's mother, the only daughter of the now wealthy descendants of the Huguenots was well educated and secure. Ingrid's father was an important Law Professor at the prestigious Heidelberg University, the oldest and one of the most important in Germany.

Ingrid was young, bright, and filled with imagination. The large home where she lived gave her plenty of interesting space in which to run, hide, and explore, the exact things she loved to do.

She associated her home with gingerbread. The mansion was constructed from local stone. It was warm and brown and was inset with dark mortar, then trimmed with an even darker brown paint. When she looked at it she smiled and thought of cookies and Christmas.

The land on which the house sat included a large grass-covered courtyard that was attached to the east side of the home. It was Ingrid's playground. The courtyard separated the formal coach or motorcar entrance, defined by a formal brick archway opening out into the street below and the main front entrance to the house. In the center of the open courtyard stood an elaborate fountain that sported four gurgling fish. The happy fish constantly spewed sparkling water into the basin.

At the front of the courtyard sat a series of open-ended brick archways, originally designed for carriage parking, horse boarding, and storage. Little Ingrid now used the area for hiding and make-believe. She chased invisible creatures and was chased in return. She played hide-and-seek with imaginary visions and exercised her vivid imagination.

When she was only three years old, she invented a game she called "crocodiles."
She used the circular wall of the fountain as her imaginary castle and inside this castle she worked in her pretend kitchen. It was filled with pretend dishes. At times, she would ask her mother or her grandmother to help her fill the dishes with food and feed the hungry crocodiles.

Step one was to pluck leaves, grass, and when she could get away with it, flowers. This "food" she piled high, one plate at a time. Then she gave the food-filled plates to mama and grandma, took one herself, and they carried them to the edge of the courtyard where the starving crocodiles sat and waited. The crocodiles were always hungry and Ingrid spent lots of time cooking and feeding them.

The crocodile game was representative of her intelligence. Her father and mother made sure that Ingrid was challenged daily with early reading and education. They lavished her with parental love. She used information learned from her encouraging parents, then went out into her childish world and used her knowledge and imagination at a very early age.

One evening her father had talked to her and mother about crocodiles. He said that some populations in the world, such as Egypt, counted crocodiles as Gods. Perhaps Ingrid didn't exactly understand what her father meant when he talked about the Crocodile Egyptian God named Sobek and Sobek's close association with the Egyptians Pharos, his violent and aggressive characteristics, those inherent to the Nile crocodile and so familiar to all Egyptians. What she did understand was when her father talked about another important characteristic of the Crocodile God.

The Crocodile God Sobek was not only famous for his harshness, violence, and cruelty, but was also known by his followers as a benevolent God. Evidence exists of Egyptian-preserved crocodile mummies, some mummified with their baby crocodiles held in their mouths and on their backs. This represents the protective and nurturing attributes of Sobek. Real-life Nile crocodiles are an example of one of the few non-mammals that actually carefully take care of their young by carrying them around protectively in this way.

When Ingrid filtered all the crocodile information she heard from her father, she was truly fascinated by the love and protection they gave their children. Her interest was triggered and crocodiles became a vibrant part of her life.

At the back of the courtyard a steep flight of stairs led further up the mountain, to a small house built by Ingrid's family for their servants use.

Ingrid had attempted many times to use her game playing and get herself up to the top of the stairs. Her mother had allowed her to climb up once or twice when they had gone up together but the rule was that Ingrid couldn't go up by herself.

Ingrid so far abided by this house rule but there was a secret desire, an intense longing in her mind to disobey. A voice called her to climb up the stairs. Her mind wasn't intent on testing parental limits. She didn't really know why she felt this need to climb up.

At some point in time, she'd stored a memory; a path existed that ran outside of the ground floor of the servants' house. Once when she went up with her Mother, she'd searched for the path, found it, and even placed her feet on it. Mother had stopped her from going any further.

"Too dangerous for my small Ingrid." Mother had smiled at her as she said it.

At that time, mother had told her that the path led up to the top of the mountain. Ingrid already loved the mountain behind her home and now she wanted to learn more about it. She was curious and wanted to understand it, to become its friend. She was fascinated.

Ingrid created more important memories for herself when she was six years old. She had heard people talking about an event that they called "The Party for German Girls." It excited her as she visualized a large birthday-like party and she wanted to be included in it. When she asked her mother if she could go, mother had said no. Then she went and asked her father. His answer was also no.

She generally behaved well, didn't try to cause trouble, but on this particular day she deliberately acted differently. First she made sure that her mother was busy sewing in her workroom. Then she quietly sneaked to the front door, and opened it slowly, just wide enough to squeeze out. With one glance back and with a mischievous grin on her face, she softly closed the door behind her.

Instinctively she hunched her shoulders forward, tucked her head down, and tried to be invisible. It was hard to do because the way into the street ran straight through the wide-open courtyard. No bushes were available to hide behind. She was out in the open but moved ahead without fear.

She listened to her heart as she ran across the open courtyard. Childlike, she believed that what she was doing was important. As she ran through the courtyard, the sweet smell of flowers was heavy in the air, invaded her senses, and linked up in her mind with adventure and happiness. As soon as she reached the exit gate, she quickly moved outside. Without a backwards glance, she ran into the wide-open world.

In seconds she raced across the road in front of her home and then onto the walking path that paralleled the Neckar River. The path led to downtown Heidelberg.

The river was her good friend. She woke up and looked down at it every morning and it greeted her with a smile of reflected sunshine, or sometimes waved at her with rowdy rough waves and flying foam. In her heart, the minute she reached the river path, she felt comfortable. For a second, she turned around and looked back. The thought that went through her mind was of the tall "Holy Mountain" that stood so close behind her home. At that moment, she imagined that her home could serve as the mountain's front door.

With a small smile, she spun around and moved forward again. As she walked along, she looked at the sunshine dancing on the small waves of the river. It shimmered in the light wind, and the river was filled with languid ripples made by the transport boats that worked their way up and down.

Suddenly she thought of her mother and felt a wave of guilt. She stopped and looked back towards home. Mother was not outside looking for her so maybe her escape was a success. She hurried forward again. On her feet, tiny red shoes caused small flashes of bright color as she marched with purpose along the path.

Then just a short distance further, she paused. She felt her name was being called.

Two swans hid in the rushes at the shallow edge of the river and screamed out loudly. They wanted her attention. She ran over to the river's edge and crouched down as close to them as she could without getting her shoes wet. The she asked them, "What's wrong?"

They answered back, screamed some more. The intensity of their screams sounded important but even as she asked them over and over to explain, she couldn't understand what they were trying to tell her. Finally she just gave up and threw them happy thank you kisses as she walked back up to the path.

Time was running out to get to the party on time.

At that exact moment she saw a man walking toward her from the opposite direction. The path was normally full of people, walking back and forth to town or exercising their dogs and themselves. Now, the only two people in sight were a little girl and a grown man.

Ingrid didn't realize that she was alone on the path with the upcoming man. She glanced forward at him once or twice, watched the distance between them get closer. When they drew even she stopped directly in front of him.

He stopped too. He lifted his hat and bowed to her, then asked, "Young lady where are you going in such a hurry today?"

With wide innocent eyes flashing blue light she smiled up at him she answered, "I'm going to the big party for the German Girls at the University."

He was very tall and as she gazed up at him she connected him with the Holy Mountain. She felt he fit perfectly into the brilliant sunlight and the blue sky. Then she thought she saw tiny shadows darting and trying to cling to the edges of his body. When she tried to concentrate on the shadows they became unidentifiable, indistinct.

Childish blue eyes stared into older blue eyes and instinctively Ingrid felt this man was important to her. She waited expectantly for his next words.

"The Party for German Girls?" As he spoke these words he smiled at her, such a friendly smile. Then he was silent as he studied the little girl. He registered her blonde curls and her friendly intelligent smile. A warm wave of affection flowed through his veins. He was totally intrigued.

Trustingly, she looked up at him and said, "I heard about a big party for

German Girls and I want to go because I'm a German Girl. I heard that the party was at the University Plaza in town and I know how to get there."

Just as these words were spoken, Ingrid and the tall man both heard a woman's voice frantically calling, "Ingrid, Ingrid! Where are you?"

Ingrid twirled around. She knew mother's voice. Yes, her attempt to go to the party was not going to happen.

Quietly she stood still and waited for mother, looked down at her red shoes. The sunshine continued to sparkle on the river and the reflected light caused her curly hair to glow. The tall man stood by her side, watched quietly. He reached out and gently placed a large hand on her shoulder, gave her a reassuring pat.

Mother saw her and ran forward. She was out of breath, full of fear for her daughter's safety, but the first words out of her mouth were not angry words. She grabbed Ingrid and hugged her tightly, "Oh, you're safe my little one! Why did you leave without telling me? You've never done that before."

Ingrid hugged her mother and smiled at her. She felt the warmth of mother's love and also felt the worry she had caused. In her mind she thought this was a happy day even if she didn't go to the party. Her mother loved her and she'd made a new friend.

The tall man bowed to mother, "It has been a pleasure to meet and talk to your daughter, and, if I am correct, did you call her Ingrid?"

"Yes, her name is Ingrid. " Mother looked curiously at the man and continued, "Please accept my apologies if my daughter has delayed you or wasted your time."

"There is no need to apologize for your daughter." He looked at Ingrid, and then looked over at the Neckar River as it flowed so beautifully off to his right. "It has been a great pleasure to meet Ingrid. I don't feel my time has been wasted. In fact, I haven't spent a more pleasurable few minutes in a very long time."

Goodbyes were said and he bowed once more, then walked past them and continued strolling east along the path. Ingrid and mother stood still and watched him walk away.

They hugged each other again, then instead of fussing at Ingrid, mother walked with her and together they identified flowers and counted ducks.

Ingrid asked, "Why don't you and father want me to go the German Girl's Party?"

Mother's face was tight with suppressed emotions as she tried to gather her thoughts, as she tried to answer honestly without overwhelming her still young daughter. She was silent for a while thinking about the Nazi Party as it enrolled the youth of the country, first the young boys and now the young girls. The purpose was to use them for the advantage of the Nazi Party.

Without elaborating Mother simply told Ingrid that her education was certainly an important thing but that her father had doubts about the quality of the education being offered by the Nazi Party.

Ingrid was six, she was happy, and she was loved, so one more time she asked, "Please, will you let me go to the party so I can get educated and have fun?"

Mother looked at her daughter and suddenly changed her mind, "Yes Ingrid. Come with me and we'll go together."

Chapter Eleven

Ana Moves to Heidelberg
Heidelberg – 1970

The Assistant Professor sat behind her desk and looked out curiously at the students seated in her classroom. Most of them appeared to be listening attentively to her as she spoke. She saw small smiles on happy faces and realized that as they listened to her, they were also definitely anticipating the fun that Friday night brings. Friday was almost over and the weekend almost here.

The students watched her too as they listened to her speak. They were curious because she was a young Assistant Professor, and also because they knew that she came from the United States.

They appreciated her youth and attractiveness at first but now they'd also begun to appreciate her intelligence and her friendly ability to share knowledge easily through challenging and interesting lessons.

Today she wore a conservative blue skirt and jacket and had pulled her long blonde hair into a tight neat roll; a perfect match for her outfit. One young man in the back of the classroom was particularly interested. He watched her speak and thought how beautiful she looked as her hair began to escape from its tight bun. A stand of gold caressed her face.

Ana Winchester had been teaching at The German International University for a few months and was now halfway through her first semester.

A short time later she ended the day's session and dismissed her students. As they hurried out the door of the classroom she sighed with relief. So far so good she told herself mentally. She was determined to encourage herself and get this new job right.

"Professor Winchester!" The unexpected call jerked attention to the classroom door. One of her students, a young man named Thomas stood there.

"What do you need Thomas?" She answered him as she began to gather books and papers and put them into her briefcase.

"Professor Winchester, a large group of students are going to a concert in the train station venue tonight and we thought to ask if you would like to join us. If you do not have plans, you might enjoy the music. Oh wait! You may not enjoy dancing and drinking as much as we Germans do." He laughed heartily at his joke and gave her a large friendly smile.

She let herself laugh too because she truly enjoyed the way he'd expressed himself. "I do love music and the concert will certainly be good but I have a lot of work that needs my immediate attention. Thank you very much though."

Thomas smiled at her again, "It was worth a try." Then he raced back out the door.

These first months had been a little stressful as she struggled to adjust to the norms in Germany, to learn different customs and sometimes to decipher the meaning of regional slang.

Her job at the University positioned her work time right in the center of the charming old town Heidelberg area. She was pleased with all aspects of her job so far. Languages were one of her interests in life and now she had the opportunity to teach others about them.

Over the course of the last few weeks, like a weird dream that won't go away, she found herself thinking about her job offer from The German International University. She understood the network and connection of people who helped her to get the job but was confused. She didn't honestly understand the lack of direct communication between the University and her. None had actually taken place.

When she was offered the job, it was exactly what she wanted, and came exactly when she needed it. But why had no one walked the normal path of interviews and conversations, made inquiries that could answer the vital question of whether or not she was the right person for the job?

When it happened, when her dream to live and work in Germany had come true, she'd recognized the abnormal method used to hire her but her desire to accept the job had overpowered the normal careful method she used when making such important decisions.

Now her mind wouldn't let it alone. The more she experienced the normal structured procedures used by the University in all its decision-making, the more she wondered about how she'd gotten hired.

Ana physically shook herself. The classroom was empty. Slowly she moved over to one of several large windows that looked down on the open square below. She watched students scatter in all directions, race toward their planned weekend adventures.

Most of the students didn't have too far to go because this old historical classroom building sat on one side of University Square and was convenient.   Most of them lived in small apartments and university housing, all nearby.

Another interesting aspect of the old town location was that the old Historical Heidelberg University Library was just a few blocks away. Plus, many different university connected classrooms were scattered throughout the area.

The street that Ana looked down on ran directly into the Hauptstrasse, one of the busiest streets in the city.   However, on this particular street, busy was measured by the number of walkers and bicyclists, not by the number of vehicles present. Only a minimal amount of automobile traffic was allowed.

All of the old brick streets were perfect for walking and talking. They were sided by beautifully detailed buildings that marched down both sides of the street. All windows sported flowers, vibrant and rich. Outdoor tables topped with colorful umbrellas offered food, coffee, wine, or beer and studded the length of the streets. Any time the weather allowed, the tables were packed with people.

Ana saw a large city bus, an important form of transportation, as it pulled over beside the square. Several large pigeons flew up swiftly from the ground to escape it. Pigeons were totally at home in Heidelberg. They gathered any food left behind by humans and as they sat on rooftops and trees, so quiet and content, they offered an additional peaceful feel to the city.

Time to get going. She knew she needed to get home and get busy with some student papers that needed her attention. The apartment she'd rented was relatively close by and gave her the ability to walk back and forth to work. She loved it and walking was quickly becoming her main means of transportation. Only if she had too many bags of groceries would she use the public bus transport system.

As she walked along the street, her mind began to change. After all, this was Friday and she felt the eagerness and the energy in the air around her. She decided not to hurry home, instead simply walk along and enjoy herself. Without actually planning to, she walked straight into the square in which sat the hotel where she'd stayed on her very first trip to Germany. She'd been a second year student, scholar-shipped over from the United States and circumstances had made her spend her first night alone at the hotel. She looked at it now and saw that it remained remarkable, as lovely as it had been so long ago.

A restaurant was attached to the hotel and it was open. A few table remained empty. The weather was cold but beautiful and the restaurant always provided soft cozy blankets for customers at outside tables. As soon as she saw the empty table, she decided to treat herself to a celebratory Friday evening. She sat down and pulled the blanket off the back of the chair and wrapped it comfortably around her shoulders.

The waiter brought her a menu and she ordered a glass of wine. At the next table down from her she recognized the face of a Professor she knew who also worked at her University. She didn't know the Professor's name and tried not to stare, but couldn't help but be interested in how the middle-aged woman handled herself as she ate alone tonight.

Ana watched as the server walked over to the Professor's table and greeted her, called her by name. She was evidently a regular. The server confirmed her order, her usual with no changes and then went to fetch the glass of wine she'd asked for.

Then the Professor reached down and opened the briefcase beside her feet. She removed several folders and placed them in front of her on the table. She pulled out a pen and began working on the papers. Ana felt they must be assignments, written by her students, and the Professor was evaluating and grading them.

A wave of peace passed through Ana. She took a deep breath, a sip of wine, then sat still and looked at the lovely river that flowed past the Alte Brücke (Old Bridge) that sat out in front of her. This must be one of the most special views in Heidelberg.

A new thought entered her mind, one she'd never had before. From what she saw and felt today, it was totally possible to live alone, enjoy her chosen field of work, and be content. She could do her job well, enjoy life, didn't need to constantly get approval from people who were supposed to love her.

Ana enjoyed her meal and thought about some of her lifetime goals.

Unfortunately intense thinking about her life triggered a difficult memory. The first night she spent in Germany.

At age 19, the university she attended in North Carolina sponsored her for a semester of study at Heidelberg University. She remembered that time so well, especially what happened during her first night's stay.

The flight out of the United States was delayed because of weather problems and of course, she didn't arrive at the Frankfurt Airport on time. She wasn't there when the shuttle she had signed up for left for Heidelberg without her. She realized that other public transportation was available and decided to use the train system. A train-stop was located at the Frankfurt Airport so she used it to get to Heidelberg.

The delayed flight caused her not only to miss the shuttle, but also miss her scheduled meeting with the person designated to take her to the student apartment she'd been assigned during her stay in Heidelberg.

With no contact information available, she got off the train at Karlstorbahnhof (the Old Town Train Station) in Heidelberg and then followed the other passengers as they left the train behind. She followed them through an elaborate entry gate into the city that appeared to have been in existence for a long time. It was lovely. As the walk progressed through more streets, many people veered off and some picked up their bicycles from nearby racks.

After about five or six blocks, she realized she was entering a small town square and off to the right stood a large old gateway that marked the opening to an old brick bridge that ran across a wide river. Across the square she saw several hotels so she walked to the nearest one. As she walked, she passed through a lovely group of outside tables, many filled with people. She heard their laughter and smelled the food as she reached the entry to the hotel. She pushed open the large heavy door and walked hesitantly up a flight of stairs to the reception desk.

A clerk sat at the desk and smiled at Ana, then asked in German if she could help her. Instead of answering in German, which she totally understood, Ana found herself answering in English. It didn't matter to the clerk, who continued taking down her information while using a perfectly understandable form of English.

Ana got a room for one night and she climbed up two more flights of stairs to reach it. When she opened the door, she was pleased to see how beautiful the small room was. It had a single bed and two large windows crowned by lovely curtains. She sat her suitcase down and walked to the windows, pulled back the curtains and gasped.

The windows looked down on the top of the square, the tall ornate gate, and the old bridge that spanned what she later realized was the Neckar River. The view was so wonderful she thought about simply staying in her room, but hunger was calling, so she locked the door behind her and went out in search of food.

The simple thing to do was to sit down at the restaurant she had walked through on her way into the hotel but the desire to explore grabbed her. She walked again through the tables of the Golden River Hotel and then turned right onto a street filled with shops and restaurants. She followed it until it branched out in two different directions at an old stone church. She decided to turn left and almost immediately found herself in another large town square. This one had a sign naming it "The City Council." Again she saw many restaurants and tables set up inside the square. She picked one and sat down.

She surprised herself. As she sat alone among strangers she enjoyed her meal, relaxed, and mellowed out. The stress of the day vanished and pure pleasure filled her mind. She felt happy.

Later she went to bed and realized that she was exhausted. Sleep was almost upon her but into the quiet, creaking sounds exploded. Heavy footsteps moved up the wooden stairs to the same floor she was on. More than one person was walking up.

The footsteps woke her up totally, sounded so close. Then she heard a woman's voice, light and content. Ana deliberately tried not to hear what she said, didn't want to pry into a private conversation.

The lady's pleasant voice didn't give her any warning of the storm that was coming.

Two people entered into the hall and walked directly past her bedroom door. She heard a door open and close further down the tiny hallway. Then a man spoke up. His voice was deep and stern. "How did you manage to show your stupidity so early this evening? How did you manage to spoil the whole evening?"

The words were precise, clear, and the language was German.

The woman's response was filled with emotion. "How can you say that? I interacted with the advisor just like you told me to. It wasn't my fault that the flight was delayed."

She moaned, cried, "What do you mean? I believed I was being everything you told me you wanted me to be. I was doing exactly what you told me to do. I thought you were happy with how I handled everything."

Ana glanced at the tiny travel clock she had placed on her bedside table. It was just past midnight.

She remained perfectly still and quiet as the angry man continued on and on. What was happening? The woman was sobbing and pain was included in the sound. Did the man hit her? The woman's voice sounded hysterical as she cried out her innocence to everything he was accusing her of.

The hotel was a bed and breakfast and the small staff had exited the building at 10:00. Ana knew this to be true because the clerk gave her a key to let herself back into the building later than 10:00, when no workers would be there. She had stayed out past that time and had unlocked the heavy red-painted door when she let herself in with the key the clerk had given her.

Alone and young and scared, she always remembered this event and felt she'd taken the coward's way out. In her short life, she'd been the target of verbal and physical abuse. She was scared and imagined the cruel man she heard would come into her bedroom if he knew she was listening to what was happening. She let the man abuse his unfortunate wife, or whoever the woman was because she was frightened and couldn't intervene, didn't know what to do.

The crying lasted more than an hour. Than all went silent. Ana lay awake for hours, careful not to move, not make a sound. He would come in and hurt her.

The next morning she climbed out of bed and sneaked to one of the windows. The heavy red-painted hotel entry door was right below her and as she looked out she saw a man and woman leave. Both were dressed elegantly, the man looked some older than the woman. The couple walked slowly across the square and to the entrance of the Old Bridge.

Another woman walked toward them from the opposite side of the bridge. She met the couple and obviously they all knew each other because they talked together for a few minutes. Then the man and woman walked on across the bridge. As they strolled calmly over the cobblestones, it looked like they were happy with each other. The woman they talked with came forward and into the square, moved toward the door to the hotel.

Ana hid behind the curtain and kept her eyes on the older couple calmly walking to the end of the bridge. What really happened last night? What were they arguing about? If these two people were the ones involved in last night's horror, maybe she had the whole thing wrong.

Ana pushed the first night's nightmare back into her mind. It was a long time ago.

Chapter Twelve

Lifetime of Confusion
Ana – Heidelberg – 1970

Later, after she watched her fellow Professor leave the restaurant, she decided to do the same. She'd finished her meal and hoped that her mind was finished delving into the confusion of her past. She was ready to go home, the physicality of the walk to her apartment called her name because it afforded her the opportunity to move forward and look at the world, not move backwards into her past.

The old bridge was one of her favorite places to walk and tonight it glowed, the darkness pushed back by the lights placed along its length and the lights of the city that reflected colorfully on both banks.

This particular night, she didn't stop to look down and enjoy the view like she usually did. She kept walking, trying to move her mind ahead. She focused on her job at the University and how it pleased her. She felt she'd made the right decision when she pulled herself away from her home to experience a different life.

Mr. Elden came to mind. She knew how he'd helped her to get this job and then to find a decent place to stay. He always took care of her, made sure she was safe.

Because he'd run his own real estate agency for years before he'd started managing Winchester Farm, she'd called and asked him how she could find a place to live in Heidelberg. He was glad to help and told her to let him look into it. A few days after they'd talked he called with good news.

He'd located an international rental service in Heidelberg and they had located an apartment that featured both a kitchen and a laundry room. In addition, it was on the second floor of a historic old home and it overlooked the famous Neckar River. She was excited and told Mr. Elden how much she appreciated his help. The apartment he described sounded too good to be true so she asked him what she needed to do to secure it immediately. He'd laughed and told her to relax because he'd handle it for her.

When she'd first asked Mr. Elden to help her get lined up for an apartment she'd explained that her contract with the University was only for one year, with the possibility of a future contract if the University was pleased with her performance and if she was pleased with her job with the University. She wanted to make sure that Mr. Elden had these details when he contracted the international rental service so that a provision could be attached that would allow her first choice to renew the rental if she needed to stay longer in Heidelberg.

Mr. Elden talked with the agent and then called and told her that the additional provision could be added with no problem. The apartment was hers. She was relieved to know she had a great place to live. Another task completed, thanks to Mr. Elden. She had a home in Heidelberg.

Now, as she smiled and walked toward it, she remembered the happiness she felt when she stepped into her apartment for the first time. It was better than she'd imagined, plus it had another great feature. It had an extra bedroom that she'd not been told about. Yes, she told herself, my Maggie would love it.

She would call her friend. The first semester was almost over and she'd have free time. It would be so good to get Maggie to come for a visit. She missed Maggie's company and it would be so much fun to share a little of her new life with her friend.

As these happy thoughts flew through her head, she heard her name called loudly behind her.

"Professor Winchester, maybe you will change your mind?"
She paused and looked back. Her student Thomas came running up behind her.

"Thomas, you never give up do you?" He hurried up, grinning from ear to ear.

"No, I do not Professor. Besides, you would love this concert!" He already knew her answer was no, so he moved past her with a quick wave and another large smile.

She looked at his back as he ran ahead and the thought drifted through her mind, "Why does Thomas run into me so often?"

Then she laughed at her silliness. Maybe he's simply a friendly young man.

The river path led her home and she crossed the highway that separated it from her apartment in the old historic building. With a lift in her steps, she gave the happy fish on the center fountain a smile and climbed up the stairs. Inside the apartment, she kicked off her shoes and looked at the clock, calculated the time difference between Heidelberg and Andrews, determined how soon she could dial Maggie's number.

Chapter Thirteen

Chaos Begins
Sam & Maggie – Andrews, North Carolina – 1971

Maggie and Sam sat comfortably across from each other at the kitchen table in Ana's house in Andrews. Sam had called and invited her to come over and she'd accepted the invitation. She'd driven up from Atlanta after work on Friday afternoon and planned to stay for a long weekend. Her supervisor had given her Monday off.

Sam got up and brought the coffee pot to the table. With an affirmative from Maggie, he refilled her cup, did the same for himself. He sat the coffee pot down and said, "Maggie it's so good to have you here! I hope the drive from Atlanta yesterday was easy and traffic not too much of a problem."

"No problems Sam. It's a beautiful stretch of country between here and Atlanta and I enjoyed the drive. It felt good to get out of the city and away from the never-ending stress of the office. The CPA firm I work for is overloaded with work right now. I was honestly surprised to be given this extra Monday off. Glad for it though."

During their conversation, Maggie told Sam that Ana had called and invited her to visit, to stay with her at her apartment in Germany if she could manage to get some time off from work.

Immediately he asked. "How did Ana sound when you talked to her on the phone? Could you tell from her voice how she's doing?"

"Honestly Sam, she sounded better than she has in a long time. Actually, maybe it's just that she sounded different. I'm having a hard time explaining what I heard but she sounded more positive. I think that's what I heard, that she seems more comfortable, more self-confident."

Sam drank more coffee, sat still, and thought about what Maggie said about Ana. He didn't respond or continue their conversation. Maggie sat still and watched him.

When he finally began to talk to her again, his voice was calm, his face solemn and shadowed. "Maggie, please understand that I'm not trying ignore you or to change the subject. Your news about Ana is good and I hope she made the right choice for herself." He got quiet. His mind was elsewhere....totally engaged.

"Something strange happened here right before you came. I haven't been able to think about anything else since it happened. It was so weird! For the first time in my life, I was told not to talk to anyone. A crazy federal agent told me that if I told anyone what he'd said or what we'd talked about, I'd be breaking the law and could be arrested. Craziness, all of it, and it's about Ana and the farm!"

She'd realized that he was worried about something but totally unprepared for his words. Her hand jerked and she spilled her coffee. "What are you talking about Sam? I'm scared by how you sound and by that look on your face. Tell me what happened! How is this about Ana?"

He got up from the table and moved around the small room. His steps shouted out nerves and restlessness. "I'm not sure exactly what this is about. Even though I was there, listened to the agent, I'm confused. From the beginning, I felt like he wasn't being truthful with me or was purposefully leaving out some of the facts. I'm worried about Ana but I honestly don't want to break the law so I've tried to keep this to myself since Friday morning when it happened. You're the first person I've mentioned it to."

Maggie was even more upset. She'd never seen Sam this confused and disturbed before. "Let's go into the other room, the living room. We can sit down together on the sofa and you can tell me exactly what happened. I'm Ana's friend just like you and between up we have her best interests at heart. You know, I work with some federal agents employed by the Internal Revenue Service as part of my job at the CPA Firm I work for. Maybe I can understand a little of what the agent said or wanted to know."

While she spoke, Maggie moved forward into the living room but before he followed her, Sam walked to the kitchen window and carefully looked out. Then he moved into the living room but instead of sitting down beside her, he walked over and opened the front door. He walked out onto the small front porch.

Maggie watched and realized that he was making sure they were alone and couldn't be overheard. She felt a twinge of fear as he came back in and sat down beside her.

He looked into her eyes. His voice sounded tight, he spoke softly. "Maggie, I'm going to tell you what happened because I need your help. I'm not going to obey the federal agent and not talk to you about this but this is strictly between you and me. We've got to help our friend."

She reached out and rubbed his arm. "Sam, I love her just like you do. Just like you, I'll do whatever it takes to make sure she's safe."

Then Sam told her what happened.

"I'd gone to work earlier than I do normally because I was over my head in some of the paperwork that I have to do as part of managing the farm. I was at my desk, working away when a sharp, unfriendly knock banged on the door. Strange I thought because everything's casual around the farm and the door isn't even usually locked. Anyway, I yelled out something like come on in, the door's not locked. I just kept on working and I heard the door open, but whoever came in didn't say a word.

"I looked up, thought I'd see somebody who works for us but instead a man I'd never seen before stood right inside the door. Even when I looked at him, he still didn't say word, just stood silent as he looked around the office. He closed the door behind him.

"That's when I stood up and asked him what he needed. That's also when I really started to feel a little nervous. Something wasn't right. I got louder and not so friendly and asked him what he wanted. He looked directly at me and instead of answering my question he asked me for my name and what I was doing in this office.

"I was stunned and decided he was nuts. He just kept looking at me and then he asked me again who I was. I decided then and there to ask him a question and if he didn't answer me then I wasn't giving him any answers either. I asked him the same question, asked him what was his name and what was he doing in my office. Before I gave him a chance to answer me, I told him real firmly that I was the manager of Winchester Farm, this was my office, and what exactly did he need from me?

"He was silent. I got even more uncomfortable. Then he asked me how long had I been the manager of Winchester Farm. That's the moment when I had enough and decided I was in charge here. He was on Ana's property, and whoever he was, he didn't have the right to act so rudely and to ask all these uncalled-for questions.

"To start with, I blurted out that if he needed information about who I was or about the farm then he'd better identify himself to me and tell me why he was asking all these questions. I asked him why my business was any of his business. That's when I got a real shock.

"The man told me he worked for the US Government as a federal agent and he'd been sent here to Winchester Farm by the government to get information on a man named Elden. According to him, a Mr. Elden was the man listed as manager of the Farm on all the government records. All of a sudden he pulled out his identification card and waved it at me.

"I was stunned in more ways than one and didn't think to ask to look at the identification card up close. Stupid me, I didn't get his name. I just stood there in shock and waited to hear what else he'd say."

Maggie jumped up from the sofa and hurried over to the window. "Sam, don't be so hard on yourself. You didn't do anything wrong here. Take a deep breath and tell me the rest of this wild story."

He continued.

"The next thing I knew he walked over and sat down in the chair in front of my desk. I ran over and sat down behind my desk and asked him what kind of information the government was looking for about Mr. Elden. He said that according to the records Mr. Elden had the legal authority to run the Winchester Farm business and to make any decisions for it. Legally he was in charge and had been placed there by the owner of the farm, Ana Winchester. What he wanted me to tell him was why Mr. Elden wasn't the manager anymore. Did he get fired? Why wasn't he still here?

"I just looked at him. I told him that Ana didn't fire Mr. Elden, had no reason to. He was her friend and had managed the farm for her for a long time. He'd made a decision that he wanted to retire from managing the farm and get back to a quieter life. That's when I was picked to manage the farm. I'd worked as Mr. Elden's assistant for lots of years.

"The man stared at me and asked me where he could find Mr. Elden today. I started right back and told him to go knock on his door. If that wasn't good enough, then try his real estate office on Main Street. I even said something like if you have all this financial and tax information, why don't you know where he lives and works? It sounded to me like he was searching for basic facts, stuff the government should already know.

"By this time I was upset and suspicious. I bluntly asked him what this whole thing was really about. I wanted to know what Mr. Elden had done to make the government investigate him. All I got for an answer was the agent telling me that he wasn't allowed to discuss this with me. He gave in a little and told me that the investigation related to funds found in the assets of the Winchester Farm. Then he told me that I couldn't talk to Mr. Elden or to anyone else about this and if I did that I'd be breaking the law and would be prosecuted.

"I thought it couldn't get any worse and then he started in on Ana. He wanted to know where the owner of the farm, Ana Winchester was at this moment. He said the government had reason to believe she wasn't living in the US anymore. Then, like the earlier conversation hadn't taken place, he asked me if she had left the country, and who had been left in charge of the farm?

"That was enough. I told him that Ana had left me as the farm manager. I'd already told him that but he acted like he didn't believe me at all. Then I told him that Ana was teaching at a University in Heidelberg, Germany. That was it, no more details from me. I just stood there and looked at him. He gave me an ugly sarcastic smile, turned around, and walked out the door."

"I was more upset than I'd realized. After a few minutes of turmoil, I ran out of the office, jumped into my truck and started driving downtown toward the police station. I just had this gut feeling that I needed help. Just at the red light on Main Street, when I was almost even with Mr. Elden's real estate office, I saw that federal agent again! He'd parked his car and was out walking but his back was towards the street and he couldn't see me. I drove past a little further then pulled into the parking lot of the furniture store across the street. I watched carefully and the agent didn't even go up to the front door of Mr. Elden's office. What he did was this. He casually snooped around the whole shopping center, pretended to be window-shopping. I just sat hunkered down in my truck until he got back in his car and drove out on Main Street. I let him go, didn't try to follow him."

Maggie and Sam stood in the middle of the living room and looked at each other. Both were thinking the same thing.

She spoke first, "Sam this is serious, really serious. From everything you've told me I think this may be the Internal Revenue Service sending an agent out to check on some problem, some large error on the part of Winchester Farms through Mr. Elden. BUT!!!! The procedure that the IRS uses in this type situation is normally quite different than what you just experienced. The IRS notifies the person or business with the problem they're examining and they set up a specific time and place to meet with the person in charge. If the problem is important enough, they will mail out notification that an audit of the tax returns related to the problem is set up and in progress. This meeting you had with the federal agent asking about Mr. Elden just feels wrong. Either the agent they sent is strange, maybe poorly trained, or somebody in charge is acting incorrectly."

Sam reached for Maggie and pulled her up directly in front of him. "Maggie I think we agree on this. I feel we need to let Ana know because something here isn't right. Is that how you feel?"

"I feel the same way Sam. In addition, I feel like I let Ana down, disappointed her because I couldn't get time off to go visit her during her semester break."

"What are you talking about Maggie? You didn't let her down and she knows that. Stop feeling guilty because you couldn't get off and go. Focus on this mess and help me figure it out. Talk to me some more about the IRS and then I believe we need to share this with Ana."

She asked, "Are you going to call her or do you want me to?"

"My Maggie, let's do this together." He put his arms tightly around her and drew her body close against his body, drew her into his heart.

Chapter Fourteen

Somewhere – 1971

Inside a small cottage hidden deep in the thick forest, a telephone rang. It was answered on the first ring.

"Your caretaker is in trouble. We caught wind of it through some of our old contacts and we double-checked. Questions are being asked. Somebody is tracking him. We wanted to give you warning because if they find him, they could also find you.

A deep voice answered quietly, "Let me know if anything else develops."

Chapter Fifteen

Night of the Burning Books
Heidelberg – Ingrid – 1933

A small emergency popped up at Ingrid's home. Her mother got sick. Mother suffered from terrible headaches, father called them migraines. They started last year and when they happened the only help for mother came from a prescription from their local pharmacist. Unfortunately, mother had used all of her pills and forgotten to refill the prescription. Now when she needed it so badly, she had none.

Father usually took care of fetching the pills from their pharmacist but he was not home to help this time. He was a Professor of Law at Heidelberg University and as part of his usual duties had gone to a conference in Munich to conduct a week-long seminar for law students. Grandmother and Grandfather were not home either. They had gone away to stay for several weeks at their country home in Bavaria. They spent a lot of time there lately.

Ingrid begged mother to please let her help. She begged to be allowed to walk into town, go to Herr Dentzinger, the pharmacist, and get the medicine mother needed. Mother was tempted to let her go because she knew Ingrid was totally comfortable with the walk into town, with the pharmacy, and with the man who owned and operated it. Ingrid often walked into town with her family, knew her way around, and recognized and was comfortable with many of the people she encountered on the walk across the Old Bridge into the Old Town of Heidelberg.

Mother didn't feel able to contact one of the employees that normally helped with the house. She didn't even know if they were around because she had let them all have time off since no one was home except Ingrid and herself. The house was empty.

Finally mother weakly answered "Yes" when Ingrid asked her again to help.

Ingrid left at once and carefully got herself to the river path. It was late in the afternoon and the day felt like weather-perfect spring. She walked fast and then almost ran along the bricks of the Old Bridge. It was not far to the Hauptstrasse, the street where the pharmacy was located. She knew it well because her father taught in a classroom off the University Square and the pharmacy was located right across the street.

All of a sudden she had to slow down. The number of people in the street increased greatly. Ingrid only noticed the increase in people because she felt the need to be polite and be careful not to bump into anyone. Otherwise, her mind was focused on getting to the pills her mother needed as fast as possible.

Finally she reached University Square. She stopped abruptly!

Students were everywhere, some piling up wood in the center of the square, others helping to pull wagons loaded with mounds of books into the square. Ingrid lost focus for a moment. She stood still and watched the students, watched all the books they were hauling into the square. She was, as usual, intensely interested in what was happening in the world around her.

Oh, Mother needed help! She remembered why she was here! She spun around and rushed over to the pharmacy door. But even as she pushed ahead, she still continued to analyze what all the stacks of books in the square meant. She walked into the pharmacy.

The owner and pharmacist was well known to her from previous visits and he was always friendly, so she looked right up at him as he stood behind the counter and asked, "Herr Dentizinger, please, do you know if the students are having a big party tonight? They are getting ready to make a big fire in the middle of the square and they are also pulling wagons full of books there too."

She asked more questions without giving him any opportunity to respond. "Do you think they are going to have a party tonight and give away free books to everyone? I want to come to the party and I want to get some of the free books!"

Herr Dentzinger seemed at a loss for words as he looked and listened to the happiness and excitement in young Ingrid's voice. Instead of answering her questions, he asked a question of his own, "Ingrid, what are you doing here all by yourself today?"

"Oh, Herr Dentizinger, my mother has another bad headache and my father is gone. My grandmother and my grandfather are gone too, so mother let me come to get some of the medicine you always give her when she is sick. She did not remember that she did not have any more of the pills and she feels so bad. I had to ask her many times to let me come get her medicine and finally, she let me. I had to promise that I would get the pills and go back home, not stop anywhere else."

Ingrid smiled up at Herr Dentzinger and waited for his answers to all of her questions about the party and the books. When he still did not respond to her, except to keep looking at her with an anxious expression on his face instead of his usual smile, she started in again, "Do you know if there is a …......"

This time he interrupted her when he rushed out from behind the counter, stopped beside her, and placed his hands on her small shoulders, "Ingrid, let me get the medicine your mother needs and you must promise to go straight home as fast as possible. Please promise me you will go home, not stop anywhere else. I honestly do not know for sure what is going to happen in the square tonight but I am sure that neither you nor I want to be there. No! From what I heard people talking about is that the students are going to give speeches and then burn all the books! The students are saying the books are not really "German" books and they are bad and are polluting out pure society."

With these words Herr Dentzinger turned and hurried into the back of his shop to get her mother's pills. He packaged them quickly and brought the small package to Ingrid. He gave it to her and she handed him the money her mother had given her to pay for it.

"Ingrid, you must promise me that you will not stay in the square. You must hurry home with the medicine for your mother's sake and for your own safety."

She looked into his eyes again, saw his genuine concern, and knew he was telling her the truth. He wanted to keep her safe.

With a tiny smile and a "Thank you Herr Dentzinger" Ingrid sped across the shop, opened the door and ran into the street. With only a last quick glance at the students and the books she ran past them. Without any stops, she flew down the path that took her home.

She was only six years old, but she believed what Herr Dentzinger told her.

Ingrid felt the danger of the event, but it was much later when she fully understood what this day was about. She was too young to understand the propaganda that told the whole country that the only correct views on any subject were "German" views.

Mountains of burned books resulted from this propaganda campaign.

Heidelberg was home to one of the oldest universities in all of Europe but even there, in University Square, students burned massive amounts of books in May 1933.

Chapter Sixteen

A Man Named Georg
Heidelberg – Ana – 1971

The last week of the semester was extremely busy. Ana had to prepare the final exam for her students, attend several administrative meetings, and answer some requests from a few students who felt they needed more detailed information and additional help as they got ready for their finals. Relief was what she felt when she realized today was the last day of the semester.

The schedule of semesters and the breaks in between differed from what she was accustomed to in the States. More off time was allowed students in between semesters and that free block of time was also there for professor's to enjoy. She still felt a little sad because Maggie couldn't get away from her busy new job and come over during Ana's break. But she understood so well the inflexibility of work schedules and hoped that Maggie liked her work with the CPA firm. She also admitted to herself though that she did feel a little lonely, missed her best friends who were now so far away.

The classroom was quiet as her students worked on their finals. She sat at her desk and attempted to begin a new plan for the next semester classes. However, she just couldn't seem to concentrate, kept thinking about what she was going to do with all the time off from work that was coming her way.

One of her students came forward and placed a completed exam in the box placed on her desk for that purpose. Only three more students left to finish up and then the classroom would be empty. Two students got up at the same time and walked forward. They turned in the exams and she nodded and smiled at them as they left the room.

The only student now left was Thomas. He must have felt her eyes on him because he looked up at her and smiled. Then he stood up, stretched, and brought his exam to her.

He didn't simply drop it off and go, but smiled and said, "Professor Winchester I wanted to say thank you for your work with this class. It has been good and I am learning a lot. I am sure, and it is confirmed by my classmates, that you are an interesting and a talented teacher. Learning is enjoyable in your class. Also, I must say that your language skill is amazing." Then he hesitated a second. "Do you have any plans for the semester break?"

She didn't answer openly with details, simply replied, "I do not have specific plans Thomas."

He still hesitated, seemed to want to say something else, but instead just said, "Goodbye."

He left and she was alone in the classroom.

Her mind was fixed on Thomas and she sat still and stared at the closed door. He was the ideal student, cooperative, kind, intelligent, and was also good looking. What she couldn't decide was what he was truly thinking or why he seemed so interested in the details of her life. She admitted to herself that she believed something was off kilter. Then she told herself firmly that she was nuts and that Thomas was just a nice helpful young man. Leave it.

She got up and walked to the window and looked down at the city below. Today she got a surprise. Large numbers of students were unloading boxes and equipment into the center of the square. Others were milling around, obviously waiting on something.

Four young men, each carrying a musical instrument entered the square and went straight to the center where the boxes and equipment lay. The pieces of the puzzle came together. Tonight a concert must be scheduled in the square to celebrate the end of the semester.

Lots of students were going to have fun tonight. Ana smiled and wished them even more fun.

Several days after the semester ended she found herself with empty time and no plans, felt a little lost. She sat in her apartment and drank some coffee. The weather was perfect and she felt that she'd definitely made a big mistake by not making any specific plans for the time off. She felt like she'd wasted the chance to expand her life and her knowledge of Europe. She could have traveled if she'd planned ahead.

As she watched the boats move past on the river below, she also happened to see the manager of her apartment, Frau Krueger, as she walked toward the house along the river carrying a tote bag. It appeared she'd been grocery shopping.

Ana sat patiently, gave Frau Krueger plenty of time to get into her apartment and unload the groceries she'd bought. The she went out and walked downstairs to the first floor of the house where Frau Krueger lived. She knocked on her door.

Frau Krueger answered the door at once and then welcomed her. "Fraulein Winchester, how can I be of help to you? Is anything wrong in your apartment?"

"Oh no Frau Krueger, my apartment is good. I want to ask you a question, to ask for your opinion, if you have time."

"Yes, I have time for you. I have returned from the market and am not pressed by anything at the moment. Would you like to come in and sit down?"

"Thank you." Ana moved curiously into Frau Krueger's apartment and saw at once how comfortable and clean it looked. It reflected the personality of an organized person. A cozy looking green chair sat in front of a window. It invited her and she sat right down. Frau Krueger chose a chair nearby. She sat down too, smiled, and waited to see what Ana wanted to talk about.

Ana began at once, "As you know Frau Krueger, I teach at the University and our semester break just started. I have some time off and I want to use it for something special. Do you have any suggestions or ideas of things to see or do here in this area of Germany? What do people do on these semester breaks?"

Frau Krueger laughed. "Oh my. Young people use this time to travel, even to other countries. They go skiing if it is the right time of year. They also enjoy hiking and some just go to their homes and enjoy their families. I am sorry not to be helpful but people use this time for things that they are really interested in doing."

Frau Krueger was pleasant and they talked some more. She honestly had no ideas for Ana but she seemed happy to spend time talking with her and when she left, Ana thanked her for her time.

At home again, Ana asked herself, "What is important to me?" The question struck a familiar chord. Maybe Frau Krueger had been more on target than she knew. Her time recently was filled with a new job, a new country to live in and adjust to, and she hadn't thought about the broader goals she'd set for herself.

She felt like her battery was now charged and said out loud, "First, get out of this apartment, get into nature and clear your mind. Then go ahead from there."

At once she changed clothes, put on her walking shoes. Without any more time wasted, she left the apartment and hurried down the stairs, through the courtyard, then up the steep staircase off to the left. The steep stairs were normally filled with students who lived in the apartment building it led up to, but today it was empty. Earlier this month, she'd walked up to the student apartment and spotted a gate that looked like it opened onto a path that ran up the mountain.

That was where she was going. Maybe she could manage to hike all the way up the mountain and then look directly down on the Neckar River and the City of Heidelberg.

She stood on the stairs, looked up at the forest path above her and her face glowed with adventure. A man walked purposefully from the street into the courtyard below her. He passed through the archway and stopped abruptly as he happened to look up and see her.

A sixth sense alert warned her that she was being watched and she looked down into the courtyard. He stood there, a tall athletic man, pale blonde hair neatly combed, and dressed like he was expected at an important business meeting. He even carried a brown leather briefcase in one hand. A spike of interest stabbed her and she kept looking at him. She wanted to know his name and why he was here.

The answers to her unasked questions were only moments away.

The man walked over to the bottom of the tall stairs and then stopped. She still watched him. A tingle of emotions swept through her as she noticed that the courtyard behind him seemed different. The water-spewing fish attached to the fountain appeared to glow, fingers of sunlight touched them. It was more vibrant, more alive than normal.

His handsome face became even more handsome when he smiled at her. "Good afternoon. I hope I did not startle you with my entry into the courtyard. Do you live here?"

So good looking, so polite and as she looked at him, she hesitated slightly, didn't exactly know why. She stood still, but let recognition of the important moment flow heavily across her mind. Then she answered him, in German, the language she'd studied for so many years of her life. Her lifelong need to become fluent felt connected with this man.

To remain in the present, she finally answered him. "Hello. You did not startle me. I was watching and wondering if the young people in the student apartment above us actually have a private gate to the path up the mountain."

She realized that he had asked her two questions. "Oh, and yes, I do live in this house, in answer to your question. I moved in last year. I teach at the German International University."

The man moved up the steps at the exact time that Ana moved down the steps. They found themselves side-by-side, bodies close. Warmth flowed back and forth between them.

His eyes looked up at the student apartment above them. "It does have its own entryway to the mountain path. That path is very old and not well kept, but it is still usable."

Ana looked into his blue eyes and he looked into hers. They both smiled.

He spoke again. "Excuse me for not introducing myself. I am Georg Schiller. I was on my way to speak with the house manager, Frau Krueger."

"I am Ana Winchester."

They both hesitated. Then she started to move back up the steps.

"Wait." He asked, "Do you plan to hike up the mountain today?"

One step above him she stopped and looked down. "Yes, I have free time during the semester break and I want to investigate the mountain and spend some time outside in nature. I want to explore Heidelberg, see what beauty exists here."

Georg looked at her intently. He seemed interested in what she had to say. "From what you just said, you are not from Heidelberg. What part of Germany is home for you?"

Surprise was clear on her face. "I am not from Germany. I am from the United States. I was hired to teach at the University because I have studied languages and qualified for a staff position." Not just surprised, she was shocked. Was her ability to speak German good enough to pass as a native? Was that what he'd just said?

Georg's face showed some surprise too when she told him she was not a native German. "I am amazed at your fluency in our language. You are very good. The University made a good decision when they hired you." His hand moved out, almost touched her arm, but he pulled it back. "Will you be back down from your hike in a few hours?"

"Why do you ask?" Her eyes sparkled with anticipation.

"I have business with Frau Krueger. Then I was wondering if we could get together later this evening and have dinner? Is this something you would like to do?" He looked hopeful, did not seem ready to say goodbye yet.

"I would like that. Shall we meet here at six this evening?" She began to move away and smiled.

"Yes. We will meet here at six." His smile matched hers.

He turned around and walked toward Frau Krueger's apartment.

Chapter Seventeen

Changes?
Heidelberg – Ana – 1971

The hike she began after she left Georg Schiller behind turned out to be much shorter that she'd originally planned. The desire to explore the mountain suddenly got pushed back to second place on her current list of important to-dos. The chance meeting with Georg Schiller had, in a short slice of time, created a new important need.

The up-coming dinner with him replaced all thoughts she had of exploring the mountain. Now, things that she normally thought of as mundane became magically important, things like time for a fresh shower, time to find something to wear that made her look her best, and all this had to be accomplished before the six o'clock time set for their evening together.

She forced herself to follow the narrow overgrown path as it wound up the hill for a while. She noticed the encroachment of nature, and agreed with Georg that it was not well kept. It was however beautiful.

During her hike she saw only one other person. A student who she'd seen earlier outside of the student apartment building, and as he passed her by he gave a polite nod and said "Guten Tag." (Good Day).

The rather steep climb was physically challenging and the exercise felt good, but excitement built as she focused on the evening ahead. She didn't feel normal, was surprised by her reaction to Georg Schiller. She thought that the clear air would also clear her mind. She wanted to calm down but it didn't happen.

All at once she knew she had to turn around. She needed to get to her apartment and she almost ran back down the mountain. When she entered the side yard of the student apartment at the gate she stopped, looked down into the courtyard to check and see if he was in sight. She definitely didn't want to bump into him again until she was ready.

The courtyard was totally empty so she hurried down the tall stairs and then zipped up to her apartment. As soon as she got inside, she raced to her closet and started looking through the clothes she had available to wear tonight.

After she'd moved to Heidelberg from the States, she carefully observed the style of clothes worn by the citizens and students there in Heidelberg. The need to blend in, dress in the style of the people she lived around, basically the need to not call attention to herself, was intrinsic. After a few days of watching, she took herself on a shopping trip to one of the local clothing stores and purchased some work/formal type of clothes that could help her blend in. Funny, but today she wanted to stand out, not blend in, wanted to look as beautiful as possible. Finally she picked something.

What, a change in attitude?

As she got herself ready, she also realized that she'd broken another one of her rules. Normally, she avoided telling anybody details of her background, always worked around it. But she'd shared the truth of her origin with Georg Schiller at once, said straight out that she was from the States. In fact, she realized that she didn't even think about not telling him. Another attitude change?

Aloud she even asked herself, "What's happening?" The habit of never sharing her background or what she was thinking was a basic structure of her life. It was as normal and as set in stone as punctuation rules are to the structure of a language. She didn't share her thoughts when she finished a task, a duty, or a conversation. Not sharing represented a period. When she had a problem or a disagreement, then not sharing her emotions represented an exclamation point. Confusion was the question mark. She punctuated minutes, hours, days, weeks, her life this way. To share was a grammatical error and she worked hard not to err. Now what was happening?

She spoke out loud. "Don't think about this right now. Please just let yourself enjoy tonight."

She was looking at herself in the mirror, attempting perfection when the knock sounded on her door. A fleck of apprehension swept across her face, she saw it and thought, "Try Ana. Move forward."

When she opened the door a smile was back on her face. Beside him as they left, she let herself admire his tall strong body. He wore black pants and a dark blue sweater and the clothes accentuated his lean muscled body. But the best thing about him was his smile, genuine and friendly as he talked to her.

"Fraulein Winchester, or maybe it is Frau Winchester? Oh, I apologize for my unintended rudeness. I honestly wanted only to address you correctly." He stood still, looked uncomfortable. What he'd done was rather awkwardly ask if she was married or single. He was embarrassed.

"Please do not worry Herr Schiller because I am not offended. I am, in fact, not married, so your first manner of address was the correct one." She laughed heartily because she could see he was afraid she thought that he'd deliberately been rude.

Then he started to laugh with her and the fun of it carried them forward on their walk into town.

"Herr Schiller, please let us make this evening together easier. My name is Ana Winchester but please just call me Ana. If it will not offend you, I will call you Georg."

It only took half a second and he answered with another laugh. "I am pleased for you to call me Georg and also let me say that you were polite when you asked. So, let me tell you that I am not married. Now you will not have to ask me." The laughter resonated in his words and she felt they totally understood each other.

"Ana, do you have a special restaurant you would like for us to visit this evening?"

She glanced at him, appreciated his niceness as she answered, "I have not lived in Heidelberg long enough to even start to know all the restaurants. I have some where I have eaten but I think for tonight, you should choose for us."

"Okay" he said. "Let us continue into the Old Town. There is a restaurant I always enjoy when I'm in Heidelberg. Actually, it is not far from the Old Bridge. Is that good for you?"

"It sounds like an excellent choice and I absolutely agree."

By now they were almost halfway across the bridge, walking the same path Ana used on her way back and forth from work.

Georg spotted a small boat that was headed toward the bridge, and then raced under it. He ran to the side of the bridge and called for Ana to come and look. The two people in the boat were both dressed as pirates and the boat was flying two skull and crossbones flags. Both people in the boat were laughing and having fun.

"I do not know what that was about, perhaps they were practicing for Fasching (Mardi-Gras)." He spoke as she came up beside him and was able to see the pirate boat. She laughed and stood close to him but not close enough. He moved even closer. She didn't back up, simply absorbed the feel of his body. Together, they shared the same feeling as they watched the pirate ship sail on down the river.

The restaurant he chose was tucked away on a small side street west of the bridge. It had existed for a long time and was especially popular with locals.

When they walked in a server stepped forward and led them to a small table. It was the only empty table in the restaurant. The number of people eating there confirmed that the food must be good.

Georg, when asked by the server what he would like to drink answered, "A weiss beer please."

The server then turned to Ana. "And for you?"

She responded immediately. "I would like a glass of white wine, half dry, please."

Quickly, the server brought the drinks then asked, "Are you ready to order or do you need more time to look at the menu?" While asking, he placed a small basket of warm bread on the table.

Georg looked at Ana and she smiled and said, "I am ready if you are."

The server asked for her order first.

"I would like beef roulade please." She ordered with no hesitation.

Georg looked surprised. Then he told the server, "I will have the same."

The server left to place the order and he asked her at once, "Have you ever eaten beef roulade before?"

Again, without thinking about what her answer could reveal about her background, she simply answered his question. "That was what my mother cooked for me on my birthday. It was my favorite meal."

Only when he asked her how her mother knew so much about German cooking did she realize that she'd been too open and too honest with him. To herself, in her mind she talked. "This is too complicated. You need to be more careful and not be so open about your life."

To him she said, "Oh in the States we have people from many different countries and we all live in the same communities. My mother had a good friend who came from Germany and who was a good cook. She taught mother how to make delicious German food. Mother even taught me to cook some of the recipes."

He was excited. "Oh so you are trained to cook my favorite dish! I think that l am lucky to have met you today and maybe one day you will cook beef roulade for me."

They laughed together and both enjoyed their delicious "favorite" meal.

The evening was still young when they left the restaurant, so he asked if she would like to walk over to the Market Square. Restaurants were located adjacent to the square tables set up outside and it was a perfect spot to sit and talk.

They picked a table on the outside edge of the square. After they sat down she found herself looking at the solid wall of tall buildings that faced and defined the square. During her time in Heidelberg, she'd observed and appreciated the beauty of the old historical Church of the Holy Spirit that occupied the west end of the square and the impressive City Hall that sat at the east end. But until this moment, she'd appreciated them only in the light of day. Tonight they displayed a dark shadowed beauty that she'd honestly never noticed before. Night revealed a different aspect of their existence.

Her eyes moved up to the top of the large brick building in front of her. The fourth floor caught her attention. Lights were shining brightly and several large windows showed everything because no curtains blocked the view.

She saw what looked like a library, with shelves filled completely with books from floor to ceiling. A young man sat at a desk, reading.

The number of books fascinated her. "Georg, look at the windows on the top floor of the building in front of me. Do you see all those books?"

He looked up and watched for a second. "I do see them. That is amazing. Either that apartment is actually a private library or the person who lives there collects books, maybe as part of a book business he operates."

She kept looking at the books in the windows and spoke softly. "Much of life is unseen, hidden behind walls and in closets. What I have seen on the streets of this beautiful city every day is not the complete picture of life here. I need to remember to think about and consider the difference between day and night, between sunlight and darkness."

He heard something in the tone of her voice. He recognized sadness beneath the words she had just spoken. "Ana, why are you sad?"

He surprised her and she instinctively disguised her real thoughts. "I did not intend to bring sadness into our time together. I was thinking about my friend back home. He had a difficult childhood and I watched him find the strength to overcome it and move positively forward. I guess my mind went from the hidden part of the city to the hidden problems in your county during the war. Sam's family was subjected to the same type of harshness that existed here during the war."

Total silence. He didn't respond to her, didn't answer, just sat still and looked down at the table in front of them.

"Oh, I am so sorry for speaking about the horrors of the war and what happened here in Germany. My mind was on Sam and the States and I talked about the Nazis without considering how that would affect you. You do not need to talk to me about this. It must feel awful to deal with and I am truly not trying to make any type of political statement. Our parents and grandparents made their own decisions during that time and our generation had no part in those decisions. We cannot change what happened."

He still looked down at the table and then slowly looked up. He spoke quietly. "We have only known each other for a few hours. I agree with you, it is extremely difficult for me and for my generation to speak about this openly. We feel that the world blames us for what happened in our country, judges us. It is almost impossible to talk openly about our hurt, our remorse, our pain."

She was not prepared for Georg. He seemed to understand her, to hear her unspoken thoughts. She felt connected to him and felt his honesty. She thought she might be a fool to think this or maybe, she simply wanted to think this. He didn't seem to be a secret keeper. Excitement surged again when she thought of the possibilities of their connection but her insecurity surfaced too. Time to slow down and learn more about him before she asked him to help her or to answer any of her questions.

At the opposite end of the square a man sat unnoticed at a table. Many people separated him from Ana and Georg, plus his dark dull clothes blended perfectly into the night. He watched them carefully as they talked.

Georg walked her back to her apartment, had refused to let her walk home alone. As they got close he stopped and put his hand on her shoulder. "Ana I do not know when I will be able to get back to Heidelberg, but if I call you when I make it, will you agree to have dinner with me again?"

Total surprise. "But I thought you lived here in Heidelberg. When we talked earlier you told me that you own the house that includes my apartment and also the student apartment above it. You do not live here?"

"No, I do not live in Heidelberg. I inherited all of this property some years ago. I was born and raised in Bavaria and I only come back to Heidelberg several times a year to make sure that everything is properly taken care of."

"Bavaria." She thought this was incredible. She needed more information. "Is Bavaria as beautiful as I have heard? I have not had any opportunity to visit there yet."

Now he smiled. "You have time off. It is semester break. Why do you not come and see for yourself? I will be happy to pick you up from the train station and I can get you reservations at a guesthouse that is run by some of my friends." He reached into his pocket and pulled out a pen and paper and wrote down his telephone number. "Let me know when, and I will be there to take care of you."

Before she could answer, he pulled her tightly into his arms and kissed her.

She didn't want the kiss to end.

Absorbed totally in themselves, they failed to feel that they were again being watched. This time the dark-clothed man was just a short distance away. This time he heard what they said.

In her bed that night, she couldn't sleep. Wave after wave of passion, pure heat, surged through her body. The kiss and intense embrace from Georg was all she could think about. As he held her she felt that she was wrapped in the arms of life. No matter how hard she tried to tell herself that she really didn't know him, she came back to the kiss. She wanted more.

In his hotel room on this last night in Heidelberg Georg fervently hoped Ana would respond to his invitation to visit Bavaria. He wanted more time with her, wanted to explore the feelings that had awakened since he met her. He kept thinking that he had known her for a long time, forever. Connected.

East of Heidelberg, in a deep forest above a small town, a man sat quietly in his cottage. He was waiting for more information before he could decide what to do next. What he'd seen already was disturbing. The plan he'd worked out so carefully and faithfully wasn't working. Could he make adjustments this late in the game?

Chapter Eighteen

The Top of the Mountain
Heidelberg – Ana – 1971

Not like normal, she overslept the morning after her night out with Georg. Rays of sunlight spilled in through her curtain, called for her to rise, but she wasn't ready to begin a new day. She couldn't bring herself to get out of the warm bed, instead snuggled down again and pulled the cover tightly around her body. Then she replayed yesterday, pretended the bed was his warm strong body forced hard against hers and his arms wrapped tightly around her. Passion flowed again.

Much later she finally left her bed and managed to step back into real time. But things had changed. Acknowledging that she saw life differently today she still felt an intense need to complete the task that she'd assigned herself. She must hike up to the top of the mountain, must see and feel it, must find out if it matched her thoughts. She needed confirmation of what she thought was true.

A little coffee, a quick breakfast, and the proper clothes and shoes for the hike, all completed in order to finish what she'd started yesterday and once again, she walked out her door and started on the hike.

The minute she stepped out the door she saw her student Thomas as he knocked on Frau Krueger's door. She stood still, said nothing as she watched Frau Krueger answer the door. She wanted to hear what Thomas said to her. But when Frau Krueger opened the door, she caught a glimpse of Ana before she totally focused on Thomas. Ana knew without doubt that she'd been seen but continued to remain quiet and still.

Frau Krueger greeted Thomas pleasantly, "Hello. Please come in and I will get the list of items that we need for the routine repairs that Herr Schiller hired you to work on and finish before the new semester starts.

71

Your help is going to make the apartments much more popular with the students who rent them."

That's when Frau Krueger deliberately looked up and gave her a friendly nod. Now Thomas knew she was there. As soon as she'd greeted Ana, Frau Krueger stepped back inside her apartment but Thomas didn't follow her. He looked up at Ana, smiled, and then said, "It appears that you are going on a hike this morning. Where are you going?"

She returned his smile but seriously considered not telling him where she was headed. He was too nosy. "Good morning Thomas. I am taking a hike up the mountain behind us. I do not know how far I will go because it depends on how strenuous the climb is. I plan to walk and see how well I do and how far up I can get today."

She walked down the stairs and as she passed him, she couldn't stop herself from smiling at him. She always found it difficult not to like him.

Before she walked out of the gate on the student apartment level she looked back to see if he was still watching her. No, he must be with Frau Krueger, getting his list of work to be done.

She couldn't help but wonder exactly when Georg had hired Thomas to work at the apartments. Thomas talked, communicated with her constantly, and surely would have told her that he'd found a job working in the place where she lived. Was it only a coincidence that Georg had just now hired him? Thomas always wanted to know what she was doing, where she was going, and now he had extra opportunities to watch her movements.

Another item got added to the list of things she needed to find out about Georg when and if she ever got the chance. Oh, hopefully soon she thought.

This time she didn't rush the walk up the mountain but took time to concentrate on everything around her, to absorb the growth and patterns of the forest. The first time she'd walked up the Heiligenberg (Holy Mountain) she'd noticed that the path was not heavily used, was overgrown, but this time she truly focused on the tall lovely trees and the ground on which they grew. Stones were everywhere, all different sizes, large, small, and all impressive as they studded the landscape sporadically in all directions. Even though the forest was dense, it managed not to feel heavy, not to crowd her as she walked through it. Instead, the heaviness of the trees and plant growth was mitigated by the generous amount of free ground, layered softly by leafy ferns and soft green moss. It was so easy to walk through, was a perfect carpet for the trees. The entire forest felt friendly and peaceful. She hoped to be able to see some of the wildlife that called the forest home. Maybe if she got lucky, a deer or a squirrel would be out and about today.

The higher she climbed the more she lost track of how far she'd moved up. There was a tremendous difference between looking up the mountain and climbing up the mountain. Just as she was beginning to think that she might not be able to make it all the way up, a small field of open grass appeared in front of her. Shortly, she found a path that moved out of the meadow and then she saw a wide, well-worn path that moved east to west. It ran directly in front of her.

The instant she stepped onto the well-traveled path, she knew where she was. It was the popular Philosopher's Way, one used daily by many people in Heidelberg. It was mid-way up the mountain and the views it provided for people who walked it were magnificent. It was possible to look down at the river as it flowed through the valley, to see the city and even the beautiful old castle that rested a ways up the mountain on the opposite side of the river. Walkers who used this Philosopher's Way got more than good exercise, they got a good dose of nature too.

Ana re-entered the original path that she was following and began to climb again. After a while, she felt weary, but told herself to move on. She must get to the top. Finally she found herself moving through an area that was more open, with more grass and less trees. The further she went, the more open it became and all at once, she walked out into what appeared to be a parking area. The sudden transition from forest to parking lot surprised her a little. As she walked along further, she saw that the parking lot was good-sized but totally empty of vehicles or people.

Now she looked around carefully. Should she leave the parking lot and follow a dirt road she saw up ahead? The road appeared to continue up the mountain so she went for it and found that it moved up less steeply than the climb she'd been on for what seemed like all day.

It only took fifteen or twenty more minutes and she saw what looked like another path, smaller than the dirt road she was on. It went off to the right and she followed it. In a few more minutes she found herself walking up to the stone side entry of a large amphitheater. She knew, from reading about Heidelberg, that the amphitheater had been built there many years earlier during the period of time in which the Nazis' controlled Germany.

The place where she entered the amphitheater was where speakers, musicians, whoever was performing entered. A little further was where they would walk out onto the large open stage.

Slowly she walked herself out and stood at the center of the stage. She looked up and out. It was so much bigger and more impressive than she'd imagined. The stage was basically built at the same level as the bottom row of circular seats directly in front and encircling it. Then the seats swept up, row after row, felt like the Roman Coliseum. What she saw took her breath away. It was powerful.

She continued to stand there and look ahead. Her eyes followed the rise of the seats and at last she saw what she'd been searching for. Straight in front of her, at the level of the highest row of seats she saw a small simple footpath. She traced it as it continued further up the mountain.

Now she moved faster, down from the stage, then up the steps past row upon row of empty seats. This was the path she needed to find, the path that continued up to the very top of the mountain.

Before she'd moved to Heidelberg and begun her new life, Ana had researched the Heidelberg area and found interesting historical information about this particular mountain. The literature she read told about ruins of an ancient Celtic settlement that was built at the top of the Holy Mountain many years ago. The article mentioned something called a Convergence Zone, located at the top, where spirits were purported to visit. This was the specific spot she wanted to find.

But when she walked into the Convergence Zone, she didn't realize that she'd found it.

In front of her stood an old broken wall and she paused. Her gut instinct told her to follow it. She went with her gut instinct and found herself beside a small parcel of open grassy ground. In the middle of it stood the remains of what appeared to be ancient buildings. A stone at the edge caught her eye and called her name. She went over and sat on it, still worn down from the day's adventure and climb. She needed to renew her will to finish the task she'd assigned herself.

Suddenly she realized that the only sound she heard was that of her breathing. The sound of birds, the soft buzz of busy insects, all the normal sounds intrinsic to the forest were absent.

Another alert. She saw above her, deep within the trees, small sparkles of light and at the same moment felt a dull soft vibration inside her. The vibration seeped softly up and into her from the stone on which she sat. Fear surged but she forced herself not to jump up, not to run away. Instead, she sat perfectly still and allowed the flashes, the almost non-existent vibration, to move up through her body and to fill her mind. Long ago, she'd felt this. It had become a hidden part of her life.

It was almost Ana's sixth birthday and her mother was trying to organize a happy family party for her. She approached her husband and asked, "Leonard, do you have any ideas about how we can make Ana's birthday special this year? Could we have a small party here and maybe invite Ana's new friend Sam?"

His answer to her question was fast and firm. "Are you nuts? Grandpa would have a fit if you invited that Cherokee kid over here for her birthday party. You know as well as I do that he's more likely to be angry, to be mean, than he's ever been before. He's been acting even worse than normal for over a week now. I think he might be sick or something and really I'm glad that he's gone up to AppleBear Hollow, though it's strange that he left so unexpectedly. Maybe time spent at his hunting cabin and killing some animals will help him get back to normal."

Mother pushed her hurt feelings as far back into her mind as possible. She felt rejected and ignored by the way her husband centered on Grandpa and didn't show concern for Ana. She responded softly, "Let me think about this some more. I'll get back to you if I come up with anything."

He didn't even seem to notice that he'd hurt his wife's feelings with his words.

She walked into the kitchen, then out the back door. Fortunately the sun was setting and the day glowed. The clouds were colored pink and she decided to concentrate on the beauty of nature, not her hurt.

Mother actually got the idea of how to celebrate Ana's birthday from Grandpa. He came back without notice, barreled in through the front door. Daddy was outside working, so only mother and Ana got to hear his harsh words.

He slammed his heavy bag down on the floor and yelled loudly. "Anybody here or are ya'll on vacation? I bet no work's been done since I left here!"

Because he'd come home, and complained about how they'd not been working the farm like he expected it to be done, mother decided in that instant that he could take over the responsibility of the farm and manage it his way. He seemed healthy enough. Since he was back now, she'd talk to her husband and convince him into talking some time off. It would feel good to leave Grandpa and the farm behind. This time, they could stay up at AppleBear Hollow and leave Grandpa behind. That way, Ana could enjoy a calm happy birthday, without grumpy Grandpa, and they could all enjoy the peace there at the cabin. Let Grandpa rule the farm.

In no time at all it was decided. Daddy approved and he informed Grandpa that they'd be gone for a week. They left the next day.

Daddy drove them, all three seated together in the front seat of his old blue truck. He'd stuffed their lightly packed suitcase into the back seat and then slowly drove them west through the valley. The drive to AppleBear Hollow, to the mountains where it stood, was always part of the pleasure of going. From the valley they climbed up and up, circling around the mountains until finally they came to the tiny mountain town of Robbinsville. The road from there was small and Daddy turned the truck back and forth, again and again until they finally turned into the final part of the journey. The last road curved even further up the mountain where, after driving straight through the bubbling stream called Shepherd's Creek, the AppleBear Cabin sat up with its back right against the mountain. From the front of the little house was a perfect view of the open valley beneath it and a wide world full of mountains. The cabin sat alone, no other homes nearby, and the only sounds heard there belonged to nature as it spoke through the hypnotic sound of the rushing creek and the haunting call of wildlife.

The three of them had stayed at AppleBear Hollow before and every night, even when the weather was cold, the windows fronting the stream were left cracked open. Mother, Daddy and Ana all loved to fall asleep listening to the sound of the water running down the mountain.

This stay was special and as soon as they got up and ate breakfast the next day, mother remembered that she'd forgotten to bring candles to put on Ana's birthday cake. She pulled daddy aside and asked, "Would it be possible for you to drive back down into town and buy some candles for the cake? I forgot to bring any."

He smiled as he answered. "Actually, I forgot to bring any lures for my fishing rod. I could get some at that little shop in Robbinsville and then I could stop at the grocery store and get the candles. I could be back well before lunch."

Mother felt happy and it resonated in her laugh. "Perfect. Maybe I'll clean up here and then I'll take Ana with me on a little hike up the mountain. We'll follow the path that enters the National Forest. It's clear and open and she can walk without any difficulties."

Daddy started laughing, he knew Mother was afraid of bears and he spontaneously decided to tease her by repeating the story of why the cabin was named AppleBear Hollow. "Hey there Monica, you do remember that the man who built this cabin and lived here for years before he granted it to Grandpa was the person who planted those apple trees that sit out back of the cabin. Remember what he saw one morning when he walked out onto the porch with his coffee in his hand? Up top of one of the apple trees sat a large black bear picking and devouring all of the ripe apples." He was having fun as he teased her.

She watched his face, recognized his happy teasing smile and responded in the mode. "Well Leonard, I'm going anyway. I know there's a tiny chance we'll run into a bear, and I admit, I will be very careful." She kept on laughing even as she cleaned up the breakfast mess.

Ana walked into the unusual laughter-filled room and she laughed too.

Right after Daddy left, Mother packed some snacks and water into a small back pack and then made sure that Ana had on her comfortable pair of walking shoes. They were both excited about the hike. It felt like an adventure.

They started out by walking across the skinny bridge that Grandpa had built over Shepherd's Creek. It allowed them to cross the stream without getting their feet wet. The path they were going to hike up was on the left after they crossed the stream. As it began, it was a fairly steep climb, but it smoothed out some as it went along, became a little less difficult.

They walked slowly and steadily and stopped for a rest where a large stone sat beside the path and served as a bench for hikers. They sat down together, caught their breath, and looked around for any animals they might see. They heard birds calling but the sound that indicated animals might be around, the rustle of leaves and bushes wasn't happening. After a few minutes they started out again.

Mother was honestly afraid of bears and really was a little nervous, but being with her daughter, both of them happy, seemed to cause the forest around her to feel warm and friendly today.

"Ana, are you tired yet?" Mother checked because they had come a respectable distance, though still a little short of their goal line, the edge of the National Forest.

"I'm not tired mama. I just wish we could see some animals."

"Maybe something will show up before we get back to the cabin little one. We've already been gone longer than I'd planned. I didn't remember it being so far up to the National Forest. Are you sure you're not tired?" Mother stopped and hugged her, rubbed her back gently.

"I'm really not tired mother. Let's just go on some more and see if we can find a rabbit."

By the time they finally reached their goal it was late in the morning. Mother didn't have a watch, but was afraid that Daddy would already be back at the cabin before they could make it there. She felt rushed because she wouldn't have time to cook the lunch she'd planned.

With her mind on being late, the loud roar that erased the peaceful quietness around them jolted Mother to a complete stop. She grabbed Ana by the arm. The roar was so close and they were both startled and afraid.

Softly mother whispered. "We must run as fast as we can! We must get back to the cabin. Right now!" She pulled little Ana along and they ran down the path.

The roar originated from the thick forest off to the right side of the path, somewhere between them and the creek, but the harsh scream felt like it surrounded them. They ran on.

"Oh, there's the path to the cabin! Fast!" Even as Mother spoke they were racing across the skinny bridge. This time the roar blasted even louder, closer. It echoed and hit against every step they took.

"Mother, something's wrong!" Ana felt more than danger, felt a direct message from nature into her heart.

Finally they were at the cabin and sped up the steps onto the porch. Mother pushed her into the door, followed, and then locked it. No time wasted, she raced from open window to open window and slammed them shut.

She stopped and looked at her daughter. "There is simply nothing else I can do to protect us. Oh, I hope your Daddy gets here fast!"

Side by side on the sofa they sat nervously and looked out the windows into the dark forest. They couldn't stop looking for the animal responsible for the roars. Recently, authorities in the area had told people who lived there that mountain lions didn't exist anymore in the forest, that they were extinct. Neither Mother nor Ana believed them. They knew, understood exactly what they'd heard.

Time passed but the mountain lion didn't speak to them again.

Ana felt strange, felt her mind escape from her body, as she gazed out the window. In the thick of the forest she saw tiny sparks of light. The sparks were directly across the creek where she knew the mountain lion still hid. Her small young body vibrated gently and in her mind she heard music-like sounds. The mountain lion was telling her something important, something bad. She simply couldn't interpret the meaning of his roar. She was nervous and sad.

Mother also acted strangely. Ana tried to ask her if she felt the vibrations too but when she said, "Mother, do you know what the mountain lion is saying?" Mother didn't answer her back, remained silent. She didn't share what she was feeling with Ana.

Daddy didn't return right away. He'd run into one of his old friends at the store and talked for a while. When his truck finally pulled into the yard, Mother got up and started to prepare lunch. Ana stood off to the side and was quiet. Neither of them told Daddy what had happened.

Even before they finished eating lunch a long black car drove across the creek and pulled up beside Daddy's truck. The sheriff got out and knocked on the door.

Daddy answered. "Well hello Fred. What brings you way up here from Andrews?"

The sheriff said, "Leonard, you and your family need to sit down 'cause I've got some hard news to tell you." He motioned them over to the couch and they all sat down nervously.

"Leonard, your house in Andrews caught on fire sometime in the early hours this morning. Your father, Mr. Winchester was evidently asleep when it happened and now he's dead. We thought you all were inside the house too, so it's taken us some time to find out you guys were up here at the cabin. We were afraid that you might all be dead too. I'm sorry to bring this awful news. I'll help you get back safely to Andrews."

Grandpa was the ruler of his world and had exercised his authority, his anger, his hatred, during his last stay at AppleBear Hollow. The animals of the forest knew all about him.

Back in Andrews, the fire chief later determined that Grandpa had forgotten to turn off the stove at some odd time during the hours after midnight. He'd gone back to bed, to sleep, and the house had burned down.

Now she was in Germany, atop a different mountain, feeling confusion and fear as she revisited the warning from the mountain lion that Grandpa was dead.

In addition, the pages filled with her Mother's handwriting were also present in her mind. Today she'd found the location, but more secrets needed to be solved. She felt the truth of her Mother's written words.

Enough! As fast as she could, she jumped up and left the vibrating rock behind. Down the path she raced, then through the Amphitheater and back to the dirt road that led to the parking lot. Again, the lot was empty. She saw a road off to the right and instantly chose to go down it. Maybe it would lead her into a normal everyday street of Heidelberg. What she needed was to find a taxi and get a quick ride back to her apartment. She desperately wanted to leave the memories behind.

Frightened, exhausted, she sadly found out that civilization was not as near she'd hoped. It took more walking to finally move into another larger parking area and then into a small street lined with homes.

By now, darkness was making its entrance, marking the day's end. She tried to stay at the edge of the street and kept walking, kept following it as it moved slightly downward. Eventually she felt the nature of the area change, with some businesses present. Now she turned onto a larger street and yes, down on the right she saw a taxi pulled over beside the road. She felt it was waiting for her.

When she walked up to it, the front door opened and the driver jumped out. "Do you need a ride?"

Thankfully, she simply answered, "Yes." Seated in the back seat, she gave the driver directions.

The drive felt super-fast in the taxi and soon she found herself in the welcome, familiar courtyard beside her apartment. She walked forward and looked up. Frau Krueger stood at the door of her apartment and Thomas was at her side.

When Frau Krueger saw her she hurried down the stairs to meet her. "Fraulein Winchester, I was worried. You were gone for so long. I checked with Thomas and we both felt we needed to go and look for you. We were afraid you were lost or hurt. Are you alright?"

Tired, serious, Ana moved up the stairs. She wanted so badly to be alone in her apartment but she managed to pause and make sure that Frau Krueger and Thomas both knew how much she appreciated their concern. She thanked them, sincerely.

She was touched by their worry but the emotions she felt from her confrontation with the past were overwhelming. She needed time to absorb and try to understand the meaning of what she'd seen and experienced today.

Chapter Nineteen

The Night of the Broken Glass
Heidelberg – Ingrid – 1938

Father called Mother and Ingrid into his study late one afternoon and asked them to sit down. He stood so tall, so caring, with a serious expression on his face instead of his usual smile. "I want to talk to you both about a meeting that I am planning to have with my good friend, my fellow Professor, Dr. Kahn. He has been having a difficult time lately, since the Heidelberg University forced him to leave his position there because he is Jewish. I need to see if there is anything that I can do to help him. He has no job, no source of income, and I want to make sure that he has what he needs to take care of his family. I asked you in here because I know that you both want to see your friends again too. Mother, you and Frau Kahn have been good friends for a long time, and Ingrid, I know how much you miss their daughter, Ana since she was moved out of your class at school."

He seemed tense and worried and he continued to stand and walk around as he talked to them. "I want to see how you feel about what I am planning. Give me your thoughts. Here is what I am thinking. What if we all three take a family walk along the river and we walk in a casual and relaxed manner. We can take the roundabout way along the river and then we end our walk at the Kahn's house. I know very well that this could be dangerous, could get us into trouble with the police if they see us entering the Kahn's house. But I truly think that if we are careful, we can do this without getting into trouble. We can be watchful and if at any time during the walk, we see or feel that we are being watched, we could just pretend that we were on the way to my office at the University. I'll say that I left some files at my office and need to pick them up, since my office is only a little further along from where the Kahn's live. After all, no one has any reason to be watching us." He paused, looked at them and asked, "What do you think of my plan? Should we try to do this?"

Mother and Ingrid both answered at once, then both stopped, and Mother said, "What an excellent idea! I am willing to take the small risk of being seen; I want to be with my friend again and I know Ingrid feels the same way."

Without time for another word to be spoken, Ingrid exclaimed, "Oh I want so much to see and talk to Ana! Yes! I say yes, we need to do what you have thought of Father."

It was late afternoon, the perfect time, so they gathered coats and hats, then went out and began to walk leisurely along the north side of the Neckar River. Father and Mother walked arm in arm and Ingrid walked more quickly, out in front, checking the edges of the river for birds. They had already decided to enjoy their family time together, walk in the beauty of the area and visit a local park located just beyond the end of their walking path. It was situated beside the Neckar River, a little beyond a large bridge that channels traffic into the Bismark Platz, the center of public transportation in Heidelberg.

As soon as they reached the park, Father selected an empty bench, one that faced the river, and they all sat down, Ingrid in between her parents. Directly in front of them was the perfect view. A large tree stood by the river's edge and a well-tended garden of bushes flourished around it. All was reflected in the background of the river.

Suddenly Ingrid jumped up. "Look! Look at the man and the squirrel!"

She directed her parents to look at a solitary older gentleman who carried a small bag filled with bits of food. He called out to a large squirrel. The squirrel scurried rapidly to his side and sat down, friendly, almost duplicating the smile that was on the old gentleman's bearded face. The squirrel responded to the man and rubbed his head against his outstretched hand. Obviously, these two were friends who met regularly and enjoyed each other's company.

Ingrid and her parents saw the friendship between the man who gave and the squirrel that accepted. They laughed quietly together and enjoyed the sight of the two friends. When the man left, the squirrel was totally content. Ingrid and Mother and Father whispered together and decided it was time to move on.

They spent a little more time and walked across the bridge toward Bismark Platz, the direction they needed to go. They walked slowly, made sure to take time out to stop and look down at the boats that ran under the bridge. According to plan, they eventually put their feet down on the south side of the river.

Now it was only another five or six blocks to reach the Jewish Plaza, their true destination. All along the way, they discreetly looked around, but could not identify anyone who might be following them. Finally they turned onto the Luberstrasse and quietly finished the last half block walk to the home of the Kahn family.

They didn't even get a chance to ring the doorbell because the front door swung open as soon as they walked up to it. Father had warned his friend that they would be visiting and Professor Kahn made sure he was there to quickly usher their friends in off the unfriendly street.

Father and Dr. Kahn shook hands firmly, and then excused themselves as they went straight into Dr. Kahn's office. Just as quickly, Mother and Frau Kahn hugged and began an animated conversation.

Ingrid looked at her friend Ana, smiled, and got a smile in return. They had missed each other and had so much they needed to catch up on. When Ana had been forced out of the class Ingrid had felt almost lost. They had been together always at school and now Ana, a Jew, was not allowed to go to school there anymore.

First the two friends walked toward Ana's bedroom but they stopped simultaneously. She shared her bedroom with her older sister, who was there now, working on homework. They both knew that if they went in, they would not be able to talk freely, would have no privacy.

They paused and then Ana whispered, "Why don't we sneak outside so that we can be by ourselves? The street lamps are lit and even though it is dark, it is not so very cold, and I know a place where we can sit and be alone and talk. What do you think?"

Ingrid's answer was to take her friend's hand and lead the way silently out the front door. If anyone saw them, they both knew that would not be allowed to go. Ordinarily they would not have gone against what they knew their parents wanted, but neither of them actually understood the danger they were putting themselves in. They deeply felt that so much had happened and they needed this private chance to figure it out between themselves, to see if the changes happening in their world made sense to either of them.

It was completely dark as they walked down the street. They were quiet and they hurried, guided by the pale light of a street lamp. They did not have too far to go because Ana and her family lived in an old established neighborhood in the Jewish Plaza where homes stood along the street, all three or more stories high. Everything was neat and the lovely old Jewish Synagogue nestled under large old trees at the end of the block.

Ana spotted the single bench that was tucked into the small garden area in the nearby corner of the synagogue. She pointed to it and they both scurried over and sat down. It was dark and they felt completely hidden away from the world.

The wind had risen and the air was a little colder, so they huddled close to each other, hands in their pockets, and began to talk together softly.

Both knew that the Nazis were the cause of the separation that had been forced on them and both suffered emotionally from the interruption of their friendship, as did their families. So far, as they grew up without any daily contact, they were already injured by the new rules placed on them by the government, but the harshness of the hatred aimed at the Jews had not really made itself known to either girl yet. They did not fully understand.

As they talked, they were aware only of themselves. They laughed and concentrated on catching up with all the important happenings in their own small world. That world was about to change.

The change was announced and accompanied first by distant sounds, glass breaking, tinkling as it crashed onto the old bricks of the ancient street. Louder sounds joined in as angry voices yelled, shouted, and wood was smashed as doors were torn apart. The volume of the crowd grew swiftly. The sounds of the crowd and its' violence suddenly penetrated their consciousness.

They shut up and looked up in alarm at the same moment. Both saw the reflection of light that came from the canyon-like street immediately north of them. In the greater darkness of their bench, tucked into the bushes, they were terrified by the encroaching nearness of the harsh voices, and the sight of shadows enlarged by the flickering torches that the angry shadowy men carried. The recognition, the actual sight of the danger paralyzed them.

Suddenly an army of mad men screamed hatred of the Jews, broke more windows, smashed down more doors, pulled helpless Jews from their homes, and then tossed flaming torches into the destruction. The mob was so very close to where they sat in fear, almost right beside them.

Ingrid jumped up, then pulled her friend up, and started forward, dragging Ana with her. The mob in the street totally blocked the way they needed to go in order to get back to Ana's home where both of their families were. Ingrid turned and ran the opposite way, still dragging her friend. With no conscious thought or plan, Ingrid was trying to reach her own home, instinctively, desperately, looking for safety for herself and her friend.

Unfortunately, a loud harsh voice behind them yelled, "Catch those two Jew girls! They just came out of the synagogue! Quick, get them!"

Ingrid screamed, "No, no you do not understand! Ana run! Run Ana!" She tried to run faster, tried to drag Ana faster.

But they could not outrun the anger of the mob.

From out of nowhere, from nothing, a tall black shadow stepped from a side street and grabbed Ingrid roughly. He jerked her, stopped her forward motion, then put his large strong hands on her as she screamed and looked up, tried to see into the shadow's face. He never returned her look, never looked directly into her face, just kept his eyes on the wild mob that was now only a step behind the girls and the tall black shadow that held them.

"Run," he said calmly, softly. "Take your friend to your home and you will be safe." The black shadow stepped forward, shielding the girls from the mob and then, as he stepped further toward the mob, Ingrid saw his black uniform.

He raised his hand and silence reigned for a moment. He ignored the girls who stood behind him as he spoke forcefully to the crowd.

Ingrid did not wait to hear what he said. She obeyed him. With Ana in tow, she ran toward the bridge and safety. Both girls cried and wondered as they ran, what about our families?

Breathless, Ingrid thought wildly for a second, "Did he know me? Do I know him?"

Ana stopped abruptly, jerked Ingrid to a halt. "Please Ingrid, I must stop, I cannot breathe. Please!"

Ingrid remained still and as she stood there, she glanced up at the window of a home that faced the street where they stood. She saw two non-Jewish faces, a man and a woman. Ingrid knew these people, saw them often, and she saw that they were crying as they watched the night's events, watched the girls running, the mob destroying the entire Jewish neighborhood. They stood hidden and afraid behind their curtains.

The night became known as the Kristallnacht, the Night of the Broken Glass. It was one of many Nazi planned attacks against Jews. The extremist beliefs of the Nazi Party resulted in the destruction of Jewish homes, businesses, and the complete destruction of practically every Jewish synagogue in Germany.

Ingrid did not lose her Mother, who was uninjured and was later allowed to return to the safety of her home. However, Ingrid's father and Ana's father were both taken into custody, along with most other males in the Jewish community. They were carried away, beaten, and imprisoned by the Nazi's in charge of the events of Kristallnacht. Neither man was ever seen or heard from again.

Ana's family was allowed to remain in their partially demolished home but they left Heidelberg almost immediately and moved to a small town to the east, where Ana's grandparents lived. They were desperately hunting for safety.

Ingrid never saw her friend again.

Chapter Twenty

Where and Why?
Andrews, North Carolina – 1971

Maggie knew a lot about finances and taxes. She'd earned a degree in accounting at University, then been hired and now worked for a large certified public accounting firm in Atlanta. On a daily basis, she worked with and understood the rules of the United States Government, the Internal Revenue Service, its tax laws and regulations. This background provided a logical basis for her to feel dissatisfied with the first assumption that she and Sam made after he shared what had happened in the encounter he had with a federal agent who claimed to be investigating Mr. Elden and the Winchester Farm. In fact, the more she thought about what happened, the less she understood what it meant, didn't understand exactly what the agent was after.

Maggie and Sam originally agreed that the agent who'd questioned him about Mr. Elden and Ana must be representing the IRS, must be investigating some sort of unpaid tax bill or maybe some figures that had been reported incorrectly on a tax return. But, with more time to think about what happened, Maggie wasn't convinced they were on the right track. She kept remembering how Sam had talked about the dark intense way the agent spoke and some of the questions that he'd asked.

Ana was so far away and Maggie felt the need to talk directly to her. She'd agreed with Sam that it was too early to tell Ana about this problem, to wait until they had a chance to get more solid information. Sam said they should probably talk to Mr. Elden, and when Maggie thought of talking to him she got slightly nervous.

For as long as she'd known Ana, she'd also known Mr. Elden, plus Ana talked about him all the time. She knew that Mr. Elden took total responsibility for the Winchester Farm, had stepped up to help Ana and her mother when Leonard Winchester had died in the wreck.

The first time she met Mr. Elden was when Ana invited her to spend a holiday week there during their first year together at University. Evidently nobody remembered to tell Mr. Elden that Maggie was coming to stay with Ana.

When he met the bus that they were riding home on at a station near Murphy, Mr. Elden only expected to see Ana and was surprised to see Maggie too. It wasn't that he treated her badly or said anything unkind, it was simply that Maggie could feel his irritation because he didn't have all the details, didn't know Ana was bringing home a friend. Maggie recognized his agitation and she remembered to this day what she thought, as he drove them both home to the farm back in Andrews. "Why did he need to know?"

She watched him from her place in the back seat and she knew then that he was a person who needed to be in charge of all the facts, and to make all the decisions based on those facts.

Even after this strange-feeling start, Mr. Elden and Maggie got on well together. She understood how much he helped Ana, and she never shared her thoughts about him with her friend.

Now, she was beginning to wonder and to worry a little. As she drove towards the farm and Sam, all she could think about was the current situation and what they should do.

Finally she turned into the main street in Andrews and drove along the valley, almost to Ana's home where she was to meet Sam. Happiness flowed when she reached the driveway. She was almost with him.

There he was, standing on the front porch. He saw her and moved down to the driveway. Even before she could turn the car off and unbuckle her seat belt, he had her door open. He reached in, helped her out, and laughed as he hugged her. "How did your drive go?"

She stretched her stiff body and happily answered him, "Sam the drive was easy but my thoughts during the drive were hard. I can't stop thinking about Mr. Elden and this mystery that's going on. We need to talk some more and maybe even call Ana."

"Wait Maggie, let's get your things inside before we start on this again." He picked up her small suitcase, grabbed her hand, and they went into the house.

The second the door closed, without wasting any more time, he put his arms around her. They kissed and suddenly everything else could wait. The depth of their relationship caused any amount of time spent away from each other to be too much. It was a while later before they got their minds back to Mr. Elden.

Later she asked him, "Sam can we go in the kitchen and I'll put together something for us to eat. I'm starved, didn't have any lunch because I just couldn't wait to see you. I only wanted to get here as fast as possible."

"Of course sweet Maggie!" He encircled her again and then ushered her forward. She walked straight to the refrigerator to see if any food might be left in it. What she saw was a fully stocked refrigerator. Just what she was looking for, some eggs were sitting inside. She grabbed them, spun around, and saw that Sam had already started to set the table.

Obviously he'd put in the food and she smiled and told him what his thoughtfulness meant. "Sam, you took time to go shopping for me, put food in the refrigerator. That was so kind, so good of you. Thanks!"

He shook his head positively at her and said, "You're important to me and I want to make sure you have what you need."

He finished the table then helped her cook their meal. They decided to have breakfast for dinner; eggs, grits, and toast. They cooked and talked and had as much pleasure fixing the meal as eating it.

Afterwards, Maggie was the one who jumped back into the Mr. Elden situation. "I think we need to find out what department of the government the agent you talked with is part of. I honestly don't think the way he acted and the questions he asked fit with the IRS. He sounds more like a FBI or CIA agent to me. I know he told you not to talk to anyone about what he said but have you considered asking a favor of your friend, Jerry, who works on the police force here in Andrews? He might be able to help us figure out what kind of investigation this is. Besides, he knows and trusts you and I bet he'd help you."

"But Maggie, I'm worried that if I ask Jerry for help, I might get him into trouble. I know he'd help me, like he has in the past, but I can't get him into something that could harm him. Ever! This is between you and me and we just have to figure it out ourselves I think."

She nodded her head in agreement and her love for Sam surged through her again. "Sam, you know Mr. Elden the best because when you grew up, he was always around. Do you think that he'll tell us what's going on if we go and ask him?" She stopped. "Oh, if you talk to him you can get into trouble with the government. Gosh, what can we do? We don't even know if he'd listen to us if we decided to go against what the agent said. Do you think that he'd know we were just trying to help, to protect him and our Ana?"

He was silent, considered what she'd said. "I've worked for Mr. Elden a long time. He's definitely a private person, keeps to himself, needs to be in charge, but having said all that, he's honestly always deeply concerned about Ana, about the farm. He was the same with Ana's mother when she was alive. I've felt for a long time that his main purpose in life was to take care of them. You know, he could have taken advantage of them since he was the one who controlled the farm, but he never even considered that. He ran the farm with complete honesty, plus he's good to all the employees too. I just don't see him doing anything dishonest."

"Maybe we should just go and talk to him, even if you're not supposed to. Can I go with you Sam? I need to see his reaction to all this and see if it sheds any light on what's going on. It feels wrong to me to keep this secret from him when he's so much a part of Ana's life. What do you think?"

He didn't hesitate. "Let's do it. How about tomorrow morning, first thing? We'll go to his real estate office and see if he's there. If he's not there, we'll head up to his house. This thing centers on him so let's be direct and talk to him. I'll do it even if I get in trouble with the government. Let's find out what he knows before we bring Ana into this."

Now that Sam was manager of Winchester Farm, he was totally responsible for the business. Ana was not present to make decisions and had left him completely in charge. This meant that he handled all facets of production, choice of crops, and also served as employee supervisor. The morning after he and Maggie had their discussion, he got up even earlier than normal so he could catch things up, get the daily chores organized, and the workers positioned and instructed. He wanted to get a little ahead of the game so that the time he needed to figure out what might be going on, what the truth was with the federal agent, would be available to him.

Later, after catching up, he stepped out of the office. He felt better, even good about getting caught up. He braced himself and moved forward. Forefront in his mind was the talk he and Maggie needed to have with Mr. Elden but he wasn't really looking forward to it. He understood that he was the person who needed to do this but he dreaded it. Then he thought of Maggie and a small spring jumped into his step, his enthusiasm renewed. She would be there beside him.

He got in and started the drive over to pick up Maggie and his mind drifted back in time. His young life had already begun to change for the good by the time Ana's grandpa died and through his friendship with Ana, her mother Monica included him in the farm business at an early point in time. She asked him to help her and Ana when they began to board and care for horses. He felt loved and accepted by people other than his Cherokee family and at that time, he began to feel good about himself. Even though the prejudice he was subjected to during his early years was sometimes harsh, he had the confidence to understand that it was practiced, believed in, only by specific individuals. Not all people were prejudiced.

Sam enjoyed life as he grew up and made new friends. One of those new friends was Jerry, who was now an officer on the Andrews Police Force. Jerry was a few years ahead of Sam in school and had happened onto an incident of bullying, with several older boys attacking Sam after school one day. Jerry stepped in without hesitation, stood up for Sam.

Because of his help, Sam escaped uninjured. Another lesson was etched into Sam's brain that day. Some people are not only your friend but will also defend you, even at their own expense.

All these thoughts raced through his brain as he neared Ana's house where Maggie waited. Now his thoughts focused on her. He admitted to himself that without a doubt he wanted her to always be the center of his life. He'd loved her since he saw her, when she'd come home from school with Ana. His memory was so clear, the tiny dark-haired beauty walking along with Ana. He felt an aura emanating from her body, bringing happiness to the world, to him. As he got to know her better, he also realized the depth of her ability to love as well as her intelligence and desire to be fair to all.

He was there, right on time. They'd agreed last evening to drive downtown to Mr. Elden's real estate office at 9:30 this morning. He stopped and looked up at the house. Maggie sat on the porch swing, ready to go. She waved, grabbed her bag and jacket, and he saw the glow on her face, accented by the sky blue shirt she wore, tucked neatly into her jeans. She was beautiful.

"How did I get so lucky?" he softly asked himself before she reached the truck. He nearly spoke aloud again, but instead thought, "I love you." He smiled happily as he opened the truck door and she climbed in beside him.

They sat, were quiet, no words needed, then touched hands and started on the morning's mission.

"Sam, you've got to take the lead on this. I'm behind you and I'll support you in any way possible but Mr. Elden knows and trusts you. You've got to be the one who does the talking and asks the questions."

He continued to look at her, full of love and concern. "I will, but if you realize that I haven't asked the right questions, you've got to help me out. I don't understand things like taxes and government rules but you do."

"We'll work together Sam. We're good together."

The drive over to Mr. Elden's office didn't take long. Sam pulled the truck into the parking lot of the tiny strip mall where it was located and parked exactly in front of the office door. Even before he left the truck he realized that the lights weren't on inside and as he approached the door, he saw that the closed sign was still up in the front window.

He said out loud, "I'll go ahead and knock on the door anyway. Maybe he just forgot to take down the sign."

So Sam walked up and knocked on the door, even tried to open it in case Mr. Elden was there. He looked into the window, verified that no lights were on and that Mr. Elden wasn't there.

He went back to the truck and got in. "Alright Maggie, we're now on our way to his home. It's a little ways from here, up where the forest begins. He bought some nice acreage a few years back and then built a good looking log cabin there at the edge of the forest. It's a great cabin, not real big and a little isolated but that's the way he likes it."

The drive actually took about 20 minutes or so, as they followed the open fields of the valley on a small road that rose up and up as they drove along. The road led them onto a tiny single-lane dirt tract that meandered through the forest. It ended at Mr. Elden's log cabin.

When she saw the cabin, Maggie was excited. "This cabin is beautiful. Look how it harmonizes with the forest, the construction is fabulous and it looks like it was built to last forever! It's so perfect!"

He agreed. It warmed his heart each time he saw it because it didn't detract from nature, rather added to its beauty. But today, he didn't give much thought to the look of the cabin, just hurried up to the front door and knocked. Silence. Then he knocked harder, tried to open the door, but it was locked securely.

Maggie jumped out of the truck and ran up beside him. One more time he knocked. Then with no words, he spun around and ran towards the small wooden barn that nestled against the forest a little distance from the back of the cabin. This time, when he pulled on the large wooden gate-like door, it opened at once.

"Oh!" Sam was totally surprised and nearly knocked over when a large yellow dog raced out of the barn and jumped frenetically onto his body. Instantly he realized that it was Sunny, Mr. Elden's dog and he hugged the excited dog, patted him and spoke to him calmly. In return he received licks of love and nudges of recognition.

Maggie ran forward when she heard Sam yell, before she realized he wasn't being attacked, was instead being happily greeted by the locked-up Sunny. "Sam, I was frightened! Was the dog locked up in Mr. Elden's barn? Does he belong here?"

Sunny jumped around, then rubbed with delight on Sam's legs again. When Maggie got closer, he ran to her and shared some of the happiness he felt for the people who had released him from his barn-prison.

With complete certainty, Sam said, "Mr. Elden never locks Sunny up in the barn. Sunny is his family and rides with him everywhere he goes." Even as he spoke these words, Sam jerked the large barn door wide open and ran inside. "Where's his car? He must have gone somewhere in the car, but he didn't take Sunny. He never goes anywhere without his Sunny. Now where did he need to go and couldn't take Sunny? Something's wrong here."

Then Sam went further, looked around, hunted for dog food or a supply for water left there for Sunny. He found nothing. "Maggie, something's wrong. We need to get in touch with the police. All I can think of is that Mr. Elden maybe got sick and drove off to the hospital. He must have been in bad shape to leave Sunny locked up here with no food or water. Let's go get the police and they can open up the house. Let's find Jerry and get some help."

Sam and Maggie loaded the cooperative Sunny into the truck with them and then drove fast, back into town and straight to the police station. Sam attached a small piece of rope to the dog's collar and passed control of him over to Maggie. They all three ran into the station.

The front office was crowded; at least that's how it felt to them as they stumbled in, dog in tow. At once every police officer in the small office stopped in their tracks. It was obvious that an emergency existed. They stood still, alert, waited to see what had happened.

Sam's friend Jerry moved from around the counter and grabbed Sam's arm, asked him, "Sam what's the matter? You look upset and by the way, what are you doing with Mr. Elden's dog? Is something wrong?" Jerry reached down and patted Sunny on his head.

Sam wasted no time. "We think something's happened to Mr. Elden. We've been looking for him today but can't find him anywhere. We went to his office, then to his house. He's not at either place but Sunny was locked up in the barn behind his house and there was no food or water with him. That's just not like Mr. Elden. And, his car is gone. It's not in the barn. That's not like him either. We don't know if maybe he got sick and drove off to the hospital or if something else is going on. Honestly though, we think something is wrong and we want to get you guys to come up to his house and make sure he's not locked up inside sick or something. The cabin is locked and dark and, like I said, the barn was closed, the car was gone but Sunny was left behind with no food or water."

"Wait. What are you saying? Do you think he's sick inside his house or gone off in his car?" Jerry stood still and looked at Sam as he tried to understand all that was happening.

"Jerry, that's why Maggie and I came here. We can't find him and it's not like him to go off and lock his dog in the barn without food or water. We need help because we think Mr. Elden needs help. If you guys can get inside of his house we can find out if he's there passed out or sick. Maybe he had a heart attack or something like that. We need you to come and help right now!"

Jerry pointed to an officer, called his name and told him to bring a car around to the front of the station. Then he hit Sam on the back and reassured him that the police were on the way. He told Sam to drive back up to Mr. Elden's house too, but to wait until the officers got there before trying to get into the house.

Jerry and the officer he'd picked to help him both grabbed their jackets and started for the door. Several more of the policemen followed them too. Evidently the day must have been quiet for the police in Andrews because two more also went along. Sam and Maggie pulled Sunny with them and raced back to the truck.

The drive back up to the cabin was fast. Two police vehicles led the way and Sam followed. They pulled up in front of the house.

With no hesitation one of the local policemen tried to open the front door. As Sam had told them, it was locked, so one of them pulled out a small device. In less than a minute he opened the door. Jerry led the police inside.

The room was neat, all in order, dark and silent. The living area and kitchen/dining room was one large room in the cabin. Jerry led the force and after a quick look around he moved over, jerked open a door. It was Mr. Elden's bedroom. He stood still and said nothing, then moved in. The rest of the police moved in behind him and Sam pushed in too. It was empty. Neat. No Mr. Elden.

A quick glance around the room and Jerry walked out, firmly said, "I want at least two of you to stand guard here and make sure no one touches anything in this house. Understand?" Then he ran for the back door, opened it and made for the barn.

The large door was still standing open, exactly as Sam and Maggie had left it. Jerry went straight in and started searching. He wanted to verify that no person, dead or alive, was there.

Sam and Maggie had started this day with the mutual resolution to clear up the mystery revolving around Mr. Elden. They planned to find out if the IRS or some other federal agency was investigating him. Well, the mystery remained, had grown larger. He'd disappeared. Now they both knew they had no choice. They had to contact their friend Ana and fill her in on what had happened. First though, Sam decided that he needed to tell Jerry everything he knew about what had happened. It didn't matter to him if he would be in trouble with the law for telling what the agent had asked him. The important thing now was to find out where Mr. Elden was and if he was safe.

Maggie held onto Sunny while Sam pulled Jerry off to the side, away from the other police, and told him what had transpired earlier in the week. He gave him every detail he could remember about the agent and admitted to Jerry that he'd not thought to get the agent's name and identification. He also told Jerry that he and Maggie were not confident that the agent was from the IRS, checking up on tax problems.

After Sam finished his confession his friend stood still, stunned. "Sam, you and Maggie take Sunny and go home. I need to do some official checking on any federal agents who've been sent into our area. Wait for me and I'll let you know what I find out."

They walked back to the truck and put Sunny into the back seat. Then they sat still, confused and worried.

Sam spoke up. "I can't imagine what this is all about. It doesn't make sense. What are we missing?"

Her answer surprised him a little. "You know what? Maybe I'm wrong, but somehow, I don't believe this has anything to do with the Federal Government. This isn't how they operate. The way that man came into your office, the way he asked all those questions and gave no real identification, I wonder if he's a criminal. Did Mr. Elden have anything valuable that someone might want to steal from him?"

Chapter Twenty-One

Eyes Everywhere
Heidelberg – Ana – 1971

The Women's Society of Heidelberg began after the end of World War II when the United States established a large military base adjacent to the city of Heidelberg. The proximity of the base to the city allowed the wives of the on-base military men to meet and form friendships with the German women of Heidelberg. This connection between the women of the two different countries, once at war with each other, but now friends, gave birth to the idea that the Women's Society could help promote mutual educational scholarships between Germany and the United States. The Society's goal for this project was to help strengthen the good connections between their two countries.

After they officially decided to work together toward this goal, their Society then worked with the leaders of Universities in Heidelberg and several Universities located in the United States. They explained their desire to help and asked for cooperation from all the Universities in order to establish a student exchange program. They were appreciated and got approval.

Cooperation grew, participation became reality, and all the participating Universities gave funding to support the student exchange program.

The costs associated with this scholarship program included items such as travel to and from the different countries, the cost of housing, health insurance, as well as the actual cost of attending the Universities. It was a major undertaking, but all those involved realized the value of this type of education and participated wholeheartedly to promote it.

The Women's Society of Heidelberg decided to provide additional help for the students coming to attend Universities there by giving each of them a small monthly allowance to help them pay for life on a day–to-day basis. They also provided each student with a member of the Women's Society who acted as their advisor, available at all times for help and advice.

In order to obtain the money needed to sponsor the students, the Women's Society requested contributions from citizens in the area, and they also held annual fund-raising events.

Ana originally came to Germany as one of the exchange students sponsored by the Society and was now, today, an example of what the Society wanted to accomplish. Because of her connection with the exchange program they all worked so hard for, Ana was now qualified for, and actually working for the German International University as an Assistant Professor in Languages.

The Women's Society had recently contacted her and asked if she would come and speak at a meeting they were having, to tell about the advantages the exchange student program had given her. She accepted at once but then discovered that the local press was also invited, as were members of the city government of Heidelberg. The event was an annual one and was published in the regional papers, discussed locally, and provided another means to advertise and raise money for student support.

Ana was a little nervous.

The event was scheduled to begin with lunch, served by a local restaurant at tables set up outside on the Market Square. Then after the lunch, a meeting room inside city hall, located right beside the Market Square, was ready for the planned event.

The food was delicious and tables were full of students, members of the Women's Society, newspaper reporters, and local politicians.

Ana sat at a table with three new students, all part of the current exchange program, just arrived to begin their first semester. They each represented different Universities in the United States and Ana had a good time talking with them in English, simply getting to know them. They were curious about her experience with the exchange program and asked for her opinion of it. She told them how much more depth and reality it had added to her education, how it had helped her get to where she was today.

Lunch lasted approximately an hour, and then Frau Klaus, the President of the Women's Society directed everyone into the impressive front door of the city hall. They climbed up to the second floor and filled up the conference room already set up for the meeting.

When she got into the large room, Ana left the students she'd been with at lunch and walked over to join Frau Klaus, along with a group of people also scheduled to speak. They all sat down in the front row of the fast-filling room.

Not so very long ago she would have been too nervous to even consider speaking at an event like this. However, as a result of the daily teaching she was now doing, she felt stronger, more confident.

The room was full. The meeting started and went smoothly. Mid-way through and suddenly it was her turn. She walked up to the podium, carried no papers or notes, and then began to speak in German, the language she'd studied so long. She talked to the room full of people, used their language, and told how powerful her experience with the student exchange program had been, how much it had helped her.

"It showed me a new culture, let me live in the midst of it, and helped me learn to speak the language more naturally. It added so much to my previous years of study and changed me, altered my life's path. I recommend this opportunity to any student who wants to broaden their perspective of this world. Also, I would sincerely like to thank the members of the Women's Society of Heidelberg for the hard work they do to help and guide us."

She smiled politely and started back to her seat when darkness invaded her thoughts, when she felt the sting of intense eyes on her body. Where were the eyes? Then she saw him. She saw his back but he'd already turned around and started out the door. She didn't see his face but knew he'd watched her before. What did he want?

Later, after the meeting was over, Ana talked to a lady she knew, a member of the Women's Society. She told her how happy she was to make the speech and return support to the Society that had supported her educational goals. Then as she walked away, she sighed with relief. She was hiding her fear about the man who'd left the room after checking her out. She tried to act like nothing happened, just wanted to get back to normal. Move ahead. He's gone. And remember! The speech is over. No more speech to worry about! She talked inside her head as she pretended to be a part of the world along with the other people in the room. Eventually she started to push the fear aside, put it behind her again. At that moment she decided to go and shop for groceries. She wanted to get back to her normal life.

Still a little shaky, but relieved, she walked slowly along the street, moved forward to a small grocery store located several blocks down. This morning, even with all the anxiety about her speech, she'd thought to tuck two cloth bags inside her purse. Honestly, her small pantry was almost empty and now she felt a strong need to cook something, a meal she really loved. She'd discovered years back that cooking relieved her stress.

The store was small but well stocked and she found everything she needed, even the fresh mushrooms. The line wasn't too long and she smiled politely at the lady who checked her out, then paid her bill and loaded her groceries into the two bags she'd brought. It was a tight fit and both bags were heavy. Time to go home and start cooking.

With help to open the heavy grocery store door from a person coming in as she was going out, she stepped into the street and took only a few steps when a familiar voice interrupted her thoughts. "Professor Winchester, hello, do you need help with your grocery bags? They look heavy." There was Thomas, right beside her. He looked and sounded as he always did, helpful and happy.

Confusion washed over her again. Why did he constantly appear in her life, always friendly, helpful, but also always curious? He asked too many questions. When she first knew him, his curiosity made her nervous but since he'd started to work at the student apartment house near where she lived she saw him almost daily. Now it felt normal to be around him so much. She deliberately watched him tackle his new job and recognized immediately that he was hardworking, totally involved in what he needed to do. In addition, he was friendly and helpful to everyone he encountered, not just to her.

Suddenly she made a decision, smiled freely back at him, no more hesitation. "Hello Thomas. Are you sure you have time to help me home with my groceries? If you are going in my direction I would certainly say yes to some help. I already have my heavy purse, overloaded today, so I would be glad to let you carry one of these heavy bags if you really want to help me."

"I am going to the apartment house up behind your place, so I am not going out of my way. Frau Krueger had told me that maybe an apartment would become available, and that happened today. I am so happy. It is convenient and decently priced and will make my next semester much easier." As he told her his good news, he grabbed both of the bags from her and together they started the walk home.

"Thomas, that is so good! The area is nice, so close to school and to town. Maybe you were lucky in more than just getting the job to earn income for school, you also got to know Frau Krueger. She probably recommended you for the vacant apartment. She is a good person."

They parted at Ana's door and as she searched for her key, she heard the telephone ringing. She tried to hurry as she opened the door and grabbed the bags, but by the time she was inside the door, it had stopped. Out loud she spoke, with instinctive worry in her voice, "I hope nothing is wrong."

She reminded herself that she received calls from the Professor, whom she assisted there at the University on a regular basis. Deliberately, forcefully, she told herself to stop worrying and live her life.

Chapter Twenty-Two

Frau Krueger
Heidelberg – Ana – 1971

Ana started cooking as soon as she got home and unpacked her groceries. She focused deliberately on nothing else as she chopped onions into long thin pieces and followed all the steps that were needed to complete her home cooked dumplings, known in German as semmelknödel, covered in crème fraiche and a mushroom sauce. It didn't take long for the smell of her cooking to permeate the apartment as it drifted up from the gently sautéing mushroom and onions. Her mouth watered.

The semmelknödel prep began when she pulled out the few-days-old loaf of bread from her cabinet. The texture was perfect because it needed to be firm and dry. Mother taught her to cook this meal and now, as she worked by herself, memories gave her an emotional lift.

One Christmas mother had given her a special present, a cookbook. It was written in English but contained basic German recipes. They'd worked together on Christmas Day and cooked exactly what Ana was working on today. One her move to Heidelberg, she'd pulled the cookbook out of mother's closet-bookcase where she found it and brought it along with her. She wanted it to be a part of her new life.

Evidently the mouth-watering smell of her cooking managed to slip out of her apartment through the open window in her kitchen, because a tentative knock sounded on her door just as she finished up and was about ready to load up her plate and indulge.

The person at the door was Frau Krueger. "Please do not think me rude, but the smell of your cooking is calling my name very loudly. You are evidently as good at cooking as you are at speaking our German language!"

"Please come in Frau Krueger. I have been cooking for myself, one of my favorite meals, but I do not think of myself as a "good" cook, or as a "good" speaker of the German language." She replied and a smile lit her face briefly, acknowledged the compliments.

Without hesitation Frau Krueger went on, "Fraulein, I can attest to your excellent ability when you speak my language because we talk to each other frequently. Now, I can also attest to your excellent ability to cook. This smell proves it."

The good-natured talk between them and the delicious smell of the food suddenly gave her an idea. "Frau Krueger, the only way to prove whether or not my cooking is as good as it smells is for you to agree to stay and have dinner with me. Oh, that is if you have not already eaten dinner."

Pleasure and anticipation glowed. "Yes, with pleasure I will accept your invitation. I have not eaten yet, but even if I had, I would still say yes to you. This is food that I like very much."

Ana began to get plates and silverware out for the meal and decided to move the food she'd cooked out of the pots and pans and into bowls and set them on the table. For herself, she had planned to eat from the pots but her guest deserved dinner on the table, ready to dig into. Frau Krueger stepped up and immediately pitched in to help. Time to eat!

Suddenly Frau Krueger stood still. "I have a special bottle of white wine in my apartment, chilled and ready in my refrigerator. I must have known I was going to get to enjoy it with your special dinner. Please wait just a minute and let me get it so we can share it together." She hurried out the door and was back with the wine almost before Ana could get the glasses out and ready for it.

Frau Krueger opened the wine and filled their glasses. They sat down, paused for a moment, then greedily filled their plates and began to devour the food. Pleasurable silence and contentment filled the room as they both ate a lot and talked only a little.

Around the time they were both satisfied, could eat no more, a question surfaced in Ana's mind. The longer she'd lived in this specific apartment, the more she recognized that it truly had been lucky that she'd been able to rent it. She saw how many people called on Frau Krueger, wanting to rent an apartment here and she didn't understand how she'd been lucky enough to get it so fast. How had she jumped in front of all the people who were waiting in line for it?

"Frau Krueger, I am so fortunate to be able to live here, in this lovely old home. It is located so perfectly, near the historic Old Town and right beside the Neckar River. I see how many people come to see you wanting to rent here and I sometimes wonder how I got lucky and got this apartment. So many people wanted it and they were here. I lived so far away and I got it. It seems unbelievable to me but I'm so happy it worked out this way. I love it here."

Frau Krueger tilted her head to the side, wrinkled up her face a little in what looked like confusion as she answered, "I thought you knew what happened, that your agent told you how hard it was. I had already agreed, as manager, to rent this apartment to a young man from Berlin who was moving here to begin a new job."

Ana was stunned but tried to look calm. "If that was the case, if the apartment had already been rented to the young man from Berlin, then why do I now live here instead of him?"

Frau Krueger's face continued to show confusion. "I only talked to your agent once and that was when I told him the apartment was rented and I could not change that. Then your agent called a person he knew here, a relative or something. I never did understand exactly what connection the lady had to your agent. She introduced herself to me but I cannot remember her name. She seemed to mumble at times, did not speak clearly even though she did a lot of talking and I did a lot of listening. She did not let it go even when I repeated that the apartment was rented already."

"Excuse me, this is not making sense to me. Are you telling me that I somehow got my apartment because my agent has a relative who lives here in Heidelberg? Even though it was already rented?"

"Yes. I guess you could say that is part of the reason that you got the apartment.   Oh, do not misunderstand me. It was not easy, was in fact a little complicated. The lady-relative paid the young man from Berlin the equivalent of one full month's rent and got him to agree to give up his right to the apartment." She groaned, gasped and clapped her hand over her mouth. "I have had too much wine!"

Extremely upset, she looked straight at Ana. "Please forget that you heard those words from me. I promised the lady, your real estate agent's person, and I even accepted a small amount of money from her when it was all settled. She said she wanted to reward me for all my help. I believe the money was to remind me to remember not to tell anyone how things had been changed, and how you got the apartment. The whole thing confused me, did not make sense."

She pushed herself back from the table and started for the door. "I must go home now. I have said too much."

Ana stood up too. She smiled gently and said, "Please do not feel so upset. This it a different story than the one I heard from my agent, but that is not really a problem. I am pleased to have this apartment. Come back and sit down with me. What you have told me actually resolves the confusion I have felt about me being lucky enough to be living here. "

She moved over to Frau Krueger and touched her shoulder gently. "You have been kind to me and we have so much in common, especially our taste for food and wine." Then she giggled.

Frau Krueger walked back over to the table and stood by Ana, looked squarely into her eyes. "Do you want the whole story?"

Now the truth came out. To ease the telling, Ana filled up both of their wine glasses again. The unfiltered version of the story came forth and Frau Krueger evidenced no more trepidation. She told the whole story.

Evidently, Mr. Elden had not engaged an "international real estate agent" to handle the search for an apartment as he had told Ana. Instead, he'd called someone he knew who lived in Heidelberg. His Relative? This "relative" handled the apartment rental, worked with Frau Krueger. Money passed hands in order to ensure the rental of the specific apartment and in addition, money was also paid to make sure that no one, including Ana, knew how she got her apartment.

Again she attempted to remain calm as she listened to Frau Krueger's story and when it ended she said, "Please accept my apology for all the chaos you went through so that I could live here. I do not really know why all this took place but I will tell you my best guess. My friend, Mr. Elden is also a former real estate agent and in addition, manages and takes care of my personal property and business. He has worked on my behalf for many years, all the way back to the time when my mother died. Honestly, I think of him as my family, call him "Uncle" sometimes in my heart. He is a good man and I think he simply wanted me to live in what he considered a special apartment. He does know a lot about Heidelberg because he was a student here at some time in his younger life, and he loves it. Maybe he tried too hard to make sure I was cared for this time. I only needed a place to live and it was not necessary that it had to be this apartment."

Frau Krueger interrupted her gently, "But what about the lady who came and did all the work with me on your behalf, the one who gave me money so I would not tell you about any of this. Does that make sense to you?"

"I do not pretend to know anything about that lady. Maybe he knew her from the time he spent here at the University. I do not know. Why they did it this way is strange to me but Mr. Elden got the apartment he wanted for me to live in and it is indeed a wonderful place. But, again I want to apologize to you for all the difficulties you had to put up with. Can we still remain friends? I promise never to mention this conversation to Mr. Elden. It does not exist."

Words between the two of them continued to flow but they decided to not talk about the rental fiasco. When they parted a little later it was obvious from her attitude and the lightness in her voice that Frau Krueger felt a heavy burden had been lifted from her shoulders.

Honesty and friendship were established.

Chapter Twenty-Three

Acceptance and Loss
Heidelberg – Ana – 1971

As soon as Frau Krueger left, Ana started cleaning up. She took her time and as she washed the dirty dishes, thought over everything she'd learned tonight from her new friend, lots of information and details that didn't match what Mr. Elden had told her about renting this apartment. What she heard tonight didn't match up with the Mr. Elden that she'd known for so very long.

Tonight's conversation left questions rambling in her head: What did Mr. Elden know? Who did he know in Heidelberg? Did he really have family here? Why had it been important enough to spend extra money so that she could live in this particular apartment?

The kitchen was clean, the food put away, and still she was thinking of him. With purpose, she walked into her bedroom and pulled her suitcase out from where she'd stored it, underneath her bed. She fetched the key from where she'd hidden it, inside a pair of her socks in a dresser drawer and unlocked it, then pulled out a large brown envelope that held mother's dairy, the one she'd found hidden in the bedroom closet.

It hadn't been necessary to purchase furniture when she'd moved into her apartment here because it came furnished. The furnishings included a small desk that sat against a wall in the living room. Ana used it as her home-office and now she went there and sat down with the dairy. It was time to read it again and try to understand what mother recorded.

Most of her words told a painful story of something that happened when she was young. She'd only written a few lines and what she wrote was hard to read. It was extremely important but, as usual, mother left out most of the facts. It was vague and shadowed.

Sadness weighed her down as she continued to read her mother's words. Somehow, she felt it was her fault that she'd never been able to persuade mother to answer her questions, to stop hiding the truth. During their lives together it never changed. Mother never shared, never answered questions about her family, about Germany, had always kept silent or just changed the subject. Even here, in her private little book, she'd still been careful not to write down any details that explained the heartbreaking words that she'd recorded.

Ana tried to connect words her mother had actually spoken during her life with what she'd written in her book. It was important, she had to figure it out because mother had left a warning at the end of her last written page. She wrote a message directly to Ana that warned of danger, said the map to wealth was where the danger lay.

After the recurring feel of eyes on her body, the lifelong feel of being watched, she finally believed it was real. For so long she'd denied it but her instincts were right. She'd told herself it was nonsense but now she definitely had to reconsider.

The telephone rang. Sam's voice was there. "Ana, I've tried to call you already but you weren't home. We need to talk. There're some strange, unexplainable things happening here." His voice was low key, sad, somehow exactly what she believed she would hear when she missed the ringing telephone just recently, evidently the first call from Sam. Bad news was here.

He didn't hesitate, just told her the worst part of the news first. "Mr. Elden is missing. Maggie and I are working together on this and decided that the best way to understand things was to talk to him, so we went to his house. We'd already gone by his office but he wasn't there. What we found when we got to his house was his dog Sunny locked up in the barn with no food or water. And, his car was gone. Mr. Elden would never leave Sunny locked up with no food or water. It didn't make sense."

He paused, thinking maybe he was dumping all the bad news on her too quickly. "Ana, are you alright?"

Shadows gathered around her as a heart-stopping roar echoed in her mind. Grief filled her heart. She knew she would never see her Mr. Elden again.

Softly and sadly she spoke. "I'm sorry for my silence Sam. This hurts. Can you tell me anything else about his disappearance? Has he been sick?"

"We haven't seen any signs of bad health. But something else happened recently. Maggie and I have been trying to figure things out and we didn't want to bother you until we had some more information. The two of us talked it over and decided to go and talk directly to Mr. Elden and get to the bottom of this but when we went to talk to him, we couldn't find him. We had to call and let you know."

She interrupted softly, "Wait. Slow down and tell me what you're talking about. What happened that involves Mr. Elden?"

So Sam gave her a concise summary of everything, from the visit of the Federal Agent to his and Maggie's realization that the agent was not telling the truth. Now, Mr. Elden had disappeared and the police were searching for him and also looking into the identity of the man who claimed to be an agent of the government.

She listened carefully and absorbed the details. "Sam, I've got something that I need to talk to you about, information about Mr. Elden. But right now I need to get home to Andrews immediately. I need to help find Mr. Elden. He's helped me so much, for such a long time."

They knew each other well and he heard more than the words she spoke. "I think that you may already have some information about this Ana. You didn't sound surprised when I told you what happened here. Now I'm worried about you too. Talk to me and tell me what you know. What's going on?"

"I do have to talk to you. I recently learned some things that I never knew but this telephone is not the place to share this information. We need to talk face to face, in privacy. I'm booking a flight home right away and I'll let you know when I'll arrive in Atlanta. Will you see if Maggie can pick me up at the airport?"

He was deeply worried and she knew it when he answered. "I'll be waiting to hear from you. Call me as soon as you get your flight booked. Don't even think about the difference in our time zones. Just call me as soon as you know when you'll land. I'll call Maggie and you can depend on her picking you up. Take care of yourself!"

Chapter Twenty-Four

A Different Life
Heidelberg – Ingrid - 1943

Across all of Germany, a country so loved and respected by its citizens, extreme changes took place. The normal everyday life that most people lived and loved changed drastically after the Nazi takeover of complete political control, and then World War II began. With each passing day, changes grew and intensified. Lifestyles, choices, were lost and the government told the people what to do. The Nazis made the decisions, and the citizens were expected to carry them out.

One example of this was the Nazi institution of specific nursing classes they set up at certain Universities around the country. Young girls of specific ages and abilities were told to enroll. The classes were difficult and intense because the Nazi goal was quick graduations. More nurses were needed now with the war causing difficulties.

In Heidelberg, Ingrid was one of the young girls required to sign up. She felt strange to be in class at the very university that she had always dreamed of attending, but instead of pursuing her interests in life, she had to do what her government ordered.

Her problem wasn't that she didn't want to help the people of her country. She simply felt sad as she walked to class each day, past the office that had once belonged to her Father. When he was alive, a respected professor, she and her mother visited him there so many times. Now he was dead, killed by the Nazis. Her entire life had changed and any optimistic plans she had for her future didn't exist any longer.

Daily life was busy. The heavy class schedule forced her to use any free time she had to complete chores, shop, cook and clean. She managed to accomplish all this, but her main purpose every day was to spend time with and try to help her mother.

Mother had changed. She wasn't the happy, helpful, busy lady who had existed before The Night of Broken Glass. She was now sick, weakened both physically and mentally after the death of her beloved husband on that horrible night, that horror that she and Ingrid had been part of.

The large happy gingerbread house that Ingrid had grown up in, filled warmly with her family, was now almost empty. She and her mother were the only ones who lived there now. The lovely Neckar River flowed past an empty house haunted by ghosts.

Ingrid's grandparents had left their home some time earlier. They made the decision to move permanently to their farm in Bavaria, or at least until the war was over. They were devastated by the horror of what happened to their family on Kristallnacht. Not only was their son in law murdered by the Nazis, along with the friend he tried to help, but he was also labeled a "Jew-Lover." This label was used personally, politically, and economically against his remaining family members. They were shunned by some of the citizens of Heidelberg and this treatment hit both Grandfather and Grandmother extremely hard. They had always been a major part of the heart of Heidelberg.

The bright happy six-year old Ingrid who had run away from home one day to go to the German Girl's Party was different. Her life was now state-controlled and she was forced into nursing classes. When she finished the classes she knew without doubt that she would immediately be transferred to a military base, hospital, or area of action, somewhere far away from everything she'd ever known and loved. She was sad and helpless. Happiness, warmth, weren't a part of life.

Ingrid walked down a hopeless road.

An amphitheater, sponsored and funded by the Nazis, was built at the top of the Heiligenberg (Holy Mountain), across the Neckar River from the famous Heidelberg Castle. The amphitheater was named "Thingstätte." The public claim was that it was built for use by Heidelberg University. Its true purpose at that time was as an additional venue for the Nazis to recruit even more disciples. Political rallies were held there frequently, with speeches made by numerous top Nazi officials.

The building site selected for the amphitheater had been originally used in early Roman times. The whole mountaintop area was recognized and celebrated as a magnet for religious meetings of many sorts, including those of the Celts. The area was believed to have strong spiritual power and perhaps that history influenced the Nazis' choice of that location for the new amphitheater.

The spiritual power historically attached to the location was felt by the

Nazis to be a powerful positive. They built the amphitheater as near as possible to the remaining ruins of an ancient Celtic settlement, known locally as the Convergence Zone, or, in laymen's terms, a gathering place for spirits.

In the years before the war, even later in the post war years, the local youth used the amphitheater area for the annual "All Saint's Celebration." It had that powerful attraction of past ghosts and spirits and made the perfect spot for a celebration of spookiness, fun, and loud music, partying, and drinking. The young people were above the city, and on top of the mountain. Part of the tradition was for them to hike up the mountain, and in so doing, they left their elders behind in the valley.

In this particular year, in spite of, or maybe because of the war and its daily threat, the young folks in Heidelberg planned among themselves to carry on with their annual celebration. That youthful hunt for a good time pushed them forward, made them more determined that they were going to follow their tradition and ignore the war.

Plans were made, information passed back and forth through the youthful grapevine. Lots of excitement circulated but a shock was imminent. The Nazis had also scheduled a "surprise" event in the amphitheater that evening. They had already dispatched several important officers to Heidelberg. The plan was for the selected officers to make speeches in specific classrooms at the university, propaganda speeches directed at the young students, in order to build more support for the Nazi Party. Later, the students would be told to attend the "Nazi Party" at the Thingstätte on All Saint's Day.

On the Friday afternoon just before the weekend of All Saint's Day, Ingrid jumped up and ran from her classroom the minute the nursing class was released for the day. She dashed through the street, and only stopped, suddenly, when she was totally across the old bridge, almost home. She felt bewildered, angry, excited.

The class was not as usual today. Mid-way through the regular session, the professor paused and told all the girls to report to one of the large university lecture halls. They did as they were told but for some reason, Ingrid moved slowly, ended up being one of the last girls into the hall. The only seat not already claimed was on the front row. Not good she thought.

Nazi officers and officials were not uncommon at the university. Because she felt intense pain and anger each time she saw their uniforms, she tried her best to avoid them all. Today, in the front row, she was in a difficult position.

Even as these thoughts went through her mind, a uniformed Nazi officer walked out onto the stage and stood behind the podium. He spoke up and told them that he was there to talk to them about loyalty, hard work, and how important it was for the young students to support their country.

As he spoke, the officer looked randomly around, scanned and addressed his audience. When he glanced in Ingrid's direction, straight out in front of him, he paused slightly. Ingrid felt his eyes change.

His style of lecturing was different from what she was accustomed to, both in content and in delivery. Most of the time, the Nazi officials displayed a confrontational style. Instead, this man spoke pleasantly, asked for their help instead of demanding it. He talked about how necessary it was for every individual to help others, and specifically of how much the country needed the young people to help the older people. The words came out of his mouth, from the mouth of a uniformed Nazi officer, but every word that he spoke rang true in her mind.

The man didn't match his uniform. Nervously, she tried to examine his face without calling attention to herself. What she saw was a tall, handsome, calm man. He seemed sure of himself, sincere in everything he said, and as she looked at him and listened to him she didn't feel the anger she had expected to feel. Instead, his belief in what he talked to them about met and connected exactly to what she believed.

During the speech, his eyes continued to touch her. They were strong. Now, as she stood at the end of the bridge, lost in time, she felt jittery. She kept feeling his eyes. With a shake of her head, she tried to push thoughts of him away, tried to focus on the old, gnarled trees, heavy with leaves. They sang with the colors of autumn and were only one breath away from falling to the ground, as was she.

She slowly started walking again and found herself near her personal refuge, her thinking spot. At one time her grandfather had kept a boat moored here beside the river but he'd sold it years ago. The ramp was never used and was blocked from sight because of the bushes that had grown up between it and the walking path. She'd long ago adopted it as her personal hiding place and now she went straight to it and sat down.

Her mind swirled as she asked herself question after question. "What does he want? What did he see when he looked at me? Why do I care what he saw, HE IS A NAZI!" She continued to sit perfectly still, knees drawn up, her head resting on them. Then she lay down and curled up on the old concrete ramp.

She let her mind wander and it slid into a dream. Something woke up, memories stirred. It wasn't clear enough or maybe she didn't allow herself to recognize the memories and their power in her life. Happiness crept in, excitement joined, and her heart beat faster.

No! No! It is wrong! My father is dead, my mother is crushed, my best friend is missing, and the Nazis did it!" She spoke the harsh words out loud, full of anger, full of pain. Her heart objected to her mind. She didn't know what truth she believed. She couldn't reconcile what she thought, believed and felt.

Later, out of the blue, she suddenly found herself trying to visualize how she looked. She'd didn't bother to look in a mirror anymore. She remembered a tall, rather thin girl with long blonde hair, naturally curling down her body, always available if she needed to hide her blue eyes behind it or to hide herself from life. With that thought, she uncurled her body, jumped up and ran from her hiding place. It was way past time to go home and help Mother by making their evening meal.

Later the same day, Ingrid tried to cheer up her depressed mother by talking to her. She had no success, so she went to the kitchen and started to fix dinner. The power of a firm knock sounded on the front door. The sound resonated not only through the air around her but also inside her body, and she knew who stood outside. She didn't take time to think further, simply ran to the front door, jerked it open, and looked again into the blue eyes that called her.

"Please come in." Her voice was soft and with no more words, she took his hand into her own and pulled him into the house, then forward into the room where her mother sat in a chair. Suddenly, she realized that even though she'd brought him to introduce to mother, she didn't even know his name. Crazy, I'm really crazy, flashed in her head.

Mother got up carefully from her chair and stepped bravely forward. All she knew was that the man in front of her was wearing a Nazi uniform. Scared, she asked, "Ingrid, who is this?"

Ingrid stood perfectly still and looked up at the tall Nazi officer.

Gently he took Ingrid by her arm and moved further into the room with her. He stopped in front of her mother. "Good Day Frau Neuschwander. My name is Max Koenig. We have met before, but long ago, and I do not know if you remember me."

Mother's face was pale. Ingrid moved beside her, "Mother, this man spoke to my class today at university. He spoke well, was kind and understanding. He was asking all of the young people to help support the older people because the war has made life so hard on them these days."

Since the tragic death of her husband, mother didn't show any emotion or engage in the real world, except she did still try to make sure that Ingrid knew how much she loved her. Today though, she acted differently. She stood up shakily from her chair and with an anger-filled voice and a look straight at Ingrid she said, "I lost my husband and you lost your father and now you dare to invite this Nazi in and you expect me to welcome him because he made a nice speech today?"

Mother was weak and struggled not to fall down as Ingrid grabbed her and helped her to sit back down. All of a sudden, in the kitchen the overheated, boiling, spitting water hissed loudly as it ran over onto the top of the stove.

Ingrid ran from the room and moved the pan off the burner, then turned off the stove. No time for this right now. She ran back and found mother wilted, almost completely passed out there in the chair. Max Koenig was on his knees in front of her. She watched as he took her mother's pulse, and then put his ear to her chest.

He saw Ingrid and said, "Does your mother have heart problems?"

"No. None that I know of." Tears were close. "Are you a doctor?"

"Yes, I am. I believe we need to take your mother to the hospital and get her tested. Let me call for some transportation from the local hospital."

Mother struggled to get out of her chair again. "NO! I refuse to go to the hospital. I will not put myself into the hands of people who helped kill my husband. If it's my time to die then I am ready to leave this world."

Now Ingrid was crying uncontrollably. "Oh mother, please let us help you. I don't want to lose you. I love you so much!" Pain and anguish filled the room. The doctor watched both women, and then he pulled Ingrid outside the room.

"I respect your mother and how she feels about going to the hospital. First we'll make her comfortable, and then I'll go get my medical equipment, then come back and take all her vital signs again. While I'm gone you can maybe sit and talk to her and possibly change her mind about going to the hospital. I agree with her, the world we live in today is not the same one we grew up with."

Together they moved mother over to her bed and covered her lightly. Max Koenig held her wrist as he again checked her pulse, then listened to her heart again too. "Right now I believe she just needs to rest. I do not see anything that tells me that your mother is having a heart attack. I believe my appearance in her house has put her into shock."

Ingrid and Max left the bedroom and closed the door softly behind them. She felt like a betrayer. How had she let this happen to her mother?

"I did not even know your name. When did you meet my Mother? How did you find me today?"

He heard the emotion in her voice, answered without hesitation, "After my speech today, I asked one of the professors at the university about you. He told me your name, and that you live with you mother here by the river. I am usually much more well-mannered and formal when I get to know people but I am only here for two days on military business and then I will leave again. I had no time to waste so I asked the professor for your information. I hope you are not offended."

Surprised by his honesty and the implication of a strong interest in her, she felt her need for him deepen.

Her emotional battle raged. The hatred and the hurt inflicted upon her family by the death of her father fought cruelly against the connection and the desire she felt when she looked, listened, even believed him.

A perfect human doesn't exist. Every person is a combination of both good and bad, and each is unique. Anyone who claims to be perfect is dangerous. They always place the "bad" on other people, never themselves. Life is imperfection. The truth must be individualized.

When Hitler and his Nazi collaborators took control of the military and power structure of Germany, they used propaganda, lies, and well-designed strategy to blame the country's problems on persons other than the perfect Nazi Party. They took control and people lost their voices because to speak up could cause death and destruction.

Now, as the good/bad, right/wrong battle raged in her mind, Ingrid experienced harsh pain. Yet somehow, she leaned toward her belief in the individual value of a person, not the political party they belonged to.

"Ingrid, I am going to town to get my medical bag but I will be back to make sure your mother is alright. When I come back, if we decide that she is well, would you consider coming out to dinner with me? I will arrange a nurse to come and stay with your mother while we are gone, just in case of emergency."

She was astonished. "You could arrange care for my mother?"

"The reason I came to your house tonight was to invite you for dinner. We could still go at around seven o'clock if you will go with me. That would give us time to enjoy our meal together and then go up to the All Saint's Day celebration at the Thingstätte tonight."

He took her hand and did not wait for her answer. "I will be so happy to see you again and go to dinner together. We won't have time for the traditional hike up but I will arrange military transportation for us both." Then he touched her face gently, turned, and walked out the door. He softly closed it.

She stared at the door but all she really saw was Max's face and his body and it was superimposed over the Heiligenberg Mountain.

Chapter Twenty-Five

The Heart Decides
Heidelberg – Ingrid – 1943

At precisely seven o'clock Max knocked on the door. Ingrid shivered with anticipation, but heard the word betrayer whisper deep inside. Happiness was on top but underneath felt she felt like Judas.

He came in and then ushered in a young woman, a nurse he had found to stay with mother provided that he found her in stable condition and they were able to go out for their evening together. Everyone went into mother's bedroom and when Max asked her how she was feeling, she didn't answer, had nothing to say to him. He accepted her behavior, and calmly took out his stethoscope and listened to her heart, then again checked her pulse, her neck. He tried to connect with her one more time. "How are you feeling?"

This time she responded. "I am fine and I do not need your help. Please leave me alone."

Ingrid was tense and at this moment all that mattered was that her mother be in stable condition.

Max picked up his bag and took her arm. Together they left the nurse behind in the room with mother. "I'm glad to tell you that your mother is not in danger. Honestly, I believe she went into a mild form of shock when we met this afternoon. I am telling you truthfully that she is not in danger here without you tonight. The nurse is good and will take care of her while we are gone."

She had already decided what she wanted to do. The internal emotional battle that she still fought continued, but she still chose Max over the Nazis. She admitted to herself that perhaps she was not logical or reasonable, but this was the path she picked, the road she wanted to walk down.

Without admitting to herself that she'd already decided what to do, she'd earlier gone into her room and picked out the best outfit she could find for her dinner out with him.

Now she walked back into mother's room and stood beside her. "I cannot tell you why but I feel this is right, that I go out tonight with Max. Please do not hate me for this. I love you and my father and all of my family." Then she turned and walked out of the room, back to Max.

The walk from her home into the city that evening, arm-in-arm with Max Koenig felt like the most perfect piece of time she had ever experienced. They talked as they walked and she felt like she'd known him forever.

Halfway across the bridge he stopped and led her to the overlook that was attached to and jutted out from that side of the bridge. They stood together and gazed down at the now dark water beneath them. He whispered a question softly into her ear. "Do you remember me Ingrid?"

"Max!" She said his name aloud and it felt so delicious in her mouth.

"Sweet Ingrid, the very first time that I saw you was when you were a small girl. I loved you then. Now I find you again by accident and now you are not that little girl, now you are a young woman. This time, I will never let you leave my life again!"

"Oh Max, I do remember you! I do know you and I have always felt a strong connection between us. I felt it was just childhood memories but you are still the tall man beside the river, the important man who engaged me as his friend at the time I was trying to run away by myself to the event that I thought was a party."

He drew her tenderly into his arms. "You do remember me. We were meant to be together, were chosen for each other. I felt that possibility that day beside the river when we met and I feel it now as we stand above that same river. We were destined to be together." His arms went around her, warm and strong, as was his tall hard body and she welcomed his heat, returned it with an intensity that shoved aside her guilt.

In life some people are bold and brave enough to receive the love they have always looked for when it is offered. No pretense or procrastination is necessary.

They got interrupted by a loud horn from below them as a barge passed slowly under the bridge. They broke apart reluctantly, but with smiles and anticipation. They continued to walk to the city.

Max led her to a popular local restaurant. They entered and the waiter led them to a nice table beside the window, with a view of the courtyard. They ordered and enjoyed a delicious meal together as they shared the food and the wine. Ingrid felt abnormal because she had not eaten out for a very long time. As a child, she'd enjoyed many meals in this very place with her family, but life had changed. Her age had changed too. She was now allowed to enjoy a glass of wine and she did. She felt she was going to ignore all the rules she usually observed, be adventurous. Tonight felt like it was meant to be and she was ready, could not wait. Max was her future.

Laughter and the drone of voices did not penetrate their personal conversation. They heard only each other. They smiled, each feeling that the evening together was far from over. Max asked for the bill, paid it, and they got up to leave.

On the way to the door they passed a table occupied by a large group of people. When they got even with the table they were startled when one of the men called out loudly, "Doctor Koenig, do you know who that girl is, the one you just had dinner with? That girl happens to be the daughter of one of the former Professors of Law at the University. He was caught aiding Jews and he got arrested, sent off to prison. I think you better check out her credentials. You may want to get rid of her company fast."

Max stopped and stared bluntly at the man. "I make my own decision about who to have dinner with. I know this young woman. Who I have dinner with has nothing to do with you and I do not need to ask for, nor do I need your advice."

He led her outside.

She could not face him. She walked away, cried, humiliated and angry. She knew that certain people called her family "Jew Lovers" because of father's friendship with Herr Kahn and because the two families were friends. Her family did love Jews, they loved their friends the Kahn family.

Max took her arm firmly and spun her around to face him, looked into her tear-dripping eyes and said, "What exactly did that man mean by that statement he made about you?"

She thought, "Surely you are a not really a Nazi?"

No choice this time, drained of happiness, filled with sadness, she looked back at him and said, "My father and another Professor at the University were good friends. He was a Jew. Both of our families were all very good friends. His daughter Ana was my best friend. One night we went to visit the Kahn family because my father wanted to see if we could help them. Dr. Kahn had lost his job at the University because he was Jewish. That night turned out to be when the Jewish community was attacked and destroyed. My Father and Dr. Kahn were taken prisoner and later killed. My friend Ana left Heidelberg with her family and I do not know where she is. Since then people have called my family Jew-Lovers. That is what happened."

She shook his hand from her arm and ran forward. Happiness had ended. She felt his rough strong hand when he grabbed her and the pulled her into his arms again. Those powerful arms encircled her tightly and he whispered into her ear again, "Ingrid, you have known you since the first time I saw you. I love you. Calm down and stay with me. We are going to go about our evening and forget the men in the restaurant. They do not matter. Remember always that I love you." He kissed her and kissed her, long, hard, hot. Doubt flew away.

Their passion, their never-ending kiss filled her body and heart. They were forever connected. They hid in an alcove near the ramp that lead up to the bridge, at the edge of a small courtyard. The alcove was secret and their passion made it hot.

It was there, when they finally parted, that Max began to talk about the rest of their evening. "We do not have time to hike up to the celebration so come with me and I'll get a car for us."

She followed as he marched over to the closest restaurant and went inside. He took advantage of his military authority to use the restaurant's telephone and order a vehicle to come and pick them up.

When the car arrived and she got into it, she again felt strange. She had not ridden in a vehicle for a long time and now here she was riding with Max and being taken up to the mountaintop.

When the car stopped, the driver opened her door and helped her out. She was in unknown territory. What was she expecting when Max had invited her to the celebration? She'd thought only of walking, drinking, kissing, music and laughter. Instead, as soon as they walked on a little, they came face to face with more Officers and Dignitaries of the Nazi Party, as well as local politicians and University Personnel.

She had no idea that the Nazi Party had planned an event here tonight. She'd somehow missed the announcement that told about it because of her immersion in thoughts of Max. She thought she was to be part of the young people planned celebration tonight, but now she found herself surrounded by Nazis and lots of political talk.

Max guided her along with him, and before she could figure out how to verbalize her disappointment and shock to him, he had moved her into a seat beside him, reserved for important people. The seats were along one side of the stage, in front of everyone out in the audience at the Thingstätte.

The Amphitheater was large and impressive, was fronted by rows of seats that rose up towards the top of the mountain. It was breathtaking, but at this point in time, she was already breathless. Of all the people here, she was seated along with the Nazis and was on stage in front of everyone attending the celebration. She shivered as anxiety built, shock crept in and brought some confusion along with it.

She turned slightly sideways and asked, "Why did you bring me here Max? I just thought we were coming to the All Saint's Day celebration. I thought we were going to have fun. How could you possibly bring me here when you know what I've been through with these people?" She whispered but she got his attention.

His face wore a perplexed look. "Ingrid this is part of what I must do tonight. I am required by the military to come here. I have no choice. This has nothing to do with our evening of celebration because as soon as this is over, we can go our own way."

The speeches began. Madness was advocated, propaganda spoken, and Ingrid shut down. She couldn't deal with the reality of the situation. Her happy time ended, and instead of experiencing love, she was ambushed again by the Nazis. They expounded their ideas from the stage, the audience applauded loudly, and worst of all was the smile pasted on Max's face when she glanced at him.

The long program finally ended, everyone stood up and moved, all except Ingrid. She sat still, so Max reached down and pulled her up and out of the seat. All she wanted was to go home.

Max walked along behind some of the dignitaries and she walked stiffly beside him. She thought they were headed back to the car to catch a ride back down the mountain. She walked along in a daze and only after they kept walking did she realize that they had gone in a completely different direction.

He stopped and touched her, bent over, and whispered in her ear, "My sweet one, just follow me. Everything will be good and you will understand why we both had to be here tonight, both had to pretend to listen."

She didn't understand anything he said but she continued to follow him as they passed seats, now empty. Instead of walking down, they started climbing up.

"Have you ever seen the wonderful things that exist above us here?" He asked her the question as he gently steered her along. He noticed that her steps were slower and she seemed physically and mentally exhausted.

She felt as tired as she looked and didn't actually understand the importance of his question. She simply shook her head and whispered back, "no."

The he began to talk about the history of the mountain. "The Monastery of St. Michael was built up here in 863AD by the Romans. They built it on top of the original Celtic Fortress that had existed from about the 5th century BC.

He led her to the site of St. Michaels and suddenly she stopped, so tired, but he insisted they press on. He told her they needed to follow the path up to the site of the Celtic Ring Wall, built to protect the settlement. She tried to follow his lead although her earlier feelings, the passion and joy, were gone. She was upset because he seemed unaware of how much his total lack of understanding for how she would feel when she got surprised into sitting with the Nazis made her feel. Now she thought she didn't make the right choice, should not have given him her trust and love.

He stopped and the Celtic Wall stood beside him. Then he gathered the exhausted Ingrid into his arms and kissed her, gently pushed his warm wet tongue against her mouth, penetrated her soft lips. She wasn't responding so he increased the pressure and tightened his muscular arms around her, forced their two bodies into one body. He attempted to absorb her, his heat burned into her. Electricity raced through her again as the exhaustion and disappointment burned away, as the heat sparked and caught fire. Instinctively she responded to him, helpless and influenced by powers greater than herself, powers that perhaps were greater than anything that could be explained rationally. Emotionally powerless, she embraced his heat and returned it.

All at once he swept her up into his arms and carried her over to a soft grassy spot beside the wall. Vaguely, as he gently laid her body down onto a blanket already in place, she had the thought that Max must have prepared this earlier. However, even as this thought drifted through her mind, the hot firm pressure of his body was on top of her. Flames and passion flowed. The sky was bright, unclouded and the ghost of a moonbeam grazed their tangled bodies as they wrestled together on the blanket. He pulled open her jacket, and started on her sweater. Her face was hidden under the sweater and he pushed his other hand down into her panties.

"No Max, please, oh please stop! Not tonight, not yet!" She was foggy. This needed to happen later, after their relationship developed.

"Ingrid this is what we are supposed to do. It has been our destiny for years, since we met by the river. I have waited for you, waited to give you my love and support. This is the time to join together forever and this is the exact place we need to be to do it. Let go. We are destined to be together. Do you feel the earth shake, the soft caress of nature around us, the power of the force that binds us together?"

Still she struggled, "Please stop!"

With the power and approval of Max and the power and approval of things not understood but present, they were joined together, their destiny fulfilled.

In the early hours of the morning after All Saint's Day, a loud knock banged on the door of the house where Ingrid and her Mother lived. The young nurse assigned to stay there and care for Ingrid's mother by Dr. Koenig jumped up from where she sat and ran to answer the door.

A bundle wrapped in blue wool lay in front of the door. When she looked closer she saw Ingrid wrapped in a blue blanket, as still as death.

The nurse knelt beside her, touched her and cried, "Wake Up! Wake Up."

The she saw the Doctor standing back a little, looking at Ingrid as she lay so still. Then he looked at the nurse.

"Thank you my sister. Ingrid is not dead, just asleep. She had an emotional evening and I gave her medicine to put her to sleep. She will sleep well into tomorrow." Then he picked Ingrid up and carried her to her bed.

His sister, the young nurse asked, "Do you want me to stay with them tonight Max?"

"Yes, they need some help. I must say goodbye to you now Eva, because I have been told that I must report to Munich tomorrow. I believe I am being transferred from Munich to somewhere else. I'll let you know as soon as I know. Please tell Ingrid goodbye for me."

Chapter Twenty-Six

Share
North Carolina – Ana 1971

Maggie waited at the airport in Atlanta for Ana's flight from Germany. She'd pick her up and then drive them both to Andrews, to Ana's house where Sam was waiting. At the airport Maggie spotted her as she walked wearily out of the exit gate, tired and depressed. Then she saw Maggie and moved forward with a little shine of happiness on her face. They grabbed each other, hugged emotionally, happy to be together again. Ana's anxiety level was almost maxed out but when she reconnected with Maggie it slacked back a little.

She slept on the drive home and Maggie was gratified that her worn out friend could get some rest so she drove the car and sang softly, to herself and to Ana.

When she finally pulled into the driveway Sam ran out the front door. As soon as the car stopped, Ana jerked awake, momentarily startled, then realized that nothing bad was happening. She was home, safe, with Sam and Maggie.

Sam helped with the suitcase and ushered them inside where all three stood for a short moment and looked at each other. Then simultaneously they hugged, grinned and plunked down on the nearest chairs. Again strong emotions flowed. Strength and balance recharged them like it has for humanity throughout its existence. Support and healing is shared between those who bond as true friends.

"I don't think we need to go into anything tonight. You two go to bed and get some rest. I'll come back over in the morning." As he spoke, Sam looked over at Maggie. "Thank goodness you were able to get an extra day off from work. Now I'll come over and all three of us can have breakfast together. Then we can catch up."

Maggie agreed. "You're right. Ana's exhausted. We'll all get some rest and then see you in the morning. I'll even volunteer to make breakfast, maybe some pancakes." The offer of pancakes was received with pleasure from both of her friends because they knew very well how delicious Maggie's pancakes were.

Sam moved to leave, then turned around with a serious expression on his face. "Make sure you lock the doors before you go to bed." He moved to the door, opened it, and looked back at them with a smile instead of a serious expression. "I'm looking forward to those pancakes!"

The smell of bacon woke Ana up the next morning. She sat right up and her mouth watered. She inhaled deeply again and even caught the light warm smell of Maggie's pancakes. At once up and out of the bed, she got dressed as fast as possible, couldn't wait to get to the food. She'd rested, had energy, and was ready for the day with her friends.

She walked into the kitchen at the same moment that Sam entered the front door. She waited for him and they greeted Maggie together as she scurried from the stove to the table, coffee pot in hand, and filled up the three mugs she'd set on the table. The strong smell of hot coffee added to the already-to-die-for smell of the bacon and the pancakes.

Anxiety and problems were momentarily pushed aside as they all enjoyed the good food and the good company.

With a clean plate and his third cup of coffee, Sam finally stood up from the table. "Sorry ladies but I've got Mr. Elden's Sunny-dog tied up in the front yard. Would it be okay if I bring him inside? He's a lonely dog lately, even though I've been trying to spend more time with him, trying to cheer him up. He misses Mr. Elden."

Silence filled the kitchen. "I'm sorry. I didn't mean to make everybody sad. Just let me go get Sunny-dog and maybe you two can cheer him up." He walked quickly out of the room and was back in just a minute with the big friendly dog.

Golden Sunny-dog ran straight to Ana, nuzzled her legs with his nose. She held him close and rubbed his back. "Okay sweet Sunny, my friends and I are going to try to find your Dad. We're going to try and get him back for you and for us."

Sam seemed energized as well, was ready to get moving, so he began to tell Ana the details of everything that happened right up until the time of Mr. Elden disappeared.

When he paused for a moment, she said, "Sam, tell me if you've found anything that you think might explain all this. Did you figure out anything that could explain what the government really wants from Mr. Elden, from

Winchester Farm? Does anything add up to a legit reason for that man to come and question you about us?"

As they talked, they moved into the living room where they could sit and talk more comfortably. Sam and Maggie sat down close together on the sofa, Ana on a nearby chair. He continued to tell her what happened and she could feel irritation and tension in his voice.

The dog followed Ana and sat beside her chair, but all at once he jumped up and moved over to Sam, stood in front of him, shook his head and attached his mournful eyes to Sam's face.

"Sunny-dog, what do you need?" Even as Sam asked the question, he realized that the dog was still sniffing the air, smelled the bacon they'd cooked. Sam got up and walked back to the kitchen.

When he came back out with the bacon-treat he held it out in front of him. "You only get a little piece Sunny-dog, because we need to make sure you eat right and stay healthy until your Dad gets home. We want him to find you in good shape."

A happy dog now rested on the floor, as Sam talked some more. "That agent had lots of questions about Mr. Elden, and right from the start they felt wrong to me somehow. He wanted information that he should have already known. You know, like where does Mr. Elden live? Shouldn't he have known that from federal records? And then he had questions about you too Ana. I mean, I understand an agent should, because after all, you're the owner of the farm, but his questions seemed off balance. Like he wanted to know if you were living here or somewhere else. It felt like he was digging for something specific, something he either didn't know or wasn't sure about."

Ana's face tightened. "Can you remember exactly what he wanted to know about me?"

"He asked about your ownership of the farm and about how and why Mr. Elden managed it. He wanted to know where you were and what you were doing, so I told him about the history of your family, the loss of your father and mother and all of Mr. Elden's help, but I also told him that you'd taken a job and moved to Germany to teach at a University just recently. He acted different, more interested, when I told him about your job. He sat still and stared at me for a few seconds. I felt uncomfortable. Then instead of asking me for any more information, he just told me bluntly that I'd be in trouble with the law if I told anybody anything about what he'd asked or what I'd answered."

Maggie had been quiet so far, but now she spoke up. "Ana, do you know something about this? I can see you've made a mental connection by how you just reacted to what Sam told you about what the agent wanted to know about you."

With a grim pretend smile Ana answered, "Yes guys, I do have some information that may connect to this situation but first I want to hear anything else you know about everything that happened."

So Sam continued, still tense and upset as he told what he'd gone through in his encounter with the so-called federal agent. He did a good job remembering things as he reached the point where the agent had left and he'd decided that he needed to follow him.

"When I saw how he sneaked around, checked out Mr. Elden's real estate office, that's when I decided to go to the police. I wanted to talk to my friend Jerry and see how all this sounded to him."

"Oh!" Ana said, interrupting Sam at this point. "I haven't seen Jerry lately. He's been with the police for a good while now hasn't he? I always liked him because he's such a good friend to you and backed you up when those boys at school were bullying you. Maybe he's the right person to give us some help."

"I'm always happy when anyone speaks good things about Jerry. He's good. I've already talked with him and admitted my big mistake, but now Ana I've got to tell you how stupid I was."

Maggie turned and looked at him, then grabbed his arm and gave it a loving shake. "You aren't to blame Sam! You didn't have any reason to believe the agent wasn't being truthful when this first happened. You were simply shocked to find yourself being asked questions about Mr. Elden and Ana, people you love and respect, and you didn't realize the importance of looking closely at the agent's identification then. You didn't know anything about what was going on and you should stop blaming yourself and calling yourself stupid. Just look at what Jerry had to say to you about what information the police could come up with in a similar situation. Andrews is a small country town and even our police department doesn't encounter this type thing much, if at all."

Ana felt her deep child-hood connection to Sam, knew he felt like he'd let her down. She got up from her seat and stood in front of him. He stood up too and then she put her arms around him and hugged him firmly. "You never let me down. You always help me. Please know that you aren't to blame for any of this, in any way."

Maggie nodded her total approval and after a few moments of silence, surrounded by love, they all settled back into their seats.

Ana asked, "Has anyone been able to figure out what interest the government had in Mr. Elden? Was it income tax related?"

"At first we thought it was." Sam got up again, couldn't sit still. "When I talked with the police they also thought it must be income tax related like the agent said. They felt maybe the IRS was investigating Mr. Elden and maybe his connection, his control, of your farm. None of the police seemed to be upset with me or tell me I was in trouble when I told them what happened. I told them what the agent threatened me with, but they said I didn't need to worry about that. They felt I was right in contacting them, especially because Mr. Elden had gone missing."

Maggie spoke directly to Ana. "Even when this first happened and Sam was worried about not talking to anyone because of what that man said, he confided in me. He knew how much I care about you and I hope you know that too. I hope you're good with me being involved with this, with Sam."

Again Ana got up and hugged a friend. This time she wanted to make sure that Maggie knew how she felt, how glad she was to have her help.

"Thank goodness Maggie's got experience working at her CPA Firm and she's smart!" Sam looked at Maggie. "She told me that the way the so-called federal agent handled everything, how he came to the farm office without an official appointment with anyone, wasn't normal. The IRS notifies the person or business they want to investigate or audit by certified mail. Then the person who gets the certified mail is required to call the IRS and then a meeting time is agreed upon, a time is chosen mutually for the audit. None of this happened here. Maggie and I believe this so-called agent was either from the FBI or the CIA because he was so secretive. We don't think this is related to the IRS, to taxes. When I told Jerry what Maggie and I thought, he agreed with us. He even told me that this whole episode is out of the norm for anything he's ever been involved in."

The room got quiet. All three looked down, each wondering what could the federal government want from Mr. Elden and how it connected to Ana.

Softly, Ana spoke. "Let's step outside, get a breath of fresh air, and see what the world looks like today. Honestly, I've got information I need to share with you, but I need to walk around and clear out my mind. I also need desperately to hear every detail you can tell me about Mr. Elden's disappearance. Any detail you saw, heard, felt, or even thought." Again, Sunny-dog was right beside Ana, ready to go outside. The dog bolted out the door as soon as Sam cracked it open.

The day was clear and cold. The mountains circled the valley, still displayed their winter nakedness. The view was pristine, complete with a small dusting of pure white snow.

The walk lasted longer than any of them had anticipated. It felt so good to be physically active, to let the body take over and the mind rest. Some of the accumulated stress faded a bit. Ana even laughed as she watched Sunny-dog scamper off the path, look for something to chase, to search for adventure.

As Sam went to the left of the path and called Sunny-dog back to them, he softly asked, "Do you think it would be safe if we talked about things out here in the open?" He carefully looked around, checked out the surrounding landscape.

"I'd love to say we could just walk and talk, but I think it might be wiser to go back to the house to finish this up. I feel strongly that it's important nobody knows what I want to tell you." Ana's voice was also low and soft, matched his tone, as she answered.

Maggie was already walking beside Ana. She reached out and took her hand. Sam came back and fell into step on Ana's other side. He also reached for her hand.

The team headed home, Sunny-dog led the way.

Chapter Twenty-Seven

Some Facts
North Carolina – Ana -1971

The walk was refreshing and instead of going immediately back to the house and the exchange of more information, they mutually decided to first get some lunch. The Burger Basket, a well-loved local hamburger café called to them. Sunny-dog heartily agreed.

The café set up was very basic. Inside, a tiny area with only a few small tables was available to sit down and eat, but in addition, the owners had placed large wooden picnic tables outside for more open eating space. Today's weather was good for a picnic, so that's where they sat down to wait for their burgers.

Their order was ready quickly, and one of the workers carried it out to them. As she brought the large bag of food to their table, the young lady suddenly yelled loudly, "Oh my, it's you Ana!" She dropped the bag onto the table and ran around to the other side of the table where Ana sat.

"Lydia! I never thought I'd get to see you today! Are you here working with your mother?" A mutual hug and Ana asked another question. "Is your mother here? I'd love to see her. She was my mother's best friend, helped her so much. Did you know she even taught mother to drive right after she married father and moved here?"

Lydia dropped back a little and gave her head a negative shake. Her body language boded bad news. "My mother had a stoke two weeks ago and she's still in the hospital. I'm trying to help my Aunt Gail because she and mother both ran this place and it's really hard for Aunt Gail to do all this by herself now."

Sadness in Ana's voice, "Please hold your mother's hand and tell her how much I care and I hope she gets better."

Lydia went inside and the group of friends was left, all quiet, with more sad news.

"Maybe we should just take our burgers back to the house to eat," suggested Maggie. "That would give you guys a little time to absorb this bad news privately. It might be hard to sit out here with people around while you absorb what happened. This delicious food was invented by and always been made by Lydia's mother. It might be hard to enjoy it when you just found out what's happened to her."

"I'm okay, Maggie. Nothing in life seems easy to me right now. I've got to accept things and move ahead." Ana unwrapped a burger and deliberately took a large bite. "It's really delicious guys. Enjoy."

They followed her example and remembered to give Sunny-dog his one taste. Then slowly, they started to walk home. Silence walked with them but it wasn't an awkward silence, not a negative silence. They were all sending thoughts and hope for the recovery of Lydia's mother.

Once inside the house again, they resumed their previous seating arrangements, with Sam and Maggie together on the sofa. Ana sat down in her chair but got right back up and walked to the window. "I have so many things to tell you but I can't decide where to start. I guess I'll just talk and if it gets confusing, stop me. Some of what I want to tell you is what I feel to be true but I don't actually have proof."

She turned from the window and looked at Maggie. "Remember that time when I was in Heidelberg as a student, and I had that scary first night there? I told you what I thought happened, what I believed to be true, but I never found out if it was really the truth. That's an example of what I'm talking about now. I feel and believe the things I'm telling you, but I can't prove them."

"Have you seen that awful man again? Has he bothered you?" Maggie's voice and face showed shock.

"I'm not just talking about "bothering" me Maggie. Since I've returned to Heidelberg, I've felt that even more than one person is watching me, following me. I have this friendly young student in one of my classes and I still can't decide if he is or isn't following me. He's everywhere I go. Also, I've caught several glimpses of an older man watching me, always making sure I can't see him directly, always hiding. He's turned up on two specific occasions lately, and each time he gets away before I can get close enough to see if I can recognize him."

"Ana, you come home! You don't need to be there by yourself! It sounds like something dangerous is going on!" Sam was angry, afraid she was in danger. "Why in this world are you being followed?"

"Well Sam, I got a little light shed on that question just recently. The lady who manages the apartments where I live came over to see me. We even had dinner together. I'd cooked something special, something she liked, and I invited her to share dinner with me that evening. It wasn't something I'd planned but it worked out to be an opportune time for me to find out that she had important information that I needed to know about."

Ana told them the story of Frau Krueger and the dinner they enjoyed together, of her honesty as she told the truth about how the apartment Ana was living in became available for her. She described the abnormal method that had been used to procure the apartment for her, the money paid for silence about how it all came about. Both Maggie and Sam were speechless. They couldn't believe what they were hearing, that Mr. Elden could be involved like that, maneuver people, people who he knew there in Germany. Why did he want Ana do have that specific apartment?

They both stared at her. Waited for more. "Yes, I've found out some more details about why people I don't even know might have an intense interest in me. I found something when I finally cleaned out my mother's bedroom, right before I left to move to Germany. I still haven't been able to understand what she meant, or the deep emotion she expressed in some of what she wrote so long ago. I'm beginning to understand that the life I've believed was mine is a lie. My mother was as good at languages as everyone tells me that I am. I think I inherited my ability from her. Sam, did you ever really think of her as German?"

His answer confirmed her thought. "I knew your dad met and married her at the end of the war. I knew she was German, but you're right, I never actually thought of her as German when I was around her. She spoke English naturally and seemed to be a local."

"Mother wrote some things about her childhood and then briefly about her youth in a small book. It was hidden away in her closet and I found it like I told you, right before I left. She didn't write down names or dates, but her words overflow with emotion. She evidently had a very hard life. At the end of what she wrote, she recorded how she accidently met my father, he asked her to marry him, and how they moved here to Andrews."

"I can't believe that your Grandfather Winchester allowed him to marry her. She was German! Remember how mean he was Ana?"

"Sam, he didn't allow it. It happened without his knowledge or his approval and he made my mother's life, and my life, a living hell."

Maggie had tears in her eyes. "I'm still confused. I don't understand why people are following you."

"Well, I never could understand it either. Mother never told me about any of my relatives in Germany. She claimed they were all dead and that she came here with father because she had no family left there in Germany. I asked more than once, and every time she said they were all dead and gone. Honestly, I didn't believe her. I still don't know why she left them all behind, what made her leave her life in Germany to move away forever with my father. It just never made sense to me, but I always felt she was hiding something important from me."

"You may be right. This is more complicated than I can even believe. How is Mr. Elden connected to all this and why is a federal agent checking up on him and his life?" Sam couldn't sit still any longer. He jumped up and walked into the kitchen, then back again. "Is Mr. Elden connected to your mother or did he just happen to connect to her after your father died? We need more information."

"Yes we do Sam." She got quiet, in pain as she thought about the disappearance of Mr. Elden.

"Let's stop right now, get some rest. I'm exhausted and need some sleep. Maybe later we can talk some more about all of this." She walked to the door of her mother's bedroom. "Maggie, I know you need to get back to Atlanta, back to work. I'll miss you."

Then she looked at Sam, "I feel a strong need to check out Mr. Elden's house. Would you go with me there tomorrow? I've got to look around, look at Mr. Elden's whole life in a different way than I have in the past. In fact, I've got to re-think many things, many people. Maybe if we look around at his house, we'll find some clue about where he's gone."

The sound of rain tapping on her window was the first thing Ana heard when she woke up the next morning. It was early so she remained comfortably tucked into her bed and thought about what she needed to accomplish today. Time here at home was limited. Duties at her University, preliminary meetings with the Professor she worked with, the need to get organized for the upcoming semester were all imminent. Suddenly she remembered that she needed to tell Maggie that she had to fly back to Germany next week. Sadness came to her as she realized she had such a limited amount of time to spend with her friend.

Another glance at the clock told her it was time to get up. Maggie was leaving early to drive back to Atlanta and she wanted to tell her how important she was and how happy it made her feel that Maggie and Sam were a team. Ana laughed out loud as she thought about how obvious is was that they adored each other. They were perfect for each other.

"Ana." It was Maggie, outside her bedroom door. "Are you awake? I'm getting ready to leave and I wanted to tell you goodbye."

Ana jerked the door open. "I was thinking of you and Sam and feeling so happy. I was just thinking how perfect you two are together. I can't believe how good this is!"

"Is it that obvious?" Love and happiness made Maggie look even more beautiful than usual. She glowed.

"When I see you two together I don't have any doubt whatsoever. You two were made for each other. I can't even tell you how much it means to me to have you and Sam in my life. Oh Maggie, I forgot to tell you last night that I have to fly back to Heidelberg next Saturday. Will I get to see you again before I go or do we have to say our goodbyes now?"

"Please don't go back there Ana. I don't want you to leave. I'm worried." Then a little excitement appeared on her face. "As soon as I can get time off I'm headed your way. You won't be alone and we'll have some fun!"

Chapter Twenty-Eight

The Horseman
North Carolina – Ana – 1971

She and Sam made plans to get together and drive over and search through Mr. Elden's home around ten o'clock that morning. As it worked out, that gave her a few hours between when she'd said goodbye to Maggie as she returned to Atlanta and the time Sam would come by and pick her up in his truck. She decided to pull out the list she'd worked on after the dinner she and Frau Krueger had together. Writing down all facts she knew was important and getting organized was crucial as she worked to identify any facts about her mother's life.

The memories mother had written down seemed to have happened during the years right before and then during World War II. She wrote about the way her normal, pre-war life totally disappeared. Almost every word she wrote was heavy with emotion. As Ana re-read the words again, she cried again. It hurt to realize that her mother had suffered through such heartbreak. Mother had even more strength than she'd given her credit for, had been able to move ahead in her life after going through everything she'd suffered.

Sam's knock sounded on the door. Ana jumped back into the present and quickly put her list and mother's book back inside the cabinet. It wasn't the right time to share any of this yet.

Some deep instinct shouted inside her, told her to go and look around Mr. Elden's house. She didn't have any idea what she could expect to find, but she knew she had to do it. Maybe she and Sam could find something that the police had missed. Another possibility also existed in her mind but she didn't share it. Maybe she could find something that would explain Mr. Elden's connection to the mysterious "relative lady" back in

Heidelberg. The police wouldn't necessarily identify anything they found that connected Mr. Elden to Germany as being important in their search for him because that information didn't have anything to do with the possible federal government investigation of his income or his job as manager of Winchester Farm. They didn't know what she knew.

On the drive to the house, both Ana and Sam were unusually quiet. This time the silence was heavy, depressed, and began as soon as Sam saw Ana's face when she answered his knock on the door. He recognized sadness. He and Maggie had just said their goodbyes and he was sad too, but he knew that Ana's sadness was something deeper. He wanted to understand and help her.

"Ana, how do you want to go about his? Do you have a plan, or do you think there's something specific that we need to hunt for?"

"I don't really know what we need to look for. I just think it might be possible we could recognize something out of the ordinary, maybe better than the police could, since we know Mr. Elden so much better than they do. That said though, how much time did either of us ever spend in this house? He was always there for us but it was hardly ever here, was always at the farm or our house. I don't remember ever being invited to come over and see him. He'd come over to the house and eat with us sometimes and he seemed to enjoy our food and company, but in the end, he was private, a loner I think."

They drove into a narrow one-lane drive and followed it through the quiet thick forest until it led them to his house. Sam drove around behind it and parked his truck in front of the barn, the barn in which he'd found and rescued Sunny-dog.

They got out at once and walked to the back door. Ana held the keys that the police had given her when they approved of the additional search by her and Sam. They were glad for additional help and also hoped for a piece of evidence that could help them locate Mr. Elden.

"I can't get the door to open." She pushed the key back into the lock and tried to maneuver it, move it around. "It feels like it doesn't fit right."

"Here, let me try." He used a little more force and the lock finally turned. The door opened.

Before he stepped inside, he reached for the light switch. "That key worked a little differently this time. When I came in with the police, they didn't have any problem getting the door unlocked, it worked real smooth." He let her in, and then scrutinized the lock. "It looks like somebody tried to open this door without the right key. They must have damaged the lock a little. This must have happened sometime after the police finished up the search out here, after he disappeared."

They stared at each other, disturbed, wondering who came into the house after the police finished and left it locked? Both of their minds spoke that it was the "federal agent" but neither voiced their thoughts.

Firmly he closed the kitchen door. "Maybe we don't have the right idea here, maybe the police damaged the lock during their investigation. Let this go for now. I'll check with Jerry later and see if they know about it. For now, let's get to it, let's search. Where do we start?"

Her face whispered concern about the messed up lock. "I think maybe just look around slowly, go from room to room like the police. I can't think of any specific item but I'm hoping we can spot something that can help us find Mr. Elden. You know, I was also thinking that you and I could maybe find something that might tell us more about his connection to Heidelberg. I remember he said that he was a student there when he was young, but he left and as far as I know, never went back. He also never talked about living in Germany, but somehow I think that time he lived there might be part of why he's missing."

Sam knew her well and realized that she'd already made some definite connection between Mr. Elden's behavior in getting that apartment rented for her in Heidelberg and his disappearance. He could see how deeply she felt, so he decided to be quiet for now, not press her for more information. Instead, he told himself to help her in any way she needed him, but only when she asked.

Gently he answered. "Why don't you look around in the house, beginning in the kitchen, and I'll go to his bedroom. We can work through the whole house and both cover the same territory, but if we work at opposite ends of the house, we won't interfere with each other's concentration and we'll also get to check the whole house twice."

"Good idea Sam. Let's get started."

She stood in the center of the kitchen and looked around. The room was compact, simple, neat and clean. Everything necessary to cook efficiently was present, but there weren't any frills or luxury items.

A small pantry was located to the left of the refrigerator and she was drawn to it immediately. It too was simple, wooden shelves, well stocked with food. She was surprised to find that Mr. Elden kept such a well-stocked, diverse supply of food on hand. Everything was organized and as she looked around, it suddenly hit her that on the bottom shelf sat a neatly stacked supply of boxed, ready to make German food, specifically semmelknödel and spätzle, German dumpling and noodles. She knew these items because mother used them a lot too.

These were mainstays of German cooking and were produced by German companies and exported around the world. Evidently Mr. Elden not only enjoyed cooking, as was obvious from his well-stocked kitchen, but he also loved to eat German food. As she continued to stare at the boxed food this thought slipped into her mind. "Didn't Mr. Elden move to Atlanta from Canada? Isn't he originally from Canada?"

At that moment she seriously believed what she had only so far suspected. Maybe before he lived in Canada, he lived somewhere else. Germany? She closed the pantry door and moved back into the kitchen, then to the living room. She didn't say a word to Sam about what she was thinking.

He came into the living room from the bedroom. "Let's do this room together Sam. You take one side and I'll take the other. This room looks basic, simple, with just a few pieces of furniture and some pictures on the wall.

He went over to the chairs and she went straight to the bookcase. It was tall and thin and filled with books. She was a book lover, so she took her time, wanted to see what type of reading Mr. Elden enjoyed. Another thought slipped into her head. "As long as I've known him you'd think I'd know what he liked to read, what he was interested in."

She scanned the titles quickly, found a great number related to history, both world and American. In addition to the history books she began to see that lots of the other books were written by German authors, some translated into English. She recognized many of the authors because she'd been a student of not only German language, but also German culture. It was perfectly clear that not only did Mr. Elden like German food, but he also interested in German culture.

"Find anything Sam?" She left Sam in the living room and took herself into the bedroom he'd just completed searching.

"Not a thing!" His words drifted back to her as he moved into the kitchen. "I guess you didn't find anything either." He paused and glanced back at her in the bedroom.

"So far nothing important. Check behind me carefully and I'll look into his bedroom. You know, it's amazing how neat and basic he is. He doesn't have clutter, just the necessities." She moved slowly around the small cozy room, even kneeled down and looked under the bed. Again nothing, so she got up and started to open each drawer of the dresser that stood beside the bed.

It was very uncomfortable to go through Mr. Elden's clothes. Forcefully she told herself, "It has to be done." She checked everything carefully but like Sam, found nothing.

His voice sounded. "I haven't found anything in this room either, so while you finish up, how about I go out and check the barn?" She heard the kitchen door open and close as he went outside.

Then it flashed. Why didn't she check there before? She raced back into the kitchen and over to the pantry. Making sure Sam was still busy in the barn, she bent down and grabbed several boxes of the German dumplings and noodles. She felt them carefully with her hands, tested for weight differences, and looked closely to see if any had been opened. The last one she checked was it. Again she checked to make sure Sam couldn't see her, and then she opened the box of food. Inside, instead of food, was a small wooden box. She slipped it out and found that it was locked tightly. There was no key.

Quickly, she hid the box in a large inside pocket of her jacket. Then she placed the remaining boxes of food neatly back on the shelf. She didn't know what the locked box contained, but she knew she had to get into it, see what it contained before she'd be ready to share the truth, even with Sam.

The box hidden in her pocket burned against her body as she walked out and joined him. He'd finished checking out the barn, found nothing, and was pacing around in the yard.

Nothing seemed out of place, nothing was missing. He thought maybe he should check with Jerry again and see if the police had found anything, to find out if anyone had spotted Mr. Elden's missing car.

"Would you like to go with me to the police station? I'm going to check with Jerry and see if they've found out anything yet."

"I'd like to go with you. Hopefully they'll have something." She walked toward the truck but her body seemed separate from her mind. As she moved forward she suddenly stopped perfectly still. She stared straight ahead of her into the deep forest that touched the back of Mr. Elden's property.

Sam watched, said nothing. He knew she was deep in the past and he hoped beyond anything that she'd tell him what was hurting her so much. He wanted to help.

"I know you understand that I'm about to tell you something bad my friend." As Ana spoke, she turned to face him but the face he saw was not the grown-up Ana of today. Instead he felt he was looking into the small young face of his good friend little Ana Winchester.

She finally told him the truth about her horrible time with Grandpa Winchester.

The small plant-filled wagon that five year old Ana sat in moved swiftly along the rough pathway, pulled by the small tractor her grandpa was driving. She sat still and held on to each side tightly with her small hands. Grandpa was on his way to his special garden, one he planted and cared for every year, where he grew the vegetables the family used regularly, part of everyday life, everyday meals, at the Winchester Farm.

His garden was beyond the open meadow that spread out from their home, so he always took his plants, tools, anything necessary to maintain the garden along in the wagon attached to his tractor.

Not regularly, but once every so often, he would demand that Monica let her daughter Ana ride with him, "to help grow the food."

On this particular morning, mother had just finished feeding the family breakfast and as grandpa got up from the table he said, "I'm going to load up what I need to plant the garden and Ana needs to be ready to go with me. She needs to learn how to grow food, how to provide for herself." He didn't wait for mother's answer, simply walked out the kitchen door.

Ana, still at the kitchen table, looked up intensely at her mother. "Do I have to go with him?"

The truth that Ana didn't want to go with him was apparent. She was suddenly nervous and unhappy. "Ana, I know you don't want to spend time with your grandpa, but sometimes we have to do things even if they don't make us happy. Just go with him, and let him teach you about the garden. Be quiet, nice, and it will be over before you know it." As she talked to her daughter, Monica continued clearing off the table, and began to wash up the dishes. "Maybe when you get back I'll have enough time so that we can go out back and play a game of horseshoes. Would you like that?"

"Yes, mother, I'd like to play horseshoes with you. I don't want to go with grandpa. He's not nice to me." Ana sat still, didn't move from her chair.

"I know he's not kind to you but we live here together, and we need to be able to get along with him. Go with him and maybe he'll begin to understand what a good girl you are and start being nice."

Ana knew she didn't have a choice, had to go with him, but she was scared.

The sound of the tractor outside the kitchen door told her that it was time to go. She got up, hugged her mother, then walked out the back door and crawled up into the wagon attached the tractor where grandpa sat impatiently waiting.

Mother waved from the open door as they started off. She called after them, "See you soon."

Grandpa was silent as he pulled her along behind him. He didn't see the man on the horse, still and quiet, off the path and partially hidden by trees. Ana saw him. She looked at him and felt his eyes on her. Although she'd never talked to him, she recognized him, had felt his eyes on her before. Several times, when shopping with mother in town, she'd noticed him.

The tractor and wagon continued down the path until grandpa rolled up to his garden spot and killed the engine.

Ana was terrified. She was confused, scared, because she knew what would happen next even though she didn't understand it.

"You get out of that wagon and come help me right now. You need to move every plant I have in that wagon over to this exact spot. You bring me the tomato plants and I'll put them in the ground." Orders from grandpa, she must obey.

"Yes grandpa." She climbed out and slowly, carefully, began to transfer the plants to him. She tried so hard not to look at his face, not see his excited cruel eyes.

The work of getting the tomatoes planted took some time. It wasn't terribly difficult, but she was so nervous it seemed like hours before the last plant was part of the garden.

Grandpa washed his hands under some water he had brought along and commanded, "Ana come over here and get cleaned up."

Her steps were slow and stiff as she did what he said. Again she whispered, "Yes grandpa" as she held out her small hands and he roughly washed the dirt away.

Then his attack began.

In a swift movement, grandpa grabbed her up in his arms and ran across to a patch of soft grass underneath a tall old tree near his garden. The same spot again. She was so scared of what would happen next. It hurt.

Carefully, but roughly, grandpa began stripping her clothes off her small body. When she was completely naked, on the grass, curled up into a tight knot, stiff with fright, only then did he take his hands away and unzip his pants. He pulled out his large throbbing penis and stroked it, added more fire to his passion.

"I like having you in my family only when I get to play this game with you. Now I'm going stretch out your body and we're going to have our little bit of fun together."

She moaned, sobbed as he pulled her arms away from her body, began to put pressure on her legs with his body, got close to her face with his hot fat penis.

"Stop! Stop! What in the hell is going on? What are you doing to your own granddaughter?" The man Ana had seen earlier yelled loudly and jumped down from his horse. He was horrified, could not believe what he saw.

For once in his life, grandpa had no answer. The horseman had the last word as grandpa jumped up, ran to the tractor, and raced away.

Ana was left naked and crying, sprawled on the grass. She didn't realize yet that the rest of the horror was not going to happen to her today. The man on the horse had saved her.

The horseman gently gathered up the little girl and began to put her clothes back on her tiny body. He cried as he dressed her. "I know that your name is Ana and that awful man is your grandpa. Can you tell me if he has done this to you before?"

She was still trembling, crying, but now felt safe. "Yes sir, he's done it to me before and it hurts so much." She cried harder.

"Look at me Ana. Look into my eyes. I promise you that this won't ever happen again. You must believe me. I will make sure you're safe."

He held her close and patted her back.

She moved away from him a tiny bit, tilted back her head, and looked into his eyes. Yes, he was telling her the truth.

Sam ran to her and caught her as she slipped down to the ground. She cried silently and tried to hide her face from him.

"I'm so mad! I knew he was the most terrible person in the world but I honestly didn't think he treated you like that! Why didn't you tell me sweet Ana? I'd have killed him for you."

Even as he spoke the words, the question raced out of his mouth. "Mr. Elden is the horseman! He saved you! Oh my! Did he kill your Grandpa?"

"When grandpa died in the house fire, I didn't even think of that. I was too young to understand the details. As I got older, I realized that the last opportunity grandpa had to take advantage of me was when Mr. Elden saved me. Then grandpa went off unexpectedly to the AppleBear Hollow cabin and he was different when he came back home. My parents thought he was sick, but now I think that Mr. Elden threatened him. Mr. Elden knew what he was doing. It wasn't a secret anymore. Soon after that, my parents and I went up to AppleBear Hollow to celebrate my birthday and that's when the Winchester family home burned down with grandpa inside it. I never had the courage to talk to Mr. Elden about what happened but later, as I grew older, I began to think that he made sure that grandpa could never hurt me again. He did as he promised me, he took care of me."

They sat together until she could control her emotions. He knew now where a great part of her sadness came from. Mr. Elden was her hero. The Horseman had saved her. Was he still alive?

Later, when they both finally made it to the police station, they found only several policemen there, but their luck was good at this moment because one of them was Jerry. He came forward to meet them and reached out to shake Ana's hand.

"It's so good to see you again. Well, maybe I didn't put that right because it's an unhappy time with Mr. Elden gone missing, but what I meant was its good to see and talk to you again. It's been a while."

She responded sincerely, "It's been too long since I've seen you Jerry. I hope all is going well for you."

"Personally, I'm in pretty good shape, but I must say, this is a bad reason for you to need to return home from your new job in Germany. We're beginning to believe this isn't a case of Mr. Elden leaving. We still don't have specific evidence, but we're beginning to think that foul play is part of the answer."

"Jerry, that's why we came by to check with you. We're both hoping the police have gotten some information that can shed a little light on this.

Also, I wanted to tell you that the lock on Mr. Elden's back door looks like it's been messed with. I didn't know if you guys had trouble with it or if somebody came by after you left and tried to get into the house." Sam seemed to still have something important on his mind.

Before Jerry could respond, he continued. "Do the police have a responsibility to find out if the man who asked so many questions about Mr. Elden was actually a federal agent? Is there a method to check with the government and get them to tell you who he is? We need to know for sure if that man was actually a federal agent. What if he had something to do with the disappearance of Mr. Elden?"

Jerry responded immediately, "Sam, we've already started that process. We've given the government the limited amount of information we have and they're checking on it. They told me they have the right to not tell us what the investigation is about, but they do have the responsibility to verify there really is an investigation in progress. Otherwise, they're contributing to possible criminal activity here."

Ana joined the conversation. "Will you be able to tell us what you find out?"

"Based on the way the agent questioned Sam about you and Mr. Elden, we'll certainly pass on to you whatever we learn about the agent's legitimacy."

"Thanks Jerry. We appreciate your help and please, if you hear anything, let us know right away." We're so worried about Mr. Elden." Sam moved, ready to leave. He and Ana walked toward the door as he said, "I'll see you later Jerry."

Back in the car they were again silent. He was worried about Ana's safety, and the safety of Mr. Elden. She was worried too, but her mind was fixed on something else….the box in her pocket.

"Do you want to come with me and get some lunch?" Gently he asked.

"Thanks so much, but I feel tired and I think I'll just get myself a bowl of soup and then rest my mind for a while. Would you like to come in and share some soup with me?"

He laughed at her. "I'm hungry girl. You better eat something more than soup, you're skinny enough as it is."

This time she couldn't help but laugh in return. He'd been telling her this since she could remember. It was one of their mutual silly sayings, like most good friends enjoy.

She waved as he drove away.

All alone inside her house, she immediately ran into the kitchen. She needed help, needed tools to open the locked box she'd sneaked home from Mr. Elden's kitchen. Underneath the sink was a small toolbox, put there years ago by mother. She pulled out a pair of pliers and a screwdriver.

Then, before she started, she made sure the doors were locked, and pulled the curtains over the two windows in the kitchen where she planned to work. She wasn't ready to take any chances today.

The small box was well made and she struggled with it. The screwdriver helped some when she first tried to pry the lock away from the box. After she managed to move it a little, she decided to try with the pliers. She used them to hold onto the lock and pry it loose. She was strong but progress was slow. She felt like she needed to do this delicately, not damage the box but then she blew that thought away and grabbed the hammer out of the toolbox. She hit the lock from the side with as much force as she could muster. This time, it worked. Now, as she put the screwdriver underneath the opening she'd made and pressed, the lock gave way. It was ready for her to open.

Tired old red tissue paper peeked out at her when she looked inside. It was neatly wrapped and even taped around what appeared, from its size, to be an envelope. Carefully she cut the tape and unwrapped the fragile paper. It tore as she pulled it away from what turned out to be an envelope. When she opened it, there were a couple of pieces of paper inside. When she pulled them out and opened the folded sheets, she held in her hand two German birth certificates.

She lost her breath, sat down at the table and held them in front of her face with trembling hands. Once, twice, she read them. Then again as she tried to understand what they meant.

Elden wasn't the name of the person documented on either of the certificates. She reread carefully and realized that both of the men were born in Heidelberg, Germany. The date of birth was the same on both certificates and that age easily matched Mr. Eldens.

Possibilities came to mind. Maybe one of the birth certificates was authentic, except for the name. Maybe neither of the birth certificates belonged to Mr. Elden. Then she wondered why everyone believed that Mr. Elden was a Canadian citizen who'd moved to the United States, even become an American citizen. Why did he have these documents? No answers in the box, just more questions.

Wait she told herself. Maybe these two certificates don't have anything to do with him. Maybe he was keeping them for someone else, for some unknown reason. Then she stopped again. It made no sense. Be honest with yourself Ana, and admit to yourself what you really think this is, that Mr. Elden deliberately pretended to be a Canadian citizen when he moved to Atlanta and started his real estate business there. He was smart and he was capable, as well as talented. He could have done it.

But most important, she now believed he'd been born in Heidelberg, Germany. His English had a slight accent but everyone thought it was Canadian. He never talked much about Germany, just to say he'd attended college there in his youth.

Chills ran up her arms as she continued to stare at the words on the certificates. Why in this world would a talented man like Mr. Elden want to live in Andrews, North Carolina? Why would he want to take care of, take responsibility for her and mother? Even though what he'd done had rewarded him financially, he'd relinquished his private goals, his life, just to help them.

Softly she said the words out loud, wondering all the while if her mother could hear what she said in the world of the dead. "Who is Mr. Elden and why is he so much a part of our life? Why did he save me and care? Why do I love him and miss him?"

The telephone rang. It was Jerry, calling from the police department. "Ana, is Sam still there with you?"

"No, he's gone to get himself some lunch. Why?"

"I'm afraid I've got some really bad news for you. Let me find Sam and send him over there to you."

"Jerry, just tell me. I can handle it. It's about Mr. Elden?"

"I'm so sorry to have to tell you that his body was found by two hikers, up the mountain, near the Trail of Tears. We've been up there and it looks like he was shot and then his body was dumped there, probably the same day Sam and Maggie found out he was missing."

"He was shot! I can't believe this!" She was extremely upset but at the same time, not totally surprised. "Do you have any more information about who did this? Is there anything I need to do?"

Jerry answered, "Ana, this is the worst kind of shock. Please sit down and take care of yourself. I'll find Sam and get him over there. Just know that right now we're making sure to follow every path that's available to us so we can find the person who murdered Mr. Elden. You don't need to do anything except take care of you. I promise to let you know if we find any clues."

On Tuesday the police reported to her and Sam that the federal government had contacted them. The government had no agent, in any capacity, working on a case in Andrews, North Carolina, or on any case involving Mr. Elden or Ana. However, the murder of Mr. Elden created a legitimate reason for the government to investigate, and they now had officially assigned agents to the case.

After an autopsy, the body of Mr. Elden was released. He was buried following a small private service full of respect and sadness felt by those who'd been closest to him, his adopted family. He was laid to rest in the Town of Andrews cemetery.

Maggie was given time off from her job and drove down for the funeral. She and Ana and Sam stayed together.

Ana flew back to Germany two days later.

Chapter Twenty-Nine

Return to Germany
Heidelberg – Ana – 1971

The flight attendant spoke a pleasant "goodbye" to her as she stepped through the exit door and onto the off-ramp passageway. Her flight back to Germany had been unexpectedly good. It went quickly, was pleasant.

Perhaps the pleasantness could be attributed to the man who sat beside her. He was good-looking and charming. In addition, he was interesting and their friendly conversation allowed the flight time to pass by enjoyably.

When she flew, she'd always attempt to respect the privacy of the any person seated next to her. Somehow that seemed to add more space to the usually close together seating.

On this flight, the man next to her started a conversation with her even before the plane took off. They spoke some and exchanged general information about themselves. She normally preferred not to engage in conversation with fellow passengers, but he seemed interesting.

During the flight he told her that he was an engineer, on his way to Frankfurt, Germany to work with the US government on the techniques and mechanics of some of the equipment they wanted to install at a military base that was nearby. He explained that he was going to live and work in Germany for as long as it took to accomplish the assignment he'd received from the company he worked for. Then he asked where she was going and she answered easily, without hesitation, that she was headed back to her job in Heidelberg, which, she told him, was very near Frankfurt. The Frankfurt airport was large and served everyone who lived in that part of Germany.

Further along, he asked her some more questions and she told him more about her job an Assistant Professor at the German International University. She explained that she had to get back soon because the next semester was about to begin.

Now as she moved ahead quickly, exited the off-ramp into the airport luggage receiving room, she couldn't resist glancing back. As she hoped, she saw him a little distance behind, perhaps ten or twelve people between them. She didn't slow down or stop but moved ahead, and wondered if he'd talk to her again, tell her goodbye.

All at once he was beside her. "Ana, please, do you have a minute? I'd like for us to exchange information, be able to contact each other again. Since you live in Heidelberg, so close to where I'll be living and working, would you let me have your number? Maybe we can get together for a drink, or a meal."

Her lips curled into a big smile. "That would be good Andrew. I'd like that."

They exchanged information and then walked a little further together. They'd both retrieved their luggage and said a last goodbye when she turned off to head to the train station that was located at the airport. She couldn't help but smile and look back one more time. She saw him turn left and then he was out of sight.

Well, that was an interesting interlude and I enjoyed it she thought as she continued walking. Now though, she tried to focus on the present. She felt positive, happy as she thought about being back in her apartment. She was ready to get back to work.

Her steps were brisk and she felt energized as she pulled her small suitcase along behind her. If she got lucky and made it to the train stop at the right time, the ride over to Heidelberg would be only about an hour. She wanted to get home, dump off her suitcase, and go get some groceries. She'd left the apartment totally food-empty when she'd flown to the US because she honestly hadn't known when she'd be able to get back.

The train pulled in at the same time she arrived and fortunately she was able to snag a seat right away. Once before she'd found the train packed to the hilt and had to stand up for the entire trip. She had to balance herself and her suitcase the whole way and it was a little exhausting. Now, from her seat, she watched the passengers get on board and subconsciously looked for suspicious people. She realized what she was doing and told herself to stop it right now, reminded herself how much she loved living in Germany and how good she'd been treated by everyone. In her mind she said, "It's time to stop thinking that everyone you meet or see is stalking you. From this moment on, you're going to work on finding out more about your mother and following every clue you have to get to the real truth so all this worry can pass."

Zip, and her mind went backwards, to the last hours she'd spend with Sam and Maggie before she'd flown away. They were worried and wanted her to promise to call them every day. They'd promised to call her as soon as they got any more information from the authorities.

In the final hours of time left to her in Andrews, she'd managed to contact a local attorney who'd done a small amount of legal work for mother in the past. He put together a power of attorney from her to Sam so that he could legally make all decisions for Winchester Farm. Mr. Elden had done this in the past, but now he was gone. Sam resisted at first but recognized that it was only logical for him to be able to make business decisions. She was too far away and would be gone too long. Sam was there, knew how to do the job, and he conceded.

Ana was usually exhausted after the long flight across the Atlantic Ocean but somehow today was different. When the train pulled into Karlstorbahnhof, the old town train station in Heidelberg, directly across from the Neckar River, with her apartment nearby on the other side, she got off and smiled the whole time she walked across the bridge. Once inside her apartment, she changed into comfortable clothes and went immediately back outside and down the stairs through the courtyard. She hurried to the grocery store.

She was just in time because the store was due to close in an hour. It only took a few minutes to fill up the bag she'd brought along. All the necessities, plus a few extras to make a good breakfast the next morning got placed into the bag. The checkout line was full and she waited patiently, simply glad to have the food and to be back in Heidelberg.

When her turn came to check out and pay, the front door opened and yes, Thomas came in. His eyes were on her. "You are back in Germany Professor Winchester. Did you have a good time? If you want to wait a few minutes, I will be happy to help you to carry your groceries home. I am going in the same direction because I now live in the student apartment house just up the staircase from your apartment."

She shook her head negatively, although she smiled at him. "Thank you very much Thomas but I have only just arrived and I want to go home as quickly as possible. I need to get this all put away and I need to get some rest."

"I understand and I will see you again soon. Welcome back."

"Thank you Thomas and I will definitely see you soon."

Chapter Thirty

Salzburg, Austria
Heidelberg – Ana – 1971

Excitement, adventure, the experience of going to a world famous city located in a country she'd never been to before, caused her mind to feel super-charged as she sat in the comfortable bus seat and looked out the large window beside her.

The bus she was riding on left Heidelberg early that morning, made stops for additional passengers at designated stations, and even with all the stops, their progress was smooth, fast, and comfortable. Already the major Munich stop was behind them and they were riding through the beautiful well-tended farmland of Bavaria. When she looked out the window she saw neat fields, precisely edged by the lush heavy trees that are so prominent, so indigenous to Bavaria. The bus moved ahead through the soothing beauty of the countryside and its passengers absorbed it all comfortably as their bus continued forward toward its final destination, Salzburg, Austria.

She almost giggled out loud when a surge of pure pleasure hit her but thank goodness remembered that she was sitting in a bus full of people who wouldn't understand her joy, might possibly misinterpret her happiness. Yes, she felt that fate or luck or a miracle had been granted her. The very idea that this was a part of her job seemed incredible. They were paying her to do this!

The second semester of her job at the University started right after she'd returned from Andrews and the deep sadness of Mr. Elden's death. So far, this semester had demanded a lot more of her time than the previous one and she was grateful for that fact. It kept her busy, didn't allow her too much free time to dwell on the murder of her caring friend.

The Professor she worked directly with at the University had requested several meetings with her before the new semester started. He'd wanted to know if she was ready to take on additional responsibilities. Specifically, he wanted to know if she was ready to go in his place, as his substitute, to a conference and meetings set up afterwards. His job always included conferences and meetings in different areas, away from the University. He needed help because it never failed that commitments he needed to attend always seemed to be set up for the same times in different places. He couldn't be in two places at one time, so he wanted her to act as his backup.

Her answer was a firm positive and from that day forward, her workload increased rapidly. Not only did she continue to teach there at the university but she also began to attend lectures and special classes in other areas as the Professor's substitute.

This new duty opened up all kinds of opportunities for her to meet people and to go to various locations there in Heidelberg, plus other cities, other schools, all she'd never visited before. Her new assignments proved interesting.

The reason she was on the way to Salzburg, Austria today was because of her new job responsibilities. She'd been scheduled to make a small speech about the history of German International University in Salzburg at a conference set up to promote and support international study.

The bus schedule showed they were to arrive in Salzburg late in the afternoon. A student from the University in Salzburg was supposed to meet the bus and show her the way to the University of Salzburg where the conference was to take place. The student was also to walk her to the hotel where a room had been reserved for her. The conference was scheduled for the next day and her speech was to start around ten or ten-thirty the next morning. She fervently hoped that after she'd completed her speech that she'd be allowed to leave the lengthy on-going conference and have the afternoon and evening off to explore Salzburg. That would be the only opportunity that she'd have for exploring it because her bus left to go back to Heidelberg early on the day after the conference ended.

All at once the bus began to slow down. Up ahead a tractor moved slowly and calmly down the road. Traffic slowed almost to a stop. Nobody on the bus seemed disturbed by the slowdown, not even the bus driver. Evidently they were accustomed to it.

The road-blocking tractor prompted a memory of her farm in Andrews where tractors blocked the roads a lot too. It jolted forward something that the Professor she worked for had explained to her when he asked her if she was ready to take on further duties for him. The traffic-slowing tractor connected Andrews, North Carolina and Bavaria, Germany in her mind and she thought again about what she'd been told.

Simply, the Professor had explained to her that even though the University had received excellent recommendations of her from her college advisor and from others, they had, in general, all been waiting to see if she lived up to what they'd been told. A specific group of individuals there at the University had made the decision to hire her. There were several other individuals at the university who were also normally involved in all hiring decisions and some comments were made. They felt that it was unusual to hire a person for this position without any direct communication with that person. The Professor admitted to her, in his straightforward friendly way, that he'd also been surprised that she'd not even been personally interviewed or even talked to before she'd been hired.

When he told her this, she decided to be forthright with him. She admitted that she'd also wondered how this opportunity came her way. She'd thought perhaps it was because of the application that she'd made almost a year before they hired her, and because they suddenly needed to fill the position she was hired for since the person who held that position had left so suddenly.

With a little more conversation but no real answers to the unusual way she'd been hired, she and the Professor agreed that the University was pleased with her and that she was equally pleased with her job at the University. They left it at that.

More suspicions confirmed.

Before starting the trip to Salzburg, she'd deliberately researched the history and geography of the country of Austria, and more specifically, the City of Salzburg. As the bus moved across a lovely river, then entered the city, she was proud to know its name. It was the Salzach River. She'd read that the City of Salzburg bordered on it, and on the northern side of the Alps. She'd already imagined the beauty that the river and the mountains would provide, but her imaginings didn't live up to the reality.

The bus went further into the city and then stopped in what appeared to be a public parking area. The passengers slowly, leisurely got off, stood still, and waited for the driver to retrieve whatever luggage they'd brought from the baggage compartment on the left side of the large bus. She felt content as she stood in line and then just as she picked up her small bag she heard a young man's voice.

"Professor Winchester? I am here to show you where the conference will take place and to take you to your hotel room." The young man spoke carefully and seemed a little timid.

"Yes, I am Professor Winchester," she answered.

He came closer and smiled as he introduced himself. "Hello, I am Hermann and I am here to show you where you need to go. Please, let me carry your luggage."

She was happy to do so and instinctively made the decision to walk beside the young man, preferring that to the feeling she knew she'd have if she let him carry her bag and then followed behind him. "It is very good of you to help me in this way." She said with a smile.

"It is my pleasure. I help the University when they sponsor conferences like this one and I enjoy it very much. I get the chance to meet many interesting people."

The walk into the Old Town was pleasant and the young student provided tourist information as they walked past and into various buildings and courtyards. Everywhere she looked she saw beauty but what caught her attention, intrigued and excited her was the large Hohensalzburg Castle perched high above the city, like it was still standing guard over all the citizens. It appeared to be medieval in style and then she was astonished as she spotted a cable car moving up the steep hill toward the top where the castle stood. She'd read a little about it but decided to ask Hermann, her student guide what he knew of its history.

"Hermann, what can you tell me about the Hohensalzburg Castle?"

He responded easily to her question. "The castle is extremely old and if you have enough time you should ride up and look at it. There is so much history to be seen and it is all interesting. I noticed that you saw the cable car going up to the top. That has been in operation since about 1892 and has provided an easy way for people to get up to the castle. Also important is the view you get to see when you get to the top. Not only do you look down upon the beauty of the river and the city, but you also get a fantastic view of the wonderful Alps. You will need to take time to enjoy and see it all."

Mentally, she put the castle on her list of things to see while she was here and she now really wanted to be given free time to sightsee after she'd delivered her speech. The mental list she'd already made was good sized for the amount of time she had. It included Mozart's birthplace, and the old historic district of the city. She wanted to experience the taste, the flavor of the old historic district. When she'd done her research it had sounded charming. She wanted to feel the charm.

She also had another historic place that she vitally needed to check out.

The hotel she'd been booked into by the university was wonderful. It was situated in the middle of the old historic district that she was so interested in, plus the rooms were comfortable and beautiful. From her windows, there wasn't much of a view because all of the buildings were joined together, forming a tall never-ending barrier to any long-distant vistas. However, after she looked out the window for a few minutes she realized that the view was still special because it provided her with a look directly down into the crowds that filled the street. She could see them plainly, follow their movement, hear their laughter, and even detect some of their attitudes.

It was time to unpack the bag that she'd packed so very carefully, just for this trip. When she found out that she'd be speaking in front of a large audience filled with prominent people, she'd decided that her normal dress code needed an upgrade so she took herself shopping and bought two new outfits. One specifically for the day of the conference and her speech, the other a really nice dress so that she could treat herself to a special dinner she'd planned for herself. She'd decided that on this trip she wasn't going to follow her self-chosen role of hiding from life. She intended to jump into it forcefully, with vengeance.

A little while later, after a warm and luxurious shower, after slowly and carefully putting on her dress, she stood in front of the floor length, gilt framed mirror and critiqued herself. Carefully she ran down her mental checklist. Usually her clothes were simple and plain but tonight was different. The slender black dress that she'd bought for herself had random sprinkles of tiny crystal beads, was designed to discreetly dazzle with tiny flashes of light that accompanied every movement of her body. Thin spaghetti straps hugged her lightly tanned shoulders and a short hemline revealed her long lovely legs. The mirror verified that her last minute purchase of a pair of sleek Italian heels had been a good investment.

Makeup came next and she applied it minimally. She approved the way it worked harmoniously with the shine of her recently styled hair as it framed her face and fell softly around her shoulders. The dramatic contrast of her golden hair as it warmly touched the black dress was perfection.

The luxurious furnishings present in her hotel room added detail and depth to her mirrored reflection, with its lush background of old gold, rich red, and classic cream, repeated in the upholstered antique chairs, ornate floor to ceiling draperies, and underfoot, vines, leaves, and flowers all woven together into a soft green-based carpet.

She put diamond-like earrings on her ears, dropped a small gold compact and her room key into a tiny sequined handbag and thought that the person who'd designed this beautiful harmonious bedroom at the Hotel Schmaus had dressed it perfectly, had achieved the goal of proper atmosphere and proper image. That was exactly the goal that she was attempting to achieve, as she got ready to take herself out into the world.

Per literature that she'd read before getting ready for her date with herself tonight, she'd found that the Hotel Schmaus was originally built in the mid-eighteen hundreds and had served the Schmaus family as a second home for over a century. It was perfectly located in the Old City of Salzburg and whenever the family had later become financially unable to maintain it, they'd sold it to a rich developer who'd restored and remodeled it and over time it had become a first class hotel. It delighted its patrons with atmosphere and service.

Again she felt how lucky she was to be here. Although she made good money working at the university, and along with that had an excellent income from her farm, she wasn't accustomed to treating herself to first class accommodations.

Experiences and memories of past years raced vividly through her mind as she continued getting ready for dinner. She felt such a big difference between how she was as the young un-experienced little girl who'd struggled through so much, and had now, finally found the job she'd dreamed about most of her life.

She approached the mirror again, and she knew that appearances could be deceiving.

Now she turned her back on the Ana in the mirror and draped a black shawl across her shoulders. When she left the room she automatically tested the door, made sure it was firmly closed and locked, unconsciously tested the security of what she left behind.

The hallway was empty and as she walked down it, she was able to appreciate the beautiful décor also present there. Like in her room, lush carpet felt soft and rich under her feet and it was paired with expensive wall-coverings. Again, the blend was right and it showcased the architecture of the lovely old family home-cum-hotel. Several oil paintings were tastefully hung at appropriate intervals along the corridor that led pleasantly to the alcove that housed the elevator. To the left of the elevator door stood an antique table, complete with a fresh arrangement of yellow roses.

The yellow roses stopped her in place as she reached out to push the brass button marked "down'. She saw the yellow roses at her mother's funeral. She was back on the front porch of the little home she'd shared with mother at the farm in Andrews. In an instant she was again a timid young girl, far removed from the sophisticated young woman she was trying to be today.

"Mother, why did you leave me? I'm alone, with nobody to help me. I need you." These words sounded at the bottom of the memory well into which she'd fallen as she stood like a statue in front of the elevator. Mentally she was overcome by dark suffocating despair.

The soft switch of sound caused when the elevator door opened propelled her back into the present. The flashback left unresolved nightmares with her again but she used force, pushed them backwards. She wasn't going to waste this chance for a pleasant evening, this chance to live. She'd done that too many times before.

She stepped into the empty elevator, shook her head and said softly out loud, "Go away and let me be. I'm trying to be happy and I don't want to remember pain and loneliness. I'm not going to think about it. I'm not!" The elevator glided softly and gently to a stop and the door opened.

Anyone who might have been looking as the elevator's door opened would have seen an exceptionally beautiful young woman, composed and slightly smiling, intent on enjoying her evening. She gracefully walked across the lobby toward the restaurant.

Chapter Thirty-One

Andrew Appears
Salzburg – Ana – 1971

Eyes observed every step she took when she left the elevator. More than one person was watching, however one person had an intense interest in where she was going.

The man sat at a small table in the open area of the hotel bar and café, drinking his first beer of the day. When he saw her get off the elevator he jumped up and left his unfinished beer behind. She moved fast and he needed to catch up with her before she had time to exit the lobby area.

"Ana, wait, do you remember me?" His words sounded familiar and friendly as he caught up with her and she turned around to see who was calling her name. Several other people in the lobby were interested too and watched closely to see what would happen next.

As soon as she saw his face she relaxed and smiled. "Andrew, of course I remember you. We just got off the plane a couple of weeks ago. What in the world are you doing here in Salzburg?"

"I was thinking the same thing. What are you doing in Salzburg?"

They both laughed and then he said. "Are you meeting someone for dinner? It looks like you're going somewhere special. You look beautiful!"

"Well thank you. I was going into the hotel restaurant, but I'm not meeting anyone. I'm here by myself and simply felt like booking myself a table and enjoying this highly recommended food. I felt like treating myself today. Hey, wait a minute. Were you going to eat here too?"

With a large smile he replied, "I don't have any dinner plans but I'm hoping that you're going to ask me to join you. It would be special for us to have time to talk some more and actually get to know each other better. Don't you think it would be much more comfortable than those airplane seats we shared?"

Conversation flowed and inside the restaurant they were seated at a nice private table. While the server was getting the menus and their drinks Andrew told her that his job with the military was working well but was much more involved than he'd imagined. He said it had taken lots of time to get hands-on information about what changes he was in charge of handling. He didn't give her details related to what his precise job was and she thought it must be related to some highly classified military project.

When he finished telling her about his job, in return she told him about the big changes that had developed in her job. She explained the reason she was in Salzburg and that she had to make a speech the next morning.

"Wow, that's something! Are you nervous speaking in public? It makes so many people really nervous. They don't want to find themselves having to speak in front of a large number of people."

At that moment their server walked up with their salads and she didn't answer his question until the waiter had the salads set up and left. "I've always had a fear of public speaking but recently, after teaching my classes at the university and being required to teach them in the German language, I feel a lot more comfortable when I talk to a room full of people."

After a few mouthfuls of her salad she asked, "But Andrew, you didn't tell me why you're here in Salzburg. Is it job-related too?"

"This salad is extraordinary. I hope the rest of our dinner is as good." He ate more and then took a slow sip of his wine. "This trip to Salzburg is personal, not work-related. I was given a long weekend off to make up for the long hours I've been working lately. When I heard that I was getting some time off, coming to Salzburg came to mind. It was close enough that I'd get a chance to check it out during my weekend and not need to spend a lot of time traveling. I've read some interesting things about Salzburg so I wanted to come and check off some of the things I'd written down on my "want to do" list. For example, I want to see Mozart's birthplace, Hohensalzburg Castle and, believe it or not, the place where the Von Trapp Family lived before they left Austria. I called my sister when I found out I was coming here and she got all excited and told me to be sure and visit the Von Trapp place. She saw that movie, "The Sound of Music." Do you know it? I bet you saw it too. It was popular in the US."

The server brought the food and as the good food continued, so did the good conversation. As dessert was being considered he asked, "Are you getting off from the conference tomorrow after you speak or are you required to stay there during the whole event? I was just thinking it would be fun to site-see together. It's always more fun when you get to share the experience of new things with someone. Could we get together?"

"I'm supposed to be off after I speak and I'd also planned to go and see some of the same things you're interested in. If I do get off after I speak,

I'll meet you here in the hotel lobby around one o'clock. If I'm not here, you'll know I couldn't get away so don't waste your time, just go on without me."

"I feel lucky. I get to come here, then I see you, we have dinner, and then we hopefully will get to tour the city together. I'll be in the lobby at one. I only hope it works out and you get off."

They said goodbye in front of the elevator. She told him that she needed an early night so she'd be rested and ready for her speech tomorrow. On the elevator up to her room she felt electrified and alert. The hallway was well lit but she still felt shadows. Small, dark and translucent, they spread out in the space between her and the ceiling. They seemed to follow her every step.

She ran over to her door and inserted the key, flipped on the light as she glanced around, then locked the door behind her. Nervous, she stood in place and looked at her room, glanced all around and then realized that the shadows had disappeared. Good. She already knew that she was being followed and not by the shadows who sometimes warned her of bad things to come.

With a sigh of relief she checked again to make sure she'd securely locked her door, then gave herself permission to go relax in the shower. When she reached up and took a towel from the rack beside the door, the soft sweet smell of her mother drifted into her face. She inhaled deeply. "My mother is here and I'm breathing her into myself. She is part of me forever even though she is far away."

The conference went well, but started out slowly and the scheduled time for her speech got delayed. By the time she spoke, it was an hour later than she'd thought. The room was filled with people and the entire program, including her speech, was well received. Although she'd told Andrew that she didn't suffer much from nerves when she talked, this time she did get nervous. As she continued she gained her confidence back and felt satisfied and relieved when she finished up. Shortly afterwards she asked for and received approval from the conference manager to leave the premises. Quickly she gathered her things and raced back to the hotel.

As she feared, Andrew wasn't in the lobby. After all, she was an hour later than they'd planned. She hesitated and looked around once again and as she did so, the lobby desk clerk gestured for her to come over.

"Excuse me, but are you Ana Winchester, and were you to meet someone here at one o'clock?"

"That is correct. I am running late, was delayed at work."

"The gentleman asked me to please give you this message from him." He placed an envelope on the counter in front of her and she smiled, said thanks and moved over to the lobby and sat in a chair.

His words. "Hi Ana. I'm so sorry to have to tell you that I can't make it this afternoon. My boss called and they need me back ASAP. Evidently, something else has gone wrong. Anyway, I can't tell you how sorry I am to miss out on our site-seeing fun. I'll call you when I get clear again and maybe we can get together for dinner again. I enjoyed seeing you. Andrew."

She remained still. The afternoon with Andrew had sounded like fun but honestly, she should be exploring by herself. That was the best way. She'd been trying to figure out ways to see what she needed to see without causing Andrew to miss something he wanted to do. His having to return to work was meant to be. Now she could go out and search for what she needed to find and not need to worry about Andrew.

She drifted over to the elevator, her mind still on the change in this afternoon's plans. She knew she had to get a few things to take with her before she started out on the site-seeing adventure and maybe while she was back in her room, it might also be a good idea to change into clothes a little more comfortable for a lot of walking.

As soon as she opened the door she felt the intrusive vibrations emanating throughout the disturbed atmosphere. First glance and all looked to be in place, looked the same as she left it. But when she moved over to the closet and pulled out her empty suitcase she examined it carefully. Yes, the zipper on one of the pockets wasn't completely closed. She'd left them closed in an exact way. With a shake of her head, she clutched the handbag she'd carried with her today more tightly. Just this morning, right before she left for the conference, she'd pulled out the envelope with her mother's secret book. She took it with her because, in a part of her last night's dream, the book had disappeared.

Back downstairs in the lobby, she asked the desk clerk if the hotel had any brochures or maps of the city made for tourists to use. He gave her a small stack of information and before she left the hotel, she again went to a chair in the lobby, sat down, and scanned it. Exactly what she wanted to know was there, all on one brochure. It told the history of the Hohensalzburg Castle, the areas of interest near it, and it gave a simple map to help tourists find everything. She placed the rest of the brochures into her pocket. She'd found what she needed. It was a good idea to start her search in a place she was sure she wouldn't find what she was looking for. Perhaps that might confuse her watchers.

The afternoon was perfect, weather-wise. A cloudy sky, but every now and then the sun opened a window and shone brightly down onto the city. The temperature was good, and the air felt fresh. Now was the time to complete this scary search. She'd put it off, was scared to find any confirmation of what mother had written. She walked resolutely out into the city.

A man dressed in dark clothing, very common looking, who blended in exactly with the people who walked along the street, watched her as she walked out of the hotel. When she appeared and turned right onto the street he put the paper he'd pretended to read into his jacket pocket and began to follow every step she took. He'd also been waiting for a chance to confirm some knowledge that he thought he'd found, knowledge he believed was correct. It if was, it would lead to the end of a mystery and would finally help him hand out the well-deserved consequences.

People were everywhere, locals shopped, tourists explored, but she just felt anxiety as she had when she'd found out that someone had been in her hotel room. Someone had searched through her things and that fact yelled out loudly that they were after her. More serious than she'd believed, she now realized that this person, or these people, felt like professionals. They were practiced and invisible and they wanted her or what she had. She walked and carefully thought through all the random facts that she'd accumulated in the past few months.

Wait, now wasn't the time to think about how she got to this place in life, it was time to figure out how to get out of this dangerous situation without being hurt or killed, and still be able to reach her goal, to verify the name her mother had left behind.

Abruptly she made the decision to join a tour group, to ride up with them to the Hohensalzburg Castle. Maybe whoever followed her might get a little confused because she joined up with all these people when they expected her to go alone to the one place in Salzburg that could help answer her question. They already thought they knew where she had to go. That realization made her body tighten up. If they knew where she was going, why didn't they just go and wait for her there? Then she wondered if the possibility existed that whoever watched her so carefully actually didn't know how much she knew, if anything. They were watching for confirmation. She mixed into the tour group and they all headed for the tram stop. She needed to figure out how to fool them into believing that the Hohensalzburg Castle was her real destination.

Everyone on the tram that had just come down the mountain got off, and the tour guide immediately held up her red umbrellas and spoke loudly, "Please pay attention and stay together. This is a large castle and we are scheduled to visit several different places. It is very easy to get confused so try to stay together as a group and follow my lead. Just follow my red umbrella."

Of course she thought! That's how she'd handle things today. The answer was to stir up confusion, get lost, and maybe disappear.

A little while later, in one of the castle's banquet rooms, extremely crowded with the tour group, she slipped to the back of the crowd. Then she slid out of the room and turned in the opposite direction from which they'd come. Maybe the person following her was part of the tour group, but she didn't think so. Carefully she followed the hallway and caught up to another tour group as they entered a different castle room. She blended in and trailed along with them as they finished up their tour.

Her hope was that she'd be hidden among the bodies of all the tourists as she followed them back toward the tram stop. But instead of getting on the tram with them, she slipped into a restroom that she'd seen earlier. Once inside, she reached inside her handbag for the soft hat she'd brought with her. Her long blonde hair was easy to see and follow, so she braided it and tucked it totally inside the hat. True, it wasn't much of a disguise but maybe it might give her a chance to get past the watcher.

When she felt sure the tram was almost totally loaded she walked over and got on. The tour leader of this group carried a yellow flag and the group was not quite as large as the one she'd gone in with. As soon as the tram stopped, she made sure she got off in a thick clump of people and she walked with her head up, straight down the street, followed the lady with the yellow flag.

The lady made a movement toward the left, then halted and told the group that they should get ready to taste the best hot chocolate in the world. She was going to take them to a famous local shop for the treat.

A smaller street, off to the right of where everyone stood, was really busy, filled with people. She stood still as the tour guide and the tourists bunched up and moved off to the left. She turned right, and at the moment she made the turn, she pulled off her hat and left her braid to hang beautifully down her back. She kept walking and once again turned right. She looked around, stopped in front of several store windows, pretended to admire the shoes they offered. Finally she saw a café ahead. Casually, slowly, she went over and walked inside, sat down at a small table toward the back of the shop.

When the server appeared at her table, she smiled happily and ordered a cup of coffee and a piece of the decadent chocolate cake that was offered on the menu.

While she waited on her order, she reached into her jacket pocket and pulled out some of the tourist brochures she'd put there earlier, at the hotel. She pretended to plan what she wanted to see next. It took a great effort to pretend to be calm, to act unhurried, not to let the fear show on her face. The coffee was good and she drank it, continued to read, and ate her cake. Part of pretending was that she couldn't look at people too much, couldn't watch out for the follower.

The coffee cup was empty and the cake all gone so she decided to go to the lady's room. A sign at the back of the café showed the way so she got up, left money beside her bill, and started toward it.

The door was solid, heavy, and as she pushed it open, she wanted to know so badly if they were looking at her. Inside she went to the mirror and looked at herself. When she looked at the face in the mirror, she saw a woman deeply involved in something she didn't understand. She felt alone.

It wouldn't be good to be gone too long, but when she opened the door and walked out, she didn't go back into the café. Instead she followed the tiny hallway and found herself in the café's busy kitchen. The aroma of fresh brewed coffee and the smell of baking chocolate cake was everywhere.

In the kitchen, a few surprised faces looked at her. One even told her that she'd gone the wrong way. She pretended not to understand the language, smiled, and quickly walked toward a door she saw at the back of the large room. She got a few looks but they evidently didn't feel she was a menace, simply let her go.

When she stepped outside and closed the door, when she saw that she was in a small passageway, she hoped an opportunity still existed for her to finish her goal. She was finally on her way to St. Peter's Cemetery.

Her steps were determined but she slowed down, and then stopped. Quietly, she turned around and walked back to the café's kitchen door. She put a large smile on her face and entered. Again, the same faces looked at her. She deliberately looked directly at the person who'd told her that she was going the wrong way.

Then she laughed out loud and said in a mixture of broken German and English, "Please excuse me. I went out the wrong door. I am sorry to have interrupted you but I did enjoy the delicious smell of your kitchen!"

She walked back down the small hallway, past the lady's room and went back into the café where she gave her server a friendly wave as she went out the front door. The only possible thing she could do right now was to forego any attempt to find out what she needed at St. Peter's Cemetery. She decided not to do it today. No matter how hard she tried, she'd be watched because whoever it was that wanted information from her would either follow her, or they'd be waiting there for her. No matter, she'd be in over her head.

The only possible way to confuse their idea of what she knew was to pretend that her agenda that had nothing to do with St. Peters. After all, she didn't have a time limit on finding what she needed to find. It wasn't going anywhere. The important thing to do right now was to window shop, spend time inside lots of stores and come out with bags of purchases. The watchers would see only a happy young woman, laden with new clothes, headed for her hotel room, and then a good dinner.

The bus back to Heidelberg left early the next morning with Ana and her purchases aboard.

A serious discussion took place late in the evening before Ana left Salzburg. Two men in a small apartment located close to her hotel talked, but neither of the men who'd been following her were convinced that she didn't have the information they wanted. However, they weren't quite as sure as they'd been previously. Both agreed to be patient. Time would lead them to the truth.

Chapter Thirty-Two

Inside the Prison
Dachau – 1944

The Sub-Commandant briskly ordered his driver to stop at the front entrance of Dachau Prison. He stepped out of the car and walked smartly toward the arched entryway that led into the prison camp. Each footstep spoke authority as it struck the ground and echoed through the surrounding air. Just a moment before he entered the building, at precisely the exact time the front door entry guard opened the door for him and snapped to attention, that's when the Sub-Commandant stopped abruptly. He stood still for several seconds then turned sharply off to the left, moved off the sidewalk he was on, and looked up at the lush, leaf-filled trees that grew sporadically and tall, marched along the prison wall.

The soldier that got left behind at the entrance still holding the open door watched the Sub-Commandant and saw a smile appear on his face. The guard had no way of knowing that the thoughts of his Sub-Commandant were in another place, thinking and making decisions. The Sub-Commandant mentally whispered to himself, "It is still summer, the grass is green and thick, the flowers are blooming pleasantly. I still have enough time."

The entry guard soldier stiffened back to attention and watched as the Sub-Commandant jerked around and marched back. He passed by the soldier and went into the building.

The main entrance to Dachau Prison featured an archway wide enough to receive vehicles, but vehicles rarely used it. Instead, the staff, workers and officers, plus any visitors granted entry into the prison, all had to pass through the camp security that was headquartered directly in front of the main door.

All aspects of security for the entire prison camp were controlled from this location. The system was impressive. It was firmly controlled, tight and harsh, but the majority of the security personnel weren't even visible. Most were in a massive part of the building where officers and their staff filled all the available space.

On this day the on-duty staff was comprised of army officers and office workers. Those visible to anyone who came in through the door were clustered around a series of ten or so desks, all filled with mountains of paperwork. This was the open-area portion of the security headquarters.

For many months, each day, like clockwork, the Sub-commandant would enter the prison, walk briskly through security, and then immediately go through the interior gate. He'd continue his brisk walk until he reached the back of the large compound where his office was located. Today, his routine changed. Instead of walking on to his office, he stepped into the security area and gave an order to the soldier behind the desk to let him speak immediately with the officer in charge.

More than one soldier at work there in the office glanced up at the Sub-Commandant and felt something shift, not tangible, but somehow it felt significant.

No questions were asked and the Sub-Commandant was taken respectfully down an adjacent hallway, into a small dark office where four young officers worked, held clipboards and wrote rapidly, as one called out names of soldiers for specific duties and another checked available hours and camp security locations. They were scheduling and mapping camp security for the next four weeks.

The Sub-Commandant walked into the room and without speaking, watched the men working. One of the soldiers looked up, intuitively felt eyes observing him. He snapped to attention and his abrupt movement caused the others to look up and immediately jump to attention too.

Instead of telling them to be at ease as was usually the case when superiors came in to ask them questions, the Sub-commandant, stern in his SS Uniform, just stood quietly. He let his rank speak, his uniform shout out his importance. A full ten seconds went by as all four young soldiers remained at attention. Routine security questions were the norm, but the Sub-Commandant didn't speak, simply slowly tilted his head and smiled. Anxiety rippled through the room.

"Which of you is Arthur Schwarz?" He asked the question as he finally moved further into the room. The expensive cane he held in his right hand tapped rhythmically on the floor as he continued. "I received a recommendation today regarding a soldier named Arthur Schwarz and I have come to meet and congratulate him and to tell him of the meeting scheduled in my office tomorrow. We need to discuss this recommendation."

Immediately the young officer who'd been calling out names from the clipboard in his hand stepped forward. "Yes, Herr Sub-Commandant Sir, I am Arthur Schwarz Sir!" Silence followed his answer.

Then the Sub-Commandant looked straight into the young soldier's eyes and continued in a low and pleasant voice, "Wonderful. Please be in my office tomorrow morning at ten o'clock and we will discuss the details of your recommendation."

The Sub-Commandant took time to smile at each officer in turn as he began to exit the room. "Our young soldiers inspire us!" He left these words behind him as he walked out and closed the door.

He'd achieved his goal in security and now he changed his routine one more time. His visit to security had been extremely important but so was his next visit, the one to the military's financial headquarters.

Normal financial routine was interrupted at that headquarters when the Sub-Commandant entered and announced that he needed to speak to one of the officers working there.

The Sub-Commandant also invited that officer to come to his office at ten o'clock the next morning to discuss the details of his recommendation.

The next morning at exactly ten o'clock, when the knock sounded on his office door, the Sub-Commandant was ready. His position at Dachau was demanding but he always felt more than equal to the task. As an SS Officer and as a Doctor in charge of all criminals at the prison camp, he was accustomed to preferential treatment and to respect from his subordinates.

"Enter." He spoke calmly and the two young officers came inside. Both were nervous, tried not to show it because each was trying to figure out the real reason for this meeting. The Sub-Commandant's visit to them to tell of their recommendations was a lie and they both knew it.

Behind his desk the Sub-Commandant sat tall and calm, dressed in the black uniform of the SS. He let his mind briefly run over the resumes of the two men in front of him. He checked them out carefully and now, he decided to keep them nervous and at attention a little longer.

One of them was here because he worked in the prison camp financial department. He handled money and paid for the camp's expenses. He was also responsible for taking and keeping an inventory of all assets confiscated from the inmates, all the money, gold, jewels. He knew what was there, in the safe, at all times.

The other officer worked with the security department where he scheduled guards for all the exits and entrances, and knew all the placements, shifts, and schedules.

Neither of the two officers understood why they were here but both knew something bad was in the air and both waited nervously for the Sub-Commandant to speak.

Suddenly he relaxed, even smiled at them and then invited them to be seated. He instructed them to "Please listen to me carefully," as he continued to sit behind his deck.

Calmly he continued. "First I want to make sure that both of you understand that I have all the necessary paperwork to see you both shot today, if I decide to use it. Second, I want you both to listen carefully to what I have to say, and to answer me truthfully. Maybe you can both still be alive at the end of this day."

Both men blanched, stiffened, and one started to speak. "Wait a minute, what do........" His sentence was never completed, was interrupted by the Sub-Commandant, who now stood up.

"If either of you ever speaks to me again without permission, I will kill you. Do you understand? I have enough proof of your stealing that should I decide to turn you in, you will both be dead men." He came around the desk and sat on the front edge, right in their faces.

"Listen to me carefully. I have a lot to say and I want your total attention. If you both play your cards right, you will not only live through today, but you will both be able to live a very comfortable life after this war is over. I have a plan and I require your assistance. If you help, you will walk away from this camp as potentially rich men. Do you hear me?" He didn't wait for an answer, simply got up and sat down behind his desk again. He acted as though this was a comfortable everyday business meeting.

"How do we know you will not kill us if we agree to help you?"

The Sub-Commandant answered at once. "I have documented evidence that you will forfeit your lives at once if I turn it over to the proper authorities. If instead you decide to work with me on this project, you will never face any charges from the military and you will wind up with more money than you ever dreamed possible. I can prove to you that I will do what I say and that you will get rewarded. You have to truthfully agree to work with me on this project."

The tension in the room dropped off a degree or two. The financial officer smirked. "Well if you can prove what you say, I believe we both stand ready to help you."

The meeting lasted for over an hour that day. The hour was used by the Sub-Commandant to explain and convince the two officers that they could depend on him to get this project completed. He planned to get himself and the two of them transferred from their current posting at Dachau to another posting in Salzburg, Austria. He had lots of work to complete to gain all the transfers but was confident he could accomplish it.

The hour together was spent listening to the Sub-Commandant as he talked about jewels, gold, diamonds, all now being stored at Dachau by orders of the Nazi Officials.

All three of the men knew that the end of the war was going to come. They planned to take measures to reward themselves now and in the future.

Chapter Thirty-Three

A Friendly Surprise
Heidelberg – Ana – 1971

The mellow glow of light that edged her curtained bedroom windows greeted her when she opened her eyes that morning. Her night's sleep had been so peaceful and when she looked at her alarm clock and saw that it was already seven o'clock she was surprised because she usually was awake much earlier.

Since it was Saturday and she didn't have any work scheduled, hadn't set up any project that had to be done, she rolled over and snuggled deeper underneath her warm comforter and relaxed again.

Embraced by the warmth of her bed, she saw the dream she'd had that night surface in her now-awake brain. Pure Happiness.

The dream started as she and her friends were on vacation and they all walked down a city street, in a city she didn't recognize, but at the same time she felt she knew it somehow.

They all laughed and talked as they walked along. Then, off to the side, an interesting old building appeared. Lots of people were going in so they decided to go in too, to check it out. Inside, everyone was having a good time as they laughed and talked and danced together. She and her friends decided to join the fun.

Immediately, one of her friends came straight over and asked her to dance. Now awake and re-living her dream, she saw him clearly; so handsome, kind, and special. They danced off on the large floor, arms wrapped securely around each other. But suddenly, unexpected and out of place, she felt something bad. Without thinking, she moved out of his arms and pulled him along, off the dance floor and over to a bed that sat at the far side of the large room.

He collapsed on the bed, lay down on his stomach and she sat beside him. Still with no thought of what was happening, she started to massage his tense muscles, his back and his arms. Slowly, gently, she slipped down beside him and sensually ran her hands all over his body. Her need was powerful and she wanted to feel all of him. She needed his love.

That didn't happen. Instead, he opened his eyes and looked at her with sadness and then pulled gently away and stood up. She got up too and simply looked at him. That's when she saw what was bad, what had gone wrong. It had happened directly in front of the bed they had been on. He stared at it too.

They were now separated from the rest of the room full of people by a large wide cavern in the floor. The hole was sided with solid brick, but random parts of the sides were harshly damaged, bricks were missing, and thick green moss hung down the sides. They couldn't see the bottom of the deep hole.

He pulled her away from it, maneuvered backwards, further away from the unknown. As she allowed herself to follow him she felt unbelievable sadness because he couldn't be beside her. He made her complete and she knew that his desire for her matched the desire she felt for him. Now though, he'd gone away and left her alone.

She knew she should have felt discouragement because he left her there, but instead she felt it told of his true love for her. Then she was awake. The dream ended.

Fully awake, she tried to relive every moment of the dream, attempted to memorize it. She didn't want it to escape into one of those secret dream files that get hidden somewhere in the brain. She wanted this dream to be available always so she deliberately placed in the front of her mind.

When she sat alone at her table a little later, ate breakfast slowly, she told herself that she needed to spend this Saturday in a positive way. She needed to leave behind the angst that was part of her life. She thought some, and finally decided to keep it simple. A walk along the beautiful river was always a positive, so that's what she'd do. She looked outside and saw that the weather was mostly sunny, some clouds drifting by. She also noticed that the wind was blustery, so she got herself dressed into something appropriate and then stepped out of the apartment.

When she got to the Old Bridge where she usually turned and went downtown she kept walking forward. This side of the river offered grassy areas where people could stop and sit on randomly placed rocks and enjoy the unblocked view. Further along another bridge that connected the north and south sides of the Neckar River could be seen in the distance. It ran from the Bismark Platz in Heidelberg, one of the main transportation centers in the city, and truly a busy center of local transit.

When she reached it, she climbed up a large wide staircase that was attached to the side of the bridge. At the top she paused for a moment and let herself enjoy the sight of two university students as they rowed along beneath where she stood on the bridge. They were probably training for upcoming races.

To go further along the river, she needed to climb down a twin staircase on the other side and she decided to do so because from the top of the bridge where she stood, she could see down into a large park that extended down to the river's edge. Benches sat all along the path that continued through the park, many were already filled with people.

Parents pushed strollers, their small children looked out brightly, and older children ran along beside. It was a lively day. Also, in the middle of the large open area, a group of young men played soccer. However, the young men weren't the only occupants of the open grassy field because it was also filled with ducks. They sat calmly and rested on the grass. They were used to being around people.

Then an older man and his small white dog appeared on the scene. The man let his tiny dog off its leash and the dog charged fanatically after the ducks. He barked, raced back and forth, around in circles, charged after the ducks. When the little white flash of a dog got too close to any of the ducks, they simply lifted up in mass and then landed nearby. The ducks weren't afraid, didn't feel danger, they were just exercising. Ana laughed out loud.

The air was crisp and the park was fun so she decided to sit down on one of the benches and enjoy the happiness around her. She wanted to watch people have fun instead of worrying about her problems.

After the little white dog moved away with his master the soccer game started up again. She looked carefully at all the players to see if she knew any of them, if one of them might be a student of hers.

Somebody scored a goal and afterwards, she casually looked off to her right as she wondered how far down the river the park ran. Then she checked the sidewalk, hoping for more young children or more entertaining dogs.

She froze when she saw them. She jumped up. Her eyes followed a couple that walked on the path that ran directly up to her bench. She felt like she was dreaming as she walked toward them. Then they spotted her and both started to run. That's when reality hit and she ran forward too. They met and gathered closely together into a tight mutual hug. All three sets of eyes were wet with tears of joy and all three faces radiated happiness.

Ana pulled back a little, but still held tightly onto Maggie with one hand and Sam with the other. Today had started out with a wild dream, then with good thoughts and a pleasant morning amidst happy families and happy animals. Now it peaked as she physically connected with two of the most important people in her world, her two best friends.

She couldn't get her questions out fast enough. "How did you get here? Why didn't you tell me you were coming? How did you know I was here, in the park?" Even as she asked the questions, she realized that she already knew the answer. That fact didn't diminish her happiness at all. She continued to smile with happiness even as she began to play along with the pre-planned "surprise" of the moment. She wasn't about to put her two friends in danger.

Maggie looked at Sam, then said, "We have a surprise for you."

Sam smiled at Maggie and then looked at Ana. "Maggie and I are married. We're here on our honeymoon. You're our family and we wanted to see you and tell you and share our happiness with you."

The announcement left her breathless! "Oh. I'm so happy for you two."

Maggie spoke up quickly. "Ana, remember when you were home and we were all so sad and upset about things. You'd already understood what was going on between Sam and me. You already knew that we were totally in love. You're the reason were found each other. You're also our best friend. We didn't want to live apart from each other anymore so we quietly got married. No big ceremony was necessary. I gave my notice to the CPA firm I worked for and we got married exactly two days ago. Now, we're here to celebrate our happiness with you."

Every word they spoke was totally true, however, their physical presence went deeper than they could tell her out in public. All three understood that. Later.

Several people were watching them, smiling at their shared happiness. Ana saw that they were being watched and said. "Guys, we need to go back to my apartment where we can talk and drink a celebratory glass of wine. What do you say?"

With no hesitation Sam said, "Ana, you lead the way. We'll follow."

The walk to the apartment was interesting. Both Sam and Maggie were apparently honestly charmed by the beauty of the area. When they finally reached the curve where they needed to cross the Ziegelhäusser Landstrasse, they both looked across the street, and they were stunned.

Maggie said, "Ana, is this where you live?" The approval they both gave confirmed her love of the place.

They crossed the street and walked underneath the elaborate archway into the courtyard. Before they got even one step up the stairs to her apartment, Ana heard the voice of her student, Thomas. "Wait Professor Winchester. How are you? Who are these people? Are they Americans, maybe your friends from America?"

Before she could respond, Sam stepped forward. "We are friends of Ana. We're here to visit with our friend. Who are you?"

Thomas knew from the tone of Sam's voice that he'd overstepped the borderline of good manners. He'd impolitely asked too many questions. "I am Thomas, a student of Professor Winchester. I feel that she is a good teacher. Please excuse me because I must meet my friends." He left quickly, without a backward glance.

The trio hurried up the stairs but Sam couldn't resist. "Wow, he's nosy!"

Ana nodded affirmatively and thought, "More on that subject later."

Maggie and Sam approved her apartment and they all sat down at the table with a glass of wine Ana poured. Sam got back up and walked all around, checked to make sure all the windows were closed. He also stepped out the door to make sure that no one was within hearing distance of anything they had to tell each other inside.

Ana watched him and then looked at Maggie. She saw a very serious face. She sat still, waited to hear what they had to tell her.

Tension was high and shared by them all, so before he got started on the serious conversation they all knew was coming, Sam first grabbed the bottle of wine and refreshed their glasses. He toasted. "Friends forever."

His care and concern was sincere but the serious information that was about to come out of his mouth kept Ana still and quiet. More bad news was coming.

He walked nervously around the room before he said anything. "Maggie and I are here because the federal government contacted us personally. Well, actually, they sent an agent to talk to us. We thought they just wanted more details from us about what happened to Mr. Elden and they did question us again, went over the same information one more time. But, there was something else that they wanted to tell us and it involves you Ana. "

She sat and watched him, full of knowledge and of fear.

"The Feds believe, from information they obtained related to Mr. Elden, that you're probably the true person of interest to some sort of secret group of Nazis who escaped from Germany at the end of the war by using fake identities. They left Germany and took lots of stolen money and stuff with them. The agent who talked to us said they're still there, all around the world and that one of the escape routes that they used was into Canada. That's where Mr. Elden lived before he moved to Atlanta, then to Andrews. The Feds tried to do a background check on him and found out that he was allowed to enter Canada during a certain point of time that was filled with postwar chaos. Seems too much was going on and nobody was able to keep track of it all. Somehow Mr. Elden helped the US Military and the Red Cross at the end of the war, there in Germany, and because of these connections, he was able to get approval to leave his country and move to

Canada. The federal agent told us that they'd checked out his passport and it was German but the information on it wasn't verifiable. While they were doing background checks, they checked out your father too. They were curious because he'd served with the US Army in Germany at the end of the war and because he'd also married a German citizen. They found out that your father's information was accurate but when they checked out your mother's passport, they weren't able to confirm that any of the information on it was correct. The record system was in a mess and the military didn't have the time or the desire to fully check records, so your mother was allowed to go with her new husband back to the US using the information she'd provided them."

Finally she came out of hiding and spoke to him. "Wait a minute. What did you mean about Mr. Elden and the Nazis? I don't understand."

"We don't have the answers yet. Maggie and I are convinced that the government knows a lot more than what they told us, has more information. We only know that Mr. Elden was taken in by Canada at the end of the war and then somehow wound up as your farm manager. The agent did tell us about something strange they found when they investigated his finances. Evidently he received foreign money on a regular basis because deposits from an unknown source appeared regularly in his bank account. After they told us this we felt that the feds didn't believe he was who he claimed to be. We think they believe his passport was a fake and they also believe he's connected to the Nazis somehow. Think back. Do you remember anything that could shed some light on who he really was, why he was in Andrews?"

All the things she'd kept hidden, the truths she'd not shared knocked around inside her as she sat still and hesitated. She had to be honest with them. They loved her, cared deeply about what was happening in her crazy life. The problem now through was that she didn't want them to be in danger. She wanted to keep that danger focused only on her. She also didn't want them to be touched by the ghosts in the past, the jam-packed closet-full-of skeletons that she felt existed somewhere in her family's history. All she wanted for them was that they go back to the farm and live together safely and happily.

She decided to keep some of the secrets hidden away for now. "My friends, I do have some information about Mr. Elden. I found it when Sam and I searched through Mr. Elden's house for clues about why he'd disappeared. Even then, I thought he'd been taken away, murdered by someone, but I had no idea who it could have been."

"What did you find? Why didn't you show it to me?" he was surprised.

I wish now that I'd told you but I was so upset and I admit, was worried about his connection to Germany and my mother's connection to Germany. I didn't understand it at all and just wasn't ready to tell you until

I could figure it out."

She got up and walked around the small room, told them about how she'd seen Mr. Elden's German cooking supplies and about the bookcase he had filled with books written in German, explained her shock because she honestly thought his slight accent was Canada-related. Then she stood still, looked directly into Sam's eyes. "I found two passports hidden in one of the boxes of German food, in the back of the cabinet. The names and the information on both of them weren't accurate for the Mr. Elden we all thought we knew."

He jumped up from the table and grabbed her, gave her a tiny shake and then hugged her. "What were you thinking? Why in this world didn't you tell me? This is exactly what the feds are hunting for! Maybe they'll be able to trace him and then we can find out what in this world he has to do with you."

Maggie's sad voice drifted to them. "Ana, do you think this has something to do with your mother? Please tell us so we can help you."

She started crying as she faced her two best friends. "I don't know, I don't understand what my mother could have to do with the Nazis. I was afraid and I wanted to try to figure it out myself before I told anyone. I've been trying to search for any little bit of information since I've been over in Germany but all I've been able to find out is that I'm being watched. Now I've got you two involved and I don't want that! You need to go back home to Andrews and keep safe."

"We want you safe too. We're your family and we won't go off and leave you here alone. We're here until we get this mystery solved." Maggie gathered both of them into her arms.

Ana went into her bedroom and retrieved Mr. Elden's hidden passports from her handbag. She'd never felt they were safe left in the apartment, so she'd accepted the risk of carrying them with her everywhere she went. Now she placed them on the table in front of her friends. "Here's what I found in his bedroom."

They looked carefully at the passports, and then both looked at her. Sam said, "We've got to get this to Andrew right away."

A gasp escaped her mouth before she could prevent it. "Andrew? Do you mean Andrew Watson? I met him on my flight back from the states. He's a government agent?"

"Slow down and take a deep breath. He's the agent the government chose to head up the investigation they've started on Mr. Elden, the investigation that they feel strongly is connected to you. Andrew booked our flight to Frankfurt, then had someone meet us there and drive us over to Heidelberg. He met us here in Heidelberg and talked to us, then drove us to a spot close to where you were, in the park. That's how we found you. He's a good man. Please don't be upset that he didn't tell you he was a fed agent. He's doing his job and let's just be glad he's on our side."

"I'm amazed but maybe I shouldn't be, especially after everything that's happened lately." The she smiled a little. "It's okay. I just need a little time to adjust to this news."

"We told Andrew that we'd get in touch with him after we talked to you. We wanted time to tell you what we knew and make sure you'd go along with letting us help." He stood up, opened his arms widely, and started to laugh. "We also want to share our new, married, happiness with you. Let's enjoy life a little instead of sitting here all worried about everything. I'm hungry!"

Finally, they laughed and loosened up.

The rest of their evening was spent at a restaurant, eating good food, and celebrating the marriage. When they left, they went back to Ana's apartment and fell asleep in the company of those they loved and trusted.

Chapter Thirty-Four

A Party
Heidelberg – Ana -1971

Early the next afternoon the telephone rang as she and her friends stepped back inside after a walk along the river. She managed to reach it before the caller hung up.

"Hello Ana. This is Andrew Watson and I've got a question to ask you. I hope the answer will be yes."

"Well, ask away Andrew."

"I've actually got this evening off and was wondering if you could meet me somewhere in Heidelberg for dinner this evening, but only if you don't already have plans. I'd love for us to get together tonight."

"Well, I don't exactly have specific plans but two friends of mine from the states are here and if it would be okay with you, I could come and bring them along with me. I think they'd love to meet you and maybe we can all enjoy the evening and have fun."

"Great! That sounds good to me. I'll catch the train over to Heidelberg and should get there at about six-thirty. If you have some idea about where we can go to eat, let me know, and I'll meet you all there."

"Well, I do have an idea Andrew. There's this restaurant on the Friedrichstrasse, sits right off the Square and specializes in fabulous mixed drinks, great wine, and best of all, a food called 'Flammkuchen.' It's like a German pizza but the literal English translation is 'flaming cake' and you won't believe how good it is! Does that sound okay to you?"

"Ana, you made my mouth water. We'll meet there but if you get there before me be sure everybody orders a drink. All the food and fun are on me tonight. I'll see you soon."

"Looking forward to it, Andrew." She put the phone down and then told Maggie and Sam about the evening's plan.

"Andrew told us when we met that he'd be calling and hoped we could all get together publically so we would appear to simply be a group of Americans having a good time together. You did a good job on the phone Ana. It sounded realistic, sounded like you were happy to go out and have fun with Andrew." Sam looked at her, wanted to believe that she was really going to let them all help her this time, not try to get through this by herself.

She surprised both of her friends when she answered, "I liked Andrew when we met on the plane. I know now that he's an agent but I still like him. I'm grateful to have him and the feds working on this situation and I'm also very curious to talk with him, see if he can give me any more information about this so-called 'connection' to the Nazis they think exists. Also, I'm warning you both about how much I adore the food we're eating tonight! It's called Flammkuchen and I eat it like a pig!" Her words encouraged her friends and left them anticipating the evening.

All worked out smoothly and the four of them walked into the square at the exact same moment. Andrew's train was on time and the three friends had deliberately scheduled their walk over to the old city so they'd be at the restaurant at the agreed upon time of six o'clock.

Just in case they were being watched, Ana made all the appropriate "pretend" introductions. "This is fun. I'm here introducing a man I met when we flew over on the same plane a little while back and my two best friends who just flew in yesterday. Maggie and Sam came to see me but here's the really best news. They just got married three days ago! They're on their honeymoon! Wow, life is good!"

None of the four had any difficulty pretending that they'd just met. They simply mixed it up with laughter and easy conversation. Without any thought of pretense, they honestly enjoyed the company of fellow Americans and the conversation grew even better.

When they entered the restaurant, the server took them over to a table off to the side. It sat one step up from the main floor and offered a pleasant view of all the patrons. He handed each a menu, then asked for their drink orders.

Before anyone could make a choice, Andrew said to the server, "Please bring us a bottle of champagne. We are celebrating tonight."

Sam and Maggie said together, "Oh no, please don't….." But Andrew cut them off, laughing.

"This is the after-the-wedding ceremony and we're going to drink champagne and toast you newlyweds. Plus, according to what Ana told me on the telephone, there's an item on this restaurant's menu that's called

'Flammkuchen' and she told me it's one of her favorite things to eat, said she loves it." Andrew continued to laugh and now everybody joined him.

Their server was fast and good. He set up the glasses and poured the champagne. After he left the table, again Andrew spoke up. He lifted his glass, they joined him, and then he said, "We celebrate you Maggie and Sam. May your life together be long and love-filled. Congratulations!" They tapped their tall glasses lightly together, drank the champagne, and celebrated happiness.

Sam, always hungry, picked up his menu. He looked at it but after turning a few pages written in German, deferred to Ana. "Maggie and I can't read German so you'll have to help us decide what to eat. I heard how much you love German pizza and I don't speak for Maggie, but I think that sounds like just what I want to eat."

"I feel the same way. I need to check with you though Ana because you know what I like and what I don't like, after all the meals we've shared together. Would I like this German pizza?" The menu Maggie held in front of her face as she talked suddenly slipped out of her hand and struck her half-full champagne glass. At the exact instant the menu hit the glass, Andrew's hand flew out and steadied it. Not a drop spilled.

Complete silence. "That was a good save Andrew. You should have been around the first time Ana and I met each other. You could have saved us from colliding and making a major food mess on ourselves and the floor of the university cafeteria." Maggie laughed and Ana joined her, both remembering the moment they'd first met and the collision and the mess and the friendship that followed.

"This time you saved me some embarrassment, a champagne soaked pair of jeans, and the rest of my glass full of champagne. Thanks!" Maggie looked at Andrew and toasted him as everyone at the table enjoyed the moment.

In the midst of all the fun, Ana couldn't help but wonder if anyone was watching. How could they think this was anything except pure fun? Because that's what it was. No spies or intrigue involved. Andrew fit right in and no agenda was visible, other than to have a good time.

"My turn now." Ana picked up her menu, waved it teasingly at Maggie, then opened it and said, "I'll answer your question about the German pizza Maggie, now that your champagne is safe. You asked if I thought you'd like it so I'll describe it and then you decide. First though, I have to tell you that the crust is perfect. It's thin, flaky, and tastes wonderful. Now listen you guys, sometimes men think that thin crust isn't the way to go but the diameter of the pizza is really large. The crust is generously spread with crème fraiche, which is similar to sour cream, but it's more subtle than sour cream, actually, not as sour. Last, but definitely not least come the toppings. Flammkuchen is traditionally topped with bacon or ham and onions, but here's the best part. You can top it with whatever you like. They have a list of things like fresh mushrooms, different types of cheese, peppers, and so many more choices you can make. It's left up to you. Since the first time I tasted flammkuchen, I've become addicted to it. It's great!"

Their server came to get their order and left with four orders of flammkuchen, all marched to the four distinctively different tastes at the table.

The rest of their time together was filled with laughter, German pizza, and lively conversation. In the middle of the food and fun, Ana reached into her pocket and retrieved the enveloped passports that she'd found in Mr. Elden's house. In the middle of a sentence, as she talked directly to Andrew, she gave him a warning, a slight downward look of her eye. He understood at once and reached his hand under the table. She handed him the passports. The conversation wasn't interrupted and if anyone was there in the darkened restaurant, they couldn't have seen the handoff.

They finally decided to leave the restaurant, after eating all the pizza and consuming more drinks. Andrew insisted that he pay the tab and eventually they all gave in. He paid the server and they rose to go.

"We'll meet you guys outside. We need to visit the lady's room, at least I do."

Ana agreed with Maggie and they moved toward the restroom.

Sam and Andrew walked outside and stood in the square talking. Andrew had intentionally positioned himself so that he could look into the large window, inside the restaurant, and see if he recognized anyone suspicious seated there.

When the girls came out, Maggie walked straight over to Sam and snuggled up against his body. "I had so much fun and I also love flammkuchen!" Laughter followed them as they all walked toward the train station to see Andrew off.

As they walked along, Andrew positioned himself beside Ana and whispered in a soft voice, as he put his arm around her and smiled, "We need to talk. I've got some information I need to share with you. Do you know of any place we could all go together and anyone watching would think we were continuing to simply have a fun evening?"

She followed his lead and smiled, flirted back at him as she whispered back. "Why don't we go to this interesting little place that I found recently? It's actually right across the road from my apartment, sits beside the river. From what I can tell, it was originally a boat launch with a large slab of concrete on the ground. It's not been used for a long time and I spend time there thinking and resting. It doesn't have any benches but we can sit on the concrete and also, we'll be able to see if anyone gets too close for comfort."

"Sounds perfect. Let's pretend to run in front of Sam and Maggie and whisper to them to simply keep having fun and follow us."

They got their message across and then the four enjoyed themselves as they walked to the old boat ramp.

Ana got another idea. "What do you all think about me going up to my apartment and bringing down a fresh bottle of wine for us to enjoy while we sit by the river?"

She got an enthusiastic "yes" from everybody. When they finally reached the private old spot she'd found, she showed them how to move over to the left through a few bushes and then make themselves as comfortable as possible as they sat down on the concrete pad.

"Sam and Maggie, you newlyweds, you stay here and be romantic. Andrew would you be kind enough to come up and help me bring down the wine and the glasses?"

"I'll be happy to help. Let's go get that wine."

They left together, crossed the street, and made their way to her apartment. As far as both could tell, no one was in their area. She turned and looked up at the student apartment to see if Thomas was watching her but she saw no one.

The wine was already chilled so Andrew opened it while she collected the wine glasses and added in a few napkins and a small bag of pretzels. A little snack with the wine would be good.

They used their little piece of time alone to speak softly to each other. He thanked her for giving him the passports and she thanked him and the government for intervening and trying to resolve the mystery of why Mr. Elden was murdered and why she was important to the Nazis.

But she still didn't share the information she'd found that caused her to think that the few lines written by her mother could be at the bottom of the mystery. She also said nothing about what happened to her in Salzburg just recently because she wanted to make sure she knew what the truth really was. She wanted to protect her mother's reputation.

When they left her apartment carrying the wine and pretzels, Frau Krueger walked out of her door. "Hello Ana. I am happy to see you. You look like you are in the middle of a party. I saw that you have young people staying with you. Are they from America?"

Ana introduced Frau Krueger to Andrew and then followed up by telling her about the visit of her friends and the celebration of their marriage and honeymoon. Frau Krueger was delighted and wished them happiness.

They said good evening and went down the stairs. Ana then stopped, turned around and called softly up to Frau Krueger. "We're having a private party on the old boat ramp. I hope that is all right. We promise not to get loud. We simply wanted to have a little more fun together this evening."

Frau Krueger looked toward the river and laughed. She wished them again a happy night.

They got back to the ramp and settled down. Ana passed out the glasses and Andrew filled them. They did another toast and then were quiet as they sipped the wine.

Andrew stood up slowly and stretched, pretended to exercise his body a little, the whole time spent scanning the area for intruders. When he leisurely sat down, he was very close to Ana and that was when he started telling them some of the important facts that the feds believed were related to the murder of Mr. Elden and the unknown interest of the Nazis in Ana.

"First, remember that we're supposed to be partying here so don't let anything I say cause you to look or sound upset or unhappy. Keep up the partying spirit, laugh at everything I say because it's extremely important that you know what we know."

Then he began. "I'm not sure what you know about the Nazis and what happened with them prior to and at the end of the war. Activities they instigated then are still in existence today.

"Maybe you've heard of the organization called Odessa? Some people know about it, but the truth about how it was organized and run is still not clear. Evidence has been documented that the Nazis knew the war was coming to its end and knew that they were going to lose. They began to organize different levels of their remaining power structure in order to make sure that SS Officers would be kept safe after the war ended.

"One of the first things they tried to do was to move everything that had value, like art, jewels, and gold out of Germany. This process took place for quite a while prior to the war's end. Lots of clever officers skillfully moved Nazi capital to other places in the world where it could be keep under their control and help those who survived the war. Their plan was to form a new Nazi regime in the future.

"At the war's end, as few as possible SS officers were captured by the Allied Forces, and money was already in place to be used to finance their new lives. In order to be safe from prison and legal prosecution they escaped through different routes designed for that purpose.

"Most importantly, they left Germany and were sent secretly into many countries around the world. After the war was over, many of their escape routes were uncovered and were given the name of 'Ratlines.' The Ratline-users were supplied with fake passports and with money. The exact number who escaped is not known, but the estimate is large, maybe even over a thousand people.

"Having said all that, some of those Nazis decided to stay in Germany, hiding in the chaos with false identities, documents and money. They were willing to take the risk of discovery in order to remain home in Germany.

"At the end of the war, the turmoil of life was extensive and the Nazis took advantage of the confusion. They even worked, without anyone realizing it at the time, with groups like the Red Cross, the Roman Catholic Church, and the Allied Military forces in order to help their members escape."

Maggie stood up too fast and pulled Sam up with her. "Listen friends, I can't sit still anymore." She yawned largely. "I need to move because I think that I drank too much wine. I'm sleepy." Then she and Sam laughed and hugged each other.

"I think you're the only one who drank too much Maggie. It's because you're so tiny, it doesn't take much wine to make you feel like this." Sam teased her and in return, she pretended to punch him.

Andrew and Ana took advantage of the interruption and laughed along with them. Then all entered a few more minutes of ordinary conversation and supported the fact that they were all having a fun time. Ana even went over to the river's edge and looked out over the water as it flowed past.

They settled back a little and Andrew took a deep breath and picked up where he'd left off. "I wanted you to understand the background behind what we think caused Mr. Elden's death. His murder has been possibly tied to an imposter who claimed to be a government agent but who was in fact a Nazi in hiding.

"My agency began investigating the money issue. We started by tracing Mr. Elden and we found that he came over to Canada as a refugee from Germany, close to the end of World War II. He got himself established there in a small town and started a real estate company. Then he moved to the US, first Atlanta, then to the small town of Andrews, North Carolina. This process of moving took place over a number of years and we can't establish any reason for him to leave Canada. He was doing well there.

"We looked closer into his life during this time, checked into his finances, and according to official bank records, he received significant sums of money on a pretty regular basis.

"We were able to check and see if any of this money was funneled into the Winchester Farm business account, but we found no evidence of that. Evidently he didn't use the Winchester family business to sneak money into the United States for his own personal, maybe illegal use. However, truly the most important thing we've found is pretty conclusive evidence that Mr. Elden was a former SS Officer. The money he was funded with came from capital that had originated, we think, from the Nazis.

"That's when they put me on this case. Ana, your family was connected so closely to Mr. Elden, and, in addition, your family has German connections through your mother. I was assigned specifically to track your movements because the feds are concerned about your safety. I know this all sounds complicated and it is, but I wanted you all to know that I'm here to help, not to hinder. I'm trying to find the reason you're so important to the Nazis."

Time to go. Sam and Maggie got up. "Guys, we need some sleep. It's been great!"

Andrew whispered to Ana. "I'll check out these passports and let you know what I find." He got up too, as did Ana. They all walked away from their party place.

"Sam and Maggie, I enjoyed meeting you. Thanks for tonight. Congratulations!" He waved and walked back across bridge to catch his train.

"I like him," said Maggie. They walked across the street.

Ana answered, "I like him too."

Chapter Thirty-Five

Danger in the Wind
Heidelberg – Ana 1971

All good things must end, so trite, so true. Ana boarded the train to Frankfurt, led Sam and Maggie to a seat and explained again how to transfer from the train to the airport once they arrived in Frankfurt.

Last night bad news flew in and destroyed the harmony of the conversation they were enjoying together at her apartment. The telephone rang and the man Sam had left in charge of the farm while he was gone was on the line, so upset he could barely speak about what happened in Andrews. A tornado, almost unheard of there in the valley, struck earlier in the day and its path of destruction brought severe damage to Winchester farm. Trees were blown down, the barn and the office building were severely damaged, and farm equipment was destroyed. Some was even missing. He needed help immediately.

Ana called the airline and arranged flights, Sam and Maggie packed up, and now they sat side by side in the train. Ana stood with them, ready to get off before it left but wanting to spend every possible second with them. All were silent, sad, as the damage to the farm weighed them down. The reality was harsh.

Sam reached out to her. "Now we're forced to leave you alone here. I can't believe this happened!"

"Stop worrying about me. The farm needs you Sam. It's our home and we love it. You've got to check on all our employees and try to get the business up and running again. We all have to do what we need to do and this must come first."

Maggie looked up at her, face damp with tears, "Please know we love you and we're only leaving because we have no other choice. I feel like

181

some powerful force is dragging us away from you, forcing you to be on your on again."

She didn't argue with what Maggie said. She'd felt something other-worldly too. Usually she called it "gut feelings" or sometimes a phrase she'd heard others use, a "sixth sense." She acknowledged to herself the existence of a power that seemed to sometimes show up in her life.

The last goodbye was hard. She watched the train pull away and with her mind in another place, walked back home.

Again her telephone rang. She rushed to it, afraid of more bad news from the farm. "Hello."

"Hello, Ana. This is Andrew. I've been thinking about all the fun we had and I wanted to see if we could all get together again for dinner and a concert? There's a good concert scheduled there in Heidelberg this Friday evening. Interested?"

"Andrew, it's good to hear from you but let me tell you what's happened. Sam and Maggie left to fly back home this morning because a tornado damaged our farm. Sam's the farm manager and needed to get back to handle everything. The farm suffered some serious damage, but luckily, no injuries to any people."

"Wow! I'm sorry! I haven't heard anything about it here at the base, but I don't really have time to watch much news. It must really be hard to not be able to leave and go home with your friends. Your job makes it hard to just leave on the spur of the moment. Listen, I know you don't feel like a concert, but let's get together for dinner on Friday. It will do you good to get out and eat, maybe even help with your stress level a little."

She thought for a second, realized he needed to tell her something. "I don't promise to be happy company but yes, let's get together on Friday."

"Tell me where you'd like to eat. Would some more flammkuchen make you feel better?"

She did smile a little at his joke. "Let's just meet at the Market Square if that's okay with you. It's convenient and easy and has lots of food to choose from."

"Sounds great to me. Is six-thirty too early for you?"

"It works for me. See you there, Andrew."

Friday morning dawned sunny and clear, a perfect start for the end of the week, the beginning of the weekend. She stood at the bottom of the stairs and looked out into the courtyard below her, then gazed upwards and took in the glowing mountains all touched by the rays of sunlight as they chased away the night's darkness from the valley. She had a full day of work ahead of her today and was glad for it, felt better to be teaching and helping her students. Maybe today would be a better day than she'd experienced since the tornado. As she thought about her upcoming classes, she knew that most of the students would be happy because they'd probably planned to go to the concert tonight, the one that Andrew had talked about taking her to. She tried to tell herself that today would to be a good day as she headed off to work.

"Ana!" Frau Krueger called her as she walked quickly down to the courtyard.

She responded immediately and started back up to see what Frau Krueger needed. She'd left for work earlier than normal so she wasn't worried about being late for her first class.

"I am so sorry to stop you because I know you are going to work but I promised Georg that I would give you a message from him. He called me last night about business, and after we talked he asked me to do him a favor. He told me that he had been hoping to hear from you but never had. I told him how busy you have been, traveling to Salzburg University and then spending time with your American friends here on their honeymoon. Anyway, he wanted me to please ask you to call him, but he insisted that was only if you wanted to." Frau Krueger sounded slightly out of breath, exhausted after earnestly passing on the information from Georg.

Ana smiled, completely at ease, "Frau Krueger, it was so good of you to give me this message from him. I honestly meant to call him but as you said, my life has been busy lately. I have his telephone number and I will call him. Again, it was very good of you to get his message to me. Thank you!"

"Oh, you are welcome." She smiled, gave a tiny wink, "I think you will make Georg very happy when you call him." The she waved her off to work.

She did now feel a little better and she immersed herself in nature and felt happiness start to bloom inside her as she walked along to work.

Friday classes went by quickly and when she left the classroom building to go home, she almost bumped right into Thomas again. They both stopped and then she looked at his face and smiled.

"Professor Winchester, please excuse me. I was thinking instead of paying attention to where I was walking." He smiled back at her but with less enthusiasm than was normal for him.

She heard his quieter voice and thought about the last time he'd spoken to her, when he'd run into her along with Sam and Maggie. He'd asked too many questions too quickly and Sam, by the tone in his voice had more or less told him he was rude. Now she knew that Thomas had understood exactly how Sam felt at that time.

Even though he'd seemed way too interested in her life, she liked him. He'd offered to and in fact had helped her out several times. Today she felt sad for his embarrassment.

"Thomas, I have not seen you much lately. How is school going for you this semester? Do you have any classes that you really like?"

He was surprised at her interest and answered with a little more of his normal enthusiasm, "Yes, I am pleased with all my classes. They are going well for me."

She remembered the time he'd asked her to go to the concert with him and some students, so she asked, "Thomas, are you going to the concert tonight?"

"I am going with my friends. Do not tell me that you are going too?"

"No, not this time. I am having dinner with a friend tonight. I got some very bad news from my home in the States recently. A storm damaged the town where I live and also damaged my family farm. My friends who you met recently had to leave and get back to handle the destruction caused by the storm. I am feeling sad and really do not feel like a concert tonight."

He expressed his concern about what happened. "I am so sorry and I hope it will all get fixed again. I am also sorry that your friends had to leave before they planned. You all probably had so much more you wanted to see and do."

His voice was genuine and she gave him another small smile and said, "Thomas enjoy the concert tonight. See you around."

She moved off as he said, "You try to enjoy your weekend too."

Without doubt, Andrew had something important to tell her. Lots of practice lately, pretending to have fun but really discussing secrets with him and her friends had taught her to read between the lines, to translate what Andrew was really talking about.

When they met at the Market Square, they both had their happy faces in place and with a little bit of talk, picked a restaurant they both approved, then chose a table.

After they sat down, she spoke quietly to him. "Please know that I'm still sad and upset about what happened at the farm. If I look or act unhappy, it's perfectly normal to anyone who knows what happened." Translated, she told him it was okay if they weren't happy and cheerful tonight. They didn't need to "act" so much. He understood her at once.

Friday is a busy night in the square but they were a little earlier than the norm, so a few empty places were still available. After they ordered their food, while they waited for it to come, he decided to go ahead and tell her what the federal investigators had uncovered. The square was not as crowded as it was going to be, so now was the best time to quietly tell her what he knew.

"I need to update you about those papers you gave me."

He had her undivided attention.

"We've investigated the passports, talked with the Canadian officials, and they gave us all the info they could find. So far, we see two men were allowed to migrate to Canada because they were homeless after the war. They were recommended for the migration because they'd helped the Allies get things under control in Heidelberg after the war ended and the Allies were left in charge. According to the records, they were brothers, residents of Heidelberg, Germany. When we checked with German officials, they weren't able to find any family of that name that existed in the Heidelberg area. Everyone now agrees that the name "Elden," the two brother's name, is a fake. The passports were all fakes, evidently backups in case of emergencies in the future. Also, records show that one of the brothers disappeared after they migrated to Canada. Your Mr. Elden filed a missing person report with the police in Canada. We don't know positively, but think that the missing brother purposefully left for some specific reason and didn't want anyone to know where he'd gone. We think he's the source of the funding that his brother, your Mr. Elden, received all these years."

She didn't know what to think, just gave him a sad smile and reached out and lightly touched his arm.

The server brought the food. The smell of the roast beef drifted up and they both started to eat.

In between mouthfuls, he added something. "We're glad to get the details we found, everything is important, but we still don't have any information that tells us who these two brothers really were. What we've found so far points to the Nazis' Odessa pattern, and we do believe that Heidelberg is at the center. We're certain that somewhere out there, somebody knows exactly who Mr. Elden was because they went to North Carolina and murdered him. Relax and try to think back really hard and see if you can remember anything your mother might have said about where she lived in Germany."

"My mother refused to talk to me about her life before she met my father. Even when I got older, asked her directly, she'd only repeat that all of her family was dead and that I should focus on the present and forget about the past." She stopped eating, stared off into the distance.

"It sounds like your life was a little tough. Sorry to make you think back to sad times, but can you think of anything your mother said, maybe accidently, about a place or anything about Germany?" He'd finished his meal, empty plate in front of him, as he focused on her gently.

She appreciated his kindness as she pushed her plate aside. "I remember one time at Christmas she'd baked some gingerbread. She told us that she loved gingerbread, that it reminded her of home and of Christmas. Now, all these years later, I still don't know where she lived and enjoyed gingerbread and Christmas. I will say this though, and you can call me weird if you want to, but I feel a deep intense attachment to Heidelberg. I feel like it is a part of me."

She expected him to laugh off what she said but instead he answered, "I credit your instincts and I'm going to focus on this area. We'll keep going until we get this figured out."

Chapter Thirty-Six

Friend Devil
Heidelberg – Ana – 1971

Andrew asked that she let him walk her home after they finished their meal together, but she stood firm. "I'm safe walking home by myself. There are lots of people around this time of day so please don't worry about me. Go on back to work and if you find out anything else, let me know. I want you to understand how much I appreciate your help and also your concern about what happened to my farm. Call me again as soon as you need me for anything, or if you find out something else."

He watched her as she walked towards the street that led out of the square. He was deeply concerned about her safety.

When she walked into her apartment, emptiness echoed. With Sam and Maggie there, it had been so warm, full of friendship. She felt exhausted. The day had started with a pop of optimism, but now she felt the weight of her past heavy and thick, blocking up her life again.

Although tired, it took a long time for her to fall asleep that night. Then, in what felt like only one minute of sleep, she woke up. A dream forced her up and out of the bed, caused her to tremble slightly, and to hear a whisper in the air, but she couldn't identify it or logically believe it was real.

Wide-awake, the dream still surged through her mind and she sank down onto the side of her bed. In the dream she was riding her beloved horse Devil, the animal she'd raised, cared for, and loved since she was a young girl. He was her friend, the one she shared her emotions with, the one who accepted her love, and reciprocated. Once again, they were flying along the road, alone, fast, and feeling carefree.

The dream ended when the telephone screamed out in the living room. She tried to steady herself, and then walked slowly to answer the call. She felt like she'd been shot and she knew it was Sam.

Her hand hesitated, and then picked it up. She whispered, "Hello Sam."

She recognized the sorrow in his voice as he answered her. "Hello Ana. I wanted to let you know that we got back home all safe. Before we got home, I was hoping to be able to call and tell you the damage wasn't as bad as we feared, but it's even worse. I want to be honest with you and I need to tell you something. That's the reason I'm calling you right now, in the middle of your night. I knew I had to tell you now, not wait."

He paused and she softly spoke to him. "I'm sitting at the kitchen table, Sam. I know you have bad news for me. I know it's my Devil. You knew I was already worried about him when we got the phone call. I've been waiting. Just go ahead and tell me."

"I wish we were there with you right now. It wouldn't change anything but I would sure feel better telling you this if I could reach out and touch you and take care of you." He paused again. "Ana, Devil is dead."

She didn't answer, made no sound, and he was afraid. "Ana, are you there? Can you talk to me?"

"I'm here, Sam. I already knew before you called that Devil was gone. He came to me and told me goodbye in a dream just before your phone call came through. Can you tell me how he died?"

His voice was muffled, pain-filled, as he answered, "This is hard for me to tell you. The barn was totally destroyed and when I saw it I felt Devil was already gone but we didn't find him in the rubble that was there. Just a little while ago I got a phone call from Mr. Davis, the farmer who lives on the other side of the main highway. He told me that a horse was in his pasture, almost dead, and he thought he recognized it as yours. I went over and there was Devil, down flat in the pasture. He opened his eyes when I got to him, but he continued to lie completely still. Ana, all his legs were broken and I think his back was too. He was most likely in lots of pain. No vet would be able to help him so I did something that was so hard for me to make myself do, but that I honestly believe was the best for Devil. I confess to you. I shot Devil. I killed him and removed his pain." Then he was silent.

Tears ran silently down her face and her voice was thick. "Please Sam, you know I trust you with everything I love in this life. I believe you did the right thing. You took away his pain and released my broken Devil from this world. Thank you for helping him. I love you Sam."

"I know how much he meant to you Ana, how much you loved him. I'm just so sorry this happened."

"Death and separation are part of life, hard and difficult to accept but I'll make it. Right now, I'm simply going to sit here and remember all the good times and the love that Devil and I shared. You go get some rest, if possible, and also please tell Maggie that I love her too."

After she hung up the phone, she walked to the window and stared down at the river. She let her tears flow unchecked.

Some miles away, a young man and an old man sat together on a bench that faced the river. They talked softly, the old man asking the questions, the young man answering, sharing information he gathered recently about Ana Winchester, about the tragedy of the tornado, and about the return to the States by her two friends.

The old man listened intently. He didn't look pleased with the young man's words.

Chapter Thirty-Seven

Georg Appears
Heidelberg – Ana – 1971

Mid-morning the next day, someone knocked on her door. She was
listlessly sitting on her sofa, remembering her Mother, her North Carolina
home, and her horse Devil, totally immersed in memories.

When she opened the door, Frau Krueger stood there smiling sadly, her
arms loaded with covered dishes balanced precariously in her hands.

Ana couldn't help but respond to her sympathetic smile and said,
"Good morning. Please let me help you. What have you got here?"

Frau Krueger gave her another tiny smile and announced, "I've made
some food for you to eat. I heard about what happened to your home and
I want to help you. I want you to know that I am concerned. The food will
help you to maintain your strength."

She was overcome, hadn't expected anyone here to understand the
sadness she was swimming through. "I simply do not know what to say,"
she said as she took hold of some of the dishes and ushered Frau Krueger
into her apartment. "This is very kind of you. I appreciate it and thank you
very much."

They both sat down and then she asked, "But how did you know what
happened?"

"Thomas came by and told me yesterday evening. He was sorry for
what happened and he wanted me to know too." Then she got up from her
chair, went over to the table and made sure she'd remembered to bring all
the food that she'd prepared.

She turned around and looked at Ana. "You have been a friendly, good
person and I am happy to know you. Of course I want to help you at a
time like this. Now you will not need to worry about shopping and cooking

for yourself today. Maybe you can get some rest."

Frau Krueger didn't stay long. She respected Ana's feelings and as she left she said, "If there is any way that I can help you, please let me know." She quietly let herself out the door.

That same afternoon Ana received a call from the Professor she assisted at the University. "Fraulein Winchester, I was contacted by a member of the Lady's Society that sponsors students to our University. She told me about what happened to your home in the United States. I am calling to tell you that the University is sorry for the tragedy and also to see if you require any time off, either to travel home to handle the situation, or to give yourself time to recover from the shock of what has happened."

Again she was surprised. "Professor, thank you very much for your concern, but I have friends in the United States who are taking care of the situation for me. I admit that I am upset but I do not feel that I need any time off. I will continue my normal work schedule with the University. I believe that keeping to my work schedule will help me to get over what has happened. However, I must tell you that I appreciate the kindness of the University's offer."

They exchanged polite goodbyes and suddenly she wished that she'd thought to ask the name of the lady who'd told the University what had happened. She again had the distinct feeling that too many people knew too much, or sought too much, information about her life.

That evening she sat at the table and slowly ate the food brought to her by Frau Krueger, and was amazed by the concern and the desire to help her shown by some of the people she'd gotten to know in Heidelberg. This stunned her because she'd always struggled to get beyond all the rejection and isolation she dealt with from some members of her family. It had been difficult not to just give up. Since her move she felt better about herself, felt more self-confident. Honestly, she felt different.

The sky darkened and the stars shone brightly against the blackness. She looked out and suddenly felt the need to get out, to leave the confines of the apartment. She felt a deep need to walk freely along the river.

Her steps were quick and she moved forward with no plan or destination. It felt good to breathe deeply as she walked and felt even better when she stopped again to gaze up at the beautiful sky full of stars. From habit, she turned onto the Old Bridge and walked over the well-worn bricks. She veered over to the edge and paused, leaned against the bridge and stared down at the river.

A large hand touched her. She spun around and Georg was close beside her.

"Ana, I am here to help you if you need me." He still held onto her arm and he looked straight into her eyes.

"I got here as soon as I could. I am sorry it was not sooner but after I heard what happened, I had to finish up some work before I left my home in Bavaria."

"Oh Georg, it is so good to see you. I cannot believe that you came all this way to see about me." She spoke gently and didn't break the connection of their eyes, instead reached out her own hand and touched his arm.

"Were you going into town? I will go with you." He said.

"I was not going anywhere in particular, just needed to get outside and breathe some fresh air." She waited for his response.

"Let me walk you back to your apartment. I will not keep you up late tonight. I just felt the need to come and knock on your door and tell you I was available if you need me for anything. My plan is to stay here in Heidelberg for the next few days, until I am sure that you are okay. I have booked a hotel room but please remember that I can extend that time if you need me."

She'd felt slightly amazed earlier in the day at the concern shown her by others. Now she felt something of greater importance. The feeling was not logical because how did she even know that he wasn't involved in everything that was going on secretly in her life? She didn't know him, yet she felt like she'd known him forever. The power of the feeling was not rational, but it was real.

Frau Krueger saw them when they walked into the courtyard together but she deliberately didn't go out and say hello. She left them alone. If she was correct in her thinking, she believed they were going to get together. She was happy with the thought and said to herself that they were meant for each other.

Georg didn't stay long, just long enough to get all the details of the tragedy straight from Ana. He saw and felt her sadness and as they talked he tried to help her, to ask if he could do anything for her.

"You have helped me greatly, simply by being concerned enough to come and see me."

He got up and went to the door. "I am going to my hotel room, because if I do not go now, I am afraid I will not leave you at all." He paused and watched her as he opened the door. "I will see you tomorrow. Goodnight."

The next days were busy and happy. Each day after her classes ended he would meet her outside the building and they would walk along the streets together, stop and have coffee, talk and get to know each other better. He also took her out to dinner several times and she reciprocated by cooking him a special meal of the beef roulade that they both had enjoyed on their first night out together.

He used the time he had while Ana was at work to get together with

Frau Krueger and schedule additional repairs, updates for the apartment house and for the student apartment building directly behind it. They reviewed all the financial records and for the first time since he had taken over ownership and management of the property, all matters were up-to-date. It felt good to be caught up and the weight of the unfinished duties lifted off his mind.

During one of their meetings together, Frau Krueger tentatively answered a question that he asked her about a forfeiture of the lease on the apartment that Ana was now living in.

He asked, "Why did this young man decide not to follow through with the agreement to lease the apartment? Was something wrong with it? Did we fail to provide repairs that were needed?"

Tentative was the exact description of Frau Krueger's voice as she hesitantly answered him. "The young man liked the apartment. He was totally satisfied with it. But, he received an offer of cash, in the same amount as one month's rent on the apartment, if he would release our company from the legal bond of the agreement he had signed already."

"What?" Disbelief from Georg sounded loudly in the one word.

"Please, let me continue. The real estate agent working for Ana called me from the United States. He was determined to get her into an apartment in this building but I had already told him that the last one was legally promised to a young man. I could not go back on the deal. Then a little later that day a well-dressed lady knocked on my door and told me that she was a friend of the real estate agent from the States. She wanted the name of the young man who had signed to rent it or, if I wanted, please call him and make an offer of one month's rent if he would let go of his right to the lease. I realized later that I had made a mistake but at the time I called the young man and he happily agreed to the bonus of a month's rent and released us from his rental. So then the lady gave me Ana's name, address and the money to finalize her lease of the apartment."

"I cannot believe this. Why did Ana feel it was so important to live in this specific place?" He paced up and down the room.

"But she did not know about any of this. I was instructed to never tell anyone what had gone on and especially I was told not to tell her. Now that I know her and consider her a friend, I have gone against that rule made by the lady and I have explained to her how she got to be living here."

He stopped. "What did she say when you told her this?"

"She seemed confused, but then she thought about it for a while and told me that Mr. Elden, her farm manager and real estate agent did not tell her about any of this. She said that he had helped her mother and her for many years, since the death of her father. Mr. Elden had managed the property and treated them with kindness. She said that maybe he had wanted to make sure she was happy with where she would live in Heidelberg."

"But why this particular home, Frau Krueger? How did Mr. Elden know it would be so perfect for Ana?"

"When Ana and I talked I asked her that too. She told me that she thought Mr. Elden had spent some time at Heidelberg University when he was a young man and maybe he knew this house and that it was a great place to live. But she had no answer for any lady he knew here. She just said maybe it was someone he knew from when he studied here." Frau Krueger was on the verge of tears. "Sir, are you mad at me? Are you going to fire me as manager?"

"You are not going to lose your job. I believe you made an incorrect decision but it has caused no problems. Also, I believe you are an understanding and kind person and a friend to Ana. Please stop worrying. In fact, let us both forget we ever had this conversation. Let us simply celebrate the fact that we have all our business responsibilities updated."

He walked over to her and patted her arm. "I am going into the city. I have a few errands to complete before I go back home tomorrow. I will talk with you later. Thank you for your help."

At morning break that day, Ana left the classroom and walked to a telephone booth. She called Andrew.

"Hello Andrew, I just have a few free minutes but something is on my mind. I forgot to tell you about how I came to be living in the apartment I have here in Heidelberg. I only just found out recently that Mr. Elden went to a lot of trouble and expense to get me in there. I promised I'd never tell this, but it's bothering me."

She gave him all the information she'd learned from Frau Krueger, even the part about the "well-dressed" lady.

Andrew listened carefully. "This is interesting and may be important. Perhaps he was more than just a student at the University. Did you get any other information?"

"Sorry I don't know more, but something else came up recently. I got a call from the University that I work for and the Professor told me a member of the Society that supports international students told them about what happened to my home in the States. I felt it was early for someone like that to know what had happened. Oh no, sorry Andrew, look at the time. I'm going to be late for class. I'll talk to you later."

She hung up and sprinted across the street and into the classroom building.

Chapter Thirty-Eight

Georg Leaves
Heidelberg – Ana – 1971

Ana released her students early that afternoon, wanting a little time to stow her papers away and freshen up before she met Georg. The bag she'd brought with her usually only held her work material but today carried more. She pulled out a small compact and brushed powder lightly against her face, then added a soft blush of lipstick. She wanted to look her best. This was the last day she would get to spend with him for a while. He was leaving tomorrow.

Quickly she finished up and put her things neatly back in the bag, then went over to her lookout window. There he stood, tall, powerful, leaning against a tree near the fountain that spurted water happily in the center of the courtyard. She watched him intently and wondered how she would feel after he left tomorrow. Deep sadness crept in because he had to leave, go back to work and home in Bavaria.

He looked up and saw her, waved. She grabbed everything, hurried down the stairs, and he met and hugged her at the door. He gently removed the bag from her arm.

"How was your day?"

"It was good, but it is better now that you are here to meet me again." She realized that she spoke naively, but even so, couldn't help it. With Georg, she felt the need for honesty.

They walked along and turned instinctively down the Hauptstrasse, into the midst of people out and about, shopping, out for dinner, or to attend a concert or the theater.

"Ana, what would you like to do on this last evening we have together?" His voice seemed muted, depressed.

"I do not know. Do you have any ideas?"

"Actually, I do know what I would like for us to do. First we should go into one of the restaurants here in town and enjoy a good meal together. Afterwards, if it is okay by you, I would like for us to go to your apartment for the rest of the time we are able to spend together this evening. I would appreciate the chance for us to be alone, to talk without being overheard by others and simply to enjoy being together. Would that work for you or are you uncomfortable for us to be alone in your apartment for that length of time?"

She stopped and pulled him to a stop, then looked at him. "Georg, something is not right with you today. Please tell me and let me help. Of course I approve of your plan for this evening. I have no objections whatsoever to being alone with you. In fact, I too would enjoy some private time together." She continued to stand still, waited for his response, hoped for a smile.

He rewarded her as he cocked his head and a gentle smile spread across his face. "I am fine, really. I just have a few things on my mind and I am trying to resolve them. Please do not misunderstand me. The best way to spend this evening is to be alone with you."

This time he moved forward and she came with him willingly, happily.

A few paces down the street she suddenly stopped again. "Oh no! I forgot! I promised Frau Krueger that I would go by the pharmacy and pick up her medicine. She has been suffering from headaches lately and called in her prescription. I told her that I would be going past the pharmacy on my way home so I would be happy to get the medicine for her. I nearly forgot! Is it okay with you if we make a small detour?"

They laughed as they turned around and crossed the street. The pharmacy was on the opposite side, near the University Plaza. "Here it is Georg. Let's go in." She opened the door and he followed her inside.

A lady was behind the counter and asked if she could help them. Ana explained that she was there to pick up the prescription called in by Frau Krueger.

"Yes, Frau Krueger did call us earlier today. We have her prescription ready and if you will give me a minute, I will get it out of the back room." The lady left through an open door off to the right, straight behind the counter.

Almost as soon as the lady walked through the doorway, an older gentleman limped a little as he came through from the back and stopped right behind the counter. He looked up and saw Ana.

"Hello, Ingrid. I am so pleased to see you again. It has been such a long time but you are as beautiful as ever." He began to walk around the counter when the lady came out of the back with the prescription.

"What is wrong Father?" she asked.

The old gentleman stopped immediately. "I was simply telling Ingrid hello." Then he looked at the lady's face and he saw that she was embarrassed.

"Father, this is an American who is staying in an apartment at Frau Krueger's and she is here to pick up a prescription. I do not think her name is Ingrid."

Ana looked directly, kindly, at the old gentleman and said, "It is kind of you to remember Ingrid in such a good manner. I am not Ingrid. I am Ana Winchester. However, it is a pleasure to talk to you."

He turned and started to go into the back room. "You look just like Ingrid. She was so sweet, so intelligent, and she always tried so hard to take good care of her mother. I apologize to you young lady." He looked at her again. "You look like Ingrid. Excuse me please." Then he left.

The lady behind the counter said in a soft voice, "That is my Father in Law. He had a stroke last year and is doing well, but sometimes he gets confused. Please forgive him."

Ana stepped up to the counter and said, "There is nothing to forgive. He was kind and he complimented me by comparing me to this Ingrid who he evidently cared about."

She paid for Frau Krueger's medicine. During this whole experience, Georg remained silent. Now he moved over, opened the door, and smiled at her as they went back out onto the street. They walked on down to the courtyard in front of the Old Bridge and sat down at the restaurant there. It was one they both enjoyed, and they had a delicious last dinner together.

They were silent for the most part as they walked toward her apartment, each thinking of how much they didn't want to separate, how much they'd miss each other.

He broke the silence. "Will you seriously think about a trip to Bavaria? I'd love to show you around and I honestly think that you would love it."

"I can say without any hesitation that I will be there to visit you in Bavaria just as soon as I can get my semester finished and hopefully will not need to fly back home to the States to finish up the repairs from the tornado. I wait to hear from my friend and manager, Sam. He is excellent and I expect he will not need me to return, but these days, I never know."

Suddenly, as she finished speaking and they came to the end of the bridge, they were startled when a voice called out, "Professor Winchester, how are you?"

Directly in front of them stood Thomas. He was evidently on his way into town.

"How is everything going with your home in the United States? Is it getting repaired? Also, how are you doing?"

Georg waited for her to answer. She glanced at him for a flash of a second and thought she saw some question in his eyes as she turned to

Thomas and said, "Hello Thomas. Everything is getting worked on and I am doing well. I want to thank you for telling Frau Krueger about what happened to me. She is so kind and she brought me delicious food to help me out. I also heard from the University where I work. They called and checked on me soon after it happened. I just wondered how they found out so quickly. Did you tell them about it?"

Suddenly Thomas was in a hurry. He took a step or two, and then answered as he moved on. "No. I only told Frau Krueger. I do not know how the University found out."

She stored that information and hoped Georg didn't object to the intrusion of Thomas into their time together.

At Frau Krueger's door they stopped and handed her the prescription. She was grateful, told them both thank you, but decided not to engage them in further conversation. She knew this was their last evening together before Georg had to return home and she wanted it to be special. She had high hopes for them.

When they finally got into her apartment, Ana headed straight for the kitchen, opened the tiny refrigerator and removed an elegant bottle of wine, a local Riesling. Without asking him, she fixed two glasses and put one in his hand. He'd silently watched her the entire time.

"This is a toast to you Georg. You came all the way from Bavaria and you helped to make my life good, helped me to come to terms with the losses I have received. I do not have any idea what to say that can tell you how much you being here has meant to me." She lifted her glass to salute him and drank a hearty sip.

He also drank to honor her toast. He was gratified by the intensity of her words and felt his heart accelerate. "Ana, I wish everything will be made right for you. I wish the best for you always." He placed his glass carefully on the table, and moved slowly toward her.

She put her glass down and moved toward him at the same time and when body touched body, passion exploded. Close just wasn't close enough, they must become one.

Suddenly he dropped his arms from around her and stepped back. Breathlessly he gasped, "Sweet Ana, I do not want to stop but I must. I must protect you from me."

She was shocked, hurt. "But Georg, do you not want me as much as I want you? How are you a danger to me?"

"I believe that I want you even more than you can imagine." He grabbed his glass and took a large swallow. "But I think I need to back away and give you time to find out things about your family, about your connection to my country. I do not understand what this is really about, but something is going on. When you figure out your past, your unknown relatives, and if you want me, then I stand with open arms. I will always want you."

He grabbed his jacket and started for the door.

"Wait Georg! What are you saying? What has my family got to do with us? I want to be with you but are you trying to tell me you do not want to be with me?"

"No Ana! I want you. I want to hold you and care for you but it is clear that you need to find out who you are first. I will miss you so much. Oh please come to Bavaria and visit me. I need you and want you and I know the perfect place for you to stay and I know how much you will love it there. This is so difficult! I must go, must leave you alone and let you find out what you need to know."

"Georg I do not know what you are talking about. Please know that I care for you." She held both hands out toward him and he came back and clasped them, then held her tightly one more time.

"I will be waiting to hear from you my Ana." Then he rushed out the door.

Chapter Thirty-Nine

Tragedy
Heidelberg – Ana – 1971

Thomas had a fun Friday night. He and his group of friends met up at a local bar, popular with the young college crowd. It was located near the University, served good food, and the drinks were priced reasonably.

After several hours of partying they were all in good spirits and absolutely ready for what happened there late that evening.

A group of eight or nine men, identifiable as Scottish by their accents and the kilts they all wore, were drinking and celebrating at a large table in the front section of the bar. Thomas and his friends were seated further back and had enjoyed listening and watching the Scotts the entire evening. From conversation they'd overheard, it was evident that the young Scottish men had come to Germany to compete in a rugby match, and from everything they talked about and the obvious happy attitudes they all had, they were the winners.

The Scotts continued to drink steadily and the more they drank, the more friendly and talkative they became. Later in the evening, one of them even came over to Thomas and his friends and asked if he could join them at their table. They were all happy to have him join in and after everybody talked, the Scottish man, beside Thomas, asked him if he was a local. Thomas answered that he'd grown up only a short distance away, so yes, he considered himself a local. The whole group bonded in a friendly way.

As they talked and drank some more, two members of the Scottish team looked out the large front bar window and spotted three young women, all dressed up like princesses. They wore long dresses and veils and pranced by on the sidewalk in front of the bar, laughing, looking in the window, obviously hoping to attract some attention from the bar patrons.

It worked. As they smiled and waved, the invitation to come out and join them was accepted by two of the Scottish men. They ran out the front door.

Lots of loud talking and laughing started up between the two men and the women. From inside, exact words couldn't be distinguished, but from what could be seen, from the moves made by the two Scottish men, the gist of the conversation was totally understandable. No words were necessary.

The girls asked a question and laughed loudly while they waited for a response from the two Scottish men. All at once, the two men turned around, their backs facing the large glass bar windows, then bent over, pulled up their kilts, and flashed their bare behinds. Indeed, their behinds were bare.

Everyone inside that saw what happened laughed uncontrollably, and in everyone's mind the question that the women asked was answered without a doubt.

The whole bar was on fire with laughter and the party continued.

When Thomas and his friends finally left, they could definitely not be considered sober, were all instead inebriated, young, and happy. Also, they were accustomed to this type of night out and all were walking home, so no danger from driving was present. They simply continued their fun as they walked along together, separating and saying goodbye only when they got close to wherever they lived.

When the group passed the courtyard beside the Old Bridge, they all said drunken goodbyes to Thomas. His way home was different from theirs because his apartment was the only one on the other side of the river. They laughed and sang and continued on.

Thomas walked onto the bridge and began his unsteady journey across to the other side. It was extremely late and although he didn't realize it, he was alone on the bridge.

As he trudged up the slightly raised mid-point that featured a large historical statue and an observation site, he was grabbed roughly from behind. A large man spun him around and threw him down onto the hard brick floor of the bridge. Thomas couldn't even realize or understand what happened, why he lay with his face crunched and painful against bricks. The attack came in a flash, out of the blackness of the night, and he was too intoxicated to fight against it.

The attacker knew his name. "Thomas, if you want to live you must tell me why you are following Professor Ana Winchester." As the man spoke these words, he sat on Thomas's back, added his weight to increase the pain. Again he asked. "Thomas who are you working for and why are you following Professor Ana Winchester?"

Although Thomas was helpless, not in total control of his mind or his body, he recognized death when he felt the pressure of his attacker. He tried to answer, spoke, slurred and slowly, "I do not follow Professor Winchester. I do not work for anyone. She is my friend and has some hard troubles. I only try to help her when I can."

One more time the attacker tried to get information. "If you do not tell me the truth right now, you will die."

Again Thomas answered, "I do not understand what you are talking about. Please do not hurt me. I do not know what you want from me."

The attacker lost patience, realized that if he did not act soon someone could come onto the bridge and see what was happing. He made a quick decision. At once, he grabbed a gun from his pocket and slammed it into Thomas's head. Thomas went limp. Then the man dragged him over to the edge of the bridge and used all his strength to throw the limp body off into the river.

Thomas hit the Neckar River and his body floated briefly.

The attacker spun around, then casually walked back into the city and disappeared.

Chapter Forty

Family Found
Heidelberg – Ana -1971

Before she left for work the next day her telephone rang again. This time it was Andrew. "Listen, we need to get together as soon as possible. I've got to talk to you. Can you possibly meet me up on the Philosophenweg (Philosopher's Way) today? It would be good if we can meet up and then find a people-free place so we can talk. There's a lot going on and this is serious!"

She answered instantly. "I'll meet you there at 3:30 this afternoon. That's as fast as I can get there from work. We'll just happen to accidently bump into each other while we're out walking."

After class she hurried out onto the street beside her apartment, followed it a little way, then climbed up the pathway designed to reach the Philosopher's Way. The popular walking path provided an incredible view of the Neckar River below it and of the City of Heidelberg, including the Castle, to all who walked along it.

With no true directional plan, she simply entered the walk and decided to turn to the right. Only a short distance down, she looked up and saw Andrew approaching from the opposite direction.

They came together and called out, "Hello. How are you? Haven't seen you in a while."

Then Andrew turned around and they began to walk together in the direction that Ana had been walking. For a short while they engaged in only surface conversation like what was happening and how their jobs were going. Soon enough they saw a garden off to the side of the path and it was empty. It also had a single bench. Perfect. They went over and sat down together.

"Have you heard about Thomas?" This question came out fast and as he spoke he reached out to steady her.

"What are you talking about? What about Thomas?" Fear filled her face.

"He was attacked last night on the Old Bridge after he left his friends. They'd all spent the evening together in downtown Heidelberg. Someone knocked him down, smashed him in the head, then dumped him off the bridge into the river."

He watched her body freeze, her face blank, no emotion identifiable. One whisper came out of her mouth. "Tell me he's okay."

"At this moment he's still alive but he's unconscious. He's in the hospital but the doctors don't know yet if he'll make it. If it hadn't been for the fact that a small fishing boat with two men happened to be underneath the bridge when Thomas was thrown into the water, he'd be dead already. They were able to pull him into their boat, then rush to shore and call for help."

Now streams of tears flowed from her eyes, but she continued to stare blankly at the trees surrounding them.

He continued. "His parents were called and are with him at the hospital. We've already met with them and explained a little about what appears to be happening, the small amount of information that we have and Thomas's part in it. They've agreed to allow the police to report officially that Thomas is dead so we can make sure that whoever tried to kill him won't try it again."

Abruptly he reached out and placed his arms around her. She was in deep pain. "I know you liked him a lot and I wish we could do something to help him, wish we knew who did this. Thankfully, the fishermen were underneath the bridge at the right place and the right time. They even heard a little of what happened. They told the police that a man's voice asked about a Professor and why Thomas was following her. They couldn't hear everything, didn't have all the details, but from what they did hear, we believe that the man who attacked Thomas wanted to know why he was following you."

Her tears didn't stop. Thomas had only ever meant to be kind to her, no matter what else was going on. She felt that it was her fault he'd been attacked. Why were the people she loved being killed and hurt?

They sat still together. It wasn't possible for her to act normal. Her mind was in chaos as she attacked herself.

Finally Andrew spoke again, "Ana, we've got to get to the bottom of this. So far our people haven't found much helpful information. We did research the history of the house where you live now, the place Mr. Elden was so insistent that you rent. The German authorities obtained the name of the family who owned it. They'd lived there for a long time, even during

World War II."

This time she looked intently at him. Tears still ran down her cheeks but she asked, "What was the family name?"

"The family name was Haupt. They lived in Heidelberg for a long time and were part of its history, helped it develop and become what it is today. We also found out from the German authorities that the owners moved away to live in another home they owned in a different part of Germany, a country home. They moved away to try to escape the intensity of the war. They left their home in Heidelberg in the hands of their daughter and her little girl, their only grandchild. When they finally were able to come back to Heidelberg after the war ended, they found out that their daughter had died and that their granddaughter had disappeared. They spent a lot of time and effort to find her but finally had to give up hope that she was still alive. Later, when Mr. Haupt died of a heart attack, his wife changed her will, because they'd lost all their family, and left all the property to a young man that they'd adopted after they left Heidelberg. His parents both died during the war and he had nobody to look out for him so they made him a part of their family. His name is Georg Schiller."

The world stood still. She could feel the movements of the wind in the trees, the sound of the leaves as they fell to the earth. For a few moments she simply went with the flow of nature, but her mind interrupted her heart. "I feel that family, feel a connection. Did you just tell me that Georg is the heir, inherited everything that belonged to the Haupts?"

"Yes. Georg is now the owner of all the assets left behind by the Haupts. But I honestly think you're part of that family too. That's possibly why Mr. Elden wanted you in this house so badly. I checked the records again and found the date your mother and father got married and it could work, but a big problem is that we still can't verify your mother's family name. The name she wrote down doesn't match the Haupt family records."

"I need to think through this Andrew. Mother didn't tell me anything, like I told you. I'm still in the dark."

"Do you think, like I do, that this family could possibly be part of you and that's why Mr. Elden wanted you to live there so badly?"

"Yes, but he's a mystery to me. I loved him and he took care of me but I can't think why anyone would murder him. I still can't believe he might have been an SS officer in the war. I'm feeling crazy, can't understand this puzzle."

"It's complicated. One more time I'm asking you, is there anything you know that could help us out here?"

It was time for more truth. "I need to admit something to you. I kept it secret because I wanted to get to the truth first, protect my mother's reputation if I needed to. Right before I moved to Germany, I found my mother's diary. It only had a few entries, but she wrote about being a nurse, taking care of wounded soldiers, and then about something bad that happened. She described how she tried to save a man and then some SS Officers came to the hospital and questioned her to see if the man told her anything. She denied that he had. Then in her private way, she wrote that if someone she loved was ever reading her words, she really did get information from the man. She said that he whispered the name on a certain tombstone in St. Michaels Cemetery in Salzburg. She said if money was needed whoever was reading her words should go to the grave."

Somehow he knew she'd been holding back information, knew she'd been raised to keep all the family skeletons hidden in the closet. "She wrote down the name that was on the grave?" He waited.

"Yes. Plus, there's more. When I was in Salzburg I was followed and someone even broke into my hotel room. I pretended to be a tourist and I think that I managed to convince whoever was following me that I was in Salzburg only for job-related reasons. I'd wanted to go to the grave because I honestly felt that if there had been any treasure hidden there, the Nazis would surely have recovered it long, long ago. I don't know how I could have known if it was there or not, I just needed to go and see the grave for myself because why in this world are they interested in me? They don't need me to lead them to the treasure grave do they?"

"This is more dangerous than you accept and I can't believe you didn't tell me all of this. Right now, you listen to me. You've got to be careful! Do you understand how deep and dangerous this is now? Your life is in severe danger."

He stopped talking and tried to get his mind around everything he'd just learned. "I think we may be able to get to the bottom of this. But to do so, you'd need to agree to go back to Salzburg, to the grave. It would definitely be dangerous for you but at least we'd all be with you, around you, protecting you. You seem to ignore danger to yourself. You secretly pursue your mission without asking for our help. Based on the fact that you don't seem to consider danger a problem, would you be interested in working directly with us to bring this whole thing to an end?"

"Honestly, right now, all I care about is getting all these questions answered. Instead of hiding my life, I want to live it. I don't want to worry about the past anymore. BUT, I have one thing that means a lot to me and I think that I'm going to ask you to give me a little time to sort this out. I've got to follow up with Georg, find out if he's trying to use me or to love me. Will you give me enough time for that?"

"This is too hard, too dangerous to put pressure on you. You get your priorities in order. I just want to get you to promise that you'll be careful at all times. You know that the unknown men are going to be watching your every step. It's also possible that Georg could be part of it. Tell me that you understand me and promise not to put your heart before your head."

"I'll try to be careful. I just know that I have to go see him and find out how he's connected to this whole thing. I've got to understand my connection to Georg."

Chapter Forty-One

A Haunted Nurse
Salzburg – Ingrid – 1944

The City of Salzburg, Austria came to life in the year 69AD, when it was built upon the almost non-existent remains of a former Roman city that had not prospered, but had in fact disappeared almost entirely. The location received the possibility of rebirth. This second chance at life was the result of a wandering Franconian Bishop named Rupert who, in looking for the perfect location to found his dream of St. Peter's Monastery, accidently came upon a beautiful spot beside the Salsach River. Salzburg was born.

Rupert's choice proved a good one for the new City of Salzburg, which grew and prospered, and also for Rupert, later named a Saint by the Holy Roman Church.

Salzburg grew quickly in its capacity as a religious center, becoming known over the ensuring years as the "Rome of the North." It also developed a sturdy business community. The accumulation of religion and people and business and money funded an extremely important and creative culture of art and music, with world famous composer Mozart being born in the city in 1756, along with many other famous musician and artists.

The structure of the city grew as well, as it sprouted row upon row of tall buildings, all perched beside the narrow, crooked, cobblestone streets. These streets wandered outward from the original settlement, connecting the courtyards, lovely baroque buildings, important churches, universities, businesses, and homes of the people who helped the city to grow.

By the year 1938, Salzburg was a popular and important center of culture in Europe. It was vibrant, filled with music, dance and art. Wealth had also found a home in the city for generations, and it was, indeed, a lovely place to be alive.

However, in that year, in March 1938, the Anschluss occurred. On that date, Austria was occupied and annexed by Nazi Germany, and it officially became a part of the Third Reich. Things changed.

Hauntingly, even after six years of war, the Nazi occupation and rule, it was still possible to walk through the closely built streets of Salzburg, appreciate the amazing Baroque architecture of the city, and imagine life as it had been prior to the war. Many of the buildings were still intact, having escaped the Allied bombing of some parts of the city. These buildings wore their original paint, the yellows, blues, pinks, now faded and worn, a testament to past prosperity, and in an unspoken way, to a still existent hope for the future.

The heart of Salzburg remained intact, though much of its life and vitality had been slowly, systematically, strangled by the war.

In Salzburg, on a night in the year 1944, a young nurse made her rounds in a military hospital. The hospital had existed prior to the Anschluss, when its purpose in life had been to provide care to patients of pre-war Salzburg. The hospital building itself had begun life as an important concert hall, built between the business district and the beginning of the residential area of the Old Town. The concert hall was built in a very grand and elegant style, and the enterprising Doctor who had converted it into use as his private hospital recognized the value of the elegant and lush surrounding for pleasing some of his more wealthy patients. It had been a prized and lucrative hospital in the midst of the rich city. Now it served other patients.

Immediately after the occupation of Salzburg, the German Army commandeered the hospital. Originally they used it as part of the Nazi-administered and ruled Salzburg-Maxglan Prison Camp, but the Nazis decided that no prisoners of that camp needed their medical help. As the war progressed and harsh battles began to produce many wounded German soldiers, the hospital was turned into one for military use.

Two rows of hospital beds marched evenly along either side of a long drab room. Most of the beds were filled. The young nurse was alone, in charge of all the hopelessness and heartbreak of the injured men lying in the ward. Alone with all this responsibility, she continued to make her rounds with purpose, stopped at each bed, attempted to push back the inevitable. She refused to give up, to stop trying to help. Her youth and vitality contrasted starkly with the near lifelessness of the patients.

The room held no color, cheer, or hope. She represented the only piece of positive energy. Young, barely looking old enough to be in the midst of such tragedy, she was, simply said, beautiful. In her life before the war and all the hurt and pain it caused, most people who saw her would immediately comment on her beautiful blue eyes and her friendly smile. The war and her life in it had caused the sparkle to leave her eyes, the smile to be almost non-existent on her lips, but it could not take away the love and care she felt for others, nor her never-ending efforts to help. Her starched nurse's uniform, required by the Nazis, was a white exclamation mark, worn in her attempt to fight against terrible odds. Her golden blonde hair was neatly coiled and pinned, hidden underneath her nurse's cap. She was calm, capable, and hardworking. Quiet and sad, she still unknowingly provided brief pleasure to those who were around her.

The men now lying in the drab hospital were, for the most part, not likely to survive. As the war drew closer to an end, some things, some people, became unimportant to those persons still holding fanatically onto power. The hospital, the soldiers, the young nurse, all sat unknowingly, helplessly, at the crossroads of intrigue on this particular evening. The power players had decided to grab anything of value, knowing already that the war was lost.

Earlier that evening, before she'd reported for duty at the hospital, the young nurse walked briskly to her job. She'd left her lodgings and stepped out into the street, her work satchel held close against her side as she pulled the front door securely behind her.

Thoughts marched relentlessly through her head as she walked down the narrow street that led from her boarding house to the hospital. She saw ghosts. She felt ghosts. The feather-soft touch of them brushed against her skin as they rushed to get to the next opera, rushed to work, rushed home from work. These ghosts were the remnants of the people who'd once lived so securely in this very street she walked on. She felt like a trespasser. The despair of Salzburg, the despair of the war, all had seeped into her soul.

Deep shadows filled the streets and the tall structure of the houses on both sides barely allowed even a glimpse of the sky. All that she could see above her head was darkness. The cloud-filled sky felt heavy. No stars were visible. The houses were dark too. No lamplight peeked through the curtains, no music spilled from the windows.

She hurried through the sad, gloomy street toward the hospital, deliberately telling herself that the presence of the nearly lost is preferable to that of the already lost.

At last she reached the hospital and entered through the main front entrance by pushing strongly against the heavy doors there. Everything was routine, normal, until the on duty nurse gathered her things together, packed her satchel, and said to her, "We have a full patient load tonight and unfortunately, I have already spoken to the other nurse who is scheduled to be on duty with you tonight. She is sick, has come down with a terrible cold and high fever and would be of no use at work here tonight. Meanwhile, you'll just have to work by yourself tonight. If you run into anything you can't handle, please send for the doctor at this address." Then she handed Ingrid a slip of paper with the information written on it.

Dismayed and disbelieving, Ingrid answered back, "I can't be expected to look after all these patients by myself! Surely, someone else must be available to come and help me."

"Sorry." The on duty nurse shouldered her satchel and made for the heavy front door. "Looks like you will just have to do the best that you can tonight." Without a backward glance she rushed out the door.

Astonished, alone, Ingrid wondered how she would be able to send for the doctor's help if she did need it. There wasn't anybody to send, she was alone. Totally discouraged, she walked slowly behind the nurse station desk and picked up the patient chart. With a deep breath she decided to start at the beginning and read the charts, see which of the patients needed her care the most.

It felt like the night zoomed by as she tried to do everything for everyone. About midnight, as she took a sip of cold coffee, the front door burst open and ushered in a blast of damp wind along with three cold, wet soldiers.

"We have a wounded soldier here. Where do you want us to put him?" asked a young soldier who wore the uniform of the German army. He didn't wait for an answer as he and his comrade dumped the unconscious third soldier they were carrying onto an examining table that sat near the front of the room.

Ingrid ran over to the unconscious soldier and said, "That will work nicely. Please leave him there, but tell me any information you have regarding his injuries. That will enable us to help him more quickly."

The two soldiers glanced at each other, shook their head, and claimed no knowledge of the soldier. They explained that they'd found him in this condition in the cemetery just a short time ago.

Before she could press for more information, the younger looking soldier blurted out, "The other soldier we found beside him was shot in the head. He was dead but this soldier is still alive. Maybe he caught a glancing shot in the head. That's all we know."

The two soldiers headed for the front door and without looking back, the older looking one said, "Maybe the SS will be by to check on this man since both the man who got shot dead and this man are SS officers."

The front door closed and Ingrid focused on the wounded man. She started to work on him quickly and realized right away that the bullet to his head would most probably prove fatal. She grabbed the doctor's address from her pocket, then realized that she should have sent one of the soldiers to get him. That was not possible now. The soldier's breathing was shallow and he remained unconscious, near death she was sure.

She gently cleaned the wound on his head, softly bathed his face. He stirred. All at once he spoke soft words. "Listen, must listen. Please, name of grave is Larson. Treasure name."

"Please, you must be quiet and save your strength. You've been shot and now I need to get the doctor here so he can help you. Maybe he can save you. Please be still until I return."

She dashed to the door then realized that she couldn't leave the hospital and all the wounded men alone. Deep sadness flooded through her as she recognized that it was impossible to get help for the dying man.

The only help she could give was to talk softly to him and tell him he wasn't alone. There was nothing else she could do. In less than a minute more he was gone.

She forced herself to get busy and cleaned his body, and then rolled it, still on the mobile examining table, into the back room that was used for dead bodies. The entire time she worked, his words ran through her mind. She tried to forget what he said, it wasn't important. Was it? Why would he want to tell her the name of a dead man? The name became etched permanently into her mind.

Streaks of dawn light filtered into the hospital windows and she looked at the clock. The tired young nurse realized that the long night shift was almost over. She felt exhausted and wanted to sleep, but once again the front door burst open wide.

This time, two SS officers entered and stood in front of her desk. Her world tilted dangerously, she lost balance, felt like she was slipping away. The senior officer looked at her for a long time before he spoke.

Eyes from the past found her own. "I need to talk to the doctor on duty here tonight. Please tell him that I must speak with him immediately."

Words were hard, didn't want to exit her mouth. "There is no doctor on duty here tonight."

Shock and displeasure showed momentarily on the senior officer's face. "Do you expect me to believe that you were on duty here, in this hospital, all by yourself last night?"

"I had no other choice. When I came on duty, the nurse here told me the scheduled nurse for the night shift was sick and that the Doctor didn't feel it was necessary for him to be here all night. That left me no choice. Yes, I was on duty by myself last night."

She'd been working on last night's paperwork when the SS officers came in and the senior officer intentionally looked down at what she was recording. He said, "Then the person I need to speak to is you."

Silence hung heavy in the air. When she didn't respond to him, the senior officer continued, "Did you receive any wounded soldiers last night or early this morning?"

Nervously, she answered, "Yes. One man was brought in with a gunshot wound to his head." She shuffled the papers and slipped them together as she spoke. "The wounded soldier was left here by two soldiers who brought him in and he died shortly after they left him. I wanted to go for the doctor but I was alone and had no one to send."

His order to her was, "I need to see the body at once."

Afraid to do anything but obey his order, Ingrid moved out from behind the desk and started walking toward the back of the ward.

"Where do you think you're going?" The younger officer called out and moved forward quickly, roughly grabbed her arm and jerked her still.

"Let me go! You asked to see the body and I'm trying to show it to you. We always move the deceased into the hall behind this ward. We don't leave the dead here among the living." Ingrid jerked her arm away from the officer and started off again toward the back of the wardroom. This time both officers let her continue but were only a few steps behind her the whole time.

Another heavy door, this one intricately carved and beautiful, stood closed at the end of the last row of patients. She opened it, fought briefly with its weight, and then entered the long corridor it opened into. She felt so weak and tried desperately to gain control of herself. Her heart pounded loudly and her breath came in silent uneven gasps.

As soon as she got into the hallway she leaned against the wall. Danger was present she knew, but she refused to give into it. She reached deep inside herself, and managed a defiant push against the wall. She stood up straight and continued forward. Her soft shoes made no sound at all in the oppressive silence.

Only a few more steps brought her to the small room on the right that was used for the dead. Before she could enter, the junior SS officer pushed past her. She decided to stand still as the officer in charge followed his subordinate into the room.

They pulled down the sheet that rested on top of the body and exposed the lifeless body of the man who had whispered his last thoughts to Ingrid not so long ago. They searched through all his pockets and then they turned away from the dead man and both looked at her with questions in their eyes.

The younger officer asked, "Was this man conscious when he was brought here? Did he say anything or did he give you anything? Did you find any papers on his body?" All these questions were asked imperiously, with the expectation of an immediate answer.

She whispered, "The soldier was unconscious when he was brought in and I attempted to help. I did the best I could, but the patient died without ever opening his eyes or saying a word and I didn't find any papers with him."

As she got quiet, the senior SS officer ordered his subordinate to leave, told him to go out front and wait.

She was alone in the room with the senior SS officer and he came toward her, got extremely close. He towered above her when he calmly asked, "Do you really expect me to believe you when you tell me he never regained consciousness?"

He took hold of her arm and pressed her back against the closed door, used his large body to push her hard against it. His strength and his heat pushed against her. The SS officer looked at her for another long moment, watched her eyes. Harder and harder he pressed into her thin body and then in a whisper, with his lips up against hers, "I'll always know if you're telling me the truth."

He backed up and she collapsed slowly onto the floor. He held onto her body until she was down on the floor, then he released her. She watched him, helpless and afraid.

He walked out into the hallway then turned back and said, "I'm watching you and I will always be watching you."

Chapter Forty-Two

Follow Them Instead
Heidelberg – Ana – 1971

A few nights went by and her sleep was constantly troubled with chaotic dreams. All centered on Thomas, who still lay in the hospital with his short life now at death's door. She needed to talk to him, tell him how much she liked and appreciated him, and how much she desperately wanted him to recover and to live a full and happy life.

Perhaps lack of sleep contributed to what she attempted to do on the fourth day after she learned of the attempt to murder him.

Up that entire night, she forced herself out of bed, got dressed, and drank a large cup of coffee. The caffeine sent her straight down to Frau Krueger's front door and she knocked a few times, even though it wasn't even 7:00 AM yet.

Frau Krueger opened the door, still in her housecoat, and had a surprised look on her face. "Ana is something wrong?" Her voice reflected her concern.

Ana faked her reply without even thinking it through, just knew she couldn't share the truth about Thomas yet. Too much danger was still possible. "Yes, you can help me I think. I just learned that one of my university students broke a leg yesterday and I want to go and visit her, want to let her know that I am concerned. Could you tell me the names of any hospitals that accept emergency cases? When I was told what happened, I got upset and didn't think to ask which hospital she was in."

Frau Krueger's face showed both concern and confusion. "Oh I am not really sure. Did she break her leg close to our area or somewhere in the Old Town?"

Ana's response was quick, "It was close to us, happened on the Old

215

Bridge. They said drinking was involved and then she fell and broke her leg."

"I am not sure but I believe the emergency vehicle would have taken her to the nearest hospital, which is the Krankenhaus Salem. It is not too far from here, just a little to the west. It is located on the Zeppelinstrasse." She reached out and touched her arm. "My friend, are you alright? You look tired, can I help?"

Spontaneously, warmly, she hugged Frau Kreuger. "Please do not worry. I am tired but I am all right. Thank you for your help about the hospital. I am on my way there right now."

She walked down the stairs and then down the street to the nearest bus stop. Right or wrong, she had to see Thomas. Even if he couldn't hear her, she still needed to tell him how sorry she was, to apologize for her being the cause of this happening to him.

Frau Krueger was right when she said that the Salem Hospital was near their home. The bus ride was quick and Ana got off at the corner of the block, then walked swiftly down the sidewalk and turned left on the next street. The hospital was large and filled up most of that next block.

As she walked toward it, she studied it intently and then shock raced through her as she realized that she could again bring danger to Thomas. The horrible person or people that hurt him now thought that he was dead. How could she not remember that they always followed her? And now here she was, on her way to the hospital to see the supposed-to-be-dead Thomas. She walked to a bench underneath some trees and sank down.

Angry with herself, she couldn't believe that she didn't think before she came out. It would be impossible to go into the hospital and ask for his room number because the police were telling everyone that he was dead in order to protect him.

The hurt and the anger were too much, and she simply leaned forward and cried, her head balanced on her knees.

A nearby voice called out to her, "Do you need help?"

Afraid, she took her hands slowly from her wet eyes and saw a young policeman only a short distance away. His bicycle was balanced in his hands while he looked at her. He saw someone who needed help.

She improvised again. "I am sorry, sir. I just received bad news about a friend of mine and I was simply overcome with grief. Thank you for checking on me but please continue your duty. I am not in need of help."

He nodded and got back onto his bicycle without asking anything else. She sat still and watched him disappear around the corner.

Her thought was that she was hurting Thomas instead of helping him. She got up slowly from the bench and followed the street back to the bus stop. In about fifteen minutes she was well on her way from the hospital. She'd taken the wrong bus. The one she was on proceeded straight across the Necker River and into the busy Bismark Platz. All at once, she decided to get off but it was too late, the doors were already closing. The bus went forward again.

She rode through several more stops, and then randomly pushed the red "stop" button. When she climbed off, she stood still for a few seconds, and then walked down a small street that paralleled the main one on which the bus rode along.

Eventually, she found herself entering the Hauptstrasse. She loved this street and walked along slowly with a quiet expression on her face. No smile was present, but also no frown appeared. She was deeply immersed in emotion.

This street always brought up memories from her past. It was a main part of her time as a university student in Heidelberg and held memories of grocery shopping, eating out, and sometimes fun with friends.

Now recent memories took over. She thought of the fun she'd had here recently with Sam and Maggie. She needed them.

One particular shop caught her attention. It was a bookstore, specialized only in antique books of all descriptions. She crossed the street and went in.

From shelf to shelf, she allowed herself time to move through all the categories, to search for any book that snagged her interest. The total concentration she exercised pushed her pain back a little. She lingered in the store a long time.

After she made herself leave, she went straight over to a clothing store, and then from there over to her favorite small grocery store. More time passed.

The end of the long street was getting close and the need to go to the courtyard that fronted the small hotel where she'd stayed on her first night ever in Germany slid into her mind. Her steps veered off to the left and she walked toward the restaurant that existed there.

The restaurant was busy, most of the tables filled with people, but she found a small table off to one side and sat down, almost hidden by the large crowd engaged in food and conversation.

Memories came again, specifically the first time she'd eaten at this restaurant. She'd thoroughly enjoyed the experience, but as that good thought flowed she was forced to remember the cruel night that happened at the hotel next door. That night, when she was so young, alone, and frightened by the voices in the room close to hers, by the harsh voice of the man and the crying of the woman.

A server approached the table and asked for her order. Without even thinking, without even caring whether she spoke in English or in German, she answered him and ordered food and wine.

While she waited for her dinner, she watched the patrons enjoy their evening and realized that she didn't care anymore. She didn't need or want to pretend anymore. She'd spent her life trying to be loved by her family, attempting to overcome the cruelty of her Grandpa and the unconcern of her father. She'd grown up confused, tried to pretend she wasn't German-connected like her mother wanted, tried not to think about the facts hidden from her, and never was able to feel secure about who she was. That was over.

The friendly conversation all around the courtyard saturated the air but entangled in that mixed sound of happy voices, suddenly she heard one particular voice, almost completely disguised by the others, and it grabbed her attention.

While she listened for it, she looked around carefully. That's when she saw him, the man from this very hotel who, on her first night here, had spoken so cruelly to the lady in his room. The same man that she'd seen with the lady the following morning, acting as though nothing bad had happened the night before.

He was finished with his meal, paid his server and got up to leave. The lady at the table with him was the same one who'd accompanied him all those years ago. They walked off and turned into the side street, moved toward the Old Bridge as they had before. This time there was a big difference. They had aged.

Ana signaled the server, paid her bill and left her table, following the man and the woman. It was obvious that they'd not seen her and had no idea she'd seen them. This time she was in control. This time she was the watcher.

At that moment, a small tour group walked past her and she took advantage of it, just as she'd done in Salzburg. She blended in behind the group and was shielded from view, just in case the man or woman decided to look backwards.

The tour group hid her all the way across the Old Bridge, then they turned right and that was the same direction the man and woman had walked. How interesting and how lucky, she thought, and kept moving forward.

It was a pleasant day for a tour group to be out. All the trees and bushes were lush and the river smooth, with ducks that sat in the calm water beside the walking path. One of the ducks quacked at her when she walked past, but she just smiled back at it and continued her mission.

Unfortunately, the tour group left the path when they came up to the next bridge that crossed back over the Neckar River. That left her out in the open. She slowed down and attempted to move forward by hiding behind any available bush or tree she could get to. She just hoped they didn't decide to look back.

The couple kept moving ahead. As Ana watched them, she saw tiny dark shadows moving around the edges of the mean man's body. She was too far away to identify what she saw and she even rubbed her eyes and wondered once more what was happening. It doesn't matter what it is, she thought, just keep them in sight.

They walked for almost two more miles. The river path led them into the outlying area of Heidelberg, to a small village that had been in existence for a long time. She saw them leave the path and walk into the small town and decided to play it safe and let them go.

She knew without doubt that they lived in this small town. She just needed to see if there was any way to identify them. They were part of the watchers she'd felt and seen over the years. They were a part of the mystery.

She needed to tell Andrew and let the government use their power to find out who these two people were.

The walk back home felt short. She was even a little surprised when she found herself at the curve in the street opposite the entrance to her apartment.

She checked for traffic, crossed the street and walked underneath the archway. The fountain in the center of the courtyard caught her eye, as it usually did, and instead of going straight up to her apartment, she found herself walking over to it. From its appearance, it was evidently original to the house and at this point in time, although it was well cared for, no water was supplied to it. It sat silent and unused.

Gently she reached out to touch the birds that sat on the fountainheads and imagined how lovely they must have been when it worked. Some forgotten thought, some old memory wiggled forward. She remembered hearing her mother ask her father if it was possible for them to get a fountain in the front yard of their new home, the one father built after grandpa's house burned down and grandpa died.

Father's answer had come forth in a voice with the same harshness that Grandpa's always held when he talked to his granddaughter. "What are you thinking? People here in Andrews don't build fountains in their front yards. This isn't Germany!"

She stood still and tried to pull more of the hazy memory out of the past but it dimmed instead of brightened.

Out loud she softly asked, "Mama, did you really say that? Are you connected to this fountain or am I making this up?"

The only response she received was a light gust of wind that drifted across the courtyard from the river. The wind was mild, warm, and softly caressed her face.

Later that night she called Sam. They talked about the farm, and the repairs, and about their lives. Then she asked him the question she needed him to answer. "Sam, do you ever worry about being a Cherokee anymore? Do people still disrespect you or cause you pain?"

He didn't hesitate. "I've found out I don't need to pretend to be anyone other than myself. I am who I am, and I'm happy. Maggie loves me and my life is good. I don't worry about that stuff anymore, I just live my life."

That's what she needed to hear.

Chapter Forty-Three

To Bavaria
Sankt Englmar – Ana – 1971

This time she didn't wait to share the information she'd discovered. She called Andrew immediately and told him about the man and woman she'd followed to the small town outside of Heidelberg. He was excited, energized, and promised to start work on the identification of the two at once. She also told him that she was going to take time off and visit Bavaria, and was going to see Georg. She was open with him about that also, even told him that Georg wasn't aware that she was coming. She said that she hadn't told him yet because she wanted to get there and settle in at the Bed and Breakfast where she would stay. She'd already made reservations.

The Pension Hill-Top was the name of the bed and breakfast she'd decided on and it was located in a Bavarian Mountain town called Sankt Englmar. Frau Krueger had recommended it when she'd told her about the trip she was taking and had explained that Georg thought highly of that specific bed and breakfast because it offered good rooms and good food.

As she explained everything to him, Andrew listened to her carefully. When she paused, he didn't respond for a few seconds, and when he did respond, his voice was tight. He told her once again that she needed to be extremely careful. Then he hesitated like he had more to say, but instead, simply wished her a happy vacation.

Ana thought she might know what his hesitation meant. He was already planning who to send and how to take care of her in the new place and the new situation. She let it go. Her top priority was to finally re-connect with Georg, try to determine if his feelings were true or if something else, some other motive, was involved.

She made one more call the day before she left for Bavaria. She called Sam and Maggie and told them that all was well. She also checked to make sure she didn't need to do anything to accomplish the repairs on the farm. At the end of their friendly conversation, she casually mentioned to Maggie that she was leaving the following morning to go to Bavaria.

Maggie understood at once. "Ana, you're finally going to get with Georg?"

Her voice contained hope when she answered Maggie. "I'm going because I want to spend some time with him and find out if it's just me he wants, or if there's something else he wants more. I'm done with mystery. I want truth, but I hope my heart doesn't get broken."

"Ana, I feel the need to be there with you. Sam and I, we're so worried about you. Is it safe for you to go to Bavaria by yourself?"

"Maggie, I've already told Andrew that I'm going and he didn't offer any objections, just told me to be careful."

The trip from Heidelberg over to Sankt Englmar took up most of the next day as she rode a train to a city in Bavaria called Plattling. After she got off the train, she asked for information at the station and managed to catch a bus that was almost ready to leave.

The train ride into Bavaria from Heidelberg provided her a good opportunity to appreciate the now-close Bavarian Mountains. They'd appeared in the distance, high and green, as the train got closer to its destination. Now the bus she was on moved swiftly up, climbed higher and higher, and gave her more personal views of all the well-tended land. Fields of grain and large, neat meadows were everywhere. She saw many animals, including goats, deer, and horses. Farmhouses generally sat well back from the road, and the farms themselves were framed by nature in the guise of tall thick trees. The countryside was wonderful.

Little by little the two-lane road got even steeper and the bus curved back and forth as it randomly passed through charming, colorful villages and houses with window boxes filled with flowers.

She saw street signs that named the small roads leading off the bus route and she looked intently out and down into rolling valleys, dotted with farms. A big red brick church topped by a tall spire stood out handsomely and fit right into the road that wound past it and on through a valley. She wanted to stop the bus and get off. She wanted to explore the beauty she was seeing.

Up high in the mountains, they turned left and entered the town of Sankt Englmar. The bus stopped and let Ana plus four other people off. She went to retrieve her suitcase, and with it in hand wondered who to ask about directions to the Pension Hill-Top. She looked around and realized that the building next to her was the City Hall.

No problem, she'd get directions there. But before she could move over to the City Hall, a man appeared from around the corner. He was in a hurry, and he scanned the bus, looking at all the passengers who'd gotten off. Then the tall man's eyes found her and his face warmed up with a friendly smile.

"Excuse me, but are you Ana Winchester? I am Peter Lintz. I am here from the Hill-Top Pension to help you with your suitcase. The climb up the hill is pretty steep, and my wife knew you would be on this bus, so I came to drive you and your luggage up."

She was happily astonished. "Hello, Mr. Lintz. I am Ana Winchester and I am pleased to meet you. It is kind of you to meet me, and honestly, I did not expect you to. You are making my life easier by your help."

She held out her hand, he did too, and they shook hands. She couldn't help but return his honest smile with one of her own.

He grabbed her small suitcase and led the way to his small red car, parked at the end of the adjoining street. He put her in the front and her suitcase in the back, got in, and they drove off through the small village of Sankt Englmar.

Mostly the streets were tiny, with houses perched on the street edges, their backs crowded against the steep hill that rose directly behind them. Along the way they passed little shops, cafes, and then a gas station. The tall steep road made a definite impression as they made their way up to the pension.

She laughed out loud. "Mr. Lintz, thank you for coming to get me. I am not sure that I could have climbed up this hill with my suitcase."

He laughed along with her as he took another left and then turned quickly into the small parking lot that sided the Hill-Top Pension.

On the ride up the hill she'd been captivated by a tall three-storied building that sat at the very top of the hill. As they'd gotten closer she saw a large open grassy lawn that extended directly down the hill in front of it. On the building's second floor a long balcony ran across. Tall trees edged an open courtyard, which was actually a large balcony that sat atop pillars. It was impressive. She got happy when Mr. Lintz pulled the car into the parking lot beside it.

"Mr. Lintz, this is a wonderful building. It is beautiful and is surrounded by nature. Plus, you have planted so many beautiful flowers everywhere. I cannot wait to step out onto that balcony and enjoy the view beneath it." As she talked, she got out of the car, then she looked up at the building again, at the small road beside it, and at the continuation of the hill as it rose even higher up the heavily forested hill behind the Pension.

Mr. Lintz picked up her suitcase. "Yes, I believe the view from our balcony is good. When the sky is clear and no fog or clouds are about, you can even see the Alps from here."

Something more to anticipate, to see the Alps she thought, as she followed him and her suitcase into the heavy old back door of the Pension Hill-Top.

"Did you find her, find Ana Winchester? She told me she would take the train so that means she would need to be on the bus to get here." The voice could be heard before the speaker could be seen. From the hallway that led to the kitchen, Peter Lintz's wife Sophie suddenly stood in front of him and Ana.

He laughed and put down the suitcase. Then he said, as he turned back toward Ana, "This is my wife Sophie." He turned to Sophie, "Sophie, this is Ana Winchester."

"It is a pleasure to meet you," said Sophie.

She addressed her husband again right away. "Peter, you help her up the stairs with her suitcase and I will come too. We have three empty rooms available and I would like for Ana Winchester to choose the one that pleases her the best."

Peter led the way up the stairs. Halfway up was a small landing that included a window with a view of the forest. The second part of the stairs led up into a large hallway with rooms on both sides.

He stopped at the beginning of the hallway and waited for Ana and Sophie. After everyone was there, Sophie stepped up and took the lead. She went to the door directly at the top of the stairs, opened it, and then invited Ana to step inside.

"Please look at all three of the rooms and then decide which one you would like to stay in. They are basically the same size, but the bed arrangements are different and the color and decorations in the room are also different. Please choose the room you like best and it will be yours." She stepped back into the hallway in order to allow Ana time to look around the room.

This room was painted off-white and the curtains and bedspread were pale yellow, light orange, and lime green. The combination was bright, cheerful, and also contained everything Ana had hoped to find. The bathroom was neat and clean, and there was a large wardrobe for her clothes.

She smiled and went out into the hall. "This room is very good and I like it."

"Wonderful," answered Sophie. "But please come and look at the other two before you decide."

Ana complied and looked at one on the left side of the hallway, but it looked out on the forest and not on the "balcony view" she was interested in. The third room, three doors down, was on the balcony side, and was also lovely. It was the same size but was decorated in muted blues and soft greens. It was calm and pretty but not as happy looking as the first room she'd looked at.

She looked at Sophie, "I thank you for the choices and I believe I like the first one I looked at the best."

Sophie responded happily, "Well you go on in the room and Peter will put your suitcase in. Oh, and here is the key. Now you just go on in and get freshened up. We begin serving dinner downstairs at five o'clock. Feel free to come down when you are ready to eat and we will have a table for you. It is a pleasure to have you stay with us."

Sophie shook Ana's hand again and Peter placed her suitcase inside the door of her room. Then they left and went back downstairs. Ana sat down and realized how happy she felt to be here. She already liked Mr. and Mrs. Lintz, already thought of them as Peter and Sophie. She also loved the Pension Hill-Top and the nature-filled world that surrounded it.

It had been a long day, but when she checked her watch she realized it was later than she thought. Immediately she unpacked and moved her clothes to the wardrobe, then decided to check out the shower. It was warm and smooth and she felt refreshed. Then, on impulse, she decided to wear the "dressier outfit" that she'd packed. It was just a step up from the casual clothes she'd packed, and for some reason it felt right for this evening.

Before she left to go downstairs, she couldn't help but go out onto her balcony. It was getting dark quickly. A chair sat beside her door, so she used it and took in the view out in front of her. It wasn't completely dark yet, but lights throughout the town below were already on and resembled twinkling stars. She couldn't wait until tomorrow's light so she could get a detailed look at the town.

Her thoughts went to Georg and she closed her eyes. For a tiny moment she allowed herself to admit all the hope she had for a future with him. She opened her eyes and saw headlights climbing quickly up the road to the Hill-Top. She feared what she might learn soon, so she told herself to go down and eat, stay in the present.

As she started down the stairs, she heard voices and laughter below. The air was filled with the delicious smell of food. She felt a little timid when she got to the closed door of the dining room, so with an extra small breath she opened it and went inside.

The room was a good-sized rectangle with tables on both sides, and most were full. At the far end, against the wall with large windows facing downhill, sat a big table occupied by a few men. They talked and drank beers and as she looked she saw above the table a sign that read, "Stammtisch."

Stammtisch was a German tradition she knew of from reading but she'd never actually encountered it. The table was reserved always for "regulars." People from the surrounding community used it as a meeting place for food, friends, and pleasure. Regulars included persons who lived there like farmers, mayors, doctors, and friends. The stammtisch helped nurture friendships and provided time for communication of ideas and interesting information. She was charmed by the concept.

Off in the corner of the dining room sat a freestanding, wood-burning stove with a glowing fire inside. Beside it lay a large, black, sleeping dog. Ana thought the black dog belonged to Peter and Sophie and again she was charmed.

Peter spotted her then and came to her side. "Please, Ana Winchester, follow me. We have this table reserved just for you." He led her to a small table in a comfortable spot, just a little out of the traffic on one side of the room. Just up from it was a bar that held a few empty bar stools, and right beyond that was the entrance into the kitchen.

"Is this table good for you?"

"This is perfect, Peter. And please, call me Ana. Is it okay if I call you Peter?"

Positive and fast he answered, "Yes, please call me Peter and I will call you Ana. While you decide what you want to eat, would you like a drink?"

The evening unfolded from there. The food was delicious and she watched and enjoyed the locals as they talked and enjoyed life together. It was also interesting to watch Peter and Sophie work so hard, wait on all the patrons, and be so good and friendly to everyone.

The dining room was well designed and decorated. It was painted a warm light golden yellow and an antique picture of a young girl hung on one of the walls beside the entrance. Fresh flowers were abundant.

She felt welcome and comfortable and wasn't in any hurry to go up and go to bed. Instead, she lingered and even ordered a second glass of wine from Peter.

The door opened and an older gentleman entered, accompanied by a large golden dog on a leash. The dog was obviously well trained and sat down right away at his master's feet. Ana tried not to stare but she loved animals, especially dogs.

The golden dog saw and responded to her face, her eyes, and her smile. He looked back, seemed to smile, and wagged his tail.

She'd really not focused on the dog's owner, but when she glanced at him, she realized that he was looking at her. His face lacked any expression, so she didn't know if he was troubled by her interest in his dog, or by something else she'd done. But he seemed displeased for sure.

At that moment Peter came over to her and his body blocked the man and his dog. "Can I get you anything else, Ana?"

She took quick advantage of the opportunity to leave. "Thank you Peter, but I am finished for tonight. Will you please bring me my bill?"

"Oh Ana, we simply keep count of everything our guests spend while

226

they are here and then when they leave, that is when we give you the bill. It saves us a lot of time." He picked up her empty glass and wished her goodnight.

She got up from the table and both of the dogs in the room paid attention. They both watched her, tails wagged, and again she felt they smiled at her.

She remembered to get her shawl from the back of her chair and went out the door. What she thought as she left was why had she bothered the man with the golden dog? Did she upset him by paying too much attention to his dog?

The next morning she woke up early, placed her feet on the floor beside her bed, and pulled apart the curtains that hid the window right beside her bed.

The Pension Hill-Top sat high up and the view down into the town below was perfect. Homes and businesses filled the small town. Most were built of stone, then painted different colors. All were neat and sat in the midst of green grass and flowers.

To the right, the church's tall distinctive tower grabbed attention where it sat at the far edge of the city landscape.

Later, after she'd explored the town, she would recognize the Kurpark that she saw now only as a big meadow with a lake, and walking paths. Smaller fields nearby supported horses, goats and sheep. Further away, after the town ended, the land slowly began to rise up, with hill after hill covered by fields alive with crops. One even had a tiny red tractor moving up and down as she watched.

She decided to take herself down and explore it all today, find out how much more there was to see.

After breakfast she walked down the steep hill into town and found her way into the area she'd seen from the balcony, the Kurpark. At breakfast, when she'd told Sophie where she was going, Sophie had gone to the kitchen and come back with a small package full of bread pieces to feed the ducks that lived at the small lake in the park.

Sophie and her family dog, named Friendly, both walked Ana out the door. Friendly butted against Ana's legs and then softly jumped up and placed his paws on her body, licked her hand.

"I am amazed!" said Sophie. "Friendly is a friendly animal, lives up to his name, but I have never seen him act like this to anyone. You seem to have a way with animals."

Ana laughed, patted Friendly again, and then went further out the door. "I simply love dogs, and maybe that's why they love me back. Thank you for the bread. The ducks and I appreciate your thoughtfulness. I will see you later."

She walked and explored for a long time, and enjoyed feeding the happy ducks. She was on a path that led out of the Kurpark when she heard a dog bark. The bark called her.

On a bench just a little way ahead of her sat the older gentleman who she'd seen last night at dinner. Beside him was his large golden dog. She had no choice but to walk past them. When she got close the dog attempted to go to her, but his master jerked him back.

She tried to ease the tension she felt, tried to be friendly. She smiled and said, "Good Day."

The man didn't even look at her, acted as though she didn't exist.

She kept walking and thought that maybe he was sad instead of mad. In her head she wished him the best and then started the steep climb back up to the Hill-Top.

Chapter Forty-Four

Forward Progress?
Sankt Englmar – Ana – 1971

Thomas stayed on her mind. To protect him she couldn't see him, and couldn't even tell Frau Krueger what had happened to him, even though Frau Krueger cared about him so much. She faced a wall of silence and had to accept the fact that she must stay away from him, move ahead and help find the man who had attacked him. Also important, she must keep hoping that he'd recover, get a chance to live his life.

She decided to ask Peter if she could use the Hill-Top Pension's business telephone. She planned to tell him that a friend of hers was sick and she needed to call and check on him. Peter could charge the cost of the long distance call to her open account.

She went downstairs and when her foot touched the bottom step Peter walked out of the kitchen. Mouth-watering smells that spoke loudly about the choices available for dinner tonight followed him.

"Can I ask you something? Do you have a minute to talk with me?"

"Sure I do Ana. We are not at the peak of our busy time yet. Come into my office and I will be happy to talk with you." He held his arm out and indicated a door, just off the entryway, beside the staircase. He opened the door and ushered her in.

"What can I help you with?"

"Peter, I have a friend in Frankfurt and he is sick. Would you allow me to use your telephone to call and find out if he is any better?"

"That is no problem. You just sit down at my desk and call your friend right now." He pulled out his chair for her to use.

Another question came into her mind, something she realized that she could ask him about. "I hesitate to ask you questions about your guests, and I am honestly not trying to be nosy, but would you happen to know anything about your guest, the gentlemen with the sweet golden dog? I feel that somehow I have offended him, although I do not understand how. Every time I happen to be around him, he shows disapproval of me. Do you know why he dislikes me, or what I could have done to gain his disdain?"

"Ana, I think you are misunderstanding Herr Schultz. He does seem to be unhappy with things. Sophie and I feel his disapproval also and we fear we are not providing him with the service that he expects. This is his first stay with us here, so maybe with time we will begin to understand what he is feeling." He chuckled a little and continued. "Maybe he is jealous that his dog, Beethoven, is so taken with you!"

She laughed in return and relief was evident in her reply, "Peter you have made me feel better. If Herr Schultz is acting as though he is not happy with the service and great food he gets here at the Hill-Top, then I now do believe that if he has a problem, it is not with me but with himself."

He was pleased with her words, her compliment, and thanked her with another laugh as he left her alone to make her phone call.

First she checked to make sure nobody was outside the door then dialed Andrew's number. It rang a few times before he answered. "This is Andrew, how may I help you?"

"Andrew, this is Ana. I'm calling from the Pension Hill-Top in Sankt Englmar, Bavaria. This is where I'm staying and I'm calling because I wanted to check and see how you are feeling. Are you better yet? You were so sick when I left and I wanted to see if anything had changed."

Instantly he knew what she wanted, so he went along with her story. "Hi Ana. It is so nice of you to call. Do you have time to talk to me, or are you busy right now? I hope you're having lots of fun."

"I have time Andrew. I'm sitting alone in the office of the people who own and run the Pension. Peter, Mr. Lintz, allowed me to use his office and his phone to call and see how you're feeling. Better I hope?"

Then he cut to the truth. "Okay we can get straight to the facts while it's safe to talk together. I think, from what you've said, that we aren't likely to be overheard. I know how worried you are about Thomas and from what I heard from the Doctor today, it looks like he may have a small chance of recovery. The Doctor was hopeful."

She tried to tone down her joy and softly answered him. "I'm so relieved to hear that. I'll continue to think positively."

"Listen, I've had my office look into the facts related to the man and woman you talked to me about earlier. So far, no names have been found but we've got a few other ideas to follow in order to get the information. I'll let you know as soon as we get anything. How is it going there in Bavaria, any problems? Have you and Georg gotten together yet?"

"So far the only thing that hasn't been happy is an old gentleman staying here. He doesn't seem to like me and I asked Peter about him. He told me that the man treated both him and his wife the same way, told me it wasn't me. And the man has a gorgeous dog named Beethoven, so he can't be all bad." She laughed a little. "I haven't contacted Georg yet but will soon."

"Well enjoy your Bavarian vacation and just remember what I told you. Be careful."

A twinge of worry nagged her as she put the phone down but she forced herself to ignore it and thought, "I'm here to find out the truth about Georg, to live my life openly, to enjoy myself."

She walked out of the office.

The next day started out perfectly again. Breakfast provided by the Pension, so fresh and good and then Sophie came to her table to talk to her.

"Peter is talking to other guests about a hike he is willing to take them on, up the Pröller, the large mountain right next to us. It is not a terribly difficult hike but it does take some time. The mountain is lovely. Peter wanted me to ask you if you were interested in going."

"What time does it start and where do I go to meet them?" The hike sounded like something she would like to do.

"You have plenty of time. They are leaving from right outside our back entrance at 9:00 this morning. The hike starts when you walk down the small street beside us, then cross the highway. That is where you actually walk onto the mountain. I believe you will enjoy it."

Sophie called her dog as she left the room. "Friendly, let us go home and do some chores there. Friendly jumped up at once, excited to be moving around with his Sophie. As they left the room, he gave Ana a quick happy glance of goodbye.

A little before 9:00 she went out the back door and saw other guests standing ready to hike. Peter was there too,

"Hello Ana, we are glad you joined us. Let me introduce you to everyone." He walked over to the three other people and began the introductions.

"This is Herr Keller and his wife, and this young man is Michael. He just arrived here last night from Munich. Everyone, this is Ana Winchester."

Peter hesitated for a second. "Ana, I am just thinking that I did not ask what part of Germany you are from. Your name honestly sounds a little different, maybe British, but you do not seem British. Can I ask what part of Germany is your home?"

Unlike her normal self, she didn't hesitate, didn't hide her background. "I am from the United States. I live in North Carolina but I am now teaching and living in Heidelberg."

Peter hesitated again. Perhaps a question popped in his mind but he realized he had a duty to all of the people present, so he put the question aside. He would ask her later.

The hike began and Peter was an excellent guide. He gave facts and interesting information about the Pröller and plants they saw as they walked along. He set a comfortable pace for the group. The heavily forested mountain caused her to feel like she was home in North Carolina again, hiking in the Great Smokey Mountains.

At the top of the mountain, a small space had been cleared and several benches placed so that climbers had the opportunity to sit down and appreciate the magnificent view so wide open in front of them when they reached the top. The mountain dropped off steeply directly at that point and left a wide-open sweeping view of the big green valley that sat below. It was even possible to see parts of the main highway, although it was distant and tiny, and then as far as the eye could see, mountains stood. Peter remarked that one of those distant peaks was the tallest in this part of Germany and was famous for its ski slopes.

The young married couple kept mainly close as a couple, only entered into conversation occasionally. They enjoyed their time together without being unfriendly to the others.

The young man from Munich seemed happy to be on the hike. He and Peter talked together a lot and this left her alone and able to enjoy things without feeling the need to keep up a continuous conversation. She listened to the others' talk and participated now and then.

Afterwards, back at the Hill-Top, the young man Michael came up to her and said, "If you do not have any plans for this evening, would you like to join me for dinner here? I know I may sound a little too forward since we only just met, but I think we got to know each other on the hike and I would enjoy talking with you and getting to know you better. Would you be interested in that?"

It surprised her but she realized it was a friendly gesture on his part, didn't mean anything else. "Well Michael, I think it would be nice to eat dinner with you this evening. Our hike was really good and I'd love to talk with you more. What time do you want to meet in the dining room?"

"Will six o'clock be too early for you? I need to eat early because tomorrow morning I am taking a much longer hike than the one we took today. It starts early and I need to get a good night's sleep."

Perfect she thought. "Six o'clock is great for me. I also have some plans for tomorrow and need to get some rest. I will see you later."

He opened the door for her and she walked inside and up to her room.

She showered, changed clothes, and then went out onto the balcony and sat down again. She had it to herself and so she sat quietly behind the waist-high rail, built from heavy wooden panels. She was practically invisible from anyone who happened to be sitting or standing in the table-filled courtyard directly below, the one that attached to the dining room and provided additional outside seating.

Slowly the light began to slip away. The town responded again with a constant twinkle of lights that offset the darkness.

Her thoughts were on Georg and she recognized that she'd been deliberately avoiding him so far. She kept telling herself that she needed to get adjusted to things here first but she was really frightened to see and talk to him again. She was afraid because she didn't want to find out he had any connection to the horror that haunted her life, didn't want him to want anything from her except her love. She loved him, she knew it, and finally admitted it.

Tomorrow she would press further forward with her honestly policy. No more pretending about Georg. Tomorrow was the day she would go and find him.

It then hit her that she was an unintentional listener of a private conversation that was taking place right below where she sat on the balcony. She started to get up but in that moment she recognized the speaker's voice and heard him say her name. It was Michael. Her attention was now completely focused and she sat perfectly still.

His voice was soft but clear and she realized he was talking into some type of mobile telephone because she could only hear his voice, not the voice of the person he was talking to.

"All is going good here. I met her today and we are now fellow guests and she has agreed to have dinner with me here at the Pension tonight."

Then silence.

"Yes sir. I will make sure to watch her. I told her that I was going on a long hike tomorrow so that will give me flexibility to watch her all day, make sure she is not in danger and all without her knowing about it. Could I ask if you have received any other information about the identity of those two people we were working on before I left to come here?"

Again silence.

"Okay Andrew. I will do my best and I will let you know if I think anyone here is a danger to her. Later."

Total silence.

She waited until she was positive that Michael had moved away, and then slipped back into her room. How should she think about what she'd just heard? Did this mean that Andrew thought that Georg was involved in the horror? Maybe he just needed Michael here to cover all possibilities.

It was only a few minutes before she had agreed to meet Michael for dinner. She hurried down the stairs and when she pulled the dining room door open, Michael was already seated at a table for two. He smiled and waved and she walked over and sat down.

"It is good to have you here. I have already ordered a beer for myself from Peter…."

He didn't get the chance to finish because Peter was at the table with his beer and asked at the same time. "Ana what can I get you to drink?"

She answered with smile and said, "Please bring me my normal, a glass of dry white wine."

Peter looked at her a little longer than normal as he left the table. She felt he was about to tell her something but instead, he smiled again and went to get her wine.

Then she put her new honesty policy into action again. "Michael, I need to tell you something important, so listen, and be quiet when I tell you. I do not want anyone else to hear what I am saying. I need you to know that I overheard the conversation you had earlier this evening with Andrew."

He simply stared at her, seemed surprised and upset.

When she saw his distress she quickly said, "No Michael, this is not bad news. It will make your job easier because I can cooperate with you. Do you not agree?"

"I am here with instructions from Andrew to watch you and protect you but I was not supposed to let you know that I was here for that purpose. My boss, Andrew, will be mad at me." His voice was quiet and he relaxed his face purposefully but she still felt his anxiety.

"I honestly believe Andrew is working with my best interest in mind. If you and I work together and pretend to be only fellow guests, then your job will be easier and so will my life." She gave him a warm smile as Peter delivered her glass of wine.

Michael relaxed and said, "It sounds like a good plan to me but I am going to inform Andrew that things have changed here. Is that okay with you?"

"Yes, that is okay with me."

They received their food and the restaurant continued to fill up with people as the evening moved along. Again, all the tables were full and in addition, the stammtisch was crowded tonight.

She was thinking that this must be the main get together night for the locals when the door opened and Georg walked in. He stood still because he saw her immediately. Then he shifted his eyes to the stammtisch table at the back of the room. He walked past her, moved stiffly to the one remaining seat at the table with his friends. They greeted him happily and he sat there with his back to the room. She was no longer visible to him. Did he really intend to pretend he didn't know her, to not even acknowledge her presence? All smiles left her face.

Peter came up beside her and quietly said, "Excuse me, but Sophie is out in the hall and needs to see you for a moment. She needs to ask you a question about tomorrow's schedule. Would you please be kind enough to go out and talk to her for a moment?"

Confused, but with an attempt to appear calm and normal she got up from the table and followed Peter out the door,

"Please forgive me for the lie. Sophie has no need to see you. I need to tell you something, something important."

"Peter, what is happening?"

His response was another surprise. "When I heard you give our guest Michael your name, and then you told me when I asked that you were from the United States and lived and taught in Heidelberg, I knew without a doubt that you were Georg's Ana."

"You knew what? You just called me Georg's Ana. What do you mean?"

"He told me how much he wanted you to come and visit here. When I realized who you were, I called and told him you were here. But he told me to keep quiet because he wanted to surprise you tonight. I saw him come in and then ignore you and I am confused and I want to let you know that I had told him you were here. I am so sorry. Are you angry with me?" Peter was nervous and sorry for her.

"Well if she is not angry with you Peter, she should be. You told Georg and then you saw Ana and Michael eating dinner together at a table tonight, looking like a couple on a date. You already knew that Georg was on his way to surprise her tonight and you should have told her that he was coming." Sophie's words to Peter were blunt and straightforward and she then walked over and punched him in his arm.

Next she talked to Ana. "I am going to go and get Georg and bring him out here. You two need to talk. I think he does not know what to think about what he just saw and needs to talk to you. Stay here and I will get him."

Once more she looked at her husband. "My man, I think you need to get back to work." Then she couldn't help herself, she grinned wickedly at him and went into the dining room.

Peter and Ana looked at each other and then he hurried away to the kitchen.

She stood still and tried to believe Sophie knew what she was talking about. Then she heard a bark. The golden haired Beethoven stood in front of his master Mr. Schultz as they came down the stairs. Beethoven saw her and saw her looking at him. He sent her another bark-hello. Herr Schultz tightened his hold on the leash attached to his dog and then brushed bluntly past her and went into the dining room.

Beethoven and Herr Schultz went in and Georg came out.

Chapter Forty-Five

Truth
Sankt Englmar – Ana – 1971

Together at last, face-to-face, the exact moment she'd ached for since their parting and the exact moment she'd feared most. She'd longed to see him, feel his arms around her but had avoided him because that allowed her to avoid the possibility of crushing disappointment if his feelings for her didn't match what she felt for him.

He spoke first. "Why did you finally come to Bavaria, stay here in the Hill-Top Pension with my friends, and choose to be with another man? Why did you even come? Why would you want to be so cruel to me?"

She said nothing, just looked at him, felt his pain. Gently she moved closer, touched his chest, and looked into his blue eyes. "My Georg, you misunderstood what you saw tonight. You don't have the facts. Please let me explain."

"Are you staying here with that man you were having dinner with?" Still his voice was tense. He didn't acknowledge what she'd told him.

"No, I am not with Michael. The identity of Michael is part of everything we need to talk about but first I need for you to understand what is most important. I am here to see you, to talk and to understand what, if anything, we have going on between us."

His face changed slightly and she saw what looked like a spark of hope in his eyes.

"Georg, let us go somewhere private. We can even go up to my room. Surely Peter and Sophie will not care."

Peter came up to them. He'd heard her last words. "You can go up to your room, but you could also go into my office and close the door. Then you would have privacy and I believe you need that right now."

He grinned, then looked at Georg and said, "My friend, you should hear all the comments and speculation from our buddies at the stammtisch. They cannot wait to find out what is going on with you and I am simply smiling, bringing them more beer, and telling them just to wait."

Ana and Georg couldn't help but smile at Peter's humor.

"Tell you what Peter, we will accept your offer of the office if you can manage to bring me a beer and Ana a glass of wine."

"Be back with your drinks really fast." Peter pulled open the office door and pushed them inside, then raced for the bar and their drinks.

Ana and Georg sat down at the small table there and both relaxed a little. The intervention and humor of Peter and Sophie helped remove a big part of the confusion and pain.

First a soft knock, then the door opened. "Here you go!" Peter set their drinks on the table and left them alone to sort everything out.

"Before we say anything else, let us toast the fact that we are finally together again." He raised his glass and she raised hers. The clink was happy and they both took a drink.

"Who talks first?" Georg wanted to know.

She took another small sip of wine then answered, "You go first. I want to know how you feel about me being here. Please ignore the confusion with Michael. We are definitely not together. I'll tell you more about him later."

"Okay, I will speak first then." He got up and walked to the window. "I have waited such a long time for you to come here, for us to be together again. When we were in Heidelberg, I wanted you but I felt your struggle and didn't know what it was connected to. I even thought you might be trying to get over a relationship you had with another man. I did not want to pressure you. I wanted you to come to me when you were ready. I must be honest and say that I felt your response to me, felt we were meant to be together." He went silent and looked at her. "Now you talk to me."

She put her head down into her hands, tried to calm down. "I wanted to be here with you just as much as you say you wanted me here. You say you felt it was important not to pressure me and you are correct. I am in the middle of some deep hard issues, things I've been struggling with my entire life. Even now, I don't have the answers. But this has nothing to do with any other man in my life. There is no other man in my life, never has been. I've never felt like this for any man before you."

He made a move toward her but she held out her hand and said, "Wait because I need to tell you so much more."

He sat down and reached for her hands. "Keep talking sweet one. I will listen."

Now tears slipped down her cheeks. "I have been afraid to see you again because I have never been able to trust the important people in my life. I loved them but they were not honest with me. I avoided you because I was afraid to be hurt again and this hurt would be the worst I've ever experienced."

No way he could wait as he saw how she felt. He went to her, pulled her up from the chair and into his arms. "I hear your pain and I also hear that you love me. Let us leave everything else right now. I want you to go to your room and get some rest because tomorrow morning I will be here to pick you up at 9:00. Tomorrow is our day, we will share everything and I will show you my world, my home, and my life. We will sort this all out together. I am so happy!"

His arms tightened and he kissed her lips gently. She responded with passion and the heat of his embrace grew hotter.

Voices erupted outside the office door, loud laughter sounded as some of the guests left the building.

They broke apart.

"But Georg, I have so much more you need to know."

"Your tears show me that you have had enough to deal with tonight. I want to take care of you. Please relax and get yourself some sleep and then tomorrow we will walk further along the hard path in front of us. Go upstairs, sleep, because tomorrow I plan to show you a whole new world."

Sleep didn't find her easily that night. Joy ran through her because she was in his arms again, but as always, worry crept back in. She needed to apply her new honestly policy to what she told him the next day but was there any possibility that he had a part in the danger? Every fiber of her being told her that he was honest and trustworthy but she kept hearing Andrew's words, to be careful and watch out for the unexpected. She didn't want to hide any of the truth from him.

Finally she knew what to do. She was honest with herself and then sleep came.

Awake really early the next morning, she followed her new routine of opening her curtains as soon as her feet hit the floor. Beautiful again, and then see saw Beethoven and now it was even better.

Herr Schultz pulled his dog to a stop as a sleek black car pulled up and stopped beside him. He moved closer to the driver's window, bent down a little, and it looked like a conversation was taking place. It was over quickly and the sleek black car pulled away and drove down the hill. Herr Schultz walked on with his dog.

She registered a small vibration that usually indicated danger was around but instead of concentrating on it, she shook her head and brushed it away. Most likely, Herr Schultz was just asked for directions by the person driving the car. Things like this happened here a lot, it was a small and friendly place.

Today was important and she needed to concentrate only on it so she dressed up as perfectly as she could. Because of last night's decision, she didn't feel weighed down worrying about Georg's connection to the danger she was in. This was to be another "honest" day and she planned to tell him everything, to clear the air and let their relationship strengthen. She couldn't wait to see his face and hear his voice.

Since she'd gotten up so early she had time to eat breakfast and then to go out for a morning walk. She was half way down the hill when she heard the sound of a car creeping slowly up behind her. It stopped.

She turned around and it was Georg. "Good morning. Do you want me to give you a lift, or to meet you at the parking lot up at the Hill-Top when you finish your walk?"

Her answer was to open the door and slide in beside him. "I am finished with my walk. I was only walking to make the time before you got here go by more quickly."

He asked if she needed to pick up anything from her room to take with her today and she remembered that she wanted her purse, so he pulled into the parking area and waited while she went up and got it from her room.

He drove, followed the small road behind the Hill-Top, where he turned onto the main highway. It slowly led them forward and dropped them softly down the mountain. This countryside, the same that she'd loved when she saw it from the bus window on the way to Sankt Englmar, was in front of her again. In about a mile or so he turned off the highway onto one of the small roads that had called her name, told her to come and explore. Now she found herself where she'd wanted to be, in the middle of the meadows, surrounded by sheep and goats and horses.

When he turned off and drove up a lane on a small slope and in front of her sat a large farmhouse, she got even more excited. This must be his home!

The car barely had time to stop before she jumped out and stood with her arms wide open, reconnected with nature. Green surrounded her. Green apple trees loaded with ripe red apples grew on one side of the farmhouse. Near the back entry sat a neat small pen with three large rabbits inside. All around in the grass, even at her feet, free-range chickens searched for food. She wanted to purr like a contented cat.

After he parked his car in the garage he walked up beside her. "Do you like what you see, all this rural landscape?"

"I cannot say how much I love it. It is perfect."

He unlocked the back door and welcomed her into his home. "Let me show you around a little."

The kitchen they stood in was bright and functional, had obviously been restored recently. She appreciated what she saw because she enjoyed cooking and she asked him, "Do you cook for yourself and use this wonderful kitchen or do you have someone local that cooks for you?"

Pleasure filled his laugh. "I cook for myself, just like you do, if I remember from our past conversation. In fact, I would like to cook for you while you are here and find out if you like what I create."

Then her took her by the hand and led her to the opposite side of the room and from there outside onto a balcony. One more step down and they were standing on an open terrace and again, the view astonished her. His farmhouse sat at the crest of a hill and down to the right, a river flowed along.

He pointed to the river. "That feeds the lake that I want to take you to today. We can walk there by following a path that winds through my property. But only if you want to will we go."

"Everything I have seen is beautiful and yes, I definitely want to go for a walk and get even closer to your beautiful property."

"Well do you need to rest a little first, let me make you some coffee?"

"Georg, right now I am full of energy and want to continue to absorb the beauty you have here. Maybe we could walk and talk together and we will be surrounded by nature, not by people."

He took her hand and they walked back into the kitchen and then stepped out into his back yard. Her happiness pleased him.

He led her to the side of the house where she'd seen the fully loaded red apple trees but they only got a few steps forward when he stopped. "I need to go back and get a basket so I can gather some mushrooms. It is mushroom season, they grow in the woods, and we should pick them as we walk along. Maybe I can even cook some of them for our dinner tonight."

"I have never hunted for mushrooms before, do not have any idea what to look for, but it sounds like fun and if we get some, also will taste delicious when you cook them."

She waited and he came back fast with a handled basket swinging from his arm.

When they got to the apple trees she stopped and looked. He saw her delight and teased, "Look girl, you and I can get busy tomorrow and you can help me pick all of these apples." Then he laughed.

She laughed back at him. "I will be glad to help you pick these apples but as payment, I get to eat lots of them."

Further along, the path led them beside a field of wheat that gently waved at them as they passed by. A light wind ran through it, the sunlight shone down, and it sparkled as it waved. The golden wheat provided a sharp contrast to the dark green of the forest background ahead.

A house sat off by itself in front of them. When they got closer he shocked her. "That is the house where I grew up. I lived there with my Mother and Father until they both died."

She fell from happiness into deep sadness. "That is so sad. How old were you when you lost your parents? Oh how very hard that must have been for you!" She put her arms around him and held him close, waited for more information.

"I do not want to put sadness into the middle of our happy day so please, let us continue on our walk. Please let me show all this to you without sadness. I want us to share happiness today."

"Wait. Please know that I am here to get to know you and for you to know me. I want and need to hear about your life, your family, happiness and sadness, all that you have experienced. We both need to share ourselves with each other."

They held together without speaking for a few moments.

"I do understand what you are saying my Ana but please know that I have accepted what happened in my life. It was not easy but truly, I am here as I am today because of the kindness and love of the family who took responsibility and who loved me after I lost my family."

He loosened his grip on her body and gently tugged her into walking forward even as he continued to talk. "My Father was the manager of this big farm. The property belonged to a man and his wife, the Haupt family. They lived in Heidelberg and visited the farm on a regular basis. They loved it here and they also enjoyed the income the farm provided to them."

She asked at once, "Did the Haupt family live in that wonderful house in Heidelberg that you now rent out, where my apartment is?"

"Yes, that is the family. My earliest memory of them is that they were what I considered "old people." I was really young and they were part of my life because they loved children. When they were here, they would invite my Father and Mother and me over for dinner and they were happy to enjoy my baby playfulness. My Mother told me later that they talked a lot about their only daughter. She and her husband lived with them in Heidelberg. The daughter and her husband had one child, a girl and she was the Haupts only grandchild.

"I feel so sad and somehow connected to the family you are talking about. Maybe because I have been living in their home there in Heidelberg."

This time he gave her a hug and again they moved ahead. "I got to know the Haupts better later on because of what happened to my parents. My Father had been pulled into the military, forced to serve as a soldier in the war. He died in battle. Even though he was no longer there to manage the farm for them, the Haupts refused to let my Mother and me leave. They insisted that we stay in this house and they took care of us. "

"They sound like really good people and cared for you like family."

"Herr Haupt finally had to hire a new farm manager and when he did, he and his wife moved me and Mother into their house, the house I now live in. That happened right before the war ended. They were very worried about their daughter and granddaughter. Their daughter's health had changed, gotten bad and then they found out that their granddaughter was sent off to a military hospital by the Nazis to serve as a nurse. I remember my Mother telling me one time that the Haupts waited for the mail every day, hoping to get any kind of information that would tell them that their family was safe."

"How sad and stressful for them! Why they did not simply return to Heidelberg to take care of their family." She wondered out loud.

Once again, sadness covered his face. "I found out later that something horrible had happened and that was why they had moved to their farm. They did not want to be in the city, hoped to find peace in the country."

Then he told her the truly difficult part. "Somehow my Mother caught pneumonia and even though the Haupts tried to help, she died. I was totally alone. They took me into their arms and into their hearts, told me to think of them as my grandparents. And I did. When the war finally ended and they moved back to Heidelberg, I went with them. When we got there, they found out that their daughter had died and that their granddaughter had disappeared. They tried so hard to find her but they never saw her again. "

Ana stood still and tried to absorb what he'd been through but the depth of family sadness he'd lived though was hard. He was just a little boy.

They held tightly onto each other.

He said, "Now listen my Ana, this is sadness I did not want to make part of our day. I want you to be happy, not sad."

"You should always tell me anything important, bad or good. I need you to understand how much I care about how you feel. Do not stop talking to me even about unhappiness."

A noise interrupted and when she looked off to her left, she saw a meadow surrounded by a high wooden fence. Several horses were grazing in the distance and evidently, one of the horses had called out to them.

"Look at the horses! They are beautiful! I love horses so very much!" Off she ran to the fence, hung onto it, and looked out at them. At first they paid no attention but then a tall one began to move forward. When he stopped right in front of her, she reached out and touched him.

"I wish I had an apple for him," she said as she wiped away her tears. Two more horses came to her.

"I am surprised. These horses are not interested in people. They know the procedure for receiving their food from the manager but I do not think they came to you for food." As he watched the horses try to get even closer to her it was clear to him that they were centered directly on her.

She spoke gently. "I had a horse in North Carolina. We grew up together. He was tall and unafraid and we were best friends. I lost him when the tornado destroyed part of my farm in the States."

He recognized pain. "Before you leave to return to Heidelberg would you please go riding with me? I ride my horses regularly and all of them need attention. It is good for then as well as good for us."

"I would be happy to ride horses with you."

Past the meadow, they moved out of the sunlight into deep shadow. They entered the tall thick forest.

"This forest is another source of farm income. If you look closely, you can see that many trees have been cut down and sold as a natural means of heating for people in this community. We re-plant a tree for each one we take down and try to not disturb the beauty of the forest."

Actually, as she looked, it was not obvious that trees were missing and the forest floor was covered with bright green moss-covered stones in addition to a blend of dried brown leaves that had fallen from the hardwoods. Bright colors sprouted as tiny wild flowers grew. Also, large red mushrooms appeared in certain places. He explained that these specific mushrooms should not be eaten, were the poison ones.

Her interest in mushrooms sparked and she started to hunt for them.

Suddenly she thought she saw one and jumped across a small ditch at the edge of the path. She reached up toward a large stone and picked it. It was brown, matched the blanket of brown leaves that helped hide it, and according to Georg, it was an edible one. She was excited.

By the time the path began to descend their basket was half-full of fresh mushrooms. Soon the trees opened up and they could see down to the lake that stretched out bluely below them.

When they got near it Georg said, "All of us who live here call this part of the country "German Canada."

A long look at the deep blue lake surrounded on both sides by tall stately trees and she understood exactly why they called it that.

Two kayaks appeared and moved leisurely over the water. Then, a little way down, at the lake's shore, she spotted a man fishing.

Life is so good.

He asked, "Would you be interested in a walk across the bridge to get us some lunch at the restaurant there? We could look at the lake while we eat."

Yes was her answer.

After they crossed the bridge he left the path, walked over to a tall stonewall, pulled up handfuls of the tall wild grass that grew there, and placed it in the basket on top of the mushrooms.

"Georg what is the grass for?"

"I am picking it for the rabbits."

Chapter Forty-Six

Facts Finally
Sankt Englmar – Ana – 1971

When they got back to Georg's home, he led her straight through the kitchen and into the large living room right next to it. The instant she entered she recognized, felt embraced, by the deep family tradition it contained. The entire room spoke of wealth, family, and happiness. She looked around before she moved further in and saw a large handsome fireplace. Directly above it hung a large family portrait, so she crossed the room to the picture. Then she forgot where she was.

The portrait was of an older couple, the Haupts, along with a younger couple, obviously the parents of the little girl who stood in front of them all. Happiness glowed on all the faces.

She couldn't stop looking at the family, and moved closer and reached out to gently touch the little girl. Then she touched the little girl's mother. She saw herself because the little girl in the picture looked just like she had as a young child.

Reality hit and she cried out in recognition. The little girl in the picture was her Mother. This was her family! That's when she started to shake and cry. Her hidden past hung right in front of her eyes. This is what she'd wanted her whole life but it felt so hard to finally see the family she'd always wanted, the family now all dead. No opportunity existed for her to bond physically with them. They were gone from this life.

Georg came right up behind her, gave her his strength and his love to help support her. He held her tightly in his strong arms and said, "The first time I saw you I felt that I should know you. I felt that I should recognize you but it was only when I happened to glance at this portrait recently that I realized the little girl Ingrid looked just like you. Ingrid was the Haupt's granddaughter. I was so shocked and wondered what was happening. I could not understand if you were really part of this family and if you were, then why did you not know it?"

He helped her over to the sofa. "Sweet Ana, please tell me what is going on here? How can I help you?"

As she'd promised herself, she was honest with him and told him about her life. She began with the Winchester Family in North Carolina, explained bluntly the cruelty she'd lived with as long as her Grandfather was alive. Then also shared that her mother had tried to hide her German ancestry. A big part of the hiding was that she never told Ana about her German relatives, in fact told her that all the German family was dead, all died in the war.

As she tried to explain all the details, the insecurity she must have grown up with became apparent. She had constantly tried to live up to everyone's expectations, pretend to be someone she wasn't, and always followed instructions.

The worst was yet to be told. She told him of the death of her Grandfather, her Father, and then her Mother and at that point, he pulled her into himself. "I had no idea that you had such a brutal life."

His love and sympathy calmed her a little and in a more steady voice, she finally told him about Mr. Elden. She didn't exclude the brutality that he'd saved her from and the fact that he was her "horseman hero." He'd truly saved her. Then she blurted out that he'd been murdered and that the authorities had uncovered a Nazi connection to his death.

When she tried to explain that the United States Authorities and the German Authorities now were convinced that she was at the center of whatever was happening, as she explained about the attempted murder of her former student Thomas, in Heidelberg, Georg was horrified.

"Wait! Please stop!" He jumped up and began to pace around the room. "Ana, you are in serious danger! If the authorities are telling you this, you are in danger!"

"The investigators are trying to get it figured out and I know I am in danger. You can call me a fool because I do not focus just on that. What I want most is to get away from all this, to live my life and not hide anymore! I hope they find the truth soon."

"I do not believe you are a fool but I am extremely worried. Go back a little and tell me anything they have discovered so far."

"The first thing they found was that my Mother used a false name when she married my Father. They met and got married in Heidelberg and evidently nobody checked or tried to verify her records. They got married right after the war ended and were sent back to the states, where I was born, in North Carolina."

She continued and told him what had been uncovered about Mr. Elden, about his escape from Germany to Canada, and she truthfully explained to him about her discovery of her mother's notebook and what was inside it, about the Salzburg mystery and the name on the grave.

By the time she finished she was exhausted and then realized that she still hadn't told him everything. She hadn't told him that the investigation team felt that the secret grave wasn't the center of the matter since the Nazis would have already recovered the treasure they'd hidden there.

Then, true to her new way of life, she told him what they thought.

He came back to the sofa and sat close beside her. "We now know exactly who your family is. I do not doubt it. You are the daughter of Ingrid, the little blond girl in the portrait. Her real name was Ingrid Haupt Neuschwander. We need to get this information to the man you told me about, the one who is leading the investigation. His name is Andrew? You are in serious danger my sweet one and we need to help solve this mystery fast!"

She used his telephone to make the call to Andrew. They both shared with him the news facts they'd discovered.

After the long detailed conversation with Andrew both Ana and Georg decided they'd had enough. Both had shared their painful family histories and now they needed to get a little distance away from their painful pasts.

They went outside and sat on the balcony. The afternoon was almost over and that special late afternoon time, when the sun cast a mellow glow on the earth was happening. Also, a light cool wind felt like perfection.

"How about a glass of wine Ana?"

"Yes, I would like that very much."

When he brought out the wine bottle, uncorked it and poured the sparkling wine into their glasses, he said, "I think we could call what happened between us today a real reason to celebrate. Do you?"

So softly she answered him, "I do my Georg."

They sat still and drank their wine and then later, he let go of her hand and moved closer to her. He ran his fingers slowly, sensually up her arm.

"Ana, I have wanted you from the moment I saw you, there on the steps of what we now know is your family home in Heidelberg. I felt that you wanted me too. Now, I know you do." His handsome face was intense.

He didn't wait for her answer, just stood up and strongly pulled her up into his arms. He pressed his tall body again her and now his hands caressed her shoulders, her back, then grabbed and cuddled her breasts. He kissed her, soft at first, then hard, wet, hot.

"Please let me show you how much I love you."

Her wet lips moved against his. "Yes, show me. I want your passion and I love you too."

Her whole body burned with desire. She'd never felt pure boiling passion, felt true love, and her body jumped forward into life. Her heart pulsed with mindless desire and emotional fire burned to match his heat, his passion, and his love.

He pulled her inside and up the stairs to his bed, then pushed her down onto the bed and the flames of their need surrounded them. Slowly he began to pull off her clothes, piece by piece, until she lay in front of him, totally naked and totally beautiful to his flame-throwing eyes. She reciprocated quickly, couldn't wait to see his magnificent chest. Shirtless, she moved straight to his trousers, pulled them down and off. She freed his hard throbbing man-rod, pulsing to push into her.

They furiously explored each other's bodies with hands and tongues. Pure emotion ruled as passion and need spiked, as he rubbed his hands against her, squeezed her butt, as she stroked and pulled his iron-hard rod. They pressed their bodies even more tightly against each other. Fire raged.

Breathing fast and furiously, as hot as the sun, he thrust his powerful rod into her wet waiting body and she screamed out again and again, ""More, don't stop, more!"

Harder, faster, deeper, nothing existed except screams and passion. They exploded and their bodies became one. Passion plus true love expressed.

Much later, in his bed, they snuggled in the after-sex warmth. They glowed.

"This is right Ana. You and I are one. Look at us, how we joined together right here in your family home with your mother, your grandparents, your great grandparents all approving."

She looked into his loving eyes. "I loved you when I saw you too but I did not truly realize how my mind kept sending me a message that you were connected to my family in some way. I tried to think you might be connected to the strange people who are after me but I never could convince myself of anything except that I loved you and we should be together. I hope you understand what I mean."

"I do understand you and now we just need to work with Andrew Watson and solve this problem. I need you safe. That is my first priority."

Chapter Forty-Seven

Kneipp Walk Danger
Sankt Englmar – Ana – 1971

During their long conversation Andrew Watson told Ana and Georg that he was going to immediately update Michael, his agent staying there at the Pension Hill-Top in Sankt Englmar, but he also asked them to repeat to Michael personally everything that they'd already told him. He wanted to make sure that no detail was overlooked and that Michael had all this new information.

They drove back up to the Pension Hill-top that same evening. They planned to get there with enough spare time to manage a meet-up with Michael and then ask him to eat dinner with them. Georg wanted to make sure that all the details they'd shared already with Andrew were passed on to Michael as soon as possible.

It would be apparent to all of Georg's friends that he and Ana had sorted out the misunderstanding they'd had and that Michael was indeed just a fellow guest at the Hill-Top. It would also appear that all was normal to any other unknown person who might be around watching Ana.

Their timing was perfect. They bumped into Michael just as he was about to go into the dining room. A friendly handshake between the two men and a happy greeting from Ana and all three moved together into the dining room.

Peter wasn't around and evidently Sophie was in charge at the moment. She came right over and sat them all down at a table, then laughed as she said, "Well I can tell from the smiles on your faces that you got everything sorted out. I am happy and Peter will be too. He will be here in a little while. But just wait until your friends from the stammtisch catch up with you Georg. They have had a lot of fun already, speculating about you and

Ana and Michael. You will have to set them straight."

Ana actually blushed and Georg just grinned. Sophie took their orders and then left them to enjoy.

"Michael, it is good to meet you and I do apologize for my incorrect assumption about you and Ana. I am sorry."

Michael quietly answered him. "That is not a problem as far as I am concerned. It was simply a misunderstanding and it is a pleasure to see you both so happy."

They ate and decided between themselves that they'd meet up later at a specific place, a bench on a nearby street. It was isolated, but it also sat out in the open. They could talk together but not look like they were hiding anything.

The plan was that Ana and Georg would walk there together, romantically. Then Michael could "accidently" run into them as he walked up from the opposite direction. They set a specific time, and then enjoyed their meal.

When Ana and Georg reached the designated bench later that evening, after walking close together in the nice darkness, they sat down and talked quietly, with a kiss added into the conversation every now and then.

Suddenly, "Well hello you two! I cannot believe we meet again so soon!" Michael came over to the bench and stood for a minute as they talked. Then they asked him to sit down with them for a minute. They scooted over and made room.

From a black car parked in a driveway further along the road, all of the activity on the bench seemed normal. It looked like an accidental meeting. The man in the car could not hear what was being said. He watched carefully and saw only friendship and heard some laughter.

What they really did was tell Michael about Ana's family story, but they did a good job of not looking serious. They looked happy together.

The man in the car sat still and watched them. He continued to watch as they walked together back up the hill to the Pension Hill-Top. All he could do was to report what he'd seen.

Over the next few days Ana and Georg left the investigating to Andrew, Michael, and the authorities. They simply spent every possible moment they could together. They walked, talked, rode horses, and cooked together, purposefully concentrated on their love.

Later in the week, mid-afternoon, Ana came down the stairs from her room at the Hill-Top. Georg had a scheduled business meeting in a nearby city that couldn't be put aside so she was on her own for a little while. As she walked down the stairs, she saw Peter.

"Peter, I have a question for you. Do you have time to help me?"

"Of course I have time for you. What can I help you with?"

"I remember you talked about different walking paths when you took us up the Pröller. You mentioned a few paths that ran down from here in Sankt Englmar to the small towns below, like the one close to where Georg lives. Is there a path that I can walk down from here and get to his farm?"

He walked to a nearby cabinet and pulled out a map. "Here is just what you need. I drew this map and had it copied because many of our guests wish to take hikes like these."

He showed it to her and said, "Just follow this and watch for the signs posted along the way. The path is well marked and you do not need to be concerned about getting lost. Also, it is not especially a difficult walk, even has some open areas now and then. There is a small building, a chapel that was built in honor of the Saint who is responsible for our little town. It is still used to honor him. Be sure you check it out. You will not miss it because it sits right beside the path."

Neither Peter nor Ana were aware that their conversation was overheard.

After she changed her shoes, she tucked Peter's map into her pocket and started happily on her walk. She loved her idea to walk down the mountain to Georg's house and get there before he got back from his meeting. She couldn't wait to surprise him.

As she walked, she thought of her recent hike up the mountain named Pröller and realized that this walk down to Georg's farm was less steep. Also, she felt rewarded to get to walk past and enjoy the same beautiful trees, stones and moss that she'd seen on her other walk.

She got a surprise though. About a mile down the mountainside she saw a sturdy wooden sign. It pointed to a tiny path that led away from the main path she was on. The sign read, "Kneipp Walking."

In the Kurpark there in Sankt Englmar she'd had the chance to look at the Kneipp Walking set up there. However, many people were usually taking advantage of it and she felt shy because she'd never done it before. This sign was great! Now she had another chance, a private chance to Kneipp!"

From her German heritage studies, she remembered reading that Kneipp Walking had come into existence from a Bavarian Priest named Sebastian Kneipp. He invented a natural method meant to boost the immune system, relax the nervous system, to strengthen the body's veins and to stimulate energy.

To Kneipp, it was necessary to have a natural stream flowing along, full of cold clear water. First, the shoes and socks come off and then pants are rolled up above the knees. Finally, step straight out into the ice-cold water and walk for a specific distance. The walk was supposed to be like a march, a lift of the knees and exercise to the legs, all in the cold water.

Now it was her turn. Even though she didn't have a towel to dry herself off afterwards, she wasn't about to not do this. Quick and determined, she walked down to the stream, sat on the bench there, removed her shoes, and rolled up her pants.

When she stood ready to step in, she first touched one toe to the water. It was so cold! She shivered and laughed out loud, then stepped in and marched down the stream, then again around the circle that had been structured for that purpose. She completed three Kneipp circles. She smiled the whole time.

When she climbed out and tried to do the best she could to get her clothes back on, she laughed again. "So I'm a little wet. What difference does it make?"

She started back to Georg's farm.

The path moved slightly up and as she reached the crest she saw the chapel Peter had told her about. "Thanks Peter" she thought. It was so small and she was curious and then surprised when she realized she could look inside it from the pathway. She moved closer and saw several fresh flower offerings. The alter inside the chapel was covered with respect.

Maybe because her attention was engaged as she read words offered in honor of the Saint, maybe because she was not her normal perceptive self, was wrapped up securely in love, she failed to instinctively feel the presence of someone tracking her.

When she turned away from the chapel to move ahead down the path, a glimpse of movement in the direction she'd come from flashed. Exactly when she saw the movement, a strong hard body struck her and a loud bark rang in her ear. In an instant, she lay flat on the ground with Beethoven on top of her as a bullet slammed into the chapel beside her. It struck the exact spot where she'd stood before the dog knocked her down.

She screamed.

Beethoven jumped off and raced down the path in the same direction the bullet had come from. His leash trailed behind him. She couldn't move, paralyzed by fear.

All at once, a man was running toward her. She whimpered, finally got up and ran behind the Chapel. She needed to get into the forest, to hide. Then she recognized a voice.

"Ana stop! It's me! It's Michael! The man who shot at you is gone. He ran off in the other direction. I need to help you, are you injured?"

She stood still and he ran up to her and then had to support her limp body with his strong arms. "Let me get you to safety."

She was in shock and he put her down on the ground and tried to warm her up, help her get in control of herself again.

Finally she choked out the words, "I cannot believe someone just shot at me, tried to kill me."

He kept his thoughts to himself. Time enough to tell her what he believed the man really had wanted, that the man wanted information first, and then, after he got the information, he'd have killed her.

Also, unless he was totally wrong, when he was able to get Ana back to the Pension Hill-Top, they would find that Herr Schultz and his dog Beethoven had disappeared.

Beethoven saved her life.

Chapter Forty-Eight

Get It Done
Sankt Englmar – Ana – 1971

Peter and Sophie did not get paid for the room they rented to Herr Schultz, or for the food and drinks he consumed. His room was vacant by the time Michael got Ana back to the Pension Hill-Top. Michael helped her up to her room and Sophie grabbed water and food and went up to take care of her.

Downstairs, Michael pulled Peter aside and told him the harsh basics of what had just happened. He didn't give details about the reason it happened, just asked for Peter's help to go up and check out Herr Schultz's room. Peter grabbed his key at once, no questions asked.

The room at the end of the long hallway sported an open door and was empty. Herr Schultz, Beethoven, and their belongings were gone. Michael requested that Peter close and lock the door and then call the police. He hoped the local police would find some scrap of evidence that might reveal who Herr Schultz really was.

Then Michael went off by himself and called Andrew.

Ana huddled undercover, very quiet and pale when Sophie came into her room with water and a bowl of steaming soup on a tray.

"Peter told me what happened and I cannot believe it! Let me help you get up so that you can eat a little of this soup. It will help you, give you some strength."

As she talked Sophie set up the soup on the small table opposite the end of the bed where Ana lay. Ana silently watched Sophie put everything in place. Her eyes remained wide, in shock, and tears covered her pale cheeks.

Sophie grabbed a tissue from the dresser, then hurried over and gave it

to her. "I do not understand this and I am so sad this happened to you. "
She sat on the side of the bed and reached down, helped her to sit up.
Then she reached further and hugged her. "You are strong and you can get
over this."

Her heart-felt words managed to penetrate the fear and disbelief Ana
struggled with, and as they fixed themselves more firmly in her mind, she
finally began to take control again, stiffened her spine a little, and sat up
straighter. Without knowing exactly what she had to face, she accepted the
reality that she must call forth determination, must force herself to stand up
and fight.

Slowly she moved to the side of the bed and put her feet on the floor.
Sophie watched as she got up and moved to the window and looked out,
then walked to the table and sat down. She sat down in front of the soup,
but before she put the first spoonful into her mouth she said, "You are
right. I am going to get this all behind me."

Downstairs Michael was busy. He used Peter's office for privacy and
called Andrew. On his first try Andrew answered.

"Andrew, this is Michael. You need to get here to the Hill-Top right
now. First, let me tell you that Ana is not injured. She is in her room
upstairs here but listen, something bad happened."

"Tell me fast!" Andrew's voice was sharp with anxiety.

"Andrew, I promise you that Ana is not hurt but you need to get here so
I can tell you everything that happened. I do not want to reveal all this
information while there is a chance that someone could overhear me.
Come fast but drive safe."

"I am leaving right now!"

Two local policemen came in through the back door and spoke easily to
Peter as soon as they came in. They all knew each other, were neighbors
and friends.

Peter explained what he knew about what had happened and then
brought them into his office where Michael was waiting for them. Peter
introduced them to Michael then politely left them alone together.

Before they could ask him anything, Michael pulled out his identification
and showed it to them. Surprise swept across both faces.

The leader of the two men spoke up. "Tell us what happened here.
This is not normal. We are a small quiet village and we do not deal with
this type of situation."

"Please let me explain a little. But before I do, I must reinforce that by
law, you cannot share any of this information without proper authorization
from both the German and American military authorities. Do you
understand and agree to this?"

While he gave this information, he watched them. What he saw supported his need to ask for their help, so he then explained briefly what had happened and also explained what was known about the people involved.

This time they were really stunned. The leader spoke up quickly. "What do you need for us to do? We will of course search the room of the Herr Schultz and perhaps we will find some evidence of his real identity. What else can we do to assist the government?"

"If you can help find out who he really is, you will help us put together another important piece of this horrible puzzle. Will you agree to maintain secrecy?"

Both of them affirmed that they wanted only to help in any way possible. They asked more questions and Michael answered them. They left and went upstairs to start their search for evidence.

The back door burst open and breathless Georg rushed in. Peter saw him first and took hold of his arm. "Slow down. She is not injured. Sophie is upstairs with her, taking care of her. Please calm yourself my friend."

Michael heard them and came out of the office. He pulled Georg back into the office with him and closed the door. Open, honest, he told him what happened. He explained that Ana had left on her walk without telling him and when he found out later from Peter, he'd run off after her. Then he told about the gun and how Beethoven had worked a miracle, had saved her life. By the time he finished explaining, Georg had bent over in his chair crying.

Michael was quiet for a few minutes, then continued, "My boss Andrew Watson talked to Ana some time back about a plan he had to draw these evil people out of hiding. She agreed to help him but she told him that she would not do it until she was able to get together with you. She came here to Sankt Englmar for that reason, because she loved you. She admitted it to Andrew. Well my boss wants to put the plan into action. He feels that danger is growing every minute and we already have death as part this thing. I found out today when I talked to Andrew that the young student who was attacked in Heidelberg died. That does it. It is time to take action and stop this."

Now more tears fell, for Georg knew that Ana would feel she was responsible for the young man's death, and she cared for him so much.

He shook himself and got up. "You tell me what you want us to do. You tell me how dangerous this is going to be. Give me every detail!"

Michael talked and Georg listened. Then they both left the office. Georg could wait no longer to hold Ana in his arms.

Andrew Watson called an emergency meeting of all agents involved in the Ana Winchester case. The meeting began early in the morning of the second day after the attempt to capture and/or murder her.

He led the group in an attempt to look more closely at every scrap of evidence, to verify that no vital fact had been overlooked. They covered everything from the death of Mr. Elden in North Carolina up to the recent attack on Ana in Sankt Englmar. Still nothing pointed to answers.

The most recent information, the true identity of Ana's family, the fact it was connected with Heidelberg, and the fact that Ana's mother had been a nurse sent by the Nazis to serve in Salzburg, all paved the road forward a little but the "why" that caused the murders remained unknown.

The one other piece of evidence that the agents looked at again was a certain written page. Ingrid Winchester, Ana's mother, had recorded the location, the grave name of a hoard of hidden Nazi treasure. This seemed to be the key. Salzburg seemed to be at the center of this mystery. However, they all agreed the problem was deeper, more complex than the location of treasure. The Nazis knew the location so why were they trailing Ana Winchester? Why did they murder Mr. Elden and the student in Heidelberg? What did Ana have that they wanted enough to commit murder?"

That's when Andrew presented his plan. They started to work on it, to define and detail what they needed to do.

Georg moved Ana into his home. Michael, still the agent responsible for her safety, protested at first but after talking with his boss, decided to abide by Georg's need to take her home. In fact, Michael also requested that he stay at the house with them. All was so much more urgent than before.

Publically, at different times over the next two days, Ana and Michael both checked out of the Pension Hill-Top. Georg picked Ana up when she checked out. Michael checked out later and then much later still, he drove to Georg's home. He was careful and made sure he wasn't followed, then parked/hid his car in the garage.

She recovered well but had to hear about the death of Thomas. As Georg predicted, she suffered badly. "He was kind, happy and intelligent. This is horrible. He deserved to live his life."

She was absolutely ready to help Andrew complete the plan he'd designed. The murderers had to be stopped. Mr. Elden, Thomas, and she feared who would die next. Georg was in danger. She must not let him die trying to save her. No.

Now she met each day with determination. She was still extremely sad and quiet but she always responded to Georg. He recognized what she feared.

Not long after she'd moved into his house, he asked for her permission to call the University of Heidelberg and explain to them that she'd suffered a fall during a climb up the mountain. That would be a way to explain her absence for a while. He also wanted to know if she would let him call Frau Krueger and tell her the same story.

She appreciated his thoughtfulness and agreed with his plan. That cleared up a few more details and helped to smooth out the road to Salzburg.

If he could have come up with any other way to eliminate the danger she faced, he would never had agreed to Andrew's plan. But there seemed to be no other way. He had to force himself to let her go forward with it, but he planned to be with her, in front of her every step of the way.

Two US agents were already in Salzburg, sent ahead by Andrew to scope out the area, get familiar with the city. Andrew and Michael were on their way there, driving together. They'd left Sankt Englmar early that morning. The Austrian government had agreed to provide cooperation and support and had already booked a hotel for them. It was near the center of Salzburg because they felt that this specific location offered the best chance for watching out for people or activities they were trying to catch up with.

The car ran smoothly down the highway as Michael asked Andrew a question. "Just how long do you think it will be before the murderers arrive in Salzburg? How long will it take before they realize that Ana is there? "

Andrew kept his eyes on the road, didn't hesitate to answer. "They already know she's going to Salzburg. I would bet that as soon as Georg's car turned in the direction of Austria they got the message."

"This is so dangerous Andrew. Do you think we can catch them without them killing anyone else?"

"I've been trying to get this unraveled and now it has gone too far. Too many people are dead and hurt. If we can't catch these people, stop them, then Ana will be the next person to die. I know that she understands the danger but she also realizes that this is the only way we can get this done. We must bring them out into the daylight, do some smart prep work, and maybe we can finish this without anyone else dying. Michael, you and I need to work harder than we ever have in our entire lives!"

Both of the men took drastic precautions before they started out for Salzburg. They'd used the talents available to them as agents and now both were almost unrecognizable. With professional help they both had different hair colors, different hairstyles, and their clothing was padded so they appeared heavier than they actually were. All the clothes they wore were of an entirely different style than was normal for either of them. They hoped they were unrecognizable except if put under intense, close-up investigation.

Ana and Georg left for Salzburg after Andrew and Michael. They'd begun the journey around mid-morning, bright daylight, to ensure that they would be followed as they drove toward Salzburg. Instead of trying to avoid being watched, they deliberately wanted to attract attention. Let it begin.

They also booked hotel reservations at the same place where Andrew and Michael would stay. This was part of Andrew's instructions.

Georg drove leisurely along the small two-lane highway and Ana looked out her window. Strangely, instead of being nervous about what the future could bring, she felt soothed as she absorbed the country they passed through, took pleasure in the deer she saw eating lunch in a meadow.

"Georg, how long will it take to get to Salzburg?"

"About two and a half hours, maybe three, depends on traffic, actually on how many slow-moving tractors we get behind." He glanced across and looked at her as he joked and was rewarded with a smile. He wanted so badly to get beyond the reason for this trip.

A little while later, she asked him some questions about her family, asked him to tell her any memories that he had of her great grandparents from the time he spent as their adopted son.

He thought for a while, and then said, "I have waited until you asked me, were ready to hear this. My adopted mother, who is actually your great grandmother, Frau Haupt, told me many things. I'll tell you one event that is very sad but I also have a happy story about your mother. I'll begin with sadness, with what happened to Ingrid when she was a young teen, in nurse training as ordered by the government. Evidently Ingrid met a man at her school one day and they went together up to the All Saint's Day celebration at the top of the mountain, a tradition in Heidelberg. Your great grandmother was upset and even cried as she told me what happened. She said that Ingrid didn't come home that night, was found lying outside the front door of her home in the early hours of the next morning. Her mother, your grandmother, called the doctor and he came right over and examined her. He then told them that Ingrid would recover but that she has lost her virginity."

"Oh no. My poor mother! Did you get any more details?

"I was told that Ingrid was not the same after that. She remained kind and caring but was quiet, sad, even depressed. After she finished her training she was sent to Salzburg to work in a hospital for the government. Her grandparents had already left Heidelberg and so when Ingrid was forced away to Salzburg to serve the government as a nurse, her mother was left there all alone in the family home."

They were both quiet for a few miles, and then he spoke up again. "Now let me tell you a happy story that will make you smile. It is also about Ingrid. Frau Haupt told me this one afternoon, after we were living back in Heidelberg. At the time, we were sitting out in the courtyard enjoying the sunshine."

Georg told her another story he'd heard from Frau Haupt about her four-year-old granddaughter Ingrid. "She loved to be outside, especially in the wide-open courtyard, the one with the bird fountain. She had recently learned about crocodiles from her Professor/Father and now she played around the courtyard, pulled up grass and picked leaves, all pretend food to feed her crocodiles. She got her grandmother to help her and they worked together gathering food and feeding the hungry crocodiles. Little Ingrid never tired of animals and her grandmother never tired of helping her have fun."

After he finished the story Ana smiled and thanked him for the happy memory. "I confess that after I had lived in my apartment for a while, I walked into the courtyard one day and the fountain caught my attention. I kept trying to grab hold of a fuzzy thought. I vaguely remembered hearing my mother ask my father if he could put in a fountain into the front yard of our house. Funny how things jump out of the back of your mind without you even realizing they were stored away there. Anyway, I heard my father tell her something about this not being Germany and that people in North Carolina didn't build fountains in their front yards."

Chapter Forty-Nine

Set the Stage
Salzburg – Ana - 1971

Day one of his detailed plan was going exactly as Andrew had hoped. He and Michael sat together at a table in the restaurant of the hotel where they were staying. A corner table allowed them to talk together, pretend to be businessmen, even as they secretly watched Ana and Georg, who sat at a table on the other side of the room.

Softly Andrew told Michael, "So our disguises are working pretty well because Ana and Georg haven't recognized us so far. I just hope we can fool the guys we're after. This way we can pinpoint and track whoever is following her. That's our first step."

Michael gave a business-like nod of affirmation and then continued to eat, continued to practice his acting skills, live up to his disguise.

Instructions were carefully given to Ana and Georg. They were specific. Andrew wanted them to sight see. That time in the open would give Andrew's agents a chance to identify who might be tracking their footsteps and maybe figure out how many people were involved. Assignment one for them: Be patient and pretend to enjoy the touristy activities.

They cooperated as told and after breakfast strolled casually along to their assigned tourist destination, Mirabell Palace and Gardens. Chosen for its apparent innocence, no connection to the cemetery, it was normally full of visitors and sat in an important historic location. The Palace had been in existence since 1606 when it was built by a Prince-Archbishop to show his love for a certain lady. It was beautiful.

It was necessary to walk across a bridge above the Salzsach River to get there and mid-way along they paused and looked down at the water. The view back toward the city was remarkable. They held hands and hugged.

Ana remembered a movie she'd seen in the early sixties with a special scene that was filmed at the Mirabell Gardens. She spoke to Georg about what she was thinking. "I saw a movie in the early sixties that had a scene from here. My friend Sam surprised me and took me to see it one night, told me he knew that I'd like it."

"I can always tell from your voice and from the way you talk about Sam that you are very close, are truly family. You grew up together but how long has he felt like a brother to you?" He wanted to see her face as she answered his question but he also felt the need to look around and figure out where they should go first to follow Andrew's instructions.

She didn't answer him right away so he moved ahead and said, "Well here we are and the gardens are lovely. Judging from the number of people here, we came to the right place just as Andrew hoped."

Still with no answer to his question about Sam, but she did say, "Maybe the number of tourists has a little to do with the film I mentioned. It won the Best Picture Award when it got released. I realize this sounds a little silly and unimportant with everything else going on but I liked the movie and would be happy to see the exact place in the garden where they sang and played."

"We will look for it for sure. I did not see the movie but I did hear some people talk about it. Some liked it but a lot of people who knew the true story of the Von Trapp family were not happy with the movie version." Then he stopped talking.

"Quietly she asked, "What are you thinking of?"

He started, "Now let us not get too serious…."

She interrupted. "Please tell me. It feels important."

He saw a few empty benches nearby and they walked over and sat down together.

The he turned to her and began softly, "Do you remember when I told you that my generation has difficult feelings about what happened in our country during the war? When I talked about the way some German people felt about the movie, it put those feelings back in my mind. Different people in different countries do not always see and feel the same about certain things. I think it depends on what you had to see, to live through, what happened to you that makes a difference of opinion. However, I honestly do not mean that one opinion is always right and one is always wrong. It is always a mix."

She continued to watch him, then responded, "The more we talk, the more I realize that we often feel or believe the same way. I love you and am so happy that you return that love to me. I will always love you." Tear welled up as she continued, "If anything happens to me I want you to know my love for you will never die. It will be in the world around you, the wind will whisper to you, the stars will smile down on you, and the rain will caress your skin."

"No. Do not even say that you might die! I cannot live without you. I have waited for you my entire life and you are my life. You must not leave me!"

She moved close and hugged him. He returned it fiercely.

"Georg I know you do not want to talk about this but I need to tell you something else important, something on my mind. I want you to be able to confirm it to Sam, in case I do not live through this."

He pulled back and moved to speak but she put her hand gently over his mouth. "I have already made a will and Sam is to inherit my farm and all my assets in the States if I die. He is the one that the land really belongs to. He is Cherokee and the land originally belonged to his family before it was stolen away by the government. By leaving my property to him I can atone a little for the suffering of the Cherokees. I can help my friend, my brother Sam."

Then she cried and he held her. Neither of them honestly cared, at that moment in time, if someone watched them. They should have.

Hidden behind a thick group of tall bushes a man stood and watched. His face did not reflect his thoughts, even as he watched the deep emotional exchange between them. However, another man, one assigned by Andrew, also stood hidden nearby and he intently watched the hidden man. Suddenly, he felt a surge of excitement. He'd spotted and followed the man all morning, saw him shadowing Ana and Georg, and now he felt sure that he'd found at least one of the suspects they needed to identify.

He stood still and watched Ana and Georg get up and go toward the Mirabell Palace. Then the suspect moved that way too. Tailing people without being discovered is difficult. Andrew had selected this man purposefully for this assignment. The reason, he was excellent.

While inside touring the Palace, Georg asked the guide how to get to the specific spot in the garden used in the film Ana wanted to see so after the tour was over, they went back outside and followed the directions given them. As they moved along a sidewalk, the US agent watched so he could confirm definitely that the man he watched was a suspect.

The suspect came out of the Palace and slowly walked after them. Confirmation! Now it was extremely important to stay a safe distance behind the suspect, who stepped off the walk and into the bushes. The agent did the same and he again saw the suspect and in the distance, Georg and Ana standing on the famous movie's garden staircase.

The whole morning went in the same direction. Georg and Ana acted, the suspect followed, and the US agent tracked him. All was tedious, exhausting, dangerous, but all per the plan.

By lunchtime when the couple headed back to their hotel, they were still followed. Enough time had gone by and the US agent now had some photos of the suspect and had already secretly radioed ahead to the other US agent scheduled to take his place. Then he confirmed to Andrew that progress had been made.

The suspect didn't follow them into their hotel, just walked on past. The new US agent took over. His assignment was to follow the now confirmed suspect and try to find out where he was staying, find the base of operations. Maybe he could also find some other suspects.

The next two days were duplicates of the first. Ana even found herself showing Georg the university auditorium where she'd given a speech as a stand-in for the Professor she worked for at the university.

The government agents hid themselves and did what they did best. At the end of the three long days Andrew called a meeting. Serious, deep discussion followed and all agreed that as of now, they had only two firmly identified suspects. Even though care had been taken and hard work completed, Andrew was still uneasy. He felt that there had to be another person, the boss of the murderous scheme, the one who gave the orders. So far, no one had been able to detect his presence.

Andrew believed that he already knew who the leader was. They' been so close to him. Herr Schultz was the most likely man behind this. Only because his dog interfered with his plan was Ana still alive. Herr Schultz wanted something specific from her and Andrew felt she did know something, but what? The name on the grave, treasure that had probably been recovered long ago, all was too inconsequential. This went deeper, another level existed somewhere.

He kept coming back to one question. Why had he/they, all the suspects, waited such a long time to find out where the treasure was located, to get the name from Ana? They could have grabbed her more than once but instead kept following her. Something vital was missing.

He tried to clear his mind and plan for the capture and arrest of the two men that they knew without doubt were part of the plot against her.

Ana was in danger because she was the only person who could motivate these murderers to action so that they could be captured. Evidence that they were trying to do harm to her was necessary for their arrest. They must be tempted and she was the bait.

He understood how brave she was, how willing to put herself in danger to find out who had killed Mr. Elden and the young man Thomas, in order to put a stop to it. It worried him a lot.

The official time was set up for the final confrontation. It was to take place right after midnight of the next day. The plan was for Ana and Georg to show up at the treasure-grave named in her mother's dairy. The agents would all be in place, armed and ready to halt the suspects before they could succeed in their plans to capture, torture, and kill Ana. Instead the murderers would be captured and hauled away.

Rest for everyone involved was essential and Andrew sent word to Ana and Georg that they should use the afternoon and evening to relax, but to stay close to the hotel. They would be guarded, kept safe, ready for the final confrontation.

They decided just to lunch at their hotel restaurant and afterward, went up to their room. Both thought a short nap might help increase their energy. They were tired of pretending.

As they stepped into the room, Georg walked over to the bed and stretched out and Ana moved over to the window. Their room was on the fourth floor and gave a good view of the city, the brick streets full of people moving about their lives.

The emotional conversation she had earlier with him repeated in her mind even though she tried to stop it. Suddenly she knew what she needed to do!

"Come over here and lie down with me my Ana." His low sexy voice drew her straight to his hard hot body. He watched as she removed every bit of her clothing and slipped up and at him. Powerful passion sensuously slid on top of his craving body.

Later they planned a celebratory dinner just for themselves. Georg picked a restaurant he'd heard good recommendations for and it was nearby. They had a lot to celebrate.

They were getting married. He'd formally proposed and she'd accepted. Neither made any attempt to plan further ahead. They simply loved each other in the present. Both understood the danger they faced, wanted it gone, and a villain-free road in front of them.

They dressed up for dinner. Happiness radiated from their bodies as they made their way to dinner. They looked fabulous and the evening was perfect. He ordered champagne and they toasted their love.

Afterward they walked along the street back to the hotel.

"Did you enjoy that as much as I did?" she asked.

"I did. I am glad we celebrated tonight and then we can celebrate again when this is finally over."

She stopped walking and looked into his face. What she saw was his fear of losing her. He did not fear for his own life. Her fear was the exact opposite. Her fear was for his life. "I love you very much," she whispered.

In the hotel, two gentlemen talked together while they waited for the elevator. Ana thought she recognized a voice and she was right because when they all got into the elevator she recognized Andrew and Michael.

No words from anyone as the elevator rose up and stopped on the fourth floor. The two men got off, then Ana and Georg followed.

"Good night Andrew" she said softly as they walked away. She didn't even turn around to see if Andrew heard her. She already knew that he realized she'd recognized him.

She made sure to see what door he went into. Good, it was only two doors down from theirs. Now she knew how to get in touch with him. She would need to soon.

Georg was sound asleep. She watched the clock carefully. When it showed midnight, she climbed quietly out of bed and put on the clothes that she had secreted in the bathroom earlier. When she came out he was still asleep so she tiptoed softly to the door, unlocked it and slipped out. She allowed herself one last look at his relaxed handsome face.

In the hallway she walked up to Andrew's door, reached into her pocket and pulled out a note to him that she'd written earlier. She slipped it under his door. Then she knocked loud enough so that the sound would be sure to wake him up. It was essential that he get her message.

No time to wait for the elevator. Instead she pulled open the door to the stairwell and ran down as fast as possible. When she got to the ground floor she stood still for a second, tried to level out her breathing, to look and act normal. Someone would be watching her.

The clerk at the desk nodded to her with a look of surprise on his face. Why did she come down the stairs at this hour of the night? Actually it was now 1:00 AM.

Guests were never questioned about things like this. He left her alone and she went out into the street.

Chapter Fifty

Push To the Finish
Salzburg – Ana – 1971

Her mind was focused, her footsteps quick and sure, as she raced toward her goal. The path she must travel was clear, burned precisely into her brain. Since her last trip to Salzburg she'd memorized it and mentally walked it over and over. Now, finally, she walked the real path. The race began.

Every step moved her closer to harsh danger but she accepted, even approved it, because she wanted to make this happen her way. Fear and worry, unknown people, unknown facts, all were left behind. Her goal in this danger-filled race was to get to the grave in St. Peter's Cemetery, the one her mother had named. The bad guys would follow her and she would lead them exactly where they wanted to go.

Too much time and too many lives had already been wasted. She'd managed to sneak away, and Georg was left behind. She'd run this race without putting his life in danger. In her heart, she wistfully wished for the company of her lost racing partner, her lost brave beloved horse Devil.

The streets provided light as she started out, but they got darker and were now also empty of people. Darkness surrounded her, but she'd thought ahead and put a tiny flashlight in her pocket. Darkness wasn't going to slow her down.

She listened for sounds, tried to detect the presence of anyone who might be following her. This time she wanted them to follow her, but she also counted on the fact that Andrew and his men would be following her too. She'd left him the note that told him what she was doing. Without Andrew's help this would end badly.

Andrew's instincts and his long years of waiting and listening, the definition of intelligence work, caused him to hear the soft knock on his hotel door. He knew it was serious.

The lamp beside his bed came to life as he reached to turn it on, and at the same time, he grabbed his shirt from the stack of clothes he'd put on the chair next to his bed. He was decently covered fast.

He ran to the door but the flash of the white envelope stopped him. A letter? Suddenly he was stressed. First he jerked the door open, weapon in hand, to see if he could catch a glimpse of the person responsible for the knock and the letter. The hallway was empty.

He ripped the letter open and what he read sent sharp flashes of anxiety through his body. Like the true professional he was, he shifted into high gear.

First he called Michael and gave him instructions to alert the other agents. Then he threw on the rest of his clothes, stashed his gun and his badge in his pockets, and ran down the stairs. The elevator was too slow.

When he reached the street, Michael was there. "Michael, did you reach the agents?" Even as he spoke, Andrew hurried forward down the street. Michael was right beside him.

"Yes. I got a call from them at the same moment I started to call them. They were at the window across the street where they've been posted and the man on lookout saw Ana when she came out of the hotel and walked off down the street. They said they also saw the man who was watching and he seemed surprised, but started after her at once. That's when they went down and they are already following the man who is following her."

"Okay. I've got to call our contact at the Austrian Headquarters. I need to verify that their men are standing watch at the cemetery like they agreed to. I've got to alert them right now!" He walked a little slower as he called and Michael went on ahead of him. Andrew would catch up as soon as he finished.

Yes! The men were there on guard. They were hidden near the gravesite and ready to protect Ana. Andrew thought, "Okay, now Michael and I need to get as close as possible but we've got to watch out. The man following her has probably alerted the others on his team, and we can't let them see us."

He caught up with Michael and they talked a little about how to handle it.

"Andrew, do you see what's happening, how dark and threatening the sky is getting? The air feels unsettled and the wind is getting stronger. Good. That extra darkness can help hide us."

Ana's body registered the change in the air too as she slowed down. She was very close to the cemetery. She stopped and stood still in the darkness and even looked up at the sky. It was filled with black swirling clouds and it felt so close, so low and heavy that she felt the weight of it on her soul.

"Slow down," she told herself. "You need to give Andrew enough time to get ready." Then she listened closely for other human movement but silence prevailed. All she could hear was the rustle of the leaves and the wind blowing snappily down on the earth. She continued to be still and to listen.

He smiled in his sleep, the warmth of his dream strong as his mind came slowly awake. He reached out across the bed to touch her, pull her closer, to share the heat of his dream. She was not in the bed.

"Just wait Georg, give her time to come back. She's probably in the bathroom."

His smile disappeared. She was gone. At the exact moment he sat up, something struck the bedroom window. The sound it made was solid but light, maybe the body of a small bird flying full-speed against the glass. He jumped up and ran to the window. What he saw was the turbulent sky, the building storm. Then he knew.

She had done what he had worried she would do. He jerked on come clothes and entered into the race. A race to save the woman he loved.

He was far behind everyone and everything. His mind raced as he got himself down to the ground floor of the hotel. Abruptly he stopped. Instead of running out the door, he ran over to the desk in the lobby. No one was there, so he smashed his hand against the bell. He needed help! The clerk, half-awake, came out.

"Call me a cab. Tell them it is an emergency." He spoke quick and forcefully.

The clerk felt his desperation and dialed a number. He spoke for a few seconds, then put down the telephone and said, "The cab can be here in less than five minutes. He is very close."

"Thank you!" Georg called as he ran out the door to wait for the cab.

Sure enough, the black cab came fast and the driver didn't even have time to get out, as was normal. Georg jumped into the back seat and started to give him directions. Again, his desperation, his need for help was understood by the cab driver. They sped away.

Several blocks were behind them quickly. The driver cleared his throat and spoke up, "Sir, do you realize that to go to St. Peter's Cemetery by vehicle, the closest I can get you is the parking lot? It is below the cemetery and you will still need to walk a small distance to get to the cemetery."

"No, I did not know, but I think that if you can get me to the parking lot very quickly I can still get to the cemetery faster than if I tried to run there instead. How long do you think it will take?"

A strong gust of wind hit the cab as it blasted down from the clouded sky. The cab driver turned on the windshield wipers as rain started to fall.

Michael and Andrew slid into the cemetery, hoping they'd made it unobserved. The weather was worse. The wind was stronger and now the rain made it more difficult for them to see or to hear what was happening.

"From what I know, Ana and the man following her should be here any moment. I hope our agents are right on their tails. You and I need to get closer and find a spot where we can see through this rain."

Ana moved again and the path into St. Peter's Cemetery was now beneath her feet. The location of the secret treasure grave glowed in her mind. Her steps slowed more as she continued to hope the authorities were all there and watching, ready to help her.

When she entered the main portion of the cemetery, a blast of wind rolled over the graves and hit her body. Then hard rain struck her. A cold shiver crept down her spine.

She kept walking through the wet grass toward her goal. Then she felt the enemy behind her. Her sixth sense had kicked in.

"I'm almost there. It's almost over. I can do this. I must!" Over and over she told herself this while she walked to the grave. She was there. She stopped and looked at the name on the marker. Yes, she was there.

The grave with the name written down by Mother, the grave once opened and used by the Nazis to hide stolen treasure, it was at her feet and she stared at it and felt sadness.

The storm continued to increase and the noise of the wind, branches thrashing back and forth, plus the noise of the heavy rain, all totally covered any sounds that could have warned her. But even with no ability to hear, she knew they were behind her, close.

In rapid succession, everything intensified. The storm took control of the earth as even more harsh cold rain fell, more wind slapped the trees and the ground, and flashes of lightening now flared wildly in the dark clouds above. The thunder shook the earth and all the people in the cemetery.

As a roar of thunder ended, she found herself looking into the face of a man, coming at her with a knife in his hand. She spun around to run but another man was there. She was trapped. Each second, each breath, each heartbeat, all took on the feel of unreality. They felt not as seconds but as hours, life morphed into concentrated slow motion.

She screamed, and like an answer to her unspoken prayer a voice returned the scream as a man ran toward her, "Leave her alone!"

The man with the knife grabbed her and tried to pull her away with him. She resisted with every bit of strength she possessed and with a quick movement of her foot, managed to trip him. But when he fell down, she fell with him. They both hit the soaking ground and suddenly he was on top of her body, his hand with the knife raised up, gaining momentum as he moved to plunge the knife into her chest.

A running, screaming Georg was almost there. He lunged at the man in front of her and attacked him violently, threw him to the ground. The man responded with a vicious kick to Georg's groin and pain shot through his body. He rolled and cursed and the man rolled away from him.

At that moment, with Ana at death's door, another flash of lightening exploded. Sparks flew from trees nearby. The man with the knife roared like a wild tiger and then went limp as his body slumped lifelessly down on top of her.

Georg managed to grab the foot of his attacker as the man tried to run. Instead Georg stopped him, held onto his foot and suddenly, that man also was halted by another silent bullet that struck his body and took his life too.

Two attackers were dead.

The swiftness of the deaths took place in the middle of the swirling chaotic blackness of wind and rain. The storm made it impossible to see what those involved, trying to help, needed to see.

The Austrian authorities, Andrew and Michael, and everyone involved ran down to the grave site, afraid they would find both Ana and Georg dead. What they found astonished them.

Two evil men were dead. How? Who fired the shots? Time was needed to work this out and right now it simply felt good that both Ana and Georg were alive.

The planning, the waiting, the outcome had all been obstructed, obscured by the intervention of nature. The violent storm had lowered a thick curtain between what happened and those trying to watch. The results were now, and always would be, cloudy.

Everyone involved in the episode was required by the Austrian authorities to stay put in Salzburg until given official permission to move on. Meetings were held between the US Military and the Austrian authorities. All accumulated information was shared in an attempt to clear up the murkiness of what had actually happened.

Andrew represented the US Military intelligence unit and made sure that everything related to the case was handed over to the Austrians. He emphasized the seriousness of past events, included the murders and the attacks.

At the end of several days, an agreement was reached between the two countries. The two men killed at St. Peter's Cemetery, the ones who were earlier identified by the US Agents as men following Ana Winchester, were determined to be responsible for the murder of Thomas, the student in Heidelberg. However no evidence actually existed to prove this, nor did they have any evidence that connected either of the two dead men with the murder Mr. Elden in the US.

The Austrians ordered that the grave be opened. They wanted verification that at some point in time it had been opened and used for storage for something other than the body it held. Proof was found that it was indeed a treasure hideout. However, no treasure was found in the grave. This information was helpful but still provided no reason for anyone to track Ana Winchester.

All agreed that something major was missing and that somehow she and her mother were involved with the Nazi-buried treasure, but no answers were found.

The case was left open, unsolved for the official records and no other options presented themselves except to wait and see if they attackers now left her alone.

Frustration and worry came along with Andrew when he talked personally to Ana and Georg. They weren't surprised, and had come to a conclusion of their own. They decided to get away from the situation, to go home, and put this behind them.

Andrew pleaded with her to consider her the danger, to let him continue to provide agents to guard her, at least for a little while longer.

Her answer was firm. "No Andrew. Georg and I decided to put this behind us. We're leaving it here in Salzburg, just where it must have started. We plan to return to Heidelberg as soon as we get permission from the authorities. I need to find out if I still have a job with the university and get things sorted out."

"You and Georg have official permission to leave, as of today. I can't force you to do anything else. I just feel that we've missed something important. Please promise to call me if anything turns up." Still worried, he told them goodbye.

They left Salzburg after an early breakfast the next morning. They drove toward a normal life together, joy and love.

She honestly needed to get back to Heidelberg as soon as possible, but agreed with him that an overnight in Sankt Englmar was an excellent plan. They'd both missed the beauty of the country, and he even asked her as he smiled largely, "How would you like to go to the Hill-Top for dinner tonight? I bet we have to answer a lot of questions from Peter and Sophie."

She remembered all the help and the teasing they'd received from Peter and Sophie. "Oh, I would love to have dinner there tonight. What a perfect way to celebrate our return home."

They didn't call before they arrived, just drove up and pulled into the parking area. When they walked in the back door, Sophie and Peter's dog Friendly saw Ana and ran over, gave and asked for attention. Ana gave warm love to Friendly and it was returned.

They didn't even make it to the dining room door before Peter saw them. "Georg, Ana, you are here! Are you good? Sophie, Sophie, they are back!" He was excited and loud as he yelled for Sophie and as he rushed toward them.

"Peter, where?" Then she came around the corner and saw them all together. With her beautiful perfect-Sophie smile, she put her hands on her hips and asked, "Where have you been? We have been looking for you." Then she too ran forward and joined them for an embrace of friendship.

"Come in, come in and sit right here." Peter was busy all of a sudden as he opened the door and led them to a table.

Sophie rushed to get menus and then hurried back to them. "This meal is on us. We are so happy to have you back, all safe, so do not say another word. Just enjoy your food and your drinks. By the way, what can I get you to drink?" Then she laughed again and they all joined in.

It felt so wonderful to be with real friends.

Peter waited until his friends finished their dinner and had a few drinks. Then he appeared at their table.

Georg looked up. "That was so good Peter. Thank you and Sophie for treating us so special."

"Well, I have something else for you. I think it will be something that will make you happy." He pointed toward the closed dining room door and then said, "Now Sophie!"

The door flew open and there stood Beethoven. The instant his eyes found Ana he ran to her. He rubbed and he barked. She responded with all the love she felt for him. Pure joy overflowed because she believed that Herr Schultz had probably killed him. He'd disobeyed and saved the life Herr Schultz wanted to end.

"Peter, Sophie, how is Beethoven here?" She was so excited she sounded breathless as she asked.

Sophie answered, "A few days ago a farmer came in and said that someone must have lost a dog. He said that he lives about five miles from Sankt Englmar and that the dog had wandered up to his house, seemed lost. He decided to come over here and check with Peter and see if maybe he knew who the dog belonged to."

Peter jumped in, "I hope I did not do wrong but I knew how much the dog loved you Ana and how much you loved him. Do you want him?"

A glowing face provided the answer. She didn't really need to speak but said, "Yes, oh yes!"

The next day three happy bodies were in Georg's car, all content to be in each other's company, and on the way to Heidelberg.

They'd decided that Beethoven should stay with Ana in Heidelberg until she got settled back in there. Later, when they officially began their future with marriage, Beethoven and Ana would move back to Sankt Englmar with Georg.

They discussed plans for their life together and both felt the desire to live permanently on the family farm in Sankt Englmar but they also decided to keep the Heidelberg home and use it sometimes. She had too many hidden thoughts, tiny bits of information about her mother's love and attitude for the Heidelberg home that she couldn't think of ever being able to totally leave it behind.

The night before they left for Heidelberg, Georg took a quick look at the personal items left behind by his adopted mother, Frau Haupt. He remembered some photo albums and gave them to Ana. She'd have plenty of time to look at them back in Heidelberg. He wanted her to see all the pictures of her family and understand them and her heritage. While he was getting the albums, he also found a small journal type book. He looked inside and recognized his adopted mother's handwriting. He nodded, satisfied with his search. This would definitely give her a look backward, to what was part of her. As soon as they got to Heidelberg he planned to give it to her.

Chapter Fifty-One

More Truth
Heidelberg – Ana – 1971

Beethoven was a happy dog, loved his new life in Heidelberg. He enjoyed his daily walks, accompanied by Ana or Georg or sometimes both. The Neckar River path was his favorite because it ran alongside the interesting river where he got to know a lot about swans and ducks and other dogs out and about on their daily walks too. He was allowed to run free during the time they generally spent at a small park a few miles down from their apartment. Whoever took him on his walk would sit down on a bench there in the park and allow him to scamper around on his own, and enjoy some freedom.

Eventually Ana and Georg had to part. She still had teaching responsibilities in Heidelberg and he had farm and business responsibilities back in Sankt Englmar. They were sad but duty called.

The day he left, she took Beethoven on his walk and when they started back from his freedom-park run her intuition clicked in a warning. Eyes were focused on her body again. She spun around and scanned the park. This time her eyes operated like radar and she focused on a spot at the far end of the park. An old man was walking away, and even though she couldn't see his face, she knew it was the same man she'd followed before into the small village a few miles further down from the park.

She and Beethoven walked back home. When they came through the entryway she saw Frau Krueger come out of her apartment. Ana and Beethoven went up the stairs toward her.

Frau Krueger saw her and called out, "Hello Ana. Did you and Beethoven have a good walk?"

"Beethoven had fun and the walk did me good too. How are you today?" Ana and Beethoven were now standing beside Frau Krueger.

"I am doing well but I need to talk to you about what has happened. Georg told me about you and your family. I am surprised but also pleased. Can we talk a little?"

Ana pulled Beethoven closer and said, "I would love to talk with you because so much has happened recently. Could you come up to my apartment? That way I can get Beethoven settled in comfortably and we can take our time and talk as long as we want to."

"That sound like a good idea." Frau Krueger answered as she followed Ana and Beethoven up the stairs.

Ana unlocked her door and they went in. She got Frau Krueger settled comfortably then put out fresh food and water for Beethoven. As they chatted together she made coffee and brought it over to the table and then sat down with her neighbor.

She passed the sugar and said, "Frau Krueger I am so glad to talk with you. From the beginning you have helped me. You befriended me, spoke to me honestly, and I trust you."

They talked and listened to each other. Ana explained what had happened since the time Mr. Elden was murdered in North Carolina. She explained that she'd been followed and even been attacked. However, the most difficult thing she confided was what happened to Thomas. They both had cared so much for him.

After they'd shared feelings and thoughts they sat silent at the table.

Finally Frau Krueger spoke up, "It is a wonderful thing to now know the truth about your family, your heritage here in Germany. It must be hard though. From what I understand, your mother deliberately kept all the family information hidden from you. When I think about that fact, I honestly believe that your mother was trying to survive and to take care of you. She obviously was trying to leave her past behind. I think she had a serious reason for doing this. I also think that your Mr. Elden was involved somehow in this. When he talked to me about renting this apartment to you, he was so insistent that you needed to stay here. He didn't want to consider any other option. I think he had a specific reason for wanting you here."

"I also believe the connection runs through Mr. Elden. He was the first person murdered in this sad mess and everything has only gotten worse from there." Ana then got up and went over to the counter.

"Can I get you another cup of coffee?"

"No, I think not. I am happy that I got this chance to talk with you and I hope you know that I am here anytime you need me. If you have questions about your family, their names, their history, please let me help. I have lived here for most of my life and maybe I can help you get more information. Then maybe you can understand why your mother ran away

from her family and her life in Germany, why she hid her past from you."
She got up, gave Ana a friendly hug, then left.

As she walked to the door Ana said, "I am so glad you are my friend.
Thank you."

It felt so good to be back at work at the University. The daily routine,
scheduling and planning classes, being in contact with her students, all
helped her get balanced again.

Any free time was spent studying the photo albums Georg had given
her, all put together by her Great-Grandmother Frau Haupt. They were
orderly and most had names and dates beside the pictures. Her great
grandmother must have been an organized person.

The information she accessed opened up a new world. So many times
in her youth she'd asked Mother for pictures and stories about her family.
Mother always said the entire family was dead and she didn't have any
pictures. Mother never shared any stories. Her answer was always that
bombs destroyed everything during the war.

Finally she had pictures with faces, smiles, and names, all in front of her.
She spent a long time getting to know her German family.

Autumn arrived and provided a suitable background for the rich harvest
of information she gathered. The trees in the valley and on the towering
mountains vibrantly changed colors and the contrast of those colors against
the blue Neckar River and the blue sky above was stunning. She was
reminded forcefully of her North Carolina home.

Today instead of pictures, she picked up her great grandmother's small
journal and started to read it again, for the third time. The words, the
events, all provided a depth of knowledge and understanding that stunned
her.

One of the entries upset and saddened her. Every time she read it, the
way she'd always thought of the war between the Allies and Nazi Germany
changed.

Her great grandmother told the story of the death of her daughter's
husband, Professor Neuschwander, at the hands of the Nazis. She didn't
give a large amount of details, but her emotions were strong and deep. As
Ana read what she wrote, she felt pain and shock. Her mother, Ingrid, had
lost her father and had also lost her lifelong best friend Ana.

The tragedy happened because Professor Neuschwander, Ingrid's father,
had tried to help a Jewish friend he cared about.

She realized that her name, Ana, was an honor from her mother to her
forever-lost best friend. She cried again.

The entire city of Heidelberg was special to her. She loved it, felt
comfortable there, and appreciated its beauty and history. She knew exactly

where the Jewish section was, knew exactly how it looked today. The empty square of land was now a small green park, a Memorial for the Jewish people killed and injured, for the destruction of their Synagogue and of their lives.

She felt the need to go there. Her mind and heart were filled by truths about what happened to her family there that one significant night.

She walked herself there slowly that very afternoon and carried with her a handful of small branches filled with leaves, all blushing with Autumn-colors. She clutched them tightly. When she reached the Jewish Square she placed them at the bottom of the memorial plaque. She wanted to honor all the people who lost so much on that Kristallnacht.

She lingered, sat down on a bench and thought of the pain her family had experienced. It was too late to change anything that had happened but she vowed to live her life helping others. She felt connected to her family and finally she belonged.

Later that week she reread another story in her great grandmother's journal. It told about the night her mother, Ingrid, had been attacked at the All Saint's Day celebration.

Only basics were written down but it was still overwhelming. Great Grandmother recorded that the man Ingrid went to the party with was an SS officer. They had originally met one time when Ingrid was just a little girl and then they accidently ran into each other at the university Ingrid was attending, taking the assigned nursing classes she'd been forced into. He made a speech to her class.

According to what was written evidently Ingrid had strong good memories of the man and was happy to go with him to the celebration up at the top of the Heiligenberg Mountain. She went against her family's warning and the next morning they found her unconscious outside the front door. She'd been raped.

The man had a name. He was Max.

Ingrid never recovered emotionally from what happened. Great Grandmother wrote down that she remained dependable, kind and caring, but all joy, all hope for happiness in life didn't exist anymore.

As far as her great grandmother knew, Ingrid never saw Max again.

Georg drove over to Heidelberg on a Friday morning and planned to stay for a long weekend before heading back to Sankt Englmar on the next Tuesday morning. They held each other, melted back together again, and attempted to make up for all the time they'd spent apart.

Emotionally he said, "We need to get married as soon as possible. We need to be together all the time. Can we make plans and pick a date? I cannot wait much longer."

Entangled together comfortably, she hugged him closer. "I agree with you. I want you with me every day. Without you I am not complete. How does the first week in November sound to you?"

Then she sat up and surprised him. "I've already talked to the university and because of all that has happened to me recently they are willing to let me out of my contract at the end of this term."

He jumped up too. "That is perfect! Let us get married the first Saturday of November."

They fell back into bed and passion roared again.

That same day she called Sam and Maggie. She wanted them to know that they were needed and wanted at the wedding if it was possible for them to come. She explained to them that the wedding would be small and private and that they would be the only people invited to witness the ceremony.

"Can you come?" she asked.

"We wouldn't miss it. We'll be there!" Sam answered, with Maggie's confirmation sounding along with his.

Wedding plans raced forward.

By the time Georg left to return to the farm they had decided the time and the location for the wedding. They would be married at the office of the German equivalent of the Justice of the Peace in Heidelberg on the first Saturday of November. Soon.

Georg contacted one of their favorite restaurants in Heidelberg and made arrangements for a small wedding dinner after the ceremony. In addition to Sam and Maggie they invited Frau Krueger to attend the dinner. They both counted her as a good friend.

About a week after Georg left, Frau Krueger and Ana walked together to downtown Heidelberg, to the specific cemetery where Ana's relatives were buried. They also had a more important site to visit, the place on the bridge where Thomas lost his life.

Both carried fresh flowers and remembered Thomas as they made their way across the Old Bridge. They stopped at the spot where he'd been beaten and thrown into the river, the place he spent the last moments of his normal life.

Frau Krueger asked, "Why did he die? Did he intentionally follow you? Do you think he was involved with the men trying to hurt you?"

Ana stood perfectly still and looked down at the river. "I do not know what role Thomas had in this but I can say one thing for sure. I was not afraid of him, and if he followed me, and I do believe he did, I only ever received goodness from him."

Sadly, slowly, they dropped the flowers one by one off the bridge and let them fall into the river as Thomas had. They let their emotions and memories of him flow freely through their hearts and minds.

It was difficult to leave but they walked on and then made their way to the cemetery where her relative's rested. Frau Krueger had helped her locate it from public records and now they walked around until they found the specific burial place of her great grandparents. She also found her grandmother, Elfriede Neuschwander there too. She couldn't help but wonder what her mother's life would have been like if she'd stayed in Germany. Gently she placed more flowers on the graves of her family.

Frau Krueger's soft voice found her, "What are you thinking?"

"Oh I was trying to tell myself that it is impossible to change the past. I feel so sad that my mother lived her life without family and is now buried so very far away, in the United States."

"It is not changeable Ana. Every person makes their own choices for their own reasons. Try to just celebrate your mother. Ingrid loved you very much."

Students were excited as usual. It was that special time of year, time for All Saint's Day. Plans were made and parties were planned. Traditionally they still gathered at the top of the mountain and had fun with the music, food and drinks. Rumors circulated that a popular band was to be part of the music for this year's celebration.

It was hard for her not to smile at the excitement of her students and so she allowed herself to enjoy their anticipation. However, when she sat alone at her desk after class that Friday afternoon before the celebration, she couldn't help but remember every word her great grandmother wrote about the attack on her mother that one All Saint's Day years ago.

That afternoon when she got home she went to Frau Krueger's door and knocked. The door opened right away and Frau Krueger greeted her. "Hello. How did your workweek at the university go?"

"It went well. I enjoyed watching and listening to all my students as they planned for this weekend."

"That reminds me Ana, is Georg coming over for this weekend? Are you two going to celebrate All Saint's Day together?"

"That is what I wanted to tell you Frau Krueger. He has obligations this weekend and cannot come. So I have decided to take Beethoven on a special walk and a picnic on Saturday. We are going to spend our day out in nature. I want to walk up to the castle, check out the gardens, and then I will find a bench with a view out over the river and we can enjoy our picnic. I wanted to tell you because I plan to be gone most of the day and I wanted to you know where I was in case Georg called or you needed me for anything."

Frau Krueger responded with approval, "You made a good plan. You and Beethoven will have a healthy and beautiful day up in the castle gardens."

Maybe because it was that time of year, All Saint's Day time, that she tossed and turned a lot until finally, she fell asleep. She dreamed deeply, was a small girl riding a cow with her friend young Sam. Then she and Devil were dangerously jumping fences and racing across the land. But best of all, she lifted her body up off Devil and then flew like a bird above the Valley River. She winged smoothly over to a mountain peak and landed on a bare flat rock. The beautiful land she loved so much lay out in front of her. She felt pure happiness, and her mother was at her side.

Beethoven woke her up by breathing in her ear and licking her face. She opened her eyes and he stood erect, like he was on guard duty. She touched him and he relaxed and said good morning with big happy lick.

After breakfast she called Georg. "Georg, I have an idea. I know where we should go on our honeymoon. We should go to North Carolina. I had a dream last night and I was back there. I woke up and thought of our honeymoon and spending some time there. What do you think?"

"It sounds perfect to me. But Ana, we cannot go right after our wedding. I have too many year-end responsibilities here. Can we maybe plan to go sometime in the early spring?"

"That would be a great time to go. It is beautiful there then."

Later a backpack sat on the counter in her kitchen while she leisurely prepared the picnic lunch and packed it. She took her time, treated herself to a no-schedule morning. She paid attention to the food because she wanted it to be tasty and add to the pleasure of the day.

Finished with the food, she got her shoes and jacket on and laughed at Beethoven. He was excited, knew he was going out into the world. She grabbed his leash and he smiled up at her when she attached it to his collar. They were ready to go.

Chapter Fifty-Two

Who, What, When, Where, Why
Heidelberg – Ana 1971

The garden area of the Heidelberg Castle was located approximately 250 or so feet up the north side of the Königstuhl (the King's Seat Mountain). The castle had been in existence since 1214, but had changed, grown, been partially destroyed by war, rebuilt and finally it had been almost completely destroyed by the French in the War of the Grand Alliance.

At one point in time its castle garden had been fabulous, designed in that beautiful Italian Renaissance style. Now, the gardens that still existed were actually the remains of the Baroque original yet the castle and the gardens remained magnificent.

The old stone castle sat partway up the mountain behind the Old Town of Heidelberg. The warm-colored stone, Renaissance Style, was charming and the gardens were well cared for with pathways in many directions all throughout. Tall full trees offered shade and benches were placed appropriately to allow people to relax and enjoy the magnificent views down the mountain and into the valley.

A funicular railway ran from the Kornmarket Square in Old Town Heidelberg, all the way up to the top of the King's Chair Mountain, with a stop partway up so people could get off at the castle.

Today Ana decided to ride the train up to the castle garden, to take an easier and faster route than the walk up she'd planned for herself and Beethoven. It was later than she'd realized because she'd taken her time getting their morning ready to go. Beethoven didn't seem to mind the short ride on the train at all. He was interested in, and friendly to, several other passengers on board with them.

When they got off the train, Ana had her hands full as Beethoven attempted to run ahead, to follow the two people in front of them who took the pathway straight into the castle. She steered him off to the right, to the garden path that circled around on that side of the castle.

Then she let Beethoven lead the way. She just held his leash and followed whatever path he chose. They had a great time walking in the fresh open air and he enjoyed all the wildlife they encountered, especially the squirrels.

Later when she finally felt a hunger pain she walked over to a nearby bench. They were lucky because the bench was placed with its back against a thick wall of trees and the view in front of them swept down the green grass to a pathway below, edged with a large stonewall. The bench she sat down on provided a perfect view of the entire city, as well as the river and the mountains. She was as happy as Beethoven as they ate their picnic lunch.

After the food, she sat still and simply relaxed.

Abruptly Beethoven's head jerked up, his nap ended as he stood and stared behind the bench and then jumped up into an on-guard stance.

She felt the man's presence, knew he was here. She continued to sit still.

He came out into the open, walked out from the trees and came to stand off to the side of the bench. She could easily see him. He was silent and as she looked at him she knew him. He was the man she'd seen in the park and once followed to a small village west of Heidelberg. He was the harsh man she encountered on her first trip to Heidelberg.

Then he spoke. His voice was quiet and firm. "You came here today because you knew that I would follow you here. You were sure of it. I must tell you that not only do you look like your mother Ingrid, but you also have her intuition, her connections to unknown powers in this world."

Still she said nothing.

"Do you know who I am Ana Winchester?"

Beethoven stood alert and ready, pressed hard against her legs offering his support. She touched his head gently as she answered the man. "You are Max. I do not know any other part of your name because my great grandmother just wrote down your name as Max."

His return was blunt, "My true name is Max Schillenger."

"Well, Max Schillenger, I wish you would tell me so many things. Why have you been following me since I came here as a young student? Also, why did you attack and rape my mother Ingrid on All Saint's Day all those years ago? How could you do that to her?"

His face flushed red with anger. "I did not rape Ingrid. She went with me to the celebration and afterwards, we got passionate. Both of us desired each other and we made love. Yes, we had sex but it was not rape. We shared a strong irresistible love. She wanted me as much as I wanted her.

Only afterwards did a problem develop. She went into a guilt driven panic attack because I was an SS officer and the SS had killed her father. She could not reconcile our love and her father's death even though she knew that I saved her life, stood between the mob and two little girls, Ingrid and her friend Ana, on the very night her father was taken away by the Nazis. Ingrid experienced a panic attack, complete with muscle spasms. Since I am a doctor, I always carry my medical bag with me and so I grabbed some pills to relax her. She took two and I watched her all the rest of the night. Then early the next morning I put her beside her front door and rang the bell. I loved her, took care of her! I did not rape her!"

He looked like an officer as he stood straight and rigid. He towered above her. "The war was on full blast. I was not in control of my life and was made to perform my military duty. I was not allowed time off, was sent to my post that same morning. It was not until the war was almost over that I saw Ingrid again. We met accidently in Salzburg, Austria, where I had been posted by the government and where, unknown to me, she was serving as a nurse in the hospital there. After we found each other again, she came to stay with me. We lived together in Salzburg for a few months and we were finally so very happy. Then the war was almost over. The military sent me away from Salzburg so I arranged for Ingrid to be given a lift by the military transport back to Heidelberg. We already knew that she was pregnant and I wanted her safe. But the last time I saw her was when she rode away in that military truck."

Ana went limp, her strength drained from her body. Her mother was pregnant when she left Salzburg. She was pregnant with Max Schillenger's child. Her mind heard and understood these words but her heart froze. She cowered back against the bench and put her arms around her Beethoven.

Finally she managed to whisper, "Are you my father?"

Straight and simple he said, "Yes."

They were both silent, self-absorbed, trying to handle the truth now out in the open.

This time he spoke differently, more gently. "I was able to use some of my influence as an SS officer to get money and a passport for myself and my brother. We sneaked out of Germany without being caught or arrested and we moved to Canada. You may recognize the name on the passport my brother used. He was then called Herman Elden.

"Wait! My Mr. Elden, my Horseman was your brother? Did my mother know this? I cannot believe this! I thought of him as family but he really was my uncle."

"Your mother never knew he was my brother. She had never met or seen him before. He was a good brother and he moved to Andrews to help me take care of the love of my life, my Ingrid. From what he told me over the years, he also took excellent care of my daughter. I totally approved of how he handled that sick, hateful grandfather you had to endure. I only wish I could have been the one to help you but your mother made the decision to put me into her past and pretend I did not exist anymore. I must believe the guilt she felt over her father's death by the Nazis and her love for me, the SS officer caused her to do this. She chose to leave her true love behind, to give her daughter a new land and a new life. I left her alone, let her make that decision without interference but I tried to always take care of her and of you too. That is why I funded my brother over the years and I never let my Ingrid know that I knew where she was, knew where my baby daughter lived."

"Did Mr. Elden kill my grandfather? Did he have anything to do with my father's death? Did he get your permission or did act on his own?"

Again his voice was filled with anger. "My brother lived his own life, his own way. I supported him but I did not tell him what to do."

She asked another question. "The young man Thomas, why did you have him killed?"

"What are you saying? Thomas worked for me, helped me to keep track of you and make sure you were safe always. I didn't kill him! The Nazis trying to find me were responsible for his death."

Beethoven's growl started slow and soft, then changed from a growl into a confused bark, strangely it had a "welcome" tone to it.

Herr Schultz raced out of the thick trees right behind the bench where he'd been hiding and listening, a luger in his hand. "Finally I have found you, Max Schillenger! You murderer! Finally Ana Winchester has led me to you. I have been working so long, so hard to find you, following her everywhere. You murdered both soldiers at that grave in Salzburg and one of them was my brother. You killed them and then kept all the treasure for yourself. That was your plan from the beginning and now I am going to get revenge for my brother."

Max answered quickly. "What are you talking about? You must be the person who attacked my daughter Ana, who killed my brother and the young man Thomas who was helping me watch and take care of her. Well let me tell you right now that you have wasted your time and money and caused a lot of unnecessary death and pain. I did NOT kill your brother or the other soldier. We were partners, were working together, and were going to share the treasure equally. Instead, your brother told one of his friends what we were doing, and the Nazi in charge of their unit overheard everything he said. That Nazi officer is the one who killed your brother and the other soldier and then stole all the treasure from the grave where we had hidden it. I had to disappear fast, get out of Germany before I was arrested as an SS officer, or he would have murdered me too! You have been chasing the wrong man!"

"I do not believe you and I'm am going to take away your treasure, your daughter, as you took mine. I want you to feel the loss of your daughter just like I felt the loss of my brother."

Max stood beside the bench and she stood in front of it. She'd turned around during the confrontation between Max Schillenger and Herr Schultz, and she saw the man's final answer a split second before he gave it.

In a smooth fast movement, Herr Schultz raised his arm and pointed his Nazi pistol, pulled the trigger. Max Schillenger flung himself in front of Ana, deliberately blocking his daughter. Ana felt something sting her body. As Max sunk to the ground before her, she looked down at where he'd fallen, and her eyes drifted to her chest. Revenge blood flowed.

Schultz blinked. Ana gasped. All hell broke loose.

"Ana!"

Andrew Watson and another federal agent rushed up the path, guns drawn and ready. Herr Schultz turned his luger in their direction and more bullets exploded.

The luger fell from Schultz's hand. He crumpled to the ground, dead.

Andrew raced to Max Schillenger and Ana, saw that Max had died instantly. Ana was still breathing, and he yelled out for help.

Ana felt herself being lifted, transported to help. Voices shouted orders all around her, but they felt distant. She drifted gently into another world where she got to see her mother Ingrid and her father Max reunite.

She didn't want to return.

Then a voice she loved asked, "Ana come back to me. Ana, I love you." Georg.

"She is lucky," said another voice. A doctor's voice. "When the bullet passed through her father, it veered enough so that it did not strike any of her vital organs. Her father saved her."

My father. Max. My real father. And he loved me.

"Ana, please."

Life and death. Future and past. One, final decision to make.

Ana opened her eyes.

ABOUT THE AUTHOR

M.S. Haber is a world traveler. She is deeply connected to family and friends who live in various parts of Germany, and has spent much time there. Her knowledge of the county and its people helps provide a deep emotional background for the story she tells in this book. Although harsh and violent, it's filled with deep emotions, natural beauty, and love.

When not traveling, M. S. Haber divides her time between Los Angeles, California and Fairhope, Alabama. She lives in and loves both LA and AL.